Praise for

How to Sleep with a Movie Star

"Kristin Harmel's fabulous book...captivated us."
—*Complete Woman Magazine*

"Editors' Pick."
—*Quick and Simple Magazine*

"Hilarious...deliciously entertaining."
—Sarah Mlynowski,
author of *Milkun* and *Monkey Business*

"We...recommend...*How to Sleep with a Movie Star*..."
—*NY Daily News*

"Kristin Harmel dishes with disarming honesty and delivers a sparkling, delightful story."
—Laura Caldwell,
author of *The Year of Living Famously*
and *The Night I Got Lucky*

Also by Kristin Harmel

How to Sleep with a Movie Star

The Blonde Theory

Kristin Harmel

5 SPOT

NEW YORK BOSTON

5 Spot
Hachette Book Group USA
1271 Avenue of the Americas
New York, NY 10020
Visit our Web site at www.5-spot.com.

5 Spot is an imprint of Warner Books, Inc. The 5 Spot name and logo are trademarks of Warner Books, Inc.

Printed in the United States of America

First Edition: February 2007
10 9 8 7 6 5 4 3 2 1

Library of Congress Cataloging-in-Publication Data

Harmel, Kristin.
    The blonde theory / Kristin Harmel.—1st ed.
        p. cm.
    Summary: "A novel about a cerebral lawyer who can't get a date and tries seeing if being a 'dumb blonde' for a month will improve her love life"—Provided by publisher.
    ISBN–13: 978-0-446-69759-0
    ISBN–10: 0-446-69759-1
1. Women lawyers—Fiction.   2. Dating (Social customs)—Fiction.   3. Blondes—Fiction   I. Title.
    PS3608.A745B55 2006
    813'.6—dc22   2006018346

Book design by Nancy Singer
Cover design by Brigid Pearson

To Karen and David. I couldn't ask for a better sister and brother. I'm so proud of both of you—for all the wonderful things you are doing with your lives, but more so for the amazing people you have become. I'm so lucky to have you both in my life. I love you!

Acknowledgments

Thanks to Mom, the biggest inspiration in my life and the best person I know, to my wonderful brother and sister, David and Karen, and to Dad, who I love very much. I'm also fortunate to have the best set of grandparents in the world—even if Grandpa insists on always telling the embarrassing story of the first time he saw me! And thanks to the rest of my great family, too—especially Aunt Donna, who helped instill in me a love of reading (and always beats me at Trivial Pursuit!). I love you all!

Thanks to all the great folks at Warner Books, especially my wonderful editor Emily Griffin (I'm so thrilled to be working with you!), Elly Weisenberg (You're not just a great publicist, but a great friend, too), Jim Schiff (I'm so glad we've stayed friends!), Rebecca Oliver, Penina Sacks, Caryn Karmatz Rudy, Laura Jorstad, Brigid Pearson, Candace Waller, Tom Haushalter, and, of course, the incomparable Amy Einhorn.

Thanks to Elizabeth Pomada, for helping give me my start in the publishing industry. I will always be grateful to you. Thanks also to superstar agent Jenny Bent, with whom I am looking forward to many adventures, and to her assistant, Victoria Horn. Thanks to my film agent extraordinaire, Andy Cohen, who has become a great, valued friend. And thanks to Linda Kuczma, the patent attorney who let me pick her brain to make Harper more authentic. I'm so glad to have met you!

One of the best things about being a writer, I've discovered, is the wonderful friendships I've developed with other writers.

I've been lucky enough to meet some of the most generous, kind women in the business. Thanks to Alison Pace, Lynda Curnyn, Melissa Senate, Laura Caldwell, Julie Dam, Mari Mancusi, Lani Diane Rich, Jane Porter, and Liza Palmer. And a special thank-you to Sarah Mlynowski, who has not only become an amazing friend, but who has also gone above and beyond to help and advise me.

Thanks to the ladies of Olive & Bettes, Shou'ture, Blue Genes, and Shopgirl for the fabulous launch parties; to Laura Baddish and Bacardi for the partnership and the super-cool "Movie Star-tini" and "Tangerine-tini"; and to Amy Tan(gerine), for your business partnership, but especially for your friendship. You're the best!

Thanks to my many friends, who have supported me, listened to me, read my drafts, and made my life happier. I am the luckiest girl in the world to know you all. Thanks especially to Gillian Zucker (it's your book!), Lauren Elkin, Kristen Milan, Kara Brown, Megan Combs, Wendy Jo Moyer, Amber Draus, Ashley Tedder, Lorelyn Koch, Kendra Williams, Don Clemence, Lisa Wilkes, Anne Rach, Andrea Jackson, Megan McDermott, Kelly McDermott, Trish Stefonek, Michael Ghegan, Michelle Tauber, Courtney Jaye, Samantha Phillips, Josh Henchey, Ryan Dean, Brendan Bergen, Eric Colley, Troy McGuire, Ben Bledsoe, Jeeves, Clayton Morris, Kia Malone, Mitch English, Lana Cabrera, Melissa Rawley Payne, Pat Cash, Courtney Harmel, Janine Harmel, Jay Cash, Tom Rottcher, Lindsay Soll, Mindy Marques, Steve Helling, Michael Kovac, the Vito crowd, Candace Craig, Jean-Marc Denis, Dave Ahern, Steve Orlando, John Kaplan, and Cap'n —and to my very favorite dogs and cats: Duke, Dr. Spots, Kitty, Tiger, Bailey, Buster, Bamboo, Jeffi, and Chloe.

And to anyone who has ever thought she has to change who she is: Believe me, if people don't like you for who you are, they're not worth your time in the first place. Be proud to be *you*—and strive only to be a better version of yourself. It's the best thing you could ever be.

The Blonde Theory

"A career is wonderful, but you can't curl up with it on a cold night."

—Marilyn Monroe, world's most famous blonde

Chapter One

I didn't know when it happened that it would be my last chance at finding love. I mean, who thinks like that? Sure, we agonize over breakups, cry with our girlfriends, drown our sorrows in too many pints of mint chocolate chip or too many martinis. But in the back of our minds, even as our hearts are breaking, we know there will be someone else. Maybe not right away, but eventually. There's always someone else just around the corner.

At least that's what I thought then. Sure, I was devastated when Peter left. It broke my heart when I came home one evening after a long deposition three years ago and found him in the final stages of packing his old suitcases. Another half an hour and I think I would have missed him entirely. I think he would have left without saying good-bye.

"Harper, I can't do this anymore," he said while I stared at him blankly, trying my best to formulate some sort of rebuttal. But I didn't know what to say. My brain was too busy trying to wrap itself around the fact that he was leaving.

I hadn't had even the slightest clue that anything was wrong. After all, we had just celebrated our two-year anniversary two weeks before with champagne, strawberries, a night of cuddling up, and drunken mumblings about spending forever together. He had introduced me to his parents less than six months earlier. We had been talking about moving into a bigger apartment when our lease was up in the spring.

"What...what...why?" I finally stammered, hoping that it was something along the lines of an appropriate response. I stared at his broad back, which was turned to me as he bent over the battered brown leather suitcase he had placed on the bed we'd shared for the last two years. I tried not to think about the last time we'd made love there, but that was awfully difficult, since it had been just four days ago, the day before my law firm announced I'd made partner—the youngest partner the old-school Booth, Fitzpatrick & McMahon had ever had. Thirty-two-year-old women weren't supposed to make partner. Not at one of the most prestigious firms in the Northeast. But in the last two years, I had quadrupled their patent business and brought in more than two million dollars' worth on my own. I'd finally had the courage to approach the partners and threaten to leave the firm if I wasn't made a junior partner by year's end. They had conferenced about it and agreed, a move that had made news all over New York's legal community. I should have been the happiest I'd ever been in my life. Peter should have been happy for me.

Instead, he was packing. To leave. To leave *me*.

"Why?" I repeated, this time my voice a mere whisper. He turned to me finally and sighed in what sounded like exasperation, as if I was simply supposed to *know* exactly why he was leaving. As if me asking him was simply some tedious formality that he had to be subjected to on his way out the door. His dark brown hair, I noticed as I stared at him, was still wet, as if he'd just emerged from the shower, and its little ends, which sorely needed a trip to the barber, were starting to curl up, the way they always did when they dried. He was fresh-shaven, so his square jaw was missing that day-old-stubble look I always found so sexy. His hazel eyes looked bright, brighter than they would have been had he any regrets about leaving. Apparently, he didn't. His posture was just as relaxed and comfortable as usual, which, in my opinion, wasn't how one should look if he was walking out on the woman to whom he'd been proclaiming his undying love less than a week earlier.

"I just can't do this anymore," he repeated, shrugging as if the situation were beyond his control, as if forces greater than he were making him decide to leave, making him pack his suitcase, making him coldly turn his back to me. "I just can't."

"I don't understand," I said, finally able to control my voice again. He turned his back again, returning to his packing as if I weren't there. I crossed the room and stood beside him, trying my best to refrain from throwing myself at his feet and hanging on to his ankles so that he'd have to take me with him wherever he was going. Because that would just be pathetic, wouldn't it? Instead, I just stood beside him, breathing hard, waiting for him to look at me. Finally he did. "Why?" I repeated.

He didn't meet my eyes. He wouldn't. But he stopped packing long enough to mumble the answer that has been ringing in my ears ever since.

"I just can't be with a woman who puts her career before our relationship," he had said, gazing straight down at his toes. All the air went out of me in a whoosh, and suddenly I felt like I couldn't breathe. I didn't understand. When had I put my career before our relationship? He worked just as hard as I did. And if he really felt that way, why hadn't he said so before? In fact, I had tried in every way I could to let him know that he was at the center of my universe. I probably could have made partner even sooner if I hadn't been so worried about making Peter feel wanted. But I had wanted to be a good girlfriend as much as I'd wanted to be a successful attorney. Until that moment, I thought I had juggled both roles just fine.

Evidently, I was mistaken.

"What do you mean?" I asked weakly, feeling more bewildered than I ever had before. Peter paused before going back to his packing. "I don't do that," I whispered. Surely I didn't, did I?

"Yes, you do," Peter said slowly, folding the last of his crisp button-up shirts, which he wore to work at Sullivan & Foley— a law firm that had once been nearly as prestigious as mine but had filed for bankruptcy last year and fired half its staff. Peter had stayed on, but he'd been forced to take a pay cut. "Besides," he added with a quick glance in my direction, snapping his suitcase shut with a resounding bang that sounded ominous and final, "we agreed when we started dating that we would never compete with each other. And now you seem determined to beat me at whatever you do. I'm just tired of it."

There were no words left. After all, *I* knew I had never *purposely* tried to compete with him or beat him. It wasn't *my* fault that I'd had an easier time climbing the ladder at my firm. It wasn't *my* fault that his firm had screwed up a few major cases, come under investigation by the SEC, and been forced into its drastic measures. Peter's career had once looked even more promising than mine, but things had changed. I just stared at him, bewildered, while tears rolled down my cheeks. So that was it. I had made partner, and it had come with a sizable raise. It apparently also came with a surprise breakup. No one at Booth, Fitzpatrick & McMahon had warned me about this.

Finally, Peter turned to look at me. Not out of respect for me, but because I was standing between him and the doorway. And he was on his way out.

"Listen, Harper," he said, the overstuffed suitcase he held in his right hand weighing down the right side of his body almost comically. "I care about you. But I'm a man. And men like to be providers. *I* should be the one who makes partner first. Besides," he added archly, "I thought we had agreed that you'd quit after a while and stay home so we could have kids."

"I...I never agreed to that," I said shakily, staring at him in shock. Besides, I was only thirty-two. What, I was supposed to have quit by thirty-two so I could bear his children? Was he delusional? I had another good ten years or so of childbearing ability left, and I couldn't exactly impress the other partners with my legal aplomb with a nursing newborn hanging from my breast, now, could I? It wasn't that I didn't want kids *someday*. It was just that I wasn't ready for them *yet*. And Peter sure as hell had never indicated that *he* was.

"I just thought we were on the same page, Harper," Peter said sadly, shaking his head at me as if I were a child and he was disappointed in my behavior. "But you just *had* to be better than me at everything, didn't you?"

I was aghast. I couldn't think of another thing to say as he walked past me toward the door. I followed him mutely out of the apartment and watched him as he made his way down the stairway to the ground floor.

He didn't look back.

AFTER EVERY BREAKUP, there's a period of mourning. Sometimes it comes in the form of a rebound fling or two. Sometimes it comes in form of a lingering semi-depression. Sometimes it comes in the form of a Ben & Jerry's Chunky Monkey carton. Or two. Or thirty-seven.

I mourned Peter. As angry as I should have been with him for leaving me just like that, with no warning, no real explanation, I was filled instead entirely with sadness and hurt. I didn't get out of bed for the next three days. My three best friends, Meg, Emmie, and Jill, sat with me in shifts. My secretary dropped by all the patent paperwork I had to do that week and canceled all my appointments and court appearances. I told her I was sick, but I think the Reese's wrappers, Pringles canisters, Bacardi Limón bottles, cigarette butts, and empty ice cream cartons scattered all over my room gave me away. As did the fact that I had Courtney Jaye's girl-power "Can't Behave" playing on repeat and was angrily singing along with the words time after time after time, inserting Peter's name in unflattering locations throughout the song.

On the fourth day, I sucked it up and went back to work, telling myself that I was better off without him. I was, obviously. Who needed a guy who walked away the moment he felt overshadowed? Certainly not me. Who wanted a guy who felt so emasculated if his girlfriend made a little more money than he did? I sure didn't.

But knowing those things didn't help much. Logic is no match for heartbreak.

It took me awhile to want to date again. I'm not the rebound type. And I just *knew* that Peter would change his mind and come back. But four months later, I hadn't heard one word from him. He had sent his friends Carlos and David to pick up the rest of his belongings—including the beautiful Italian leather sofa we'd bought two months before he left that he'd insisted on putting on *his* credit card—and then he had seemingly disappeared off the face of the planet while I moped around in a living room with no furniture.

But when I was finally ready to get out there again, to dive back into the dating pool, I found I was swimming alone.

Sure, I had dates here and there. I wasn't unattractive; at five foot six with shoulder-length light blonde hair, green eyes, a tiny nose, girlishly freckled pink cheeks, and a body that would be considered average for a woman in the vicinity of thirty, I still turned my share of heads.

But the problem wasn't in attracting the guys. The problem was that the moment they found out I was an attorney—and even worse, a partner in one of Manhattan's most prestigious firms—they ran. Far and fast. They couldn't get away from me quickly enough. A few of the braver ones hung in until date three or four, but they always jumped ship eventually.

And it wasn't that I didn't get asked on dates. I did. Men were intrigued by me. They knew they were *supposed* to like the tri-fecta of beauty, charm, and brains (okay, in my case, moderately average attractiveness, a sarcastic sense of humor, and brains). But apparently, in reality the total package—so to speak—was totally horrifying. Who knew?

I'd been so sure I'd find someone. It wasn't because I needed a man by my side; I wasn't that kind of girl. I was perfectly content being by myself. It was just that I had known that after Peter, I'd eventually find someone else, someone who would love me and whom I would love, someone who was a stronger man than Peter and who appreciated what I did for a living without feeling threatened by me, someone who understood that my job didn't define who I was.

I was thirty-two then, when Peter left. Young enough to be hopefully optimistic. Foolish enough to believe in love.

Now I was thirty-five. I hadn't had more than four dates with the same man—other than Peter—since my twenties. And my twenties were a long time ago.

Tomorrow was the third anniversary of Peter leaving me, the third anniversary of me being alone, the third anniversary of the day that I began to realize that being successful and being desirable are evidently mutually exclusive.

It was becoming increasingly obvious that as long as I kept climbing the corporate ladder, I was destined to be alone.

Chapter Two

"It's not you, it's them," said Meg at brunch the next morning—my Happy-Anniversary-of-Being-Undesirable Brunch, if you want to get specific—looking at me with thinly masked concern.

"You sound like a bad breakup line," I mumbled, still wondering why we'd had to move our usual brunch time from 11 AM up to 9. Who did brunch at 9 AM on a Sunday? This *so* wasn't brunch. This was breakfast. I felt like we were cheating.

Of course, my mood wasn't helped by the fact that, due to lingering depression over celebrating the three-year marker of my apparently endless singledom, I had been at home alone, awake until 3 AM, during which time I had polished off six Bacardi Limón and Sprites (okay, to be fair, six Bacardi Limóns on the rocks—with splashes of Sprite), had plunged headfirst into the tray of brownies my overly helpful secretary, Molly, had brought me at work on Friday, and had then proceeded to smoke an entire pack of cigarettes. And I didn't even smoke. Well, not that often, anyhow. I smoked when I was drinking too much and wanted to feel sorry for myself. I was a Sulky Smoker.

And yes, I knew it was a disgusting, terribly unattractive habit and that I was slowly killing myself. I was well aware. But I had the situation under control. I'd made a deal with Fate. Whenever Fate wanted to send me a guy who wasn't scared of me, I'd quit smoking—cold turkey. In the meantime, I didn't see the harm in lopping years off my life. And besides, what goes better with Bacardi than a Marlboro Light?

Admittedly, I was grasping at straws.

"Were you up late drinking and smoking again?" Meg asked, as if reading my mind. Her wide, gentle brown eyes bored into mine. I shot her a guilty look.

"Maybe," I said. "But in my defense, I also polished off half a tray of brownies."

The three of them—Meg, Jill, and Emmie—just looked at me. Okay, for a lawyer, I wasn't doing the best job of putting on a good defense.

"Fine, fine, so I ate the whole tray," I said, throwing up my hands in mock surrender. "So shoot me."

I had never been good at anniversaries. Even happy ones. I hated the pressure they put on me. With Peter, I had freaked out over what to get him for our first anniversary and had ended up lamely presenting him with season one of *Seinfeld* on DVD while he had bought me a beautiful leather-bound day planner, inscribed with HARPER ROBERTS, ESQ. With Chris, the guy I'd dated before Peter, I had baked him a giant heart-shaped cookie that said I LOVE YOU, CHRIS in chocolate chips, but the edges had burned, the chocolate had melted and smeared, and I basically wound up giving him what looked like a charred Frisbee with unintelligible chocolate smears.

See, I was a disaster at anniversaries. But the bad anniversaries— like today—were especially dreadful. Thus, the overeating, over-drinking, and resumption of the gross habit of smoking.

"You're never going to find a guy sitting on your terrace and drowning your sorrows, Harper," Jill proclaimed a bit smugly, toss-ing her sleek blonde hair (touched up on a biweekly basis at Louis

Licari's salon on Fifth Avenue, in case you were wondering) over her shoulder. I didn't even try to mask the fact that I was glaring at her. Since she had gotten married six months earlier, she had suddenly become very comfortable—*too* comfortable—dispensing advice, as if her status as a Married had made her a sudden expert in all things love-related. I had thus far restrained myself from reminding her of all the dating fumbles she'd had before stumbling upon the diminutive Dr. Alec Katz, who had proposed to her in less than six months with a diamond roughly the size of a disco ball.

"Honey, you're just in a slump," Meg said to me gently while shooting Jill a dangerous look. "And this isn't the day for us to pick you apart." She could always be counted on to dispense motherly nuggets of irrefutable wisdom. Sometimes I forgot she was only thirty-five and not sixty-five, an observation I had thus far refrained from sharing with her. She even *looked* like a concerned grandma sometimes, with her dark hair cut short for practicality's sake, and her affinity for collared shirts with khakis. And she wore aprons at home when she cooked, for God's sake. Aprons!

"Easy for you to say," I grumbled. After all, she was married, too. Darned Marrieds. Going on like they knew what they were talking about.

Hmph. Well, maybe they did.

It was just too early in the morning to deal with that possibility.

Then again, Meg had always seemed to know everything. Maybe it was time I started listening to her. After all, she had been right about pretty much everything in the twenty-nine years I had known her.

In what was a particularly unusual feat for four Manhattanites in their mid-thirties, Meg Myers, Jill Peters-Katz, Emmie Walters, and I had been friends since grade school in Ohio and were still as close as sisters—even if we didn't always see eye-to-eye on everything.

Meg and I had been best friends since the first day of first grade, when she sat down beside me and announced that she had Band-Aids, Children's Tylenol, and Neosporin in her backpack, should I ever fall on the playground and scrape my knee. Twenty-nine years later, she *still* carried Band-Aids and Neosporin, although the Tylenol had been replaced by Advil. She has always been the one I turned to when I had a problem—whether it be the time that Bobby Johnston stole my lunch in the second grade (Meg gave him a very threatening speech about respecting other people's property) or the day my parents told me they were getting a divorce, when I was eleven ("They're not divorcing *you*, Harper," she had explained patiently while I punched her pillow and bawled my eyes out. "And neither of them loves you any less."), or the time my first boyfriend, Jack, broke my heart by dumping me over the phone when I was eighteen. ("He didn't deserve you anyhow," Meg had sniffed while handing me a tissue.)

Emmie had come along two years after Meg and I met, a perky blonde whirlwind of energy whose parents had just moved east from LA. She arrived at James Franklin Cash III Elementary School midway through November with a dark tan and a necklace made of seashells, and all the third-grade boys fell immediately in love with her. Meg stood up for her one day when big Katie Kleegal tried to steal Emmie's lunch, and the three of us had been close ever since.

Jill Peters had been the last addition to our little group. She had moved in down the street from Emmie the summer before junior high, and despite being a year younger, she was the only one of us who knew how to put on foundation, wear a bra, and French-kiss boys, which of course made her immediately indispensable to our little group.

"Girls in Connecticut, where I come from, are *so* far ahead of girls in *Ohio*," she had said with a withering expression of boredom that made us all feel just a bit embarrassed about our affiliation with the Buckeye State. From the day we met her, she had been talking about finding Mr. Right, which baffled Meg and me. We had both been late bloomers, and the summer before junior high we still thought boys were kind of icky.

(Come to think of it, though, maybe we'd been right all along, before the teenage hormones took over our brains. Guys *were* kind of icky, weren't they? Why was it that I was just now coming to this realization at the age of thirty-five? Clearly, I wasn't as smart as I'd thought.)

The other three girls had moved to Manhattan when they were twenty-two, after we had all graduated from Ohio State. Meg had moved into a tiny, dingy one-bedroom in Brooklyn to pursue a career in magazine journalism. Emmie had moved in with Meg for a year, her old Rainbow Brite sleeping bag stretched out on Meg's living room floor, to try out for every Broadway show possible. Jill had studied interior design and had somehow moved directly into a management position at Lila McElroy, a hip, prestigious downtown firm, her first year out of school.

I had visited on weekends but hadn't made the permanent move to Manhattan until I was twenty-four, after I had graduated from Harvard Law, making our little foursome complete once again.

Now we were all living our dreams—or at least an adjusted version of them. I had a thriving career that I loved. Meg, who had originally wanted to be a writer for *The New Yorker,* was instead a senior editor at *Mod,* a trendy women's magazine, which seemed to fit her better anyhow, since it allowed her the opportunity to give young women advice every month—and there was nothing Meg liked better than dispensing advice. She had married her high school sweetheart, Paul Amato, an electrician, who had come to New York with her. She kept her maiden name.

Emmie, a tiny, adorable blonde with pixie-cut curls, had struck out on Broadway, had a string of roles in off-Broadway productions, and finally landed a role on the soap opera *The Rich and the*

Damned two years ago. Once a month or so, she was approached by a starstruck housewife from Boise or Minneapolis or Salt Lake City who recognized her and asked for her autograph, which thrilled her to no end. She also had an endless string of adoring men who were enchanted with her status as a C-list celebrity. She had collected no less than a dozen marriage proposals during the thirteen years she had lived in New York.

And Jill, whose mother had repeated the mantra *Marry well and before you're thirty, and you'll never, ever have to worry* in lieu of a lullaby, every night before tucking her into her pale pink cano-pied bed, had done the only thing she'd ever really aspired to do anyhow: married a wealthy doctor with a penthouse on the Upper East Side. (Although I should add that she hadn't gotten married until the age of thirty-three, somewhat violating the mantra. She had really been in desperation mode in the two years between the time she hit the big three-zero and the time she met Alec.)

So maybe the girls *did* know what they were talking about. After all, I was the only walking romantic disaster among us. I was so used to making faces at them when they tried to give me advice that I never really listened.

"So I added it up last night, and I've figured it out," I said to no one in particular, trying to look as if I thought the whole con-cept of my romantic meltdown was hilarious. "I've been on thirty-seven unsuccessful first dates in the last three years. I think this is a new record. Would one of you like to call the *Guinness Book*?"

"Stop being so negative, Harper," Meg said gently. "The right guy will come along. Just be yourself."

"Easy for you to say," I grumbled. "You married a guy who's been in love with you since we were sixteen. And you—" I turned to Jill. "You married a doctor with a penthouse, just like you wanted. Even before you met him, guys were falling for you all the time. And you—" I focused my attention on Emmie, who was squirming uncomfortably. "Well, I don't even know where to start with you. You're on a date every night of the week with a different guy."

"Not *every* night," Emmie said after a moment. At least she had the decency to blush. I sighed and looked at the three of them: Emmie with her perfectly golden Shirley Temple curls, perfectly perky little nose, and perfectly tanned skin; Jill with her sleek dyed golden hair, Hermès scarf, and perfect Upper East Side ivory complexion; Meg with her cocoa-and-cream skin and silky black hair, a perfect product of an African American mother and a Jewish father. And then there was me: blonde, not unattractive, but apparently less appealing to men than a visit to the urologist.

"Do you know how long it's been since I've even so much as kissed a guy?" I asked softly. "I'm pathetic."

I wasn't just whining. I didn't do that; I hardly ever exaggerated. I think it was the lawyer in me that made me want to tell everything like it was, as if under oath.

"You're not pathetic," Meg said gently. Emmie and Jill nodded, but I just shot them a look. They couldn't put one past me. I knew pathetic when I saw it. And I saw it every morning when I looked in the mirror.

The girls were silent for a moment. They exchanged looks and then turned back to me, waiting for me to go on. But I had nothing left to say. I was deflated. I sighed. I didn't know why I'd even opened my mouth.

"The right guy will come along," Meg said finally, breaking the uncomfortable silence that had settled over us. It seemed to be her fallback phrase for me, and I wondered whom she was trying to convince—me or herself. Her forehead was furrowed with concern.

"Really?" I asked, staring at her in frustration. "When? Where is he? Because the wrong guys aren't even coming along anymore."

As my thirties ticked by with no prospects in sight, I was starting to get just the slightest bit nervous that I had somehow missed the boat.

"That's not true," Jill said, interrupting my self-indulgent self-exploration. "Guys come up to you all the time."

"Yeah," I said softly. "Then they talk to me—or maybe even go out with me a few times—and find out I've got a brain in my head, which is apparently horrifying."

I swallowed hard and forced a smile, trying to look as if I thought the whole thing was funny. In a way, it was. I mean, weren't men supposed to be strong and confident and all? So what was it about me that scared them so much? I wasn't unattractive. I wasn't unkind. I was actually one of the least demanding women I knew, and I didn't think I had a diva bone in my body. But apparently men liked to be the breadwinners, the success stories, the financial kings of their relationships. And thanks to my mid-six-figure income, they never would be if they were with me.

I always knew that the trite phrase *Money doesn't buy happiness* was true. I just hadn't realized that money would actually *preclude* all my chances for happiness. Hmph, they didn't tell you this at Harvard orientation.

"You don't scare men," said Emmie feebly. I looked at her for a moment, waiting for her to continue, but her voice had trailed off, and she looked troubled.

It was no use. I knew the girls meant well. They always had. I mean, they were my best friends in the world, and I knew they only wanted the best for me. But they didn't understand how *hard* it was. Dating had always come so easily to them, despite the inevitable hiccup here and there in their love lives. I mean, I knew that dating was a roller coaster, filled with ups and downs. But the coaster of my love life had stalled at the bottom of a loop for years. And despite their best intentions, the girls didn't know how to get me out of it any more than I did.

I blamed Peter. Okay, so none of this was *actually* his fault, but I had decided long ago that I would blame him anyhow. He made a good scapegoat. I mean, c'mon, what kind of a guy just walks away one day because his live-in girlfriend gets a promotion and a raise? Why couldn't he just tell me that with every success I had, he felt just the teensiest bit more emasculated? If I'd known, I wouldn't have kept talking about the things that made me happy at work. I wouldn't have invited him to my work parties and let my colleagues talk me up. I mistook his mounting discomfort for happiness somehow, deceived myself into believing that for the first time, I was with someone who was *proud* of my accomplishments rather than terrified by them. My mistake.

And so I came home from work each day and, horror of all horrors, told him about my day, which I now recognized as tactical error number one. I told him about all my hopes and dreams—tactical error number two. And then I had the nerve, the gall, the indecency, to go after what I wanted and to make partner at my firm, which came with a lot more prestige and a nice pay hike. Clearly that had been the biggest tactical error of all. Perhaps Peter had been clinging to the hope that I would one day see the light, decide to leave my legal career, and become a stay-at-home mom, like all the good little girls his buddies were dating.

It would have been nice if he had consulted me about that plan.

Now I knew better. The more successful I was at work, the less successful I was at dating. It was a simple causal relationship, and somehow I had only recently managed to wrap my mind around its logic. Perhaps I wasn't as smart as the senior partners at my firm thought I was, or I surely would have figured this all out sooner.

The irony of it all was that none of the men at work—who were my professional peers—would ever understand how I felt. That's because they were the victors in the world's most unfair double standard. All of my male co-workers—even Mort Mortenson, with his enormous belly, ubiquitous suspenders, and ridiculous comb-over—had pretty little pixies of wives ten, twenty, or even thirty years their junior. Many of the secretaries at the firm (all female, of course) considered themselves the dating pool for the firm's young, overworked *male* attorneys, and more than one conference room secretary-on-associate scandal had inexplicably blossomed into marriage.

But wonder of all wonders, there were no men in the I-want-to-date-an-attorney secretary pool. Or at the bar in the building next door to our Wall Street high-rise, where women waited to pick up the attorneys and bankers who filtered out of our building each evening. Or in any bar, bookstore, coffee shop, or apartment party I'd ever been to in New York so far.

I was beginning to run out of options. Or maybe I already had.

OF COURSE I didn't realize then, in my hungover, brownie-stuffed state, hunched over a plate of too-runny eggs, soggy hash browns, and a mug of coffee as big as my throbbing head, that this would be the brunch that would change my life. Or at least my *dating* life. But I guess I had underestimated Meg, fresh out of any Advil or Neosporin to heal the sting of repeated rejection, who of course couldn't stand for any of the people she loved to be unhappy. I thought, sometimes, that she should run for president. We'd achieve world peace in no time, because Meg wouldn't sleep until every last person on the planet had a smile on his or her face. She would sit down personally with Fidel Castro and Saddam Hussein and Tran Duc Luong, bake them cookies, talk to them in that soothing tone of hers, and get them to see the light. They'd be having tea and biscuits in her living room and signing peace treaties in no time. That's just the way she was.

Clearly, in retrospect, I should have been wary of the pleased expression on her face as Emmie and Jill discussed my singledom and I cracked self-effacing jokes at my own expense.

"Maybe you shouldn't tell them what you do for a living," Emmie was suggesting helpfully as I tried steadfastly to ignore her unsolicited help. "I mean, that seems to be what scares them away, you know."

"What, so I'm supposed to lie?" I asked petulantly, pushing my eggs around on my plate with considerably more violence than they deserved.

"I don't know," Emmie said. She shook her head. "Not necessarily *lie*. Maybe just not bring it up."

"But I *don't* bring it up," I protested. "You know that, Em. In fact, I avoid it for as long as I can. But it always comes up. How could it not?"

"Well, maybe you shouldn't tell them," Jill chimed in. "Even if they ask."

I shook my head. "It's part of who I am," I said stubbornly. "I don't want to lie about that. Why is it so scary anyhow?" After all, even if it *was* the death knell to my love life, I was proud to be a lawyer. It's what I had wanted to do since I was a little girl, and I had done it, even though there had been lots of people who had tried to discourage me along the way. I was happy with my job, and I didn't see why I shouldn't be allowed to at least mention it. It was a part of *me*.

"Men are jerks," Emmie said simply. "They're scared to be with a woman they feel at all threatened by. And lots of them feel threatened by women who are smarter or more successful than them."

"So basically, it would be easier to get dates if I were just a dumb blonde," I muttered, reaching up to tug at my naturally blonde hair, which, almost unfortunately, hadn't actually succeeded in making me less smart. So much for the theory that blondes have more fun. I was the walking antithesis to *that*. "Because then I wouldn't be the Scary Lawyer Lady. Is that what you're saying?"

The girls were silent for a moment.

"No, not necessarily," Jill said uncomfortably. Emmie looked nervous, and Meg looked lost in thought. I knew what they were thinking, and they were right. It sure *would* be a lot easier if I didn't have anything going on north of my neckline. Whoever thought

that intelligence—and the courage to go after what I wanted—
would wind up being such a curse?

"Say that again," Meg said finally, breaking the stifling silence
and turning to me with a gleam in her eye that made me a bit
uneasy.

"Say what?" I asked, looking from Jill to Emmie, who
shrugged.

"What you said a second ago," Meg said, sounding excited.

"What, that it would be easier to get dates if I were just a dumb
blonde?" I glanced at her nervously. I knew Meg well enough to
know that I should be more than a bit worried about the look on
her face. I'd seen that look before. And it never ended well.

"Yes!" she said triumphantly, grinning at us and clapping her
hands with glee.

"What's wrong with you?" Emmie asked, staring at Meg skeptically. "You're being weird."

"Nothing's *wrong*!" she exclaimed. "I just had the best idea!
For 'Dating Files'!"

"Dating Files" was one of the sections that Meg edited in *Mod*
magazine. Each month, a different dating topic or strategy was discussed. To be honest, I thought it was sort of ridiculous. I mean,
I'd been reading "Dating Files" since Meg started working at *Mod,*
and look where it had gotten me. Absolutely nowhere. I had even
resorted to taking notes on the columns in one particularly dis-
couraging dateless slump in my late twenties—and still nothing.

"I'm trying to assign out 'Dating Files' for August, and none
of our stringers' suggestions or the suggestions we came up with at
the editorial meetings really struck me as right," Meg bubbled on.
"But this. This is perfect!"

"What's perfect?" I asked slowly, knowing Meg well enough
to be feeling just the teensiest bit apprehensive as she grinned at
me like a lunatic. I had a bad feeling about whatever was about to
come out of her mouth.

"You'll write 'Dating Files' for the August issue!" Meg said, clapping her hands again.

"I will?" I didn't have the faintest idea what she was talking about, but I knew I would have remembered agreeing to pen a column for her.

She just kept on talking, as if she hadn't heard me. "It's perfect," she said gleefully. "You can try dating like a dumb blonde for two weeks and write for *Mod* about how it changed your life!"

"What are you talking about?" I asked slowly. "And what exactly is dating like a dumb blonde?"

Meg shrugged and thought about it for a moment. "I don't know, just acting ditzy, vacant, airheaded," she said finally. "Stereotypically blonde. No offense to the three of you." The three blondes at the table—me, Emmie, and Jill (who wasn't really a natural blonde, but who was keeping track?)—exchanged glances. "We'll iron out the details later," Meg continued excitedly. "But you're not allowed to say you're a lawyer. You're not allowed to say anything smart. Just act brainless and see how it changes your life."

"Why would I want to do that?" I asked dubiously. Emmie and Jill were both grinning and nodding with what appeared to be agreement to Meg's harebrained plan.

"Because it's about time you put your money where your mouth is, Harper Roberts," Meg said, suddenly as stern and as mother-like as I'd ever seen her. "You're always talking about how it would be so much easier to date if guys didn't feel so threatened by you and your job and your intelligence. Well, let's see."

"I don't think so," I said skeptically. It sounded insane. How was I supposed to be a dumb blonde? I wasn't a dumb blonde. Besides, wasn't the whole concept offensive anyhow?

"Ooh, you should do it, Harper!" Emmie said excitedly, tossing her own blonde curls.

"We'll call it The Blonde Theory," Meg went on, also ignoring me and grinning like a lightbulb had just gone on in her head.

"The theory that acting like a dumb blonde will make you have more success with guys. We'll see if dumb blondes really *do* have more fun!"

"I love it!" Jill gushed, reaching across the table and squeezing my hand. "You *have* to do it."

"The Blonde Theory?" I asked skeptically. I looked around at the three of them. Their eyes were all gleaming—with excitement or with vulture-like hunger, I couldn't tell. They looked insane. Actually, this whole plan was insane. "No way. I'm not going to do something like that. It sounds crazy. You guys are crazy."

"Are you scared?" Jill asked, innocently cocking her head at me, a devilish grin dancing across her face.

I turned to her. "What?" I asked sharply. She knew better than to ask that. Nothing scared me. "No," I said defensively after a moment. "Of course not. I just think it's a dumb idea."

"So you're scared," Jill singsonged triumphantly.

I glared. "I am not." For a moment, I felt like we were back in junior high again.

"So what's the problem, then?" Jill pressed on. "You're always saying that it would be easier to date if you weren't smart or didn't have such a good job."

I knew she was trying to goad me into saying yes. So were Meg and Emmie, who were staying conspicuously silent as Jill pressed me.

"I don't know…," I said reluctantly, half swayed by Jill's implication that I was wimping out, half swayed by the idea that maybe this *was* the way to test the theory I was always whining halfheartedly about.

"C'mon, Harper, you'll find out once and for all if it really is easier to date if you don't have a brain in your head," Jill coaxed. I bit my tongue before I said something I'd regret, like something about how she had seemingly already proved this by batting her eyes right into the heart of Dr. Alec Katz, who didn't seem all that thrilled when Jill expressed a thought or opinion of her own. Emmie, Meg, and I didn't like him much—he seemed pompous and superficial—but we had thus far restrained ourselves from saying anything negative about him since the day Jill had announced she was marrying him.

Instead, I tried my best line of defense. "I don't know *how* to act like a dumb blonde," I declared with finality, looking suspiciously among the three girls. They'd clearly already made up their minds. I suddenly felt like the odd man out.

"I'll help you, I'll help you!" Emmie exclaimed, clearly so excited that she felt she had to announce it twice. "I'll give you lessons!"

"She *is* an actress," Jill pointed out helpfully. Then she paused for a moment, her eyes gleaming. When she spoke again, her words were slow and deliberate. "C'mon Harper. We *dare* you."

I sucked in a quick breath. Oh geez. She had said the magic words. *We dare you.* I knew from the looks on Emmie's and Meg's faces that they'd realized what had just happened, too. It was common knowledge in our group—heck, in the whole town of Worthington, Ohio, where we had grown up—that Harper Roberts *never* turned down a dare. But this was different from the dares of our childhoods, where I was sent out to trip dumb boys in the junior high hallways or to hide frogs caught at the creek in the desk of our unpleasant science teacher. This was a *real* dare with *real* consequences.

I knew I couldn't say no.

Three years *was* an awfully long dry spell, I had to admit. And this could be my chance to find out the truth. Were men scared away because I was smart and successful (horror of all horrors)? Or because I was *me*? The latter was a possibility I had been trying to ignore as long as possible, but maybe the problem was just that I wasn't attractive to guys. What if, smart or dumb, they just didn't like *me*? If I could do an experiment to control the intelligence factor, at least I'd know where the problem lay.

"Harper, you have to!" Emmie said, unaware that I had already made up my mind. "It would be so fun!"

"Two weeks?" I asked finally, trying to sound reluctant. I didn't want the girls to know that in reality, frightening as it was, I was actually starting to embrace the idea of dating as someone other than me. After all, dating as myself hadn't exactly been a resounding success.

"Two weeks," Meg confirmed with a confident nod, reaching over to begin buttering her bagel.

"And all I'd have to do is act like a dumb blonde?"

"In every dating situation," she confirmed with a nod. "On dates. At bars. At parties. Wherever."

All three of them were looking at me eagerly.

"Fine," I said finally, nodding. I took a deep breath and smiled at my friends. "I guess I'm in." The contents of my stomach shifted as I said it, and I felt vaguely queasy, but I tried to ignore it.

A cheer went up from our little table, and Meg proposed a mimosa toast. As I raised my glass and looked back and forth among my three maniacally grinning friends, I wondered momentarily what I had just gotten myself into. What if the theory didn't work and the only thing that I discovered was that men didn't like me no matter what?

"We start tomorrow night," Meg said ominously as we all downed our orange-juice-spiked champagne. "Mark it on your calendars, ladies. May twenty-third. The day that Ditzy Harper will be born."

Chapter Three

D-Day was May 23, the day that a new and infinitely more datable Harper Roberts would hit the streets of New York, the day that all my luck would change.

Right?

I sure hoped so. Because the alternative would be that I'd spend the next two weeks acting like a complete idiot for no reason whatsoever.

Oddly enough, that did not exactly appeal to me.

Having already established that naïveté and empty-headedness wouldn't go over very well in the law offices of Booth, Fitzpatrick & McMahon, I had received "permission" to act like my normal self at work, where I was operating under the assumption that the corporate attorneys, engineers, and chemists that I dealt with on a routine basis as a patent attorney would be less than enthusiastic trusting their financial futures to a half-wit. Elsewhere, in all other situations, I was to become a vacant Barbie doll. Well, a Barbie doll without the 39–21–33 to-scale measurements, of course. Mine were 34–29–36. More Raggedy Ann than Barbie. But I digress.

I was thankful that I could at least act normally at work, because it was the only place in the world where I truly felt at home. I know, that's a sad statement, right? But they say home is where the heart is. And due to my conspicuous lack of any guys worthy of giving my heart to (okay, or any guys who actually stuck around long enough to consider such heart giving), I had thrown all my energy—and all my heart—into my job, which I really, truly loved.

I once read that only 1 percent of Americans had what they considered a "dream job," a job that made them excited to go to work every morning and let them leave entirely satiated at the end of the day. I knew without a doubt that I was one of those lucky few. I had become a patent lawyer because I couldn't decide between chemical engineering (which I loved because of the fascinating interaction between chemicals, but I won't go into the details...I've been told that when I start rambling about ionization and the periodic table, I'm a really dull conversation partner) and rhetoric (I've always loved talking circles around people by using logic and spinning my thoughts into cohesive, convincing phrases). So after earning my bachelor's in chemical engineering and graduating summa cum laude from Ohio State in just three years, law school felt like a natural fit. I graduated at the top of my Harvard Law class then went on to study for the patent bar, because chemical engineering and law were inextricably wed in my mind. And patent law was the best way to combine my two loves.

Little did I know that the marriage between chemicals and legal terminology would be the only successful wedding I'd personally experience in my first three and a half decades of life. But again, I digress.

I felt like the luckiest girl in the world, because I got to do something different every day. Okay, it probably sounds boring to you, but I got such a rush out of hearing a chemical engineer at 3M tell me, his eyes shining excitedly, about a new adhesive he'd discovered to make tape seven times stickier. Or a pharmaceutical engineer at Mabry tell me about the new compound she'd engineered that would make headache medications work up to three times faster. Or the chemical engineer at BakersGrain tell me about the new preservative that would double the shelf life of cornflakes.

Seriously. It was awesome because I *understood* it all. And I loved helping engineers and chemists secure patents for their developments. I loved knowing that I played a small role in all sorts of new products and designs that made differences—however subtle—in the world. I loved the intellectual stimulation of being surrounded by both scientists and lawyers, tickling both the creative and logical sides of my brain. I loved arguing cases in front of the patent board, convincing them that my clients weren't infringing on other patents and should have full rights to their ideas. I loved it with all my heart.

But loving your job wasn't cool. At least not when your job involved complicated chemical formulas and legal intricacies and netted you three hundred grand a year. Nope, then it was just intimidating. In terms of dating, I'd be much better off with just a high school diploma.

Thus, The Blonde Theory.

AFTER A RELATIVELY normal morning of using my man-repelling brain to write a quick brief and begin work on a series of contracts associated with a bizarre "miracle cream for breast enhancement" that one of my clients had brought me last week for patenting, I headed to the set of *The Rich and the Damned* to meet Emmie for a quick lunch. She had said she wanted to talk with me about The Blonde Theory, and I figured I had nothing to lose. Who better to take dating tips from than my friend who seemed to be a pied piper of men, leaving a trail of broken hearts behind her wherever she went?

"I only have an hour," I said when she met me at the stage door, which she opened to let me in so that we could avoid the bleached-blonde, gum-snapping receptionist, who always took at least twenty minutes to issue security "clearance" to visitors, which consisted only of photocopying their IDs and giving them a visitor's badge. "I have a mound of work to do at the office. Maybe we can grab something quick at the deli on the corner."

"Oh, we're not eating today," Emmie said, grabbing my arm and yanking me inside. The stage door shut behind us, rather ominously, I thought.

"We're not?" I asked suspiciously. Emmie was in full makeup for the show, as she often was when I visited her, and I couldn't help but feel like I was being led down the hallway by an overly enthusiastic clown with a face full of matte pancake makeup and bright red lips. The only thing missing was a big red nose.

"No," she said cheerfully.

"Then why am I here?" I looked at her blankly. "I thought you invited me to lunch."

"No time for small talk. We have to get right to work," Emmie said mysteriously, ignoring my question. "Follow me."

Checking my watch and trying to shush my grumpily grumbling stomach, I followed her down the darkened hallways. Still holding my hand, as if she were afraid I would dart away if she let go (well, maybe I would have), she click-clacked in her high heels past doors decorated with actors' names inside stars, then on past Sound Stage 1, currently set up to look like a hospital room.

"One of the characters is in a coma," Emmie explained hurriedly as we passed by. Of course. One of the characters was *always* in a coma. Except during the times when one was *awakening* from a lengthy coma or returning from the dead or some such thing.

For two years now, Emmie had played the assistant to the devilishly handsome Dr. Dirk Doubleday on the soap, and she was convinced it was the first step toward her big break, the role that would lead to her being noticed and cast as a lead on a prime-time drama series, which would, of course, lead to her being cast as the lead in next summer's box-office-breakout romantic comedy.

She already had her sights set on the mansion next to Tom Cruise's. Seriously. She had a photo of it pinned to the mirror in her dressing room.

Emmie turned down the hall leading to the makeup room with me following two paces behind, wondering where she was taking us. My nose told me we were leaving the general vicinity of the tempting buffet table.

"Wait here for a moment," she said, pulling to a halt before we reached the dressing room she shared with several other minor characters on the show. Of course, I would never refer to them as minor characters. *Supporting actors,* Emmie called them.

"What are you doing?" I asked as she opened a door off the hallway.

"Shhhh! " she hissed at me. "I'm just making sure the coast is clear." She looked from side to side suspiciously, her blonde ringlets bobbing around her face, and slipped inside the room beside her dressing room.

I sighed and leaned back against the wall of the hallway, crossing my arms. I was hungry, and it had been a long morning. I didn't have time for Emmie's dramatics today. She was always making a bigger deal out of things than she needed to. I mean, I guess that was her job. But I'm the complete opposite: practical and sparse in my antics.

In a moment, an elated Emmie reemerged from the room, grabbed my arm, and pulled me inside.

"It's safe. C'mon," she said. She flipped on the light, revealing a massive closet lined with racks and racks of clothes, shoes, wigs, and accessories. "Welcome to the Wardrobe Closet," she said with dramatic flourish, gesturing around us grandly. I blinked and stared. It was what I'd always imagined Heaven would look like.

The room seemed to go on forever. The walls were lined with shelves six feet high, filled with every color, shape, and size of shoe I could imagine. Clear cabinets were filled with a sea of denim in every shade, and endless racks were lined with hangers full of shirts, pants, dresses, skirts, and jackets in every color, shape, and size ever created. Carrie Bradshaw would have a field day here. Well, she would if she weren't a fictional character, anyhow. I gulped and tried to appear nonchalant, although my little shopper's heart was beating rapidly.

"What are we doing here?" I asked, trying to sound grumpy instead of impressed. I refused to admit that I was trying not to salivate. "I'm hungry," I said instead.

"Har*per*," Emmie said in exasperation. "Can you not think about food for, like, thirty seconds? We're trying to get you outfitted for the Blonde Theory experiment."

"Outfitted?" I asked suspiciously, my gaze finally drawn away from the endless rows, shelves, and racks of beautiful clothes. I focused on Emmie with some reluctance. "What are you talking about? We didn't say anything about outfits."

Emmie sighed, clearly exasperated with me.

"Harper," she began slowly, as if she were talking to a child. "In acting, the first step to *being* the part is *looking* the part. And you're not exactly going to *look* the part in *your* clothes, are you?"

I looked down at my body. I was dressed in a slim, pin-striped black Armani pantsuit over a crisp white blouse with Jimmy Choo stiletto pumps peeking out from beneath the slightly flared bottoms of the pant legs. I looked all business. My favorite necklace, a sterling-silver Tiffany heart on a slim silver chain, dangled in the cleft of my collarbone.

"I can see your point," I admitted reluctantly. Although I loved my clothes.

"So I've taken the liberty of picking out several outfits for you," Emmie announced. I just stared at her. She pulled out one of the sliding racks.

"Smart Harper," she said, grinning at me, "meet Dumb Harper." She gestured grandly to the rolling rack.

It was a veritable sea of acid-trippy tight pants, clingy dresses, halter tops, and shirts that looked suspiciously like bras.

Oh no. I could *not* wear any of this. No way.

"A tube top?" I asked skeptically, pointing to the first outfit that Emmie held up.

"Yep," she said proudly. "And don't worry; everything's a label."

I groaned. "Yeah, the label of ugliness," I muttered.

She rolled her eyes. "No, look." She pulled out one of the dresses, a short, white, nearly transparent one. "See," she said, showing me the tag. "Versace. And this one," she said, replacing the white dress and pulling out a little turquoise number, "is Stella McCartney."

I quickly leafed through the rack, and indeed, nearly every item on it seemed to be from an expensive designer label. Not that I could imagine anyone spending that kind of money on these kinds of designs.

"Emmie," I said flatly, turning back from the rack to face her. A slightly ill feeling rose inside me as I tried not to picture myself in some of these dresses. "I would never wear any of this."

"Exactly," Emmie announced triumphantly. "Harper Roberts, meet the new you."

TEN MINUTES LATER, I was poured into a strapless fuchsia dress that was long enough to keep me from looking like a streetwalker but clingy enough in all the right places to leave little to the imagination. It followed the curves of my hips then flared out into a flowy tulip skirt that ended well above my knees. I frowned at myself in the mirror.

"I look like a prostitute," I groaned, knowing very well that I didn't. Actually, I was ashamed to admit that I looked a lot better in the dress than I had expected. Not that I would say that to Emmie. I wouldn't want to encourage her.

"You're exaggerating, Harper," she said dismissively. "Besides, do you know any prostitutes who wear Dolce?"

"I suppose I'm supposed to wear this to the firm dinner tomorrow night?" I asked wryly, ignoring the fact that Emmie was right about the dress's label as I turned to stare at myself in the mirror from another angle. No, this was definitely not working for me. "You know, the dinner I don't have a date for yet?"

She laughed. She knew me well enough to know I was just trying to deflect attention from the real issue. It was my oldest trick.

"I wouldn't exactly recommend wearing this to dinner with the other partners, Harp," she deadpanned. "I think that falls into the category of time off from The Blonde Theory in the interests of keeping your job."

"Great," I said, rolling my eyes at her. "Lucky me."

Not that it mattered. If I couldn't find a date—which was beginning to look like a distinct possibility—I'd be ostracized like a leper anyhow. Seriously. I had tried going stag before, and the stigma still hadn't worn off. The implication, of course, when you showed up alone was that you were not actually capable of getting a date. In my case, this was true. But it's not like I wanted my co-workers to *know* that. It was one thing to *be* an undatable loser. It was quite another to have the entire office *know* you were an undatable loser.

"Besides, stop changing the subject," Emmie said, swatting me lightly as I turned to look over my shoulder at myself in the mirror. "This is about the dress you have on, not about your firm dinner. We'll get you a date. And right now, you look hot."

Okay, so I did look hot.

If you were into that whole slutty look.

Which I wasn't.

But who knew I could pull off trampy so well? Hmm, this was a new side to myself.

"I looked hotter in my Armani suit," I said antagonistically. Besides, what did she mean when she said she'd get me a date? So now she was my stylist *and* my pimp?

"Well, I think you look a little masculine in your Armani suit," Emmie said with a grin. I frowned at her. "Besides," she added, "you look *dumber* in this, and that's the key."

"For what it's worth, I think you look hot, too," said a deep voice from the direction of the door. Emmie and I both whirled around, startled.

Framed in the doorway stood Matt James, one of the big-name stars of the show, a thirtysomething actor with jet-black hair, sharp green eyes, a strong jaw, and boyish dimples. He played defense attorney Patrick Carr, the embattled Good Samaritan whose plotline currently had him embroiled in some sort of conflict with the mother of his identical twin brother's baby. I'd never admit it to Emmie, but I didn't catch *The Rich and the Damned* often, even with my new ability to TiVo it and watch it at night. I just found soap operas far-fetched, melodramatic, and boring. Imagine that.

But the actors on them sure were cute. I had the uncomfortable suspicion that I was blushing.

As for Matt James in particular, I was embarrassed to say that I'd had a bit of a crush on him—inconceivably illogical as that was—since we'd first met at one of the show's wrap parties just after Peter and I had broken up. I had still been deep within my post-Peter depression and hadn't been looking to date anyone at all, but I would have had to be blind to have not noticed Matt. I mean, obviously, a guy who plays a hunky lawyer on a daytime soap is going to be attractive. All of Emmie's co-stars were. But there was something about Matt that struck me so deeply from the beginning, I turned into a blushing fool nearly every time he was around. And that was *so* not me. I usually stayed cool, calm, and collected no matter what. Matt somehow always seemed to turn my brain—and my knees—to mush just by existing in my general vicinity.

Unlike the other actors on the show, most of whom struck me as stuck-up and kind of empty-headed, Matt had always seemed to have an unexpected depth. He sounded intelligent when he spoke.

His eyes sparkled intently, and he tilted his head thoughtfully when he listened. He had a smile for everyone. His happiness and kindness appeared genuine.

Then again, as I constantly reminded myself whenever I saw him, he was an *actor*. It was his *job* to make people think he was a genuinely good guy. I wouldn't be fooled. There was no such thing as a genuinely good guy. At least not a genuinely good soap-star guy.

Of course, it was ridiculous to have a crush on some random daytime soap actor. I had never even told Emmie about my attraction because I knew she would laugh at me. I knew she found him attractive, too, but she had dated another star on the show when she'd first started there—an actor named Rob Baker—and learned the hard way how difficult it was to work with an ex after a breakup. It still bugged her to see him around. She had vowed she would never date another co-worker. Easy for her to say. She never had a shortage of men throwing themselves at her away from the set.

"Hey, Em," Matt said cheerfully as he approached us, eyeing us warily as we dug through the wardrobe closet. He appeared to be smirking a bit, though I hardly noticed. I was trying desperately to control my blushing, but it appeared to be futile; my cheeks felt like they were on fire.

"Well, what have we here?" he asked, turning to me with sparkling eyes and putting a hand on my elbow to hold me at arm's length. His eyes ran up and down the length of my body, still clad in the skintight fuchsia dress, and I suddenly felt the urge to cover up. I crossed my arms and looked at him defiantly, giving him my best reserved-for-the-courtroom hard-ass glare—which, for the record, is a little hard to do when your cheeks are lit up like Rudolph's red nose.

"Nice to see you again, Harper," he said with just enough of a glint in his eye that his words didn't sound entirely genuine. "Nice dress." Okay, now it was a full-out smirk.

"Stealing from the wardrobe closet?" he asked Emmie, an eyebrow arched.

"Not stealing," she said defensively. "Just borrowing."

"Hmm," Matt said thoughtfully, turning back to me, grinning like a little boy now. Emmie and I were both squirming uncomfortably, and he seemed to be enjoying every second of it. "Harper, with your hot-shot lawyer job and all, I'd think you'd have enough money to buy your own clothes. Or are you considering a career change?"

"Shut up, Matt," Emmie snapped, shooting him a warning look.

"So what *are* you doing?" he finally asked, cutting to the chase. I tried to ignore the way his big green eyes sparkled with amusement as he looked back and forth between us. Big green eyes are my weakness. Well, one of my weaknesses.

"None of your business, Matt James," Emmie said. Uh-oh, she was full-naming him. She clearly meant business. I, of course, was staying silent, trying to think of all sorts of cold things—ice, the North Pole, sticking my head in the freezer—to cool my cheeks. This was beyond embarrassing.

"Hmmm," Matt said again, his green eyes twinkling with infuriating adorableness as he looked at us slyly. "And yet it strikes me that it *is* my business, seeing that I'm now inadvertently an accomplice in your little steal-from-the-wardrobe-closet scheme."

"Borrow," Emmie corrected impatiently. "Borrow-from-the-wardrobe-closet."

"Ah," Matt said, arching an eyebrow. "*Borrow*. Of course."

"Anyhow, it's still none of your business," Emmie said sourly.

"It would seem not," he said finally, looking back and forth between us. He grinned again and raked a hand through his thick, dark hair. "I have the feeling that when I find out about it, though, I'm going to get a kick out of it."

"There's nothing to find out," Emmie snapped.

"Right," Matt said. He winked at me and I forced myself to glare back at him. Glaring seemed so much classier than drooling. He smiled at me, apparently unfazed. "Okay, well then, ladies, I'll leave you to playing dress-up. I'm due on Sound Stage Two. It seems that young Mrs. Cohen's eighty-five-year-old husband is in a coma and she needs a lawyer to help her figure out how to legally pull the plug."

"Important stuff," I muttered.

"Ah, I knew you were listening," Matt said, turning to me. "Apparently that dress hasn't squeezed all of the brain cells out of you yet."

I made a face. He grinned back, his gaze even.

"Just one more thing, Matt," I heard Emmie say innocently beside me. There was something in her voice that made me turn and look at her. She was smiling in a way that made me suddenly uncomfortable.

"Yes?" Matt asked, waiting expectantly.

"What are you doing tomorrow night?" she asked. Suddenly, I realized exactly what she was leading up to. I opened my mouth to say something, but it was too late. Oh no. I felt my cheeks heating up again.

"Nothing," Matt said with a shrug. "Why?"

"Harper has a firm dinner tomorrow night," Emmie said, refusing to look at me because she knew very well that I was currently shooting death-ray stares in her direction. "She had this really hot, really great guy lined up to go with, but the plans just fell through." She shot me a look, and I made a desperate face at her. She grinned. "Apparently he's some big-shot lawyer in DC, and the president just called him away." I rolled my eyes and shook my head, but Emmie ignored me. "Anyhow, it would be a shame for Harper to go alone. And I thought that maybe spending the evening with a bunch of lawyers would be great research for your role on the show. Do you want to go with her?"

"Oh," said Matt, looking temporarily unsure as he glanced at me and then back at Emmie. I felt an unexpected lump in my throat, and suddenly my knees seemed weak. I knew I was still blushing furiously. This was humiliating. He didn't even *want* to go with me. Of course he didn't. I was sure he had much better things to do than take pity on some frumpy lawyer who couldn't get her own date to events. Emmie's story hadn't even sounded remotely truthful. Sheesh.

"Actually, I'd love to go," Matt said, turning to look straight at me, his green eyes boring into mine. I felt my eyes widen with surprise. "That is, if it's okay with you, Harper," he added cautiously.

"Uh, yeah, it's fine," I said, caught totally off-guard. What I wanted to say was, *You don't have to come with me just because you feel sorry for me and because Emmie put you on the spot.* But of course, I couldn't say that. Emmie was grinning triumphantly beside me, I noticed out of the corner of my eye. I made a mental note to strangle her later. "But don't feel like you have to come," I said, suddenly defensive. "I mean, I can get a date on my own, you know."

Okay, so that just sounded childish. Not to mention the fact that it was entirely untrue. Embarrassing as this fix-up was, at least I'd have a date to the dinner.

"No, I'd love to go," Matt said kindly, a little too hastily to be believed. "Emmie's right. It would be great research."

Despite myself, I could feel my heart sink. Of course. That's what this was about. He could kill two birds with one stone: He'd be the humanitarian of the evening for escorting the undatable lawyer to the dinner, and he'd also score some free lawyer lessons. It was Matt James's lucky day.

But I was too humiliated now to change my mind and turn him down. On top of that, I really *did* need a date.

"Great," I finally said softly. "Thanks." I gave him my address and phone number.

"So I'll see you tomorrow night, then," Matt said, turning back with a grin after he reached the doorway. "Oh, and Harper?"

"Yes?" I asked cautiously.

"Don't wear that dress," he said with a grin. "I don't know much about being a lawyer. But I don't think the senior partners would approve." He winked. "See you tomorrow night."

Then, with a wave over his shoulder, he was gone, leaving me to stare after him openmouthed. Finally, I turned to Emmie, ready to tear into her.

"Are you blushing?" she asked me suspiciously.

"Uh, no," I said. I was a terrible liar. I could feel my cheeks get even hotter. "Emmie, why did you do that? I'm humiliated."

Emmie just shrugged. "You needed a date," she said casually. "And I'm sure Matt is happy to go with you. It will help him with his role. Besides," she added, giving me a sidelong glance, "he owes me a favor."

"Oh," I said, trying not to sound disappointed, because of course that would be stupid. "Of course. A favor."

"Okay, Harper, I know you're in a rush, so we have to do this quickly," Emmie said, snapping me back to attention. She looked wholly oblivious to what she'd just put me through.

"Do what?" I asked, trying to snap out of the feeling-sorry-for-myself haze.

"I have to teach you how to act like a dumb blonde," Emmie said impatiently. "And we need to start right away."

"Can't it wait until tomorrow?" I asked, tugging at the top of my fuchsia dress, wondering why they didn't build more support into these things. Suddenly, I didn't feel like talking about dating anymore. I just felt defeated. But I suppose that was all the more reason to get to work on The Blonde Theory, wasn't it?

"Patience, Harper, patience. And no, we can't wait until tomorrow. Tonight's the first night of The Blonde Theory, and that means you have to start playing the part today. The girls will kill me if we show up and you're still the same old Harper. I promised them a dumb blonde, and a dumb blonde they will have."

I sighed. She had a point.

"Okay," I said reluctantly. I took a deep breath and resigned myself to whatever it was I had gotten myself into. "What do I have to do?"

Chapter Four

By the time I had left the soap-opera set, the promised roast beef sandwich in hand, Emmie had taught me how to insert the word *like* into sentences every few words instead of speaking concisely, to bat my eyes shyly rather than stare people down confidently, to carry myself with my bosom thrust perkily upward instead of standing with my shoulders back and my head held high. She had taught me how to gaze at someone in consternation over simple points rather than following every move in a conversation, to exclaim, mystified, "I don't understand!," and to speak an octave higher than normal instead of keeping my voice low and assured. She had even talked me through fictitious backgrounds in my new profession. I was now Harper Roberts, New York Knicks City Dancer.

Not that that was even realistic. Thirty-five-year-old women who hadn't seen the inside of a gym in months couldn't pass for NBA dancers, could they? But Emmie dismissed my objections out of hand.

In short, Emmie had taught me how to be the complete opposite of me. And I was doing a frighteningly good job of it. As I'd looked at myself in the mirror, the fuchsia dress clinging to my curves, my hair teased with a can of Aqua Net and false eyelashes that looked like giant spiders glued to my eyelids, I almost believed that I was a few tuna cans short of a Jessica Simpson. I even *felt* dumber as I trudged back to my office that afternoon—having changed back into my suit—chomping hungrily on my sandwich and dreading the evening ahead.

You might wonder why I feel that I need to resort to something as drastic as The Blonde Theory. After all, you might say, *She seems to have it pretty much together. Why does she feel like she has to fake being someone else?*

Easy for you to say. You don't have a dating history that reads like a train wreck. Or maybe you do. But if that's the case, you probably wouldn't be asking me why I'm trying out The Blonde Theory. Right?

Okay, let's just study this for a moment:

Boyfriend Number One: Jack. I'm eighteen; he's twenty-two; we seem to be a perfect match. He looks into my eyes, tells me he loves me, sends me flowers, writes me love letters...and then seven months into our relationship announces that he'd like to get married and have kids soon. "But, Jack," I say, "I want to finish college. I want to go to law school. I'm not ready for kids yet." He protests; I relent and say that maybe I'll think about it once I've finished college, because after all, I'm only eighteen, and I don't realize that you aren't supposed to give up all your dreams just because the guy you stare dreamily at says so. No, he tells me, I want kids within a year. "But, Jack," I say again, "I'm not ready." Three weeks later, Jack calls and tells me that God spoke to him in the car and told him that Southern Baptists (which he is) shouldn't date Catholics (which I am). Two months later, he's planning his wedding to Southern Baptist Suzy, a month after that they're married, nine months later they welcome Jack Jr. into the world. *Okay,* I think. *It's not me. It's a religious thing. It's not about me.*

Boyfriend Number Two: James. I'm nineteen. He's twenty-three. The complete opposite of Jack. Probably never seen the inside of a church. *Good,* I think. *God won't speak to him in the car.* We date for two years. James works as a newspaper reporter in Columbus. When I find out the spring of my final year that I've gotten into Harvard Law, I'm ecstatic. James is upset. "But you were supposed to stay here and go to law school in Ohio," he says, sulking over the celebratory champagne I ordered to break the great news to him. I never said that, I protest. It's always been my dream to go to Harvard. "But now I'm in the picture," James says angrily. "Your dreams should take me into account." They do, I assure him. You can come with me and work at a newspaper in Massachusetts, I say. Or I'll visit all the time and move back as soon as I'm done with school. "I hate Boston," James tells me, although I know he's never been there. Two weeks later, James leaves me a message on my answering machine. "I love you, but I'm not *in* love with you anymore," he says cheerfully. "I'm ending this. I'm sure we'll stay friends." I try calling him back, but he never answers his phone. *Okay,* I think. *It's not me. It's because he doesn't want to move. It's not about me.*

Boyfriend Number Three: Dusty. I'm twenty-two. He's twenty-three. He plays guitar in a rock band. I meet him at Ned Devine's Irish Pub in Faneuil Hall. I'm drunk—too drunk to realize that I am not exactly compatible with a rock guitarist who hasn't been to college. *I'll go out on a limb,* I think the next day when I'm sober and trying to rationalize my new crush. *I've never dated a musician before. Maybe I need someone creative.* Soon, creative translates into alcoholic, which translates into unreliable. We date for a year. Clearly, I should break up with him, since I'm fairly sure he's cheating on me, and he spends much of his time stumbling around in a drunken stupor. But I feel sorry for him. And so I am caught off-guard when *he* breaks up with *me* on our one-year anniversary. "You spend too much time with your nose buried in a book," he says, then belches. "Would you mind asking the bartender to send me another Jäger Bomb on your way out?" *Okay,* I think. *It's not me. It's because he's an alcoholic who spends his life in smoky bars. It's not about me.*

Boyfriends Numbers Four, Five, and Six: Greg, age twenty-five; Brad, age twenty-seven; Griff, age twenty-six. After Dusty, I go the other way and date three Harvard students for a few months each. Greg is in a few of my law classes and breaks up with me after three months the day after our professor calls me up to the front of the class to announce that I've earned the most prestigious internship in the whole class. "You're always trying to one-up me, aren't you?" Greg mutters sourly on the way out. "Don't bother calling." Brad is getting his master's in public policy and has already spent some time work-ing on Capitol Hill. We differ in our political opinions and after a lengthy fight two and a half months into the relationship, he explodes at me. "The other girls I've dated all share my viewpoints! What's wrong with you that you don't?" he yells at me. I have opinions of my own, I shout back. "Well, I wish you didn't!" he yells back. For once, I am the one to dump the guy. But I notice he doesn't seem too upset about it. Then there's Griff, another law student. It works out fine for a while. Then one day, when things seem to be going beauti-fully, Griff tells me curtly that he can't see me anymore. Why, I ask, stricken. "I shouldn't have to explain it," Griff says, glaring at me. "You're supposed to be the smart one here, aren't you?" *Okay,* I think. *It's not me. It's because they all have issues. It's not about me.*

But by the time I get to Peter six years after breaking up with Griff, I'm beginning to wonder . . . *Is it me?* After all, the common threads among the breakup speeches are that I'm too smart. I don't know my place. I'm not ready to have kids. I'm too driven. Are we starting to see a theme here?

Maybe I should just give up, buy five or six cats, subscribe to *Reader's Digest,* and commit to being an old maid. Or the neigh-borhood's resident Crazy Old Cat Lady. But I'm not ready to do that yet. I'm only thirty-five. I'm not horrible once you peel back all the layers of my scary lawyerness. Surely there's a nice, smart, successful, cute guy who could like me for me if my job doesn't get in the way. Right? Besides, I'm allergic to cats.

This is the only reason I've allowed Emmie to persuade me that a tube top, a miniskirt, and masquerading as an NBA dancer are the way to go this evening. Against my better judgment, The Blonde Theory is on.

WE MET AT 7 PM at the trendy rooftop bar of the Hotel Gansevoort in the Meatpacking District. Meg came in a rumpled black linen dress, straight from a late evening at the *Mod* office; Emmie came with a full face of makeup, an Amy Tangerine LOVE tee, and a worn pair of Robin's Jeans with the signature wing stitching on the back pockets; Jill came in a slim-cut crisp white shirt, a black pencil skirt, and, of course, her diamond wedding ring, roughly the size of a disco ball and no less attention grabbing.

I, on the other hand, slunk out of the elevator, feeling humiliated, in a tight pink halter top, a short white denim skirt, and nude sandals with three-and-a-half-inch stacked heels—all of them designer labels, of course, although I still couldn't fathom how any designer in his or her right mind would make clothes like this. And what if I ran into someone I knew? I didn't think any of the partners at my firm were hip enough to come here, but it would be horrifying if they did. How had I let my friends talk me into this?

"Tell me again why I have to wear this outfit," I growled at Emmie as the three girls collapsed in giggles. I mean, this was *humiliating.* Worse than humiliating. Ordinarily, I wouldn't be caught dead in an outfit like this...and yet here I was, proudly sporting it at one of the trendiest bars in Manhattan to the apparently endless amusement of my three best friends.

"Because a real dumb blonde wouldn't have the taste to pick out the clothes that hang in your closet, now, would she?" Emmie asked between giggles.

"Besides, you look hot," Meg choked out between full-out laughs. I made a face at her. "I'd take you home, hot mama," she sputtered out before doubling over again.

"I cannot believe I am doing this," I muttered to no one in particular, feeling none too amused. While they giggled, I adjusted the halter top to make sure I was as covered as possible and yanked down on the hem of the white skirt, trying to conceal as much thigh as I could. I wasn't sure this outfit was such a good idea, as the color of my thighs more or less matched the color of the white denim. But Emmie, who was still doubled over, had assured me that I looked good.

"Okay, okay," I said, sitting down at the table with them. "I'm not going to get any of these supposed dates tonight if the three of you are cackling like lunatics." I took a deep breath and looked at them reluctantly. "So what's the game plan?"

Apparently, Meg, the boss of this absurd operation, had decided that I would start off our little experience with a big bang—acting as ridiculously dumb as possible from the outset. She started to explain.

"Do I really need to act that bad?" I interrupted, looking around the table for support but finding none among the girls, who were all grinning at me broadly. So I took a big swig of the Bacardi Limontini they had ordered for me. At least it gave me *some* kind of support, albeit not the very tangibly helpful kind. "Can't I just be borderline ditzy?" I asked, trying not to sound like I was begging. "I mean, I've known lots of girls who weren't exactly rocket scientists, but they weren't laughingstocks, either."

"Nope." Meg shook her head firmly. "Tonight we have to kick this experiment off the right way. Full-on ditziness, as dumb as you can possibly be. Those are the rules."

"Now, are you in?" Jill chimed in, her eyes sparkling. "Or are you chickening out?"

I glared at her for a second, then sighed in resignation. My friends obviously knew me way too well. They knew all the right buttons to push—and they were currently pushing them with glee.

"So what do I have to do?" I asked carefully. Meg rubbed her hands together, her eyes sparkling. She actually looked surprisingly like a cartoon villain—or one of those scary guys from those Old West movies, plotting mercilessly against the heroes. So was it any wonder that I felt like the hero who was about to take a major fall?

"Tonight, you're Harper Roberts, New York Knicks dancer," Meg said, clapping her hands together as Emmie and Jill giggled. I moaned. I mean, I'd known it was coming, but I still couldn't exactly envision myself as a high-kicking, split-doing, bouncy dancer type. Was it too late to talk my way out of it? I mean, hey, maybe the girls would take pity on me and let me slide by as, say, a waitress or a bartender or something.

"You know, I don't exactly *look* like an NBA dancer type," I protested, gesturing down to my admittedly un-dancer-like body. Not that I was fat. Actually, I was pleased at how slender I had managed to stay at thirty-five—a result, no doubt, of the long hours I often worked while forgetting to eat. But see, when I went to basketball games—which was actually pretty often during the NBA season each year—I eat hot dogs and drink beers in the bleachers. I don't leap across the court in acrobatic displays. Heck, I sometimes had trouble climbing the bleachers without getting winded. Hence the less-flexible-than-the-average-pom-pom-girl body and lack of dancer-friendly body parts.

"That's true," Meg said with a frown. Hey, wait a minute. She wasn't supposed to agree with me so readily! I made a mental note to add an additional fifty sit-ups to my morning exercise routine. Eh, who was I kidding? I'd be lucky if I rolled out of bed with enough energy to walk to the Starbucks on the corner, never mind actually do exercises, despite the stack of hand weights, yoga mats, and encouraging-looking Denise Austin DVDs currently gathering dust in the corner of my living room. I had long operated under the theory that buying as much workout gear as possible was one step closer to actually having that perfectly fit body I dreamed of rather than the slightly round-around-the-edges and jiggly-in-all-the-wrong places one that nature—and my own laziness—had bestowed upon me.

"How about you be a *retired* New York Knicks dancer?" Jill asked, smiling at me.

"Unh-unh, no way, I'm thirty-five," I said, shooting her a look. "I'm too young to be a *retired* anything."

"I guess that just leaves *current* New York Knicks dancer then," Meg said, her eyes twinkling mischievously. Rats, she had me trapped.

"Gooooooo Knicks!" squealed Emmie, loudly enough that the people at the adjoining tables turned to stare. "She's a Knicks dancer," Emmie explained loudly to their questioning glances. They smiled tentatively at me as I groaned.

Just what had I gotten myself into?

I QUICKLY DOWNED a second Limontini—under the very wise notion that playing dumb would be easier if I was a bit intoxicated—and set to work.

"Don't forget to toss your hair a lot, like I taught you," Emmie whispered to me as I set off to the bar with a giggling Jill. The three girls had decided that if we *all* went up to the bar, I'd be too intimidating to approach. So they drew straws to see who'd come with me.

"Let's go find you a date!" Jill enthused, grinning at me and reaching over to squeeze my hand encouragingly as we approached the bar.

"I should warn you," I said, only half kidding. "I don't find dates very easily."

"We'll see," Jill said mysteriously, brushing her silky blonde hair back over her ears with one perfectly manicured hand and smiling at me.

Ten minutes later, I was eating my words.

"So your friends over there tell me you're dancer for the Knicks," said the tall, dark, and admittedly handsome stranger who approached me at the bar. He gestured to Emmie and Meg, who waved and grinned. Great, so he had hit on them first and they had sent him here. He was their leftovers.

But I had to admit, for a leftover, he looked pretty good. He appeared to be in his late thirties, about six foot four with broad shoulders, dark, piercing eyes, and a wide smile. His dark hair was close-cropped in a way that made me think he might have been in the military at one time, an assumption supported by the at-attention way he was standing beside me rather than lounging against the bar.

In other words, just my type. Tall, masculine, probably successful. The type that usually rejected me as soon as they found out I was a lawyer instead of a garden-variety bimbo.

"Yes, I am a dancer," I said primly, then I caught Jill's threatening look. Oops, I had answered him like I normally would have. I raised my voice an octave and tried not to roll my eyes at myself. "I mean, uh, yeah. I, like, totally dance for them." It was my best dumb-Valley-girl impression, and actually, I'd done pretty well. I'd nearly convinced *myself* that my IQ had slipped fifty points in the last few minutes. I choked back a giggle.

For an instant, I wondered if I'd gone overboard, acted too vacant. But Mr. Tall, Dark, and Handsome didn't seem to be turned off by my apparent stupidity and lack of mastery of the English language. Instead, he slid in a bit closer and smiled.

"Is that right?" he asked, his voice thick as syrup.

"Totally," I confirmed in my best chirpy, perky voice. "Like, I totally love doing those cool split jumps in the air, you know?"

I snuck a glance at Jill, whose face had turned beet red as she valiantly struggled to keep her laughter in. She looked as if she might explode at any second. Hey, I wasn't half bad at this! I was surprising even myself.

"That's fascinating," the guy murmured, leaning even closer and dazzling me with his big, white smile. Perhaps this fake me *was* fascinating. So I smiled back and batted my eyes, trying hard to recall the way that Emmie had batted hers at me in front of the dressing room mirror this afternoon. I *thought* I was being sexy. Then I realized that Tall, Dark, and Handsome was looking at me with apparent concern.

"Are you okay?" the guy asked, taking a step closer and looking worried. "Do you have something in your eye?"

I stopped batting. Okay, clearly I was going to have to ask Emmie for a follow-up tutorial on the finer points of eyelash flirtation.

"Uh, I'm fine," I chirped in my elevated-octave dumb-blonde voice. "Just a little problem with my contact lens." I tittered softly in that high-pitched giggle Emmie had taught me. I thought I sounded like one of those squeaky toys dogs played with. But instead of look-ing startled, the guy seemed to like it. He took a step closer, until he was effectively blocking my view of Jill, who was just feet away from me.

Note to self: Apparently squeaking is hot. Who knew?

"I can take a look at it for you if you want," he said. I looked at him, startled, and he grinned. "I mean, I'm an ophthalmologist. An eye doctor. My name's Scott Jacoby."

Hmmm, an ophthalmologist. (How nice that he had defined the term for me. I guess the dumb-blonde act was working.) For a moment, I almost wanted to drop the act right there and let him know that I was his intellectual equal, not some high-kicking floozy with bad contact lenses. Think of the conversations we could have: Politics! Business! Science! Technology! But then I remembered that the *real* me didn't attract tall, dark, and handsome doctors. Pushing down the resentment bubbling up inside me at the unfairness of it all, I forced a smile at Scott.

"No thanks, my eye's fine," I chirped. "But it's, like, totally nice to meet you. I'm Harper."

"Wow, what a pretty name." Scott grinned down at me. "Are you named for Harper Lee, by any chance? The author?"

Of course I was. Both my parents had been attorneys, and they had both been moved by Harper Lee's *To Kill a Mockingbird*, the twentieth-century classic about lawyer Atticus Finch, his daughter, Scout, and the racial turmoil boiling in their small Southern town. But, I reminded myself, a dumb blonde probably wouldn't know about the book, would she? And her parents probably wouldn't have been two well-read lawyers.

"Who?" I asked stupidly, widening my eyes at him and looking as vacant as possible.

He laughed, but it was in a decidedly *Isn't-it-cute-she's-so-dumb* kind of way. "Never mind," he said, leaning in and placing a hand on my arm.

I snuck a glance across the room at Emmie and Meg, who were watching us from their table. Jill, clearly shut out of my conversation with Scott the Eye Doctor, had rejoined them, too, and when they saw me looking, all three of them shot me the thumbs-up sign. I resisted the urge to make a face at them and quickly redirected my attention toward Scott, trying to think of what a dumb blonde would say next.

"Wow, so you're an eye doctor," I breathed excitedly in my high-pitched voice. A dumb blonde would be excited to meet a doctor, right? I mean, wasn't that the gold star atop the Men-to-Be-Desired list? "That's, like, so awesome. You must be, like, really smart."

I tilted my head to the side flirtatiously and tried not to giggle. I couldn't believe words like this were coming out of my mouth, but the more I talked, the more I got into the groove of being a dumb blonde. It wasn't as hard as I'd thought it would be. Or perhaps the Limontinis had just greased the wheels of my stupidity. Either way, I was a natural! It occurred to me that perhaps I should be concerned about how easily the stupidity seemed to come to me. But I had plenty of time to worry about that later.

Scott laughed.

"Nah," he said in a way that really meant *Yes, I'm very smart. And rich.* "I wouldn't say that. I've just worked hard, you know? I have an office just off Fifth Avenue."

"Wow, Fifth Avenue," I breathed, widening my eyes at him. "That's like, where Saks is. I totally love Saks."

Sadly, this was true. Perhaps this was where Dumb Harper and Smart Harper intersected.

"I'm right near there, sweetheart," he said, rubbing my arm now as he leaned even closer. I resisted the urge to back away, because that's what a self-respecting lawyer would do, not a dumb blonde trying to pick up a date. "Maybe you can come by sometime after you go shopping."

"Maybe," I giggled back, pretending that I liked his touch on my arm. Actually, I didn't hate it as much as I thought I would. Sure, it was presumptuous, and I definitely had invasion-of-my-personal-space issues. But he was cute. And it had been a long time since a guy had seemed this in to me right from the outset. It was kind of nice, for once. Even if he was calling me *sweetheart,* which was sort of getting under my skin. Still, his presumptuousness was offset by his cuteness—and the fact that he was already staring at me with adoring eyes. It had been so long since I had seen that look, I hardly recognized it. I was accustomed to deer-in-the-headlights terror.

"So can I buy you a drink, Harper?" he asked.

"Sure," I giggled. "A Bacardi Limontini. *All* the dancers drink those."

"Oh, do they?" Scott asked with a lift of his eyebrow, looking amused. He turned to the bartender and ordered, then turned to me a moment later with a frosty, clear, lemon-twisted martini for me and a dirty martini for himself. "Cheers to the prettiest NBA dancer I've ever seen," he said, clinking glasses with me and taking a long sip from his.

I blushed—a real blush this time, because I wasn't used to being called the prettiest *anything*—and took a sip of my drink. Scott was smiling at me when I lowered my glass.

"So what's it like dancing for the Knicks?" he asked. "I love basketball. I try to make it to a few games a season."

"Oh, it's awesome," I enthused, smiling flirtatiously at him like Emmie had taught me. Ah, she'd be so proud. "I'm a big fan of..." My voice trailed off and I stopped, lucky to have caught myself before I continued. I was *going* to say that I was a big fan of the Knicks' aggressive offense, because I was. I actually loved basketball—I always had. When you were born and bred just down the street from the home of the OSU Buckeyes, there was sports in the water, sports in the air, probably sports in the breast milk. Every Ohioan was born loving sports. But it wouldn't sound very dumb-blondish of me if I admitted my hankering for hoops or passion for the pigskin, would it? So instead, I tittered lightly and started again. "I'm a big fan of the way all the guys run really fast and all. But I don't really *get* what goes on on the court. It's way confusing."

I grimaced, practically choking on the words. Surely I'd just gone over the top and sounded stupider than I'd intended to.

But Scott was still grinning and nodding. "Maybe I can teach you more about the game someday soon, baby," he said, giving me a conspiratorial wink and rubbing my arm in a way that was apparently meant to be seductive.

I smiled back brightly, not quite believing that I'd managed to convince him. "That would be, like, really nice," I said, feigning shyness and attempting to bat my eyelashes again.

"Are you sure you don't need me to take a look at your eyes for you?" Scott asked with concern. Obviously, I needed to officially retire the eye-batting move for the evening.

"I'm fine," I said. "But thank you. You're, like, really sweet."

Scott smiled down at me admiringly. Then he looked at his watch.

"Damn it," he said, turning back at me with a pained expression. "Listen, I have to get going. I promised a friend I'd meet him uptown at ten. But look, could I maybe take you out sometime? I'd really like to hear more about what you do. I've never gone out with a Knicks dancer."

"And I've never gone out with an eye doctor," I said with a smile. I couldn't believe it! I'd only talked to him for fifteen minutes, and he had already bought me a drink *and* asked me for a date! That had never happened while I was being myself—not even *pre*-Peter. Clearly there was more merit to this Blonde Theory than I had anticipated. I just wasn't sure whether that was a good thing or a bad thing.

"So is that a yes?" Scott asked, looking a little nervous, if I wasn't mistaken.

"Yeah," I said with a confident smile. Hey, I was hot stuff as a dumb blonde. I was completely unused to this feeling of attracting men rather than repelling them.

"How about tomorrow night, then?" he pressed on. "I mean, I know it's soon. But if you're free..."

"I would love to," I said, beaming at him. Then I remembered: Tomorrow night was the firm dinner. The one Matt James had agreed to go to out of pity for me. The one I was dreading. But I still had to go. And it's not like I could tell Scott that. "Um, I mean, I'm actually busy tomorrow," I corrected myself. "A dance squad meeting. But maybe the next night?"

"Sure," Scott said with a smile. "Wednesday it is."

"Wednesday it is," I echoed. The girls would die. I was going on my first Blonde Date the day after tomorrow! And Scott was just my type: smart, cute, self-confident. The plan was working!

Maybe I could get to like the dumb-blonde version of myself after all.

Chapter Five

"For the hundredth time, Harper, it's not really a date," Emmie's voice bubbled from the phone, which I was currently holding a few inches away from my face and glaring at. "So there's nothing to worry about."

"I *know* it's not a date," I said sharply as I returned the phone to my ear, wondering if she was picking up on the tension in my voice. It wasn't like I was lying. I *did* know it wasn't a date. It's not like I was delusional. It was just one of those irrefutable laws of the universe—like gravity and $e = mc^2$. Newton or Einstein had probably also cataloged the fact that hot soap actors were never attracted to stuffy, brainy thirty-five-year-old lawyers.

"So why are you worrying?" Emmie pressed on. I pulled the phone away to glare at it again. Too bad I didn't have a videophone yet. I felt that Emmie deserved to see the death rays I was currently shooting in her general direction.

"I'm not," I grumbled, saying each word slowly and distinctly. But of course I was. It was hard not to feel a little spark of something as I sat in my living room, dressed in a black Armani dress and a string of pearls, waiting for a soap star to come pick me up for my firm dinner. But that *something* was actually an abundance of patheticness. Seriously, I knew Matt James didn't have any inter-est in me; either he felt sorry for me, or he was just looking for an opportunity to be exposed to a roomful of lawyers so that he could study for his role on the show. And here I was, dressed up, looking rather hot, if I do say so myself, waiting for a knock on the door from a guy who would never look at me as anything but his co-star's dorky, pathetic lawyer friend.

I had tried to express this to Emmie earlier, but she had taken it all wrong, and I had gotten embarrassed. I mean, it wasn't like I could tell her that I actually had a minicrush on Matt, because of course that was immature, illogical, and downright embarrassing. So my mumbled explanations had somehow come out sounding like I was afraid of this date or something. Emmie had laughed and started joking about how Matt and I would never work out anyhow. "As *if* he would ever ask you out!" she had added with a giggle, completely unaware that she was offending me.

Emmie was right; I wasn't his type. I was sure of it. And you know what? That was fine, because he wasn't my type anyhow. He probably hadn't even gone to college. He probably wasn't settled in his career like most of the guys I dated; I suspected that to him, the soap opera was just a step on the ladder of fame, and he hoped to move on to Hollywood sooner or later. And I'd decided in my midtwenties that I wouldn't date any more men who were still try-ing to "find themselves." Inevitably, while looking for themselves, they seemed to find a reason to discard me. Then they promptly moved on and married the next woman they stumbled across. Seriously. Before Peter, it had happened to me three times in a row. Not that it mattered then: I was young myself, and I wasn't ready to get married to anyone. But now, at thirty-five, the stakes were higher and I didn't want to be an inadvertent surrogate mother to any more guys searching for their identity. It never ended well. For me, at least. For my exes' new girlfriends-turned-fiancées, I sup-posed my "mothering" worked out beautifully.

After a few more moments of faux-encouragement from Emmie, she wished me luck and we hung up. I sat back against the couch, trying to rid myself of all signs of attraction to Matt James, because it would be entirely futile. Not to mention self-destructive. And of course I was an attorney, so logic was my forte. All I had to do was come up with the reasons why I shouldn't like him, and I'd be fine.

Okay, so he was cute. But the cute ones were always the ones you had to worry about. They'd have all the girls looking—and they usually looked back. And sure, he was friendly and flirtatious. But surely he flirted with every woman he met—not just me. And those snappy comments he was so fond of making? They *sounded* smart, but I bet they were just lines he had used on the show or something. No way was he a witty brainiac walking around in an actor's admittedly hot body. He was just some con artist who liked to make girls think he was smart and sexy and witty all rolled into one. Real guys were *never* like that.

Just then, as I was deep in the midst of the little game I liked to call Pass Judgment on a Guy Before He Has a Chance to Pass Judgment on Me, the doorbell rang.

"Coming!" I yelled, leaping to my feet a little too eagerly for someone who had just convinced herself that there was no compelling reason to be attracted to Matt James.

I opened the door and there he was, standing on my welcome mat, larger than life. His dark hair was tousled—but in that sexy way that made me want to run my hands through it. (Would that be wrong? Okay, yes.) He was wearing a charcoal suit with a maroon shirt underneath, the top button undone. He looked polished and professional—but at the same time laid-back. It was a look only he could pull off. His eyes looked greener and brighter than usual today, and his teeth were so white they seemed to sparkle in the hallway lights when he smiled.

I was dismayed to find that he looked really good. Hot even. Really hot.

"Hey, Harper," he said, smiling that wide, white toothy grin at me from the doorway.

"Hey, Matt," I said. Or at least that's what I intended to say. But in my effort to remain calm and casual, I think the words came out in sort of a gurgle instead.

Matt looked confused for a split second, then the perfect grin returned to his face. "You look gorgeous," he said, looking me up and down appreciatively. His gaze made me blush just as it had in the dressing room. Damn my excitable cheeks. "I really mean it, Harper," he said, his green eyes returning to rest on mine. "You look really nice."

"So do you," I said. And of course, that was the understatement of the year. It was getting hard to focus on him thanks to the increasing tempo of my heartbeat.

"Come on in," I said finally, stepping aside and holding the door open for him. I tried to deactivate the pitter-patter in my chest. But so far, I couldn't seem to locate the off switch. Matt grinned again and crossed over the threshold, taking in my apartment appreciatively.

"Nice place, Harper," he said, nodding with apparent approval as I led him down the narrow hallway into my living room, which was actually quite spacious for a Manhattan apartment. Well, that's what a $300K salary could buy. "You have great taste."

"Thanks," I said, smiling at him shyly.

The living room walls were painted a pale beige with one broad accent wall a deep maroon color. The sofa and love seat, which I had bought after the Peter breakup to replace the sofa he'd taken with him, were made of overstuffed taupe leather with accent pillows that matched the wall. I had a teak coffee table and two teak end tables with tall, chrome lamps on them, and the walls were filled with large, teak-framed photos of Paris, Venice, and San Francisco, my three favorite cities in the world. The tables and two metal magazine racks were piled high with old issues of *InStyle*,

Real Simple, W, Mod, Vogue, Wine Spectator, and *Time,* all of which I devoured the moment they arrived in the mail.

I led Matt over to the sofa and asked if I could get him a drink while I finished getting ready. He thanked me and said he'd make it himself, so I pointed him toward the bar in the corner of the small dining room, which was stocked with Grey Goose, Bacardi Limón, and Tanqueray, as well as a large selection of wines I'd picked up here and there when a label interested me. I was as obsessed with wines as I was with shoes and often made impulse purchases based on *Wine Spectator* ratings or simply the interesting names on bottles (Fat Bastard wine had become a favorite of mine, oddly enough). While Matt mixed a Grey Goose and cranberry for himself and a Limón and Sprite for me, I went back into my bathroom and applied one more coat of lipstick. Then I just stood there for a moment, looking at myself in the mirror.

What was I doing? I stared into my green eyes reflected in the mirror. I wasn't bad looking, even though my hair hadn't wanted to cooperate with me today and was currently sticking out at moderately funny angles. And I wasn't that hard to get along with. I wasn't unpleasant or mean or anything. At least I didn't think so.

But I'd been dating for more than twenty years, and some things never changed. From the time I'd had a crush on Ryan Patterson in the sixth grade and he had told me to my face that it wasn't cool to go out with nerdy girls, to the last few years when every date ended with guys running scared, I was slowly learning that I was just undatable, unlikable, and clearly downright threatening to every male ego in Greater Manhattan. Maybe rather than hating Peter, I should have been commending him for sticking around so long in the first place.

That was a depressing thought.

"Get ahold of yourself, Harper," I said sternly to my reflection.

"Are you talking to yourself in there?" came Matt's muffled voice from the other side of the bathroom door. I froze and widened my eyes at myself in the mirror. Great. Now Matt probably thought I was a lunatic who talked to herself in the bathroom. The night was clearly off to a stellar start.

"Uh, I'll be right out," I said quickly, cringing once more in front of the mirror before opening the door.

When I stepped out of the bathroom, Matt was standing a few feet away, holding two glasses. He handed me the one with the clear liquid and raised his own glass in a toast.

"To the most beautiful attorney in town," he said with a wink.

I arched an eyebrow at him skeptically as we clinked glasses. "You don't have to butter me up," I said flatly after I'd taken a long sip of my drink.

Matt looked surprised. "I'm not buttering you up," he said, clearly feigning hurt. "I mean it."

"Whatever," I scoffed, still feeling pathetic. I averted my eyes and took another sip of my martini. When I looked back at Matt, he was staring at me. "What?" I asked.

"I just don't understand why you do that," he said, shaking his head.

"Do what?" I asked suspiciously.

"Put yourself down like that," he said. "You always do that."

I looked at him in surprise. "Matt, I've maybe had three or four conversations with you in my entire life," I protested, feeling suddenly defensive. What, like he thought he knew me or something because we'd said hello to each other a few times at cocktail parties and at bars? "I don't *always* do anything."

Matt shrugged. I noticed with some surprise that he didn't look unpleasant or aggressive. Just concerned. That was worse, somehow.

"I didn't mean to offend you," he said matter-of-factly. "I just meant that you should give yourself more credit."

I glared at him, still defensive, even though on some level I knew he was trying to pay me a compliment. It didn't feel like it, though. He didn't know what he was talking about.

"Thanks for your input," I said drily. "But that doesn't carry much weight when you're just here out of pity for me. Or as a favor to Emmie because her friend can't get a date to her firm dinner on her own."

The second the words were out of my mouth, I regretted them. Even I knew that one of the cardinal rules of dating—not that this dinner with Matt was a *real* date, but still—was never to tell the person you were going out with what an abysmal failure you were with the opposite sex. And I had just broadcast it loud and clear.

"Harper," Matt said slowly, looking at me strangely. "I'm not here as a favor. I'm here because I want to be here. See, you're doing it again. Putting yourself down."

What was he, a psychiatrist? Well I wasn't interested in any dime-store amateur psychoanalysis tonight, thank you very much.

"Okay, whatever," I said quickly, because I didn't want to be having this conversation anymore. I took a long sip of my drink, draining the glass. I suddenly felt a little light-headed. "Are you ready to go?"

Still peering at me strangely, Matt nodded and took a long sip from his own drink, finishing it off. In silence, he took my glass from me and carried them both into the kitchen, where I could hear him rinsing them in the sink and setting them on the counter. He returned a second later. As we stepped into the hallway and I locked the door behind us, Matt put a hand on my arm. I turned to look up at him

"I really do want to be here, Harper," he said softly, looking at me with such intensity that my heart started doing that crazy pitter-patter thing again. I forced myself to look away. Those green eyes were deadly.

"Okay, thanks," I said brusquely, studying the floor. Whatever. He was an actor. I didn't believe a word he said.

Besides, wouldn't he have asked me out long before now if he wanted to date me instead of waiting for Emmie to practically beg him to go out with me?

Of course he would have.

I rest my case.

I HATED FIRM dinners. Really, I did.

But there was virtually no way out of them. Partners were required to go. I would have had to fake a death in the family or something if I couldn't come up with a date. And believe me, I had done so in the past. More than once.

Booth, Fitzpatrick held these firm dinners four times a year, once a quarter. I firmly believed that they were simply institutionalized forms of torture.

For example, the dinners were always on weeknights. Did it make any sense for one of the most prestigious firms in the city to hold dinners on nights when all the associates and most of the partners should presumably be staying up late, holed up in the office, reading legal briefs? No. It just meant that everything was thrown into disarray for the week for everyone but the senior partners, who didn't do a lot of hard work anymore and wouldn't be caught dead in the office after 6 PM anyhow. Clearly they had forgotten what it was like to be lower down on the totem pole.

Another reason that I strongly believed this was just some cruel form of torture was that I didn't really care for most of the people I worked with. It's not that I *disliked* my co-workers. But with a few exceptions, the people around me were really competitive. I wasn't. Okay, that might sound nuts, because obviously I had a little bit of a competitive streak in me, too. But really, the only competition I've ever felt is an internal one. I competed with *myself* to get good grades and ace the LSATs. I pushed *myself* to get a great job and succeed at it. I was happy for my co-workers when they got promoted, not jealous of them. And when I'd made partner, it hadn't been at anyone else's expense; I was the only patent attorney in the firm who concentrated in chemical engineering. It was such a specialized area of law that few people went into it. And because there were fewer sharks swimming in my pond, I was worth more to the company and moved up more quickly. It wasn't that I was any better than them; I just went into a different area of law. And I worked hard to be good at what I did. End of story.

But many of my co-workers didn't see it that way. Most of the attorneys I'd been shoulder-to-shoulder associates with my first few years at the firm were senior associates now. None of them was a partner yet. And although I had never been particularly close to any of them, the day I had made partner had also marked the day that any friendly camaraderie they had shared with me had vanished. I'd even overheard a bathroom conversation once in which Kendra Williams, a property associate, was telling Wendy Jo Moyer, a tax associate, that she knew for a fact that I'd slept my way to partner. The rumor had spread like wildfire, and I'd heard it repeated behind my back several times.

But ever since that rumor had spread, people had treated me differently. I think they were glad to assign a reason to why I had ascended the law firm ladder more quickly than them. And because that "reason" involved me being a corporate slut, they felt they had me pegged. It didn't seem to cross anyone's mind that I had perhaps *earned* my promotion. Nope, there had to be a sinister explanation.

So firm dinners were awkward, to say the least. At work, I could remain professionally friendly to the attorneys who gossiped about me without really getting into any sort of conversation with them. But at dinners—well, you were expected to talk. To socialize. And I had trouble doing that with people who didn't seem to like me all that much. I'd been a partner for three years now, so the initial sting had faded, and I was on decent terms with everyone. But they treated me differently. I no longer fit with the associates. And I didn't really fit with the partners, either. I was one of the only women, and I was the youngest partner by more than a decade. So just as in my dating life, I was the odd man out. Or rather, the odd woman.

The third reason I believed that these dinners were institutionalized torture was that it just underscored the firmwide divide between the Marrieds and the Singles. If I didn't fit in with the partners to begin with, believe me, my singleness made matters ten times worse. They didn't know what to make of me. The one time I had bravely shown up at a firm dinner without a date, I had been mostly ostracized because, it turned out, the partners whom I worked with every day at the office suddenly felt it was inappropriate to chitchat with a dateless woman—it made their wives uncomfortable. The wives, meanwhile, didn't want to chitchat with me because I was one of the attorneys, not one of the spouses. So I had literally wound up at a table with no one on either side of me—and the attorneys and their wives across the table all but ignoring me.

Very comfortable.

Since then, I had always managed to find a date of some sort. Tonight was the closest I had come to being dateless, so in a way I was grateful to Emmie for pressuring Matt into coming. At least I had *someone.* I could usually rely on my friends to set me up with a bad blind date who was a friend of a friend of a friend or something. Usually, the guy and I wouldn't have anything in common, but my date always wound up at least semi-content, because the dinners were always held at nice restaurants, and they got a nice free meal.

Who said men weren't easy to please? Now, if only I didn't up and ruin it by, horror of horrors, being intellectual and successful. Terrifying, I know.

"Harper!" exclaimed William Bradley as Matt and I walked through the door into the back room of The Lotus Room, an upscale restaurant on 24th Street that often hosted corporate events. William was one of the senior partners, a thin, balding man in his midsixties who had unsuccessfully experimented with wearing a toupee a few years back before it flopped off his head once during his closing arguments in a multimillion-dollar civil trial.

"Hi, William," I said, extending my hand. We shook hands firmly, then he turned to smile at Matt.

"And who might this be?" William asked, nudging Matt jovially. I rolled my eyes. At every firm dinner, William basically accosted my poor, unsuspecting date the moment we walked in the door. "Are you the man who's finally going to make an honest woman out of our old maid here?"

I forced a smile. I mean, who didn't just *love* being called an old maid by her co-workers?

You'd think an attorney would realize that this was an inappropriate way to talk to a colleague, especially given all the sexual harassment and gender discrimination rules in place in the American workplace these days. But apparently I was giving William Bradley too much credit.

"This is my *friend* Matt James," I said to William in a strained voice.

"Pleased to meet you, Matt," William said warmly, slapping Matt on the shoulder as if they were old friends. Matt looked vaguely startled, and I felt even more embarrassed. I hadn't known that was possible. "Our Harper here is quite a catch, don't you think?"

What was he, my embarrassing dad or something?

"Um, yes sir, I'm sure she is," Matt said, shooting me a confused look. I just shook my head and closed my eyes. Two more hours. I had to be here for two more hours. Then I could leave. Time had slowed to a crawl.

"She can't seem to hold on to a man, though," William continued. This time I groaned aloud and looked at Matt in horror. I was nonplussed to see that he was clearly stifling a laugh. Not that

I blamed him. "It's the darnedest thing, son," William continued, oblivious to my obvious humiliation—and Matt's obvious amusement. Not to mention the inappropriateness of this whole conversation. "No one here can understand it. A nice girl should be able to be married by the time she's . . . how old are you, Harper?"

"I'm thirty-five, William," I said through gritted teeth. "Just like I was when you asked me at the last firm dinner."

"Of course, of course, thirty-five," he said, shaking his head in wonder. "Why, my wife had already had three children by the time she was thirty-five."

I refrained from asking him which wife he was referring to. The first one—Pamela—had been his age and had given him his three adult children. I had liked her. The second one—Mitzi (I kid you not; her name was really Mitzi)—he had married three weeks after his divorce to Pamela was final four years ago. Seven months later, she had given birth to their first child. Yeah, you do the math.

"We're going to go find our table now, William," I said with a sigh. *Please, just let this be over quickly.* "Nice seeing you."

"Yes, nice to meet you, sir," Matt said, smiling at William and shaking his hand.

Still internally cringing, I led Matt away from William and toward the tables in the back of the room. I hoped we wouldn't have to mingle for too long before Jack Booth and Franklin Fitzpatrick, the two founding partners, tapped their glasses and asked us all to sit down.

"Nice guy, that William," Matt said into my ear as we crossed the room. I turned to scowl at him, hoping my embarrassment wasn't too evident. He was smirking at me. Not that that was any surprise.

"You have no idea," I muttered. "These firm dinners are horrible."

"I don't know," Matt said with a shrug, still smirking. "I think they seem pretty fun."

"I bet you do," I said under my breath. He grinned at me, his green eyes sparkling. I glared back, wishing I could slink out the back door without anyone noticing.

By the time we sat down thirty minutes later to a first course of salads with some sort of red wine vinaigrette, Matt looked so amused that I feared he was about to burst. Thankfully, he managed to contain himself. As we'd made our way to the table, before finally being saved by the clink of Booth's and Fitzpatrick's glasses, Matt and I had been approached by three partners, two senior associates, and a junior associate—all of them men and all of them married—wanting to know how serious Matt and I were about each other. Not that I was surprised; every guy I'd brought as a date to one of these dinners had been subjected to the same. Who knew that my colleagues cared so much about my social life?

Actually, it wasn't that they cared. It was that I unsettled them. They didn't know what to make of a thirty-five-year-old single woman who was a partner in her firm and, horror of all horrors, wasn't in a race to the altar.

Little did they know I wasn't even in the running. But when they saw me with a guy at the firm dinners, I think they felt a bit better, like they had me pegged just a little bit more or like I was fitting into their ideal-lawyer mode just a little bit better. In their narrow view of the world, I supposed I was intended to be at home, barefoot and pregnant in the kitchen or something. Not that that would ever happen. Pregnant: maybe someday. But barefoot? No, I liked my shoes too much. And in the kitchen? No, I was the world's worst cook. Nope, this law firm was just where I belonged, whether they liked it or not.

"Your co-workers sure are interested in your personal life," Matt said quietly to me as we picked at our salads. Around us at the ten-seat table, four other partners and their spouses talked comfortably in quiet conversation. I glanced over at the only female partner at our table, Mildred Mayhew, a fifty-something tax attorney, whose husband seemed thoroughly absorbed in what she was saying and not at all ill at ease at a table full of his wife's colleagues. I felt a momentary pang of envy. Would I ever have that?

Then again, Bob Mayhew was a mousy little man with a comb-over and a complete lack of assertiveness. I was pretty certain I didn't want *that*!

"They just don't know what to make of me," I said softly. "I'm sorry. I'm sure this is embarrassing for you."

"Not at all," Matt said, shaking his head. "I'm just surprised that they're that pushy. It's strange. It's like they desperately want you to get married."

I nodded.

"It's the weird politics of this firm," I explained quietly. "Actually, it's probably like this at any big firm."

"Like what?" Matt asked. I glanced at him and noticed that his expression appeared to be truly curious. I sighed.

"Socializing is a big part of getting ahead here," I explained, careful to keep my voice low so that the other partners at my table didn't hear me. Matt nodded, listening carefully, and I went on. "I've made partner already, but that's just because I threatened to walk out, and they couldn't lose the only attorney they had who special-ized in chemical patenting. But I'm never going to fit in on the next level if stay single. I'm never going to be thought of as one of them. It's weird. I never get invited to any of the other partners' private dinners or anything—the ones where the *real* politics of the firm are discussed—because I'm single. They have all these little couples din-ner parties where nearly everyone is invited but me…because they don't know what to make of me. I don't come as a set of two."

"That's ridiculous," Matt said softly, staring at me. He almost looked like he felt sorry for me, which made me squirm uncom-fortably in my seat. I didn't want his pity.

"That's the way it is," I said with a shrug, averting my eyes. "It's no big deal."

"But it's the twenty-first century," Matt protested.

"And as with probably every major firm in the city, the mentality here is stuck fifty years in the past," I said immediately. I glanced around the table to make sure no one was listening. Of course they weren't; I was generally the social leper at firm functions.

"But isn't that sexual harassment or some sort of discrimination or something?" Matt asked, looking confused. "Wouldn't a bunch of lawyers know better?"

"None of it is overt enough to sue over," I said with a shrug. "Not that I'd sue anyhow. But it's not like anyone ever says, *Harper, you're being excluded because you're single*. Or *You're being passed over for promotion because you haven't tied the knot*. It's just the way it is."

"But there are other female partners, obviously," Matt said, looking around the room, then back at me. "Surely they all didn't get married right out of school or anything."

"They were all married by the time they made partner," I explained softly. "And they've stayed married. Unlike the men here, most of whom are on wife number two or three. One of the guys"—I paused and nodded at an overweight sixty-something man at the next table over who was sitting with a blonde woman who looked younger than me—"is on wife number five."

"So there are different rules for the men and women?" Matt asked incredulously. He was staring at me with those gorgeous green eyes, and for a moment I felt sad in a way I couldn't explain.

"Yeah, the rules are different," I said.

"That's fascinating," Matt murmured, and all of a sudden I realized that he wasn't interested in me and my predicament; he was interested in the underbelly of firm politics so that he could enhance his performance on *The Rich and the Damned*. Of course. My heart sank. For a moment, it had felt like he actually cared about *me*. But that was silly, wasn't it?

By the time we got to the main course, the other couples at our table had started talking to us, comforted, apparently, by the fact that Matt seemed to be an attentive date—an actual half of a couple with me, instead of simply a blind date one of my friends had stuck me with. Little did they know that whatever chemistry they thought they perceived between us was simply Matt doing what he did best: acting. Granted, he was doing a pretty good job of it. He had even slipped his arm comfortably around my shoulder a few times, and I had caught him gazing at me adoringly once when I was talking to Bob Livingstone across the table about a complicated case I had worked on last month. Matt had looked away as soon as I glanced at him, but I was impressed at all the work he was putting into making this look like a real date. I would have almost been convinced—if I didn't know better.

Three hours after the ghastly firm dinner had started, Matt and I were standing back on the doorstep to my building.

"Thanks for inviting me, Harper," he said. I was touched that he had gotten out of the taxi to walk me in. Apparently, he was taking this acting gig very seriously, playing the part of the attentive date right up until the end.

"Thanks for coming, Matt," I said with equal formality, reaching out to shake his hand. He looked confused for an instant, then took my hand and shook it slowly, a strange look on his face that I couldn't quite figure out. "Sorry about all the weird questions and stuff. I should have warned you about how awkward it would be."

"I didn't mind," he said, shaking his head. His green eyes looked so earnest as he gazed at me that I started to feel a little uncomfortable. He cleared his throat. "Can I walk you inside?"

I laughed.

"I think I can make it to my door okay," I said, shaking my head at him. "Besides, you can drop the act now. There's no one watching anymore."

"What act?"

I rolled my eyes. No wonder he had gotten the gig on Emmie's show. He was good. "You know, pretending to be an attentive date hooked on my every word," I said. I shook my head again, trying to suppress the hurt I was feeling over the realization that no one would probably ever *really* look at me the way Matt had pretended to that evening.

"Oh," Matt said, looking slightly confused. "Well, I guess I should go then."

"I guess you should," I agreed, feeling suddenly uneasy. I was embarrassed that Matt had gone to so much effort tonight, putting on such an elaborate act for my colleagues' benefit. How humiliating that he would feel he needed to do so. I was even more humiliated by the fact that it *had* made me feel better.

"Harper," Matt began, taking a step backward and looking me square in the eye. "What I said before, about you not giving yourself enough credit? I meant it. I think you were amazing tonight."

My heart skipped a beat but I ignored it. I rolled my eyes at him.

"Great," I said, making sure that I sounded sarcastic. "Okay, seriously, Matt, you can stop acting now. I appreciate all your help, but the night's over."

He looked at me for a long moment, his stare so intense that I started to feel a bit uncomfortable. I was just about to start squirming when he spoke again.

"Yeah, I guess the night *is* over," he said, shaking his head. "Thanks again."

Then, with a terse nod, he turned away from me and started walking east, toward Third Avenue.

I watched him until he hailed a cab and climbed in. He didn't turn back once.

Not that I thought he would. They never did.

Chapter Six

The faux-date with Matt had unnerved me and mortified me. I couldn't believe I'd ever expected it to go any differently.

Of course, usually this would have made me hole up in my apartment for several days, grumpily smoking on my terrace, eating Chunky Monkey ice cream in an attempt to freeze over the mortification, and emerging only to go to the office.

But with the Blonde Theory experiment in full effect, I actually had a task to put my mind to, although the task itself was somewhat ridiculous. Nonetheless, instead of having to hibernate for days to forget the awkward nondate with Matt, I could throw myself into a *new* date...a first for a girl who hadn't had back-to-back evenings with different men since Clinton was in the White House. Hurrah!

Resolving to erase the humiliation of the smirking (and infuriatingly gorgeous) Matt James from my mind, I used my lunch hour at work to get a manicure and a bikini wax (okay, so this was far too optimistic of me, but that's beside the point), and, although I'm embarrassed to admit it, I actually sat in my office with my door closed all afternoon, practicing dumb-blonde-isms between patent paperwork.

I just hoped Molly, my secretary, couldn't hear me through the door as I repeated phrases like "It's, like, so great to see you" in various high-pitched tones and practiced my giggle. I even got out the compact I kept in the top drawer of my desk and spent a full fifteen minutes hair tossing and eyelash batting in the mirror (so that Scott wouldn't offer free eye care again, much as I appreciated his generosity).

I stopped when Molly buzzed me on my intercom to nervously ask if I was okay.

"Um, yes," I responded, then, realizing that I was still speaking in an elevated octave, I cleared my throat and amended in my own voice, "Um, I mean, yes. Yes, I'm okay."

And strangely, I was. Very okay.

I couldn't believe I was actually *excited* about my date.

I mean, that was silly, right? Because it's not like Scott Jacoby wanted to go out on a date with *me*. He wanted to go out on a date with a ditzy, brainless Knicks dancer who just happened to look like me. But still, I was going out on a date. A real date. With a man who wasn't scared of me. With a man who wasn't a slickly smarmy soap actor who probably thought I was a total nerd. I had to admit, that had a certain appeal.

Emmie called at four o'clock on my direct extension.

"You're still in the office?" she demanded. I assumed it was a rhetorical question, as I was *clearly* in the office; she had just called me there. "You need to be at my place by five thirty," she continued, without waiting for me to answer. "Scott will be here to pick you up by seven, and we have a lot to go over before then."

Emmie was apparently taking her job as my dating-slash-acting coach very seriously. She had decided that when Scott called me to set up our date, I was to give him her address and not mine. After all, it wouldn't make sense for a brainless dancer to be living in a spacious Upper East Side apartment whose sale had required a patent lawyer's salary, now, would it? Emmie's tiny East Village third-floor walk-up was much more realistic.

"Why can't I just arrange to meet him somewhere instead?" I had asked what seemed like the obvious question.

Emmie had sighed impatiently. "*Because,* Harper, the dumb blonde you're pretending to be isn't the same empowered twenty-first-century woman you are," she had explained, like she was talking to, well, a dumb blonde. Hmm, my act was apparently already working. "Pay attention, because if you're going to play the part, you're going to have to do it right."

"Okay," I said.

She went on to run through a laundry list of dumb-blonde rules. The dumb blonde will not talk politics. The dumb blonde will not disagree with her date. The dumb blonde will not bring topics up, but she'll cheerfully discuss anything her date brings up, to the best of her rather limited ability. The dumb blonde will always speak in breathless, high-pitched tones. The dumb blonde will speak no more than ten words at a stretch without inserting the word *like*.

Who knew that being a dumb blonde was so hard? I suddenly had new respect for the women who were cursed with too little intelligence and too-easy access to bottles of peroxide. Walking a mile in their stilettos was harder than I had suspected.

I quickly finished the remaining work on the briefs I needed to have ready for a meeting the next day and gathered my things. I was walking out the front door of my Wall Street office building by four forty-five and pulling up to Emmie's place in a cab by five twenty.

"See, no need to worry," I said as she opened the door and stared at me. "I'm ten minutes early."

Emmie looked at me suspiciously. "You also look *way* too smart to be going out on your first dumb-blonde date in an hour and a half." She shook her head in what appeared to be disappointment with me. I raised an eyebrow at her. "Come on in," she sighed. "Luckily I brought some blue eyeshadow and bright lipstick home from the set yesterday. I *knew* you couldn't be trusted to prepare well enough on your own."

"Blue eyeshadow?" I asked, stepping inside. "You have *got* to be kidding me."

"Nope!" Emmie said cheerfully as I followed her back toward her bedroom. "It's very dumb-blonde chic. Besides, blue is back in a big way, if you believe what the fashion magazines are saying."

"Great," I muttered. "Just when I thought we'd left the eighties behind." As far as I was concerned, this opened the door to leg warmers, tie-dye, and those little clippy things that tied '80s T-shirts on the side. Not to mention side ponytails. No, it was better if the door to the '80s stayed closed. But clearly it was too late for that.

In addition to the blue eyeshadow and bright red lipstick Emmie was about to massacre my face with, she had also brought Dumb Blonde Outfit Number Two home from the set of *The Rich and the Damned*. The moment she pulled it triumphantly out on its hanger to show it to me, I was horrified. The dress was bright blue and skintight, which I was more than a bit concerned about, even after Emmie produced a Spanx girdle—a *girdle*!—to help hold me in. The dress was low-cut on top and short on the bottom, and I knew it would barely cover my back end before coming to an abrupt halt midway down my upper thighs.

"You've *got* to me kidding me," I said. This was beyond humiliating.

"Nope," Emmie chirped. "Afraid not."

Growling at her, I took the horrible outfit into her bedroom to change and came out ten minutes later—after summoning Emmie to help pour me into the girdle—looking like a completely different person. Gone was the buttoned-down attorney who had entered Emmie's apartment; instead, standing in her living room, was a full-on stereotypical nightclub princess in a man-hunting dress. Well, an expensive, designer, man-hunting dress.

"This is horrible," I said, looking down at my body and wincing. However, I was secretly pleased that the dress fit me and actually didn't look as bad as I thought it would clinging to my curves. I never wore tight clothes, so sometimes I forgot that I *had* curves, albeit unimpressive ones. Once the girdle was in place—and I had donned Emmie's water bra that made me look like I had generous C cups instead of my own less-than-impressive small B's—the dress didn't look half bad on me. Not that I would *ever* wear it voluntarily.

"Actually, you look pretty hot," Emmie protested, looking at me admiringly. "Who knew that inside that lawyer facade there was a hottie itching to get out?"

"Don't jump the gun," I mumbled, wondering vaguely why it had never occurred to me to dress a little more sexily in the past.

MEG AND JILL arrived at six forty-five with amused grins that only grew wider when they saw the ridiculous outfit I'd been stuffed into by the very talented Emmie.

I waited with the girls in Emmie's living room, not sure why I felt so nervous. But my heart was doing that pitter-patter, pitter-patter it sometimes did before I walked into the courtroom to face a tough judge or before I had to argue a thorny case in front of the patent board.

Was it possible I actually liked Scott Jacoby? I mean, at face value, the pairing made sense: Smart young lawyer meets smart young ophthalmologist and they hit it off. The only thing wrong with this scenario was that the smart young ophthalmologist in question thought that I was a dumb, slightly over-the-hill NBA dancer. So unless I intended to come clean—which of course I didn't (I had been *dared,* and I took that very seriously)—I was stuck pretending to be someone I wasn't.

Well, it was worth a try, I had to admit. Acting like the person I actually was hadn't been working out so well lately. And tonight,

I figured it was better to *be* the one pretending rather than being out with an actor pretending to like me.

"So how are you going to convince him you're dumb?" Jill asked as she and Meg settled into Emmie's raggedy-looking beige couch.

"I don't know," I shrugged. I felt embarrassed as I added, "I practiced some blonde-isms in my office today with the door closed."

"Blonde-isms?" Meg asked.

I shrugged. "You know, just speaking like a dumb blonde." I could feel my cheeks heat up a bit. "Saying *like* every few words. Giggling. Acting vacant."

"Sounds like a good start," Meg mused, nodding thoughtfully. "I think you have to have a better plan than that for tonight, though."

Jill nodded. "Since it's your first blonde date and all," she added wisely.

I looked back and forth between the two of them, then glanced down at my watch. "He'll be here in ten minutes," I said. "Do you really think I'll have time to prepare more?"

"I think you'd better," Meg said with a solemn nod.

Emmie came back into the room and squeezed onto the sofa with Meg and Jill. For the next ten minutes, they sat and stared me down like a harsh tribunal while drilling me on blonde responses, making suggestions about how I should fawn over Scott because he was a doctor and quizzing me on all things blonde.

"But do I really need to act so over-the-top?" I asked hesitantly. I hadn't thought this was what I'd signed up for. Jill and Emmie looked uncertain. Meg shrugged.

"Look," she said. "We've never done anything like this before. Why don't you give it a try acting really ditzy and see what happens? If it's a total disaster, you can scale it back on future dates. But this guy, this Scott, he liked you because you acted like a total ditz at the bar the other night. You have the perfect opportunity to follow up on that and see what happens."

"I guess so," I sighed. I could see her point. I just wasn't sure how acting outlandishly ridiculous would help anyone.

The doorbell rang at precisely 7 PM.

"At least he's punctual," Emmie said with a smile. She uncrossed her legs and stood up from the couch. "Extra points for that."

"Good luck!" Meg murmured excitedly. Jill nodded eagerly beside her.

I rolled my eyes and got up to answer the door—after all, we were pretending that this was my apartment, not Emmie's. As I unlocked her four deadbolts and swung the door open, I was greeted with the sight of an even more handsome Scott Jacoby than I had remembered. Despite my best intentions, I could feel my heartbeat pick up.

He was freshly shaven and dressed in a charcoal suit with a tie-less pale blue shirt, with the top two buttons sexily undone. His dark brown hair was tousled—with some effort and lots of pomade, I suspected—and I could smell just a hint of some sort of musky cologne, not too overpowering, but just present enough to reveal that he'd put some effort into all the little touches.

Unfortunately, as I had suspected, this was *just* my kind of guy—which might make things difficult. After all, I was only testing out this stupid theory, right? I wasn't supposed to actually *like* the guy. I had to remind myself that he actually didn't like me, either. He liked the gum-snapping, eyelash-batting, lowered-IQ, dancer version of me. Still...

I was suddenly nervous. I wasn't sure I could convincingly pull off the blonde act.

"You look beautiful," he said with a smile as I invited him in.

"Thank you," I said demurely. Then I remembered I was supposed to be speaking in a higher octave in a voice peppered with giggles and *like*s. Fortunately, I had practiced all afternoon.

I took a deep breath and threw myself into the act. "You, like, look awesome, too." I giggled for emphasis. He grinned back, apparently flattered, and for a moment I let myself bask for a moment in the glow of his perfect smile.

Inside the apartment, I could hear Meg saying something softly and Jill giggling. Scott apparently heard it, too.

"Are those your roommates?" he asked hopefully.

"No," I said, remembering to keep my voice high-pitched. "Just some friends of mine. We were just, like, having a drink. Want to, like, say hello?"

Wow. It was getting easier to throw random *like*s around. I gave myself a mental pat on the back.

"Sure!" Scott enthused before looking at me hopefully. "Are they dancers, too?"

I giggled as if he'd said something funny and tossed my hair over my shoulder with exaggerated enthusiasm.

"No, silly," I squealed. "I usually just, like, go out with the other dancers after practice, of course."

"Of course," Scott said with a nod as if my answer had been the obvious one. We rounded the corner into the living room, and the girls stood to greet us.

"This is Scott Jacoby. He's an ophthal—" I quickly stopped myself before completing the word that would clearly contain two many syllables for a dumb blonde to process. "He's, like, an eye doctor. You know? Like Monica's old boyfriend? Richard? On *Friends*?"

Woo-hoo. Score one blonde "cultural reference" for me.

"This is Emmie. She's on my totally favorite soap opera, *The Rich and the Damned*," I said as Scott grinned at her and shook her hand. "This is Meg. You already met them at the bar the other night. And this is Jill. Her husband is a doctor, too."

"Nice to meet you girls," Scott said, shaking hands all around.

"So, Scott, what are you and Harper up to tonight?" Meg asked politely after the introductions were complete.

"I thought we'd start off with dinner at a nice little French bistro in Midtown called Café le Petit Pont," he said with a charming smile. "It's one of my favorites. Then we'll see where the evening takes us."

"That sounds wonderful," Meg said. She turned to me and gave me a wide-eyed look that I assumed was supposed to have some sort of significance. I just wasn't sure what she was getting at.

"I thought it would be a perfect little romantic spot," Scott said, draping a protective arm around me. I snuggled close to him, like I figured a dumb blonde would do, and beamed stupidly at my friends.

"Can I see you in the kitchen for a moment, Harper?" Meg asked innocently. "I have a quick question for you." I nodded and followed her into Emmie's kitchen as Scott continued chatting with the girls.

"What is it?" I whispered once we were safely out of earshot.

"You have a perfect opportunity to act like a dumb blonde with the menu items at the restaurant," she whispered back, her eyes gleaming.

I arched an eyebrow at her.

"This is perfect!" she continued excitedly. "I can't believe he's taking you to a French restaurant! You *have* to mispronounce your way through everything."

I looked at her for a moment and shrugged. "Do you really think that's a good idea?"

"Yes, yes!" Meg exclaimed, her voice still low, her eyes still shining. "Okay, and you also have to order frog legs or escargots or something and make a really big deal out of it, like you didn't know what it was ahead of time."

"Isn't that too dumb?" I asked, not convinced.

"No, no!" Meg bubbled. "It's perfect. It will be so funny!" Hmph, easy for her to say.

I stared at her for a moment then nodded in resignation.

"I guess I have to," I said. "I signed up for this, didn't I?"

"Oh, Harp, it's going to be so great!" Meg exclaimed. "Now, get back out there and go on your date!"

"Do I have a choice?" I grumbled.

AFTER HUGGING THE girls good-bye and asking them to lock the door behind us, I was out on the street with Scott, who already had a town car idling by the curb. I was suddenly nervous now that the safety net of my girlfriends had been removed. It was somehow easier to act like a dumb blonde when I knew they were right there with me, prepared to play along. Suddenly, I was flying solo. But hey, I was used to working alone on major legal cases, right? I could do this. I gave myself a little internal pep talk. I took a deep breath and resolved to do my best to sound as empty-headed as possible.

"You have, like, a chauffeured car?" I breathed, looking at Scott with wide eyes as we approached the town car. I twirled my hair and looked up at him.

He laughed, his smile lighting up his chiseled face again. "Not exactly," he said. "The hospital where I work has a car service. I just figured we could use it tonight for our date rather than trying to get taxis."

"Like, definitely," I agreed, still pretending to be incredibly impressed with the car service. Of course, in reality, I had a car service at my disposal, too, and I used it most nights when I worked late. It was one of the perks of being a partner at Booth, Fitzpatrick & McMahon. But I supposed that a professional NBA dancer wouldn't be using one on a daily basis unless she had a sugar daddy. Like Scott. "This is, like, so awesome," I breathed as the driver, dressed in a navy suit and matching chauffeur's cap, hopped out to open the back door for us. I let Scott take my hand and "help" me into the car, resisting the urge to tell him I was perfectly capable of getting into an automobile by myself.

On the drive uptown, I concentrated on tossing my hair as many times as I thought was believable (until my neck started to hurt) and keeping my eyes so wide and vacant that I was sorely in need of eyedrops within the first few moments. Scott asked me questions about myself, but I deflected most of them as Emmie had suggested—by commenting minimally and then turning the spotlight back to him. Fortunately, this worked beautifully, as Scott's favorite subject was apparently himself. By the time we got to the restaurant on 39th Street, I had learned that he was thirty-eight, that he had gone to Yale, that he and a partner had a private practice associated with Montefiore Regional Medical Center, that he was from Connecticut, and that his dad had been an ophthalmologist, too.

"You haven't told me anything about yourself, Harper," Scott said as he helped me out of the car in front of the restaurant. A big maroon canopy with the restaurant's name extended the length of the building, and little bistro tables were set up outside on the street. "You'll have to fill me in once we get a table."

I giggled nervously.

"There's, like, nothing really interesting to tell," I said as he opened the door to Café le Petit Pont for me. "I've just been a dancer for, like, as long as I can remember. It's, like, always been a dream of mine."

I hesitated, hoping that Scott wouldn't ask more. Because as much as I had prepared to behave like a dumb blonde, I'd run out of time to craft a convincing backstory. The fact was, I didn't know much at all about dancing. Fortunately, Scott seemed to accept that as an answer. He took my hand as we approached the hostess stand.

"We have a reservation," he announced to the hostess. "Under *Doctor* Scott Jacoby." I swear, he stressed the word *doctor*. I wanted to laugh but resisted. Why would he have to throw in the fact that he was a doctor? That would be like me introducing myself to people loudly as "Harper Roberts, *Esquire.*" But the bubbly hostess seemed thrilled to be in his presence, giggling at him flirtatiously, despite the fact that I was standing right there beside him.

"Your table will be ready in just a moment," she said. Then, I swear, she batted her eyes at him (more successfully than I had, I might add)! "So what kind of doctor *are* you?"

"An ophthalmologist," Scott answered, puffing his chest out proudly. "That's an eye doctor."

"Wow, cool," the hostess bubbled, completely ignoring me. I should have been annoyed, but it seemed like a better use of my time to take mental notes. Although brunette, the hostess seemed to have the dumb-blonde thing down a lot better than I did. I reminded myself to act more impressed with Scott's status as a doctor during dinner, because, I supposed, that was what a dumb blonde would do, right? The hostess seemed like a pretty good person to emulate.

We were seated and Scott ordered a bottle of wine—without consulting me, which was the first thing of the evening that really got under my skin. I had such high hopes that Scott would turn out to be my type of guy. But my type of guy would at least be polite enough to consult his date about the wine selection. Right?

I tried valiantly to overlook the lapse. Maybe he'd just been nervous and forgotten to ask me.

"You'll like it," he reassured me, reaching across the table to pat my hand confidently. "Trust me." I smiled and giggled, but inside, I was fighting a feeling of creeping annoyance. Yes, I knew I would like the wine—it was a Domaine de Mourchon Côtes de Rhône-Villages Grand Reserve, and I had actually stayed just outside the Domaine de Mourchon vineyard during a trip to a culinary school in Séguret, in the south of France, six years ago. But I knew I couldn't tell Scott any of that. It wouldn't quite fit with my dumb-blonde image, would it? Instead, I nodded tightly. After all, maybe this was the one area in which he was mannerless, and he'd be perfect in everything else. Besides, I *was* acting airheaded.

I supposed it was understandable that he'd assume I didn't know my wines.

"This wine looks really expensive, so it must be good," I said in my best little-girl voice, giving Scott a little pouty face and bat of my eyes. Thankfully, I had perfected the eye-batting technique in the mirror, and Scott didn't seem to be about to leap over the table and pull out an optical scope this time.

Instead, he nodded and reached across the table to give my hand a squeeze. "Nothing but the best for you, baby," he said with a patronizing wink.

I smiled back, but only because I didn't know what else to say. He was calling me *baby*? Because I approved of his selection of wine? Did guys really talk to women like that? No one had ever talked to me that way. But was it because, as my normal self, I intimidated and scared them? Was this what dating was like when you weren't me?

I resolved to stop getting offended and to instead simply enjoy being as vacuous as possible. After all, maybe he wasn't that bad. Maybe he was just picking up on my blonde cues and responding accordingly.

Steeling myself for more blonde ditziness, I opened the menu, which was all in French, and began flipping through.

"Do you need any help reading the menu, baby?" Scott asked, leaning across the table and putting a hand on my arm.

"No, I'm okay," I assured him in a chirpy voice. "I, like, took a year of French in my high school. I'm, like, practically a native speaker."

"Oh, are you?" Scott asked, looking amused.

"Oh yes," I said dismissively and giggled. "I mean, I know *lots* of French words. Like *bonjour* and *au revoir*." I purposely pronounced the words "boon-joor" and "ow reev-oyr." Boy, I was good at this. Perhaps I should apply for an acting job on Emmie's soap. Actually, I was glad Meg had suggested that I butcher the

French language. It was easier than thinking up my own stunts. Scott looked at me solemnly and nodded.

"Yeah, that's almost perfect, baby," he said, looking amused. I nodded enthusiastically. "But are you sure you don't need my help translating the menu?" Scott asked again, studying me with what appeared to be some level of genuine concern.

"Oh no, I'm fine," I said with my cutest little grin, relishing the all-too-perfect opportunity to mispronounce my way through the appetizer, the salad, and the entrée courses.

The waiter appeared beside us a moment later, and I knew exactly what I wanted to order.

"I'll start with the *cuisses grenouille,*" I said, pronouncing it "coo-ee-ess-ess gren-oo-ee-lee." The waiter raised a curious eyebrow and I pretended not to notice. I was about to give my salad order when Scott interrupted.

"Baby, are you sure you want to order that?" he asked, looking concerned. "Do you know what that is?"

"Of course I do," I said, doing my best to look wounded. "And yes, I want it. Is that okay?" I giggled.

Scott hesitated for a moment then relented, leaning back in his chair. I ordered the *salade de la maison,* mispronouncing the words, of course, then the *coquilles Saint-Jacques,* pronouncing it "cock-ay-lees saint jack-ess."

Scott looked a bit concerned, but he didn't protest this time. Instead, he ordered his own meal—a much less adventurous one than mine, I might add—and settled back in his chair as the confused-looking waiter walked away to bring us our appetizers.

I wish I could say that the date went wonderfully from there; that Scott was the charming gentleman he had, at first, appeared to be. But sadly, he wasn't. Not at all. As he downed one glass of wine and then another, he loosened up a little, and his larger-than-life ego began to rear its head. I nibbled on the bread the waiter had placed on the table and slowly sipped my wine, trying to appear as vacant and wide-eyed as possible, while Scott launched into a monologue about his wealth, his fabulous job, and all the other things that were apparently supposed to make me believe he was the greatest man in the world.

Meanwhile, I struggled to keep my eyes big and round as I oohed and ahhed over the things he told me while trying to suppress my gag reflex.

I learned that Scott owned his own two-bedroom on the Upper East Side (on a cheaper block than mine, but of course I didn't mention that); that he had two cars—a BMW he drove around town and a Jag he kept in a garage outside the city for his "weekends in the country"; and that he owned a summer share in an enormous house in the Hamptons. "Play your cards right, baby, and you might get to be my 'plus one' this summer."

Did girls really fall for this?

"Oh good," I muttered, not caring that I sounded sarcastic, because Scott was already far too absorbed in telling his stories to notice me much anyhow.

He told me all about his boat, *Lady Luck;* his mid-six-figure income; and his wild weekends in Vegas with his buddies, "where we drop tens of thousands like it's nothing, baby."

"So do you get to the gym much, Harper?" he asked, switching tracks rapidly. I blinked at him and almost said no (because in real life, I didn't even own a gym membership, depending on my collection of workout DVDs to tone my body effortlessly, through osmosis or something), but then I remembered that I was supposed to be a dancer.

"I, like, get to use the weight room?" I said, remembering to add question marks at the ends of my sentences, as Emmie had advised. "At Madison Square Garden? Where the players work out? We're, like, allowed to use the gym when they're not using it."

"So you must be in some shape," Scott said approvingly, not even bothering to hide the fact that he was looking my body appreciatively up and down. Despite myself, I glanced down skeptically, then noticed that my body actually *did* look pretty toned in this skintight dress (with the hidden help of the girdle, thank you very much). Well then! Who needed the gym—or to actually *watch* her workout DVDs—when she had some Spanx in her wardrobe?

"Thanks," I chirped. "That's, like, really cool of you to say that."

"I'm in great shape, too, you know," he said, leaning across the table conspiratorially. I peered at him strangely, but he didn't seem to notice. Okay, this conversation was taking an odd turn. For once, I didn't have to fake confusion; I really had no idea where he was going with this. He didn't leave me wondering long.

He took my hands and looked into my eyes. "I'm like a well-oiled machine," he whispered in a manner that I supposed was meant to be seductive (although I'd be quite alarmed if anyone was successfully seduced by this sort of talk). "I can go all night, baby. All night."

Startled, I struggled not to laugh and looked at him as blankly as I could manage. I wasn't exactly sure what the proper dumb-blonde reaction to this kind of information would be. But if he was going to be so bizarrely offensive, I might as well have a little fun with him.

"Wow," I said, widening my eyes. I feigned ignorance. "You can go all night to the gym? I didn't even know there were gyms that were open all night!"

Scott looked at me for a moment, startled. Then he shook his head as I tried valiantly not to collapse in laughter.

"No, baby," he said, sounding frustrated. "In bed. I can go all night in *bed*."

"You have gym equipment in your bed?" I breathed, struggling my hardest to continue looking completely blank, which was difficult, because it was getting more and more difficult to hold back my laughter. "That is, like, such a great idea. You can work out *and* sleep at the same time! That is *so* smart! I never think of things like that!"

Man, this stuff was coming to me with frightening ease. Perhaps I had missed my calling. Perhaps deep down, I *was* a dumb blonde who just happened to have been more educated than fate had intended.

Then again, perhaps not.

"No, no," Scott said loudly, starting to look so exasperated that his cheeks were turning pink. He sat up a bit straighter and banged a fist on the table. "I can have *sex* all night!" he clarified loudly.

Thankfully, our waiter chose that moment to arrive with our appetizers, saving me from having to address Scott's boasts. Of course, he also arrived just in time to hear Scott's last words and as a result turned an amusing shade of scarlet himself.

"*Mademoiselle,* your *cuisses grenouille,*" he said, pronouncing the name of the dish much better than I had. He set down a tantalizing-looking plate in front of me, garnished with parsley. I pretended not to look too closely at it; I still wasn't entirely convinced that creating a scene about my food, as Meg had advised, was the best route to take. But it was hard not to think about it and giggle as the *cuisses* swam delicately on my plate.

"And *monsieur,* your *moules à la crème,*" the water said, sweeping in with a delicious-smelling dish of mussels in white wine cream sauce for Scott. "*Bon apétit,*" he added before vanishing, his cheeks still a deep red.

As soon as the waiter left, I made a big show of examining my plate, making sure that Scott was watching me. His face was filled with trepidation as he awaited the inevitable—my dumb-blonde reaction to the dish in front of me.

"Like, what *are* these?" I asked finally, touching the edge of one of my *cuisses,* which were bathed in a delectable-looking sauce of butter, garlic, and chopped parsley. I looked up at Scott in mock disgust. Of course I knew what *cuisses* were. But clearly my dumb-blonde alter ego didn't.

"Um, that's the appetizer you ordered, babe," Scott said nervously. He looked far less comfortable than he had a moment earlier while boasting of his sexual prowess. I looked at him incredulously and then turned my attention back to the plate.

"They look like"—I paused dramatically and poked at the *cuisses* again, lifting half of one up experimentally with my fork— "frog legs," I concluded with disgust.

Scott just looked at me nervously.

"Are they?" I demanded a bit more loudly, relishing his reaction. He looked so uncomfortable, not exactly the "well-oiled machine" he had just claimed to be. "Are they *frog legs*?" I persisted in a high-pitched squeal.

"Well," Scott paused, as if considering the question. He cleared his throat. "That depends on your definition of frog legs."

"What?" I asked, my voice rising an octave (to heights previously unknown to my vocal cords). "What do you mean, my *definition*?" I paused and tried to look both haughty and dumb at the same time, which was no easy feat. And yet somehow, I seemed to be pulling it off. Hurrah for me! "Are they, or are they not, the legs of a frog like Kermit?" I asked, keeping my voice slow and deadly—but still up an octave.

"Um...yes," Scott finally said meekly, avoiding my gaze while he nervously twisted his napkin into a knot.

"Ewwwwww!" I exclaimed, loudly enough that the diners at the tables around us turned to stare. Ordinarily, I would have been self-conscious, but in slipping into the dumb-blonde persona, I had also apparently checked my embarrassment at the door. For a second, I actually reveled in the liberty of it all. Then I remembered that I was supposed to be freaking out. I pushed my plate dramatically away and stood up.

"This is disgusting," I said, contorting my face into a mask of repulsion. Heck, I should win an Oscar for this performance. "I can't believe you would bring me to a place like this," I continued, putting my hands on my hips angrily and striking a pose that I hoped looked both stupid and defiant. "A place that would...that would"—I drew a big breath, pretending that the words were difficult to say—"that would murder innocent frogs!" I concluded.

Concealing my giggles as sobs, I pushed my chair back from the table as Scott stared at me.

"I'm going to the ladies' room," I announced before grabbing my purse and stomping off in the direction of the restrooms.

In the bathroom, I finally allowed myself to giggle, and once I started, I couldn't stop. I doubled over with peals of laughter, ignoring the woman washing her hands at the sink, who was making no effort to conceal the fact that she was staring at me with blatant disdain. Not that I blamed her. I looked like a complete tramp in my clingy blue dress, and I'd just made a scene that had turned heads all over the restaurant.

I was impressed, frankly, at how well I actually seemed to be doing. Once I had started acting like a dumb blonde, it had started coming more easily to me, helped, no doubt, by the fact that Scott was falling for my act hook, line, and sinker. I was a bit disappointed, actually, to see just how easily he had been convinced—and just how much he seemed to *still* like me, even after my abominable behavior thus far.

But at the same time, this kind of act wasn't answering any *real* questions for me. Sure, it was evident that as ridiculous as I acted, I could still keep Scott's interest, because apparently a brainless ditz in a skintight dress has that certain je ne sais quoi. But I couldn't go through the rest of my life—or even the next two weeks of this Blonde Theory experiment—acting like a space cadet. Besides, I had a hard time believing that most men would be as easily convinced by my bimbo act as Scott was. No, I would have to refocus The Blonde Theory and tone down the stupidity on future dates. But for now, I had to finish out this date with Scott. Well, at least I'd get a decent meal out of it.

I reapplied the hideously pink lipstick Emmie had given me and made my way back to the table, where Scott was gazing at me with concern.

"Are you okay?" he whispered nervously once I sat back down. He looked swiftly from side to side, as if to see if anyone was watching us. Evidently, he expected another explosion. But, I noticed as I looked down at the table, my beautifully sautéed frog legs had been whisked away.

"I'm fine," I chirped, blinking at him blankly as if I had no idea what he was talking about. "Why?"

"Oh," he said, looking confused. He obviously didn't know how to approach me. Not that I could blame him. "Um, our meals should probably be out in a moment," he finally said helplessly.

"Great!" I bubbled.

By the time our main courses arrived five minutes later—sautéed sea scallops in creamy tarragon sauce for me, and filet mignon in cognac sauce for Scott—he was back on track, bragging like a pro, my frog-leg outburst already apparently forgotten. His resilience was impressive.

Inconceivably, he still seemed to be attracted to me. What an interesting observation: As my normal brainy self, I could act polite and socially acceptable yet still routinely freak guys out. But as a dumb blonde, I could create a huge scene and guys would still apparently come back for more. How odd.

As we made our way through our meals, Scott chatted comfortably about his job, his income, and the fact that he thought he was irresistible to basically all members of the female gender.

"I don't know what it is," he said with a forced sigh and a little grin. "But women love me. My patients, my nurses, my office staff, and women I meet out in bars."

"How nice for you," I said drily, wondering what he was getting at.

"Obviously, Harper," he said, "that makes it difficult to choose just one woman to be with. I'm sure you understand."

"Of course," I said flatly.

"But you, Harper." He sighed and shook his head at me in what appeared to be wonderment but was probably feigned. "You might just be the one woman who can capture my heart."

I simply stared at him. I didn't know what to say. Did he use that line on all the women he went out with? And if so, did they fall for it? Or was he simply using it on me because I had seemed more empty-headed than the rest?

"Um, lucky me," I said finally, not having to fake the hesitance in my voice. Scott nodded heartily and winked.

"You *are* lucky," he confirmed. "There are lots of women who would give anything to trade places with you tonight."

Well, at least he was humble.

"Like, I am so lucky to be here," I chirped finally, not sure what else to say.

"You are indeed," he confirmed with a nod and a wink. "Now," he said, waving his hand to the waiter to indicate that we needed our check. What, no dessert? I'd been craving crème brûlée! "What do you say we go back to my place?"

Ew. Double ew.

"And do what?" I asked blankly, batting my widened eyes although of course I knew *exactly* what he was suggesting.

He smiled patiently. "I don't know," he said. "There are *lots* of things to do. I could show you my bedroom..."

He let his voice trail off in a way that was evidently meant to be seductive, then reached across the table to intertwine his fingers through mine.

"Um, won't the gym equipment in your bed be in the way?" I asked the only thing I could think of. He looked momentarily frustrated.

"No, I told you, I don't *have* gym equipment in my bed, Harper," he said, an edge to his voice. I continued to force myself to look at him blankly.

"But you said…" I stopped and let my voice trail off, then shook my head in consternation. "I just get so confused."

Actually, what was confusing me the most at the moment was that an apparently intelligent man like Scott couldn't tell he was being duped. He really thought I was this dumb. And he was seemingly growing more interested in me by the moment, apparently not *despite* my stupidity but *because* of it. It was enough to make me want to toss the remainder of my red wine all over him and his perfect suit. But I refrained.

"So, do you want to come home with me?" Scott asked again. Well, you had to give him credit for trying. But really, I was done playing these games. Amused as I was by how easy it was to fool him, it also annoyed me that stupidity would be so appealing to a man who was so educated and successful. He *should* have wanted an intellectual equal, like me. Instead, he was looking to take home an empty-headed floozy.

I thought about my response for a moment, then, without saying anything, reached into my purse to get out enough cash to cover my portion of the dinner. I plunked it on the table, smiled at Scott, and stood up. He looked panicked.

"What…where are you going?" he asked, standing up, too, and looking at me desperately.

"Home," I said simply. I smiled sweetly at him and prepared to turn away. I was on the verge of blowing my blonde cover.

"But…but we were having such a great time!" he exclaimed, desperation shining in his eyes. "You can't leave now! Look, I bought you this nice dinner. You have to come home with me."

"I *have* to?" I inquired sharply, turning to stare at him incredulously.

He shook his head. "I don't mean *have* to," he stammered. "Just that you should. You should. You won't regret it. Besides," he tried again, "I just took you out to a really nice dinner."

"I've paid my share," I said softly, letting my real voice shine through for the first time this evening. I looked at Scott long and hard, then smiled again. "Besides, I have some briefs I need to get through tonight so that I can file them in the morning. I've had a lovely time, but I have a lot of work to do."

Scott stared uncomprehendingly.

"Briefs?" he asked finally. "What are you talking about?"

"Legal briefs," I said nonchalantly. I snapped my purse closed with a tight grin.

"I...I don't understand," he said desperately, stepping out from the table and moving in my direction. "You're a dancer." I just arched an eyebrow at him. All of a sudden, his face darkened. "Aren't you?" he asked hesitantly.

"Sure, Scott, I'm a dancer," I said. I paused and looked him straight in the eye. "And you're a gentleman."

It was his turn to look blank.

I looked at him for a second longer, smiled—more to myself than to him—and turned to walk away. I could feel him watching me as I turned the corner out of the dining room and pushed through the doors of Café Le Petit Pont onto the bustling street outside.

Chapter Seven

O kay, this isn't going to work," I groaned to the girls over dinner at Spice Market the next night after recounting my evening with Scott. "It's too much. Acting like a complete moron isn't going to help anything. The guys attracted to that kind of thing aren't my kind of guys at all."

"But that's what the whole thing is all about," Emmie protested, looking hurt. It took me a moment to realize that she probably felt like I was rejecting *her*, since she had "taught" me how to act like a dumb blonde. "Weren't you convincing?"

"Yes, I was convincing," I said. I sighed. "That's the problem, though. If this Blonde Theory experiment is about seeing if my job and my intelligence scare guys, then that's all I should change, right?"

Three confused faces looked back at me. I took a deep breath.

"Look, I lost it with Scott last night because I was acting *so* stupid, and he still totally ate it up," I said, trying my best to explain a feeling I couldn't quite put a finger on. "That's not going to tell us anything. I would *never* go out with a guy that shallow. The whole thing was just fundamentally off from the beginning."

"What do you mean?" asked Jill, wrinkling her brow in consternation. Meg and Emmie looked equally confused.

"He was attracted to me because I acted so completely stupid and moronic at the bar," I said. "Fine, so we've already proved that it's easier to get a date as a dumb blonde than as a lawyer. That wasn't exactly surprising. But what I really want to know is whether guys will be attracted to me for who I am—as long as who I am isn't a lawyer or a Harvard grad or anything."

"So you don't want to act like a dumb blonde anymore?" Meg asked slowly.

"No, that's not what I'm saying. Not exactly, anyhow," I hedged. "I think I'd learn more if I acted like a dumbed-down version of myself rather than a full-out ditz. I mean, this isn't some crazy chick flick. This is my life."

The girls stared back at me. Meg reached for a spring roll, and Jill took a delicate bite of her lime noodles. Emmie took a long sip of her kumquat mojito.

"You're right," Meg said finally. The other girls nodded thoughtfully. "But," she continued, "how are you going to meet guys? As you mentioned, it's harder to meet them when you're not acting like a blonde ditz."

"Yeah, it's not exactly like they're coming out of the woodwork to ask me out," I muttered.

We sat in silence for a moment, mulling that over. I took a bite of pepper shrimp and waited for someone to say something to make me feel better. No answer seemed to be forthcoming.

"The Internet!" Emmie exclaimed suddenly, as if the thought had just popped into her head. We all swiveled our heads to look at her.

"What?" I asked as my stomach began to swim uneasily. After all, the three of them had tried to persuade me more than once in the last three years to give Match.com or one of the other sites a try. But I hated the idea. I knew lots of women who loved the ease of meeting men online, but I was still a bit old-fashioned and didn't quite believe that a lasting connection could begin in cyber-space. Plus, what if one of the partners at my firm somehow saw my profile and knew I was trolling for dates on the Internet? That would be humiliating!

"Internet dating!" Emmie declared triumphantly with a toss of her short blonde curls. "It's perfect!"

"No, no," I said quickly, shaking my head. "No, no, no, no." I looked to Jill and then to Meg, expecting to find some sympathy and support. Instead, they were both nodding enthusiastically. My heart sank.

"It's actually not a bad idea," Meg said, nodding sagely.

"It's not?" I asked skeptically. Because online dating sounded like a *very* bad idea to me.

"No," she said eagerly. "No, it's not a bad idea at all. It's per-fect. I think this is it."

"It... it is?" I asked skeptically.

"Sure!" she exclaimed. "It gives you the chance to flesh out your personality in your dating profile—but without saying that you're an attorney or that you're as smart as you are or as successful as you are or anything."

"So be me, for the most part, but leave out the things I feel drive guys away?" I asked. The three girls nodded enthusiastically.

"That's the whole purpose of The Blonde Theory, isn't it?" Meg asked softly. "To see if those are the things that scare guys away? To see if they're attracted to you for who you are—without all the so-called problems of your success or your intelligence?"

"I guess it is," I mumbled, feeling a strange blend of deflated and somewhat hopeful. After all, maybe this was the answer. Maybe I could meet guys who were marginally more normal than Scott. It would be a good chance to tone down the stupidity a notch but still attract guys without scaring them away through mention of my job. It was worth a try, I realized resignedly.

For the next half an hour, with Jill taking notes in a pink notebook with her bubbly handwriting (complete with hearts over the i's), we outlined what we wanted my profile to say. In the end, I was relatively happy with the wording we had come up with; I still sounded like me, but I didn't sound like a particularly accomplished or successful version of me. It was perfect. Well, as perfect as I could get while lopping off an entire aspect of who I am.

Meg took a cab uptown with me to my apartment. We sat down together, and I entered the information dutifully into NYSoulmate.com, a hot New York dating site that had debuted several months before with a mass advertising campaign in *New York* magazine, the *Times,* and the *Post.*

INTERESTS: I like spending time with my friends, traveling, shopping, talking on the phone, and aerobics.

(Meg had insisted I leave "reading" off the list, because it sounded too intellectual, and of course I'd been smart enough to leave off "chemistry," "physics," "particle matter," and "researching legal precedents" on my own. Oh yes, and in real life, I didn't *exactly* love aerobics. But it sounded good.)

OCCUPATION: Bartender.

(Meg and I had mulled this over for a while before deciding that "bartender" didn't sound stupid, but it didn't necessarily sound intelligent or educated, either. It left it up to potential dates to judge me for themselves without knowing ahead of time that they were going out with someone smart—or not.)

LAST BOOK I READ: I hate reading. Why read when you have a TV?

(Meg had again insisted that I couldn't sound like I liked to read or do anything intellectual, which just killed me because reading was one of my favorite pastimes. "Isn't that part of my fundamental personality?" I had argued, trying to convince her to let me put *My Sister's Keeper* in as the most recent book I had loved. "No way," Meg had responded firmly. "Too intellectual.")

> ABOUT ME: I totally love to have fun. I like going out with my friends, meeting new people, and having a blast. I don't have a college degree, and I never did that well in school. I'm more street smart than book smart, I guess.

(I wasn't crazy about the wording, and it pained me to leave out the entire lawyer side of my personality, but Meg made a strong argument for staying as vague as possible. As for the "admission" that I didn't have a degree, Meg had insisted that I needed to lay it on the table that I wasn't very smart if this Blonde Theory was going to work. I argued that nobody was likely to respond to me if I put that in there, but she just shrugged mysteriously and said, "We'll see.")

> WHO I'D LIKE TO DATE: I'd like to meet guys who want to get to know me, who want to talk, who want to listen to me, who want to go shopping with me, who like to dance, and who want to share some fun experiences. I like guys who have good jobs, are self-confident, know what they want out of life, and want to get to know me, too.

(Well, at least that part was mostly true.)

"Anyhow, I brought my digital camera," Meg said after we had finished with the profile. "Let's take your picture to go with the profile, okay? Then I've got to get going. Paul is going to start wondering why I'm taking so long getting home."

For the next five minutes, with the assistance of a can of Aqua Net she had bought at the Duane Reade drugstore outside her office building, Meg teased my hair into heights previously unknown to my head (then again, my normal hairstyle was conservative and slicked-back). Then she insisted that I use the bright pink lipstick Emmie had provided me with, as well as putting too much blush on my cheeks. I reluctantly obliged and added an extra layer of mascara on my own. When I was done, I looked in the mirror and saw a dumb blonde looking back, which I supposed meant I had done my job.

Finally, we went back to the living room, where Meg snapped a series of photos. We uploaded them onto my laptop and chose the best—one where I was staring vacuously off into the distance with a decidedly empty expression on my face. Thankfully, with all the piled-on makeup and teased hair as well as the angle from which the photo was taken, you could barely tell it was me.

We logged on to NYSoulmate.com and uploaded both the photo and the profile Meg had written for me, choosing BlondeBartenderHotti as my screen name. A thought had begun creeping into my mind while we worked, though, and when we were done setting up my profile, I turned hesitantly to Meg.

"Would you mind taking a few more photos of me?" I asked, feeling stupid for even suggesting it.

She tilted her head to the side. "Sure," she said. "But why? Don't you like the one we chose?"

"Well, I'm just thinking about it, and it seems like maybe I should put on a *real* profile, too," I said slowly. "I mean, not that I would ever use an Internet dating site. But just for comparison's sake, you know? Like, put up a similar photo—without the hair spray and lipstick— and write my *real* bio and see how many hits I get."

"That's a great idea!" Meg exclaimed. "I can't believe I didn't think of it."

I shrugged, a bit embarrassed. It wasn't as if I was going to meet the love of my life on the Internet. But it would be interesting to compare. After all, maybe The Blonde Theory was wrong and I was just meeting the wrong guys. Maybe an equal number of guys would respond well to my *real* profile—complete with horrifying lawyer stats. That would certainly be a relief. It was worth a shot.

I wiped off the lipstick and blush and combed as much of the spray out of my hair as I could, then I returned to the living room, where Meg sat waiting with her digital camera. She took a series of photos, and I chose the one that most closely resembled BlondeBartenderHotti's photo (for comparison purposes)—just without the overdone makeup, teased hair, and empty expression.

"Need help writing your profile?" Meg asked once we were done with the photo.

"Nah," I said with a sigh. "I think this is something I have to do myself."

Meg nodded and stood up to leave.

"Thanks for being a good sport about this, Harper," she said as we walked toward the front door.

"No, it's fine," I said. "I hate to admit it, but I'm kind of enjoying this whole thing. A little bit, at least. It's kind of interesting to find out what these guys are really thinking. Even if it turns out that they're just the jerks I always expected they were."

"Try to keep an open mind," Meg said sagely.

I hesitated, then nodded. "I'll try." We hugged good-bye, then I opened the door to let her out. "Say hi to Paul for me."

"I will." With a little wave, Meg was gone down my hall.

I shut the door and walked back to my living room, approaching my laptop with trepidation. I wasn't crazy about the idea of pouring out my likes, dislikes, and dating desires to strangers on the Internet. But I knew I had to, for the sake of proving or disproving the theory, at least. Anyhow, it wasn't like I had to actually go out with any of these guys, right?

I got to work and spent the next hour writing a profile for NYSoulmate.com. I chose the user name UptownAttorneyGirl. By eleven thirty, I had finished a profile I was happy with, beginning with: "Wanted: A man who isn't scared to date a lawyer and wants to have good times with a woman he can carry on thought-provoking conversations with." I changed my occupation to "attorney" and kept the appearance info the same—it wasn't like my height, hair color, age, or body shape had changed with my IQ level. And I put a lot of thought into the bio. Finally I had one I was happy with.

INTERESTS: I like spending time with my friends, reading, traveling (especially to Europe), and the occasional shopping trip.

FAVORITE HOT SPOTS: The Union Square Cafe. Spice Market. I like to dance at Manahatta. And I like the Pink Martini.

LAST BOOK I READ: *The Lovely Bones:* Thought provoking and moving. I loved it.

ABOUT ME: I graduated from a prestigious law school and have a good job as a partner at a big law firm in town. But these things don't define me. I'm also fun and warm. I'm a good friend. I enjoy going out with my friends, meeting new people, and just relaxing and having fun.

WHO I'D LIKE TO DATE: I'm looking for someone who can look beneath the surface and see me for who I am, and who isn't intimidated by my job or my education. That's just one part of me, and I want to find a guy who understands that—and a guy who has lots of dimensions, too. I'd love to meet someone who is open to getting to know me without any preconceived notions or expectations of who I am.

By the time I was done, I felt mentally exhausted in a way I never did after finishing legal briefs. I had just poured out the real me onto some anonymous dating site. I sighed and clicked on the icon to upload the photo and profile. I waited for the little confirmation *beep* telling me that the upload was complete. Then I turned off the computer, got ready for bed, and waited for my social life to take off in cyberspace.

When I got into the office the next morning at seven thirty, the first thing I did was sign on to NYSoulmate.com and check my profiles to see if I had gotten any messages yet. I checked my "real" one first. In less than twelve hours, UptownAttorneyGirl had gotten thirty-one hits and received three messages. I stared at the numbers for a moment, shocked. This was my *real* profile! The one where I said I was me! Hmm, maybe I wasn't as scary as I'd thought. Maybe I should have tried this Internet dating thing a long time ago. Who knew I was such hot stuff in cyberspace?

I was excited to read the e-mails I'd received from potential suitors, but first I wanted to see how many hits and messages BlondeBartenderHotti had gotten. I figured the ditzy profile had probably received two or three times as many letters from cyberguys. After all, my whole life had been testament to this inequity, and I was sure it extended to cyberspace.

I signed out of UptownAttorneyGirl's profile and signed back on under BlondeBartenderHotti's screen name. The page took a moment to load, but when it did, my jaw dropped.

In the twelve hours that the profile had been posted, my blonde alter ego had received 256 views and fifty-seven new messages.

Fifty-seven new messages?

I sat stunned for a moment. The photos I had posted to the two profiles were virtually identical, although in the second one, I had been sans fuchsia lipstick and teased hair. Still, the only real difference was that BlondeBartenderHotti's profile had sounded blatantly unintelligent. The UptownAttorneyGirl profile? It had sounded just like me.

I stared at the screen. BlondeBartenderHotti's overflowing inbox stared back at me as if taunting me. There it was, in the stark black and white of NYSoulmate.com's messaging system: the answer to The Blonde Theory. If I were summing this up as a mathematical equation, I supposed I could quantify the results by saying that for every one man who would be interested in dating an intelligent attorney, there were *nineteen* who wanted to date a dumb blonde. *Nineteen.* The figure made me—the real me—feel really pathetic.

I sighed and clicked back to UptownAttorneyGirl's inbox to read the meager assortment of messages.

The first was from JaysonArchieNYC, who said he was a thirty-eight-year-old firefighter on Staten Island who liked to date "smart chiks who are smokin hot because I've never been out with a smart chic." The second was from DinoRichie who said he was a forty-five-year-old mortgage broker who didn't get out much and wanted "someone who wants to stay at home and listen to NPR with me on Friday nights and go on perfect dates to the Museum of Natural History to see the dinosaurs." The third message was from a sender who'd called himself DrMcDream101, so I opened it feeling optimistic, visions of Patrick Dempsey dancing in my head... but it was just an ad for breast-enhancement cream, which promised me that it would "Double your dating success overnight—guaranteed!"

I sighed. Perhaps my alter ego had fared better.

I logged out of UptownAttorneyGirl's inbox again and signed back in as BlondeBartenderHotti. I spent the next thirty minutes scanning the messages, reading each one quickly. In the total of fifty-seven messages, there were four ads, including one from the DrMcDream101 of breast-enhancing fame. But that still left fifty-three genuine responses to the dumb-blonde profile.

Some were ridiculous, but just under half sounded like guys I could actually consider going on a date with, although I supposed this was the first sign that I was going insane. I cut and pasted the best twenty answers into an e-mail that I sent on to Meg, Jill, and Emmie with a note from me asking them to pick their favorite ten. Meg had said I needed to go on at least five more blonde dates, and although I felt like the answer to The Blonde Theory was just as simple as the 1:19 ratio, I knew I couldn't let her and the girls down. For that matter, I couldn't exactly let myself down.

At noon, after I had met with a new client, an independently wealthy man who wanted to patent a "viable alternative to shoelaces," as he called the strange sticky device he had plunked down on my desk, I called Meg, who conferenced in Emmie and Jill. Together, the four of us picked our favorite ten guys from BlondeBartenderHotti's list and agreed that I would e-mail them back in descending order, trying to make a date with five of them, one for each of the next five nights—including tonight.

"You never know," said Jill, ever the optimist. "My friend Anne met her husband through Match. There *are* good guys on these Internet dating sites."

"They just happen to be few and far between," I grumbled. "And I don't think any of the good guys are writing to BlondeBartenderHotti."

"Don't be so negative," Meg said. "After all, you agreed to this experiment. Maybe it will help change your perspective on dating."

I snorted. "Yeah," I said. "It will erase any doubt in my mind that I'll wind up a spinster. Now it's a certainty."

"There's no such thing as a spinster anymore," Emmie chimed in, her voice bubbly and enthusiastic as usual. "You're just a fabulous thirtysomething with a fabulous job and fabulous shoes."

"You're like Carrie Bradshaw!" Jill chimed in excitedly.

"Yes," I said. "Except that this is real life, not some TV show that wraps up neatly in thirty minutes and ends with my Mr. Big sweeping me off my feet."

The girls wished me luck, and we said our good-byes. I spent the remainder of the hour drafting quick e-mails—in my best dumb-blonde writing style, of course—to the top five guys on the list: GeorgeEdwards38 (a thirty-eight-year-old engineer), MarcoPolo (a thirty-six-year-old Italian buyer for Prada), HighAltitudeFlyer (a forty-year-old airline pilot), CorporateColin (a thirty-seven-year-old mortgage broker who owned his own company), and DavidDunnNYPD (a forty-one-year-old NYPD detective).

By the end of the workday, I had heard back from CorporateColin, whose real name was Colin White; MarcoPolo, whose name was really Marco Cassan; and HighAltitudeFlyer, who was really Douglas McDonnell. Colin had agreed to meet me for dinner tomorrow night at eight, while I'd made a date with Marco for Sunday night and one with Douglas for Monday. And all three guys who had responded by the end of the day sounded decent, in their e-mails and profiles, at least. How could I go wrong?

Why did I have the uncomfortable feeling that those were famous last words?

Chapter Eight

I awoke the next morning to the sound of running water.

For a moment, in that foggy place between sleep and consciousness, I couldn't remember where I was. I'd never heard running water like this in my apartment, but the sound conjured up the image of a trip I'd taken with Peter to Brazil during the time that our relationship was going well. We had stayed in a little cottage at the edge of a rain forest and had awoken every morning to the sound of a little waterfall nearby. For an instant, I was back there, listening to the flowing falls and waiting for Peter to roll over and spoon me, holding me tightly against him like he never wanted to let me go.

Then, blinking my eyes into the harsh sunlight that was already pouring in my window, I realized in an instant that I was indeed not in Brazil, on a romantic vacation with a man I loved. Instead, I was in someplace far less exciting: my own bed. Alone. As usual.

As I lay there trying simultaneously to forget the trip to Brazil and to go back there again in my mind, I realized that the sound of rushing water was closer than the waterfall had been to our Brazilian cottage. And in the middle of Manhattan, in a fifth-floor apartment, I shouldn't be hearing rushing water in any kind of proximity.

This was not good news.

Hmm, maybe I had finally cracked and was going whole-heartedly insane. Ah well, at least it would get me off the hook for The Blonde Theory. The girls couldn't very well expect me to conduct self-deprecating dating experiments from the loony bin, now, could they? Although dating mental patients would add an interesting new dimension to this whole thing.

I sat up in bed and looked around. I couldn't *see* any rushing water, which I supposed was a good sign that I hadn't totally cracked up yet. But I could definitely hear it. And it was coming from the direction of my bathroom. Not a good sign.

I slid out of bed, cringing a bit as my feet touched the cold hardwood floors and adjusted to the temperature. I kept my apartment very cold at night, because I loved wrapping myself in several blankets while I slept. But stepping out of the warmth of the blankets into the Antarctic-like conditions of my bedroom was always a shock. I pulled on a robe over my boxers and gray Harvard-insignia tank, and, wrapping my arms around myself, I shuffled to the bathroom.

I turned the knob and pushed open the door. I immediately wished I hadn't.

But it was too late. The six inches or so of water that covered the tiled bathroom floor came gushing out into the bedroom, seeping immediately into my beautiful hardwood floor, no doubt warping it. Trying to close the bathroom door again proved to be useless; the water was already pouring out.

"No!" I moaned as I noticed the bottom of my bathrobe absorbing the flow. I peeked my head around the corner of the bathroom and immediately saw the source of the early-morning waterfall, which was significantly less appealing than the one I'd had outside my window in Brazil. The torrents of water were spilling over from the bowl of my toilet, which must have started to overflow during the night.

I closed my eyes for a moment, still standing in the puddle of water, and wondered just how cursed I was. I mean, whose toilet starts to spontaneously overflow for no apparent reason during the night? This could only happen to me.

I took a deep breath and shuffled over to the toilet, trying not to think about the fact that I was currently standing in toilet water. It didn't get much grosser than that. I tried to remember what I could about fixing toilets, but all I could come up with off the top of my head was jiggling the handle. So I reached over and did that, jiggling the metal grip firmly. I paused and listened for a moment, waiting for the flowing water to shut off, thanks to my miraculous handyman solution.

No such luck. Okay, so I wasn't destined for a career as a plumber.

I took a step closer and removed the top of the tank, setting it gingerly on the edge of the bathtub. I peered inside hesitantly, not sure what I'd find or, for that matter, what I'd do with what I'd find. The inside looked fairly simple. I gave myself a little pep talk. *You're a smart girl, Harper. You graduated from Harvard, after all. Surely you can figure out how to stop your toilet from overflowing.*

I took off my robe, as I wasn't crazy about the idea of sticking my robe-clad arm into the toilet, then I reached into the cold water, fishing around for something that would make the running water stop. I was heartened to discover that the flow ceased temporarily when I lifted the narrow lever attached to the thin chain in the middle of the back toilet basin. I was just about to go pour myself a congratulatory glass of orange juice and give myself a pat on the back for solving the problem when I realized that the moment I let go of the lever, the water started flowing again. And it seemed heavier this time. So unless I planned to stand in the bathroom holding the lever for the rest of my life, I was still stuck.

Okay, I could handle this. *Stay calm*, I told myself. *You aced the New York patent bar exam. You can figure out a toilet.* I plunged my arm into the back of the basin again, feeling around for anything else that might have triggered the unwelcome flow of water. There was a little tank-looking thing on the left with a metal pin attached. I lifted the pin, crossing the fingers on my other hand optimistically. Nothing. I jiggled the little white tube shooting a steady stream of offending water into the cylinder that fed the toilet bowl. But it just squirted out toward me, making me jump back in disgust, because now not only were my feet and arms covered with toilet water, but I had been squirted in the cheek with it, too. I took another deep breath and plunged my arm back in, pulling at the little floating bulb that I assumed was supposed to indicate when the bowl was full and didn't need any more water. That, too, just made the speed of the flow increase.

I felt for anything else that might stop the flow. I jiggled the handle again with my other hand. I tried jiggling it while holding the little black lever up, while pushing the bulb down, while jiggling the little white tube.

Still, nothing.

"It's a toilet!" I finally said aloud to myself, scowling at it. "How can it be this hard?" I kicked the base of the toilet for emphasis, which evidently sent some sort of signal to the water shooting from the tube to double its flow immediately.

Okay, I could handle this. I thought for a moment. Right. I could just call my landlord. He'd have someone come up and fix it right away. Sure, he'd probably look at me like I was a brainless idiot, which in fact I was at the moment, but at least the water flow would stop. Every second I wasted was one more second that the water was seeping into my expensive hardwood floors, no doubt damaging them beyond repair.

I made my way to the kitchen, too discouraged to even think about the fact that I was now tracking toilet water all over the apartment. I felt like screaming. This should be something I could handle. I was a single girl, not an incompetent dolt. Why couldn't

I figure out the damned toilet? I couldn't help but think that if I had a boyfriend—if Peter or anyone else were still here—the problem would already be solved. Men just seemed to be born with the innate ability to fix things and mow lawns and hook up electronic devices, didn't they? What was wrong with me that I could figure out the intricacies of extremely complicated patent laws but I couldn't figure out how to stop a simple toilet from running?

It wasn't until I was in the kitchen with my portable phone in hand that I realized that I *couldn't* call the landlord. Why? Because I didn't *have* a landlord. That's what happens when you *buy* your apartment. Damn it. And I thought I was being so smart and independent by purchasing a place two years ago—sort of a knee-jerk reaction to Peter leaving. *Who needs a man?* That was my theory. But that was before my toilet broke and I realized how incompetent I was. What was I going to do?

I could call Meg and have her send Paul over, but by the time he got here from Brooklyn, I'd already be floating away in a sea of toilet water. I'd be better off spending my time building an ark. I could call Jill, but I had the gut feeling that Alec was conspicuously missing the home-repair gene. And even if he *did* know how to fix a toilet, he'd no doubt make excuses about how he had to go into work instead. I couldn't imagine him dirtying his hands with toilet water. I could just hear his nasal voice: *Harper, I save lives. I don't have time to fix toilets.* Okay then.

That left me one choice. Sad as it was, I'd just have to call a plumber. I felt like an idiot; it would cost me hundreds of dollars to have some guy come over and do something that an independent woman like me *should* be able to do myself.

"Idiot, idiot, idiot," I cursed myself aloud. But I didn't have a choice. I grabbed the yellow pages from the drawer below the phone and skimmed through the plumbing section quickly until I found a location close to me. *Handymen on Call: The 24-Hour Answer to All Your Plumbing, Electrical, and Household Problems,* the entry read. I immediately dialed the number. It rang three times before a gruff voice answered, growling the business's name into the receiver.

"Um, yes," I said, feeling like a complete fool. "I live on Seventy-fourth and Third. My toilet is overflowing, and I can't get it to stop. I need someone to come over and help me as soon as possible, please."

The guy snorted.

"Our minumum charge for a house call is seventy-five dollars," he growled, sounding amused. "And since it's before ten AM, that's an extra twenty-five. And that's before you add on our hourly rate."

"Fine, fine," I said hurriedly. Whatever. I didn't care. I just wanted to solve the problem quickly, and if I had to throw money at the problem to make it go away in a timely fashion, then so be it.

"All right, ma'am," the guy said. "I'll have Sean there in fifteen minutes. He's the closest to you right now. Let me have your credit card number."

I read it to him hastily, then I gave him my exact address, hung up, and waited for the handyman to arrive.

Less than ten minutes later, there was a knock on the door. I waded back out from the bathroom, where I had been standing, peering into the toilet and trying to figure out its mysterious ways. Of course I hadn't bothered to use the time to brush my teeth, run a comb through my hair, or put on any makeup, which I immediately regretted, despite myself, when I opened the door to find a sandy-haired guy about my age standing outside.

He was looking down at a notepad in his hands when I opened the door, and when he looked up and grinned pleasantly at me, his blue eyes wide and sharp, I felt momentarily self-conscious about my matted hair, makeup-free face, and braless tank top.

"Um, Mrs. Roberts?" he asked, glancing back down at his notepad, his deep voice thick with an accent I couldn't immediately identify.

"Yes," I said. "*Miss* Roberts," I corrected, not sure why I'd felt like I needed to clarify that. "But please, call me Harper."

The handyman, dressed in faded jeans and a collared pale blue shirt that said HANDYMEN ON CALL over the left breast pocket in red stitching, smiled at me and extended a hand.

"I'm Sean O'Sullivan," he said. Okay, so that solved the mystery of his accent's origins. He was obviously Irish. I took his hand and he shook mine firmly. "Pleasure to meet you, *Miss* Harper Roberts. You say you have a toilet overflowing, so?"

"Um, yes," I said, self-consciously. "Right this way, please. Thanks for coming on such short notice."

"That's what we do, ma'am," he said cheerfully, shutting the door and following me down the hall toward my bedroom. Of course I'd hadn't made the bed or picked up last night's outfit from the floor. I hurried ahead to the bathroom, hoping he wouldn't notice my bra and panties lying in a heap beside the corner of my bed. Not that it mattered; he was the handyman, not some potential date. I guess my senses were just going haywire because it had been so long since I'd actually had any kind of man in my bedroom at all. We rounded the corner toward the bathroom, and when he saw the pool of water extending out into my bedroom, he groaned.

"Ah no, you have a bit of a mess 'ere, eh?" he said, shaking his head.

"It happened while I was sleeping," I said, a bit defensive. After all, it wasn't like I had clogged the toilet myself. "I just woke up and found it like this, and I couldn't figure out how to turn it off."

Sean turned and grinned at me again, then stepped into the bathroom, wading through several inches of water. He bent down beside the toilet and in one twist of his left wrist turned off a knob behind the toilet that I hadn't even *noticed* when I was fishing around *inside* the toilet. The water immediately stopped.

"Well, this will stop the water for now, then," he said, standing back up and looking at me with an amused expression.

"I feel like an idiot," I mumbled, shifting from foot to foot and looking at the ground. "I didn't even notice that knob there. You mean I could have fixed this myself?"

"Not to worry, miss," he said cheerfully in his thick Irish brogue. "You'd be surprised how many calls we get like this. If you've never had an overflow, you don't even think to look for the faucet handle. Now let me have a look inside the belly o' the beast 'ere." He bent at the waist to look inside the back of the toilet. After a few seconds, he reached in a hand, fished around for a second, looked down, and twisted something inside.

"That should do it, now," he said, straightening up. "Let's just see what happens when we turn 'er on, right then?" He bent down and turned the faucet handle back to the left. We both listened for a moment. No more running water. He flushed the toilet, and we both stood in silence as it went through its normal cycle and then shut off, as it always had in the past.

"It's fixed?" I asked incredulously. "Just like that?"

The handyman turned around to face me and nodded. "Yeah, it's back to right normal, so," he said. "Now we just have a bit of a mess to worry about 'ere."

"Wow," I said, blinking hard. "That took you like two seconds. I could have done that myself."

"Like I said, happens all the time. Those toilets are tricky little bastards. Excuse the language, ma'am."

Damn it. He'd *ma'am*ed me. Again. I hated that. Come to think of it, he did actually look a few years younger than me— maybe twenty-nine or thirty—and without my makeup, I'm sure I looked like quite the old bat to him. Not that it mattered anyhow. He was just the handyman whom I'd never see again. I was thankful for that, because I didn't want word to leak out that I was such a hopeless idiot, I couldn't even fix my own toilet. Although that kind of rumor would certainly do wonders for my dumb-blonde image.

"Don't worry," I said. "Anyhow, thanks. I appreciate it. I'll let you out." I started to head into my bedroom, where I hoped to find a ten-dollar bill in my wallet to tip him for his time. Of course, this was in addition to the hundred-dollar up-front fee and the hourly charge that would appear on my credit card for a job I could have done in under a minute if I'd known how.

"Hold on a second, ma'am," the handyman said, following me into the bedroom, which made me blush, just a bit, for no apparent reason. I guess it was that whole unfamiliar-cute-male-in-the-vicinity-of-my-bed thing again. I was more than a bit rusty. "Let's get some towels first and try to salvage this floor."

I looked at him, surprised and a bit confused.

"No, I'm fine," I said, shaking my head and peering at him carefully. "Thanks for your help. But *this* I know how to do."

"I'm sure you do, ma'am," he said with a polite nod. "No disrespect intended. It's just that you're paying the company for an hour of my time anyhow, so. I might as well help you while I'm here."

I hesitated.

"Are you sure?" I asked finally. It sure looked like it would take a lot of effort to sop up all the water by myself. Not exactly my idea of an ideal way to spend a morning. And I suspected I'd be nearly as hopeless at sopping up water as I had been at stopping the leak in the first place. I had been blessed with neither the home-repair nor the home-maintenance gene.

"Ay, I'm sure," Sean the handyman said with a grin. "I've got nothin' else to do at the moment. I'm happy to help ya out. Just point me in the direction of your towels and we'll get to work right away."

"Okay," I mumbled finally, embarrassed to need a stranger's help and surprised that he was offering it. "Thank you." I grabbed my entire stack of spare towels from the linen closet in the bathroom and handed him half. We lay them down on the wet floor in silence and watched as they sopped up less than a third of the standing water. We wrung the towels out in the tub and went back to try again, but they were already saturated and barely picked up more water.

"You're going to need more dry towels than this, it looks like," he said, looking concerned, once we had thoroughly used up my admittedly meager stack of towels. "I'll go get some more from my apartment, okay? I just live about five minutes away."

"You do?" I asked, surprised, before realizing that the question had probably sounded immensely rude. I knew he could read in my face exactly what I was thinking: *How does a handyman afford the Upper East Side?* I instantly felt like a snob and blushed again. "I'm sorry, I didn't mean..." My voice trailed off as he shook his head.

"Not to worry," he said, looking rather amused. "No offense taken. It's actually not my place anyhow. I just moved here from Ireland a few weeks ago and one of the lads from back home is being kind enough to let me stay on his couch till I get on my feet." He smiled at me. "That's the great thing about we Irish. We stick together. He came over here three years ago and has made it as a bigshot banker. So his couch is a bit nicer than you might expect."

"Oh," I said, feeling terrible for inadvertently insulting him. But he didn't seem bothered.

"Anyhow, I'll be back with some towels in ten minutes, all right?" He started toward the door, his stride long and purposeful.

"But you don't have to...," I began.

"I know I don't," he interrupted firmly. "But I'm happy to help. Seems crazy for you to pay the company for an hour when I'm only doing five minutes of work. Besides, what kind of a gentleman would I be if I let ya drown in a pool of yer own toilet water? Me ma would kill me. So unless you have an objection, I'll let myself out and see you in a few minutes."

I stared after him as he walked down my front hall and disappeared out my front door, closing it gently behind him.

I looked down and realized he'd left his toolbox here. He really *was* planning to come back. I wasn't exactly sure why that made my stomach swim uneasily.

Ten minutes later, I had thrown my discarded undergarments and dirty clothes into the hamper, quickly made the bed, changed into a Newcastle T-shirt (with a bra underneath, thank you very much) and jeans, and had combed my hair back into a ponytail and applied some mascara, a bit of pink Tarte lip gloss, and some concealer to hide the ubiquitous dark circles under my eyes. Not that I cared what some random handyman thought of me. I just didn't want to look like a total mess. The doorbell rang and I hurried out in the hall to answer it.

"Newcastle is shite," the handyman said by way of greeting when I opened the door. His arms were piled so high with folded towels that I could barely see his face.

"What?" I asked blankly. Clearly I was not the only one who appeared to have gone insane this morning. Then he nodded toward my chest, his chin squishing into the top of the towel stack as he did so.

"Your shirt, Newcastle beer. It's shite."

"It is not," I said, vaguely insulted and more indignant than I should have been. "It happens to be my favorite beer."

"Then ya clearly haven't tried enough beers," he said simply. He grinned at me and I rolled my eyes.

"I suppose you're going to tell me that Guinness is the only way to go," I said, placing my hands obstinately on my hips.

He shook his head. "No, Guinness is shite too," he said. "I'm a Murphy's man. You haven't had a beer till you've had a Murphy's."

"I've never heard of it," I said sourly.

"Well then, you can't call yourself a beer drinker," he said promptly. "Murphy's is the best. I'll be drinkin' it all the way to the grave, I will. Anyhow, are you goin' to invite me in? Or do you want me to just stand here with my arms full o' towels?"

"Oh," I said, stepping aside and trying to conceal the flush that had once again spread up my cheeks for no apparent reason. "Sorry. Thanks for bringing the towels over."

"Not a problem," he said. I shut the door and followed him down the hall. "I'm not sure the lad whose couch I'm sleepin' on would be so thrilled that I'm using his towels this way. But if we get 'em washed and dried, he'll never know the difference, will he?"

I shook my head, and he passed me half the towels. Silently, we each went to work, me sopping up the water that had spilled into the bedroom, the handyman concentrating on the water pooled on the bathroom floor. Feeling guilty for needing his help, I struggled to think of something to talk about while we sopped.

"So what brought you over to the States?" I asked. The handyman looked up and smiled, his well-defined cheekbones rising as he did so and his eyes crinkling at the corners.

"Ay, you want to know my story, do ya?" he asked. "Well, here's the condensed version, then." He bent and put down more towels, scrubbing and sopping up water as he spoke, his back turned to me. "I'm from Cork, in the southwest of Ireland, the second largest city in our great nation, third largest if you count Belfast, which I do. After I finished with school, I stayed there in town and supported me ma. I'm all she had." He was looking at the floor, sopping as he spoke.

"It was a decent life," he continued. I worked slowly while I listened to him. "All me mates were there. I had lots of friends, lots of good times, lots of great nights at the pubs. But I was never really happy, you know? I had never traveled much. I couldn't afford to, not with me ma to support there, you know."

"Wow," I said, because I didn't know what else to say. Sean shrugged and continued, his back still to me.

"Anyhow, me ma got real sick last year," he said, his shoulders slumping a bit. "Cancer, you know. I had to sell the house to help pay for her care. And when she passed away this spring, I couldn't stay there. Too many memories, and no kin, no ties keepin' me in Ireland. I wanted to see the world. So a couple o' months ago, I bought a one-way ticket to the States. And here I am."

"I'm sorry to hear about your mother," I murmured, straightening and looking in his direction.

He shrugged his broad shoulders and continued sopping the water up. "'Tis all right," he said. "'Tis the natural course of life. I miss her, but she's not in pain anymore. And she's with me every day, in my heart at least. You know, I wasn't happy in Cork. Not with my job there, not with my life there. I'd realized that some time ago. But the time was never right to leave until after she was gone. I know me ma would want me to be happy. I'm trying to find that happiness now."

"As a handyman?" I asked before I could stop myself. I clamped my hand over my mouth the moment the words were out, fearing that I had offended him again. But he just laughed.

"Not really," he said. He turned to me, and his face looked friendly. "This is the means to an end, so."

I nodded, chastised. I was afraid to ask more, because apparently I had lost all control of my manners. What was wrong with me? Talk about putting my foot in my mouth. I'd basically just inserted it up to my shin.

"I really am sorry about your mother," I said softly.

"And I appreciate that," Sean said with a smile before turning back to the towels and the bathroom floor, which was finally looking drier. "So what's your story, then? You live by yourself in this big apartment?"

I hesitated, not sure what to say. Of course, common sense dictated that a single woman wasn't supposed to tell a man she didn't know that she lived alone. But there was something that stopped me from lying to Sean.

"Yes," I said simply. "I do."

"Ay, that's class!" he exclaimed. "Good for you, then. What is it you do that lets you afford such a place?"

I sighed. Here we go. If stockbrokers and doctors freaked out as soon as they heard what I did, revealing the truth would probably have Sean the handyman racing out the door in record time. Even though sopping up toilet water before 10 AM didn't exactly constitute anything remotely resembling a date. Not that I could ever imagine myself dating the guy who came to fix broken toilets. Even though he was gorgeous.

"I'm an attorney," I sighed finally, turning off the crazy voice in my head and bracing myself for whatever response was to come.

"Oh, class!" Sean exclaimed immediately. I turned to stare at him, shocked. "Good for you, then! You must be good at what you do. I love the law, you know. Fascinatin' field."

I couldn't believe it, but my words hadn't scared him off. He didn't seem to notice my gaping mouth and impolite stare. He stood up, his arms full of wet towels.

"Well, I'm just about done in your bathroom," he said. He heaped the towels into the bathtub, then stepped out into the bedroom. "All the water's come up. How're you doin' in the bedroom, then?"

"Um, okay," I stammered. He joined me on the hardwood floor and helped me sop up the rest of the moisture. Then he bent to look closely at the floor, lying on his stomach and looking at the hardwood at eye level.

"Not to worry," he said finally, straightening back up. "I don't think the water was there long enough to cause significant damage. Let it dry a day or two and then layer on some Thompson's Water Seal, and you should be as good as new."

"Thank you," I said, looking from the floor to him.

"Not a problem," he said cheerfully. "You might want to give your floors a good clean, then. Not sure what's swimmin' around in water from the loo, you know."

I laughed and nodded. "I'll mop it today," I assured him.

"Ay, I figured as much," he said with a nod. "Well then, I'll be on my way. It looks like you can take it from here."

I glanced toward the bathroom. "I'll wash and dry the towels for you today, okay?" I said, feeling guilty that he'd brought so many.

Sean shook his head. "Nah, that's fine. I can take 'em home and wash 'em myself."

"No, I insist," I said firmly. "It's the least I can do. Besides, I have to wash mine anyhow. Just leave them in the bathtub, and I'll have them done for you by tomorrow. I can even bring them by your place."

Sean laughed. "Now you make house calls, too, eh? All right, then, I'll let ya wash them if you insist. I appreciate it. But I'll come back and get them myself tomorrow, if that's okay. Say six PM? No need for you to come by my place."

I nodded, assuming he didn't want some client of the handyman service seeing the apartment he lived in with a friend. I didn't want to push.

"Thanks again," I said. Sean nodded and ducked into the bathroom to scrub his hands with soap and water. When he finished, he glanced around for a towel, then, apparently remembering that there were no clean or dry ones available, simply dried his hands on his jeans and shrugged.

"No problem," he said. "Nice to meet you, Miss Harper Roberts. Call us again if you ever need anything else, so."

"I will," I said, meaning it, although I hoped that I wouldn't be such an imbecile in the future that I'd need to pay a hundred dollars to have some guy come over and fix my home-maintenance problems in under five minutes. Not that it had been an unpleasant way to spend the morning, all things considered. "Thanks again."

"No problem," Sean said again. I walked him to the front door, where he picked up his toolbox. "I'll be seein' ya then. Slán."

"What?" I asked.

"Slán," he repeated. "It's Irish for good-bye and good luck. It's me wishin' you the luck o' the Irish, so."

"Oh," I said. "Slán to you, too, then."

Sean grinned and waved as I shut the door behind him. Little did he know that I'd be needing more than the luck of the Irish to make it through the next week and a half of this dumb-blonde experiment.

I felt more demoralized than ever as I walked slowly back to the bathroom to heap the wet towels into a basket to take down to the laundry room in the basement of the building. I'd just been everything I hated—a stupid, helpless woman who couldn't do the simplest of tasks by herself. I never wanted to *need* a man, and this morning, I had. It left me feeling powerless and pathetic.

Even worse was the fact that I'd had a better time kneeling in toilet water with some random handyman than I had on any date I'd been out on in the last three years. This did not seem to be a good sign. Nor did it reflect well on my dating life. I resolved to throw more energy into The Blonde Theory. Sadly, it seemed to be my last chance.

Chapter Nine

*T*hat evening, after half an hour of scrubbing my bedroom floor after work, I arrived a few minutes before eight at the entrance to Semana, a trendy new Zagat-rated Spanish restaurant a few blocks from my apartment that changed its menu each week based on the produce and herbs that were currently in season. Colin White, the first guy from NYSoulmate.com, had called my cell earlier in the afternoon to make sure that I liked Spanish food, which earned him extra points in my eyes, because a guy like Scott Jacoby (sorry, that's *Doctor* Scott Jacoby) wouldn't have bothered to ask. Colin had made a reservation for us at eight and asked me to meet him outside the restaurant.

By the time I arrived, I was actually feeling optimistic about the date. Sure, I wasn't going as *me,* but Colin White had sounded nice on the phone, and his NYSoulmate.com profile photo had looked downright hot. Maybe there could be some sparks between us if I didn't screw it up by getting all lawyerly. His sexy baritone was still ringing in my ear after our phone conversation earlier in the day.

"I'm looking forward to meeting you," he had said on the phone, his voice low and deep. "You sound like just my type."

Hmm, I doubted he'd be saying that if he knew what I really did for a living. Let's face it: The Colin Whites of the world just didn't go out with lawyers.

"You do, too," I had said peppily, carefully to keep my voice elevated an octave, as Emmie had trained me to do. After all, Colin sounded nice. And wasn't there just something about that name that conjured up sexy images of Colin Firth and Colin Farrell—rolled into one? Now *that* was worth acting dumb for.

Besides, after my morning, I was feeling a renewed sense of urgency as well as the pressure to maintain the blonde persona throughout the date, without cracking under the pressure of agitation, as I unfortunately had with Scott. And if I could have a good time sopping up toilet water with a handyman, then I shouldn't have a problem having a good time with a hot mortgage broker who had already expressed an interest in me, right? And I wouldn't even need to act as blatantly empty-headed as I had with Scott the other night. Hurrah for me!

Emmie, under duress from me, had also conceded a little ground on the outfit issue and had let me dress a bit less ridiculously when I had reminded her that not all dumb blondes dress like cheap hookers. In retrospect, I was starting to realize that perhaps she was deriving a bit too much enjoyment from dressing me in a way that, let's face it, made me look like a total fool.

I still wasn't dressed the way I normally would for a date—far from it, in fact—but Emmie had relented and allowed me to wear a short, low-cut black Diane von Furstenberg wrap dress and decent black heels instead of the lime-green skintight sheath and clear sandals she'd had in mind. I'd drawn the line at clear heels (I was playing a dumb blonde, not a stripper), and now I was thankful I had taken a stand.

My dress was still tighter than I was comfortable with, but all things considered I looked relatively normal—for a brainless blonde.

Emmie had insisted on overdone makeup again (although I had put my foot down on the blue eyeshadow issue, and we had compromised on a copper color with thick eyeliner), and it actually didn't look too bad. I didn't usually wear much makeup—except to darken my light lashes and to conceal my under-eye circles—and as much as it pained me to admit it, Emmie did have a way with a set of makeup brushes. She'd made me look more glamorous than I had expected, although I was still resenting the too-bright pink lipstick she insisted I wear. ("A *real* dumb blonde would never be without bright lipstick or teased hair," she had said sternly.)

So, looking far more presentable than I had the other night, and shifting nervously from foot to foot, I waited in front of Semana, scanning the crowds for my approaching date.

"Harper?" came a deep voice from behind me as I scanned the street uptown. I spun around and found myself face-to-face with a man who looked like he'd just been cut from a magazine ad.

I recognized him immediately from his profile photo and for a moment found it difficult to breathe properly. In person, he was even more attractive than I had expected. His hair was jet black, his eyes were bright blue, and his tanned skin was perfect, stretched over sharp, handsome features. When he smiled, he had deep dimples. I almost wanted to pinch his perfectly sculpted cheeks. But that probably wouldn't have been appropriate, would it? Thankfully, I managed to refrain.

"Yes," I said with a smile, extending my hand out of habit before I remembered that dumb blondes probably didn't shake hands. Fortunately, he saved me from having to fake a limp-fish handshake by picking my hand up and kissing it instead.

Ooh, points for heart-melting charm. It was almost a shame that I'd have to spend the night acting instead of simply drooling at the man across the table. Then again, I reminded myself, the real me would never have been his type. Or at least I assumed. Fine, so an empty-headed bartender I would be. Maybe this Blonde Theory would be worth it if this was the caliber of the guys I'd get to go out with. My heart hadn't stopped thudding in my chest since he'd arrived.

"How did you know it was me?" I asked him as he looked up at me after kissing my hand.

He winked one gorgeously piercing eye at me. "You looked so beautiful in your profile photo," he said without missing a beat. Boy, this one was suave. Almost too suave. Especially considering that my face was partially obscured in the photo. But this was interesting. Did he really think *I* was beautiful? I flushed involuntarily. "And you are the most gorgeous woman on Third Avenue right now," he added, sounding slicker by the minute. "How could I miss you?"

Okay, I knew when I was being given a line. I mean, I was just *pretending* to be a dumb blonde, remember? I wasn't supposed to genuinely buy this stuff. But still, his words made me blush. It wasn't every day that guys like this complimented my appearance. Heck, it wasn't every day that *any* guys paid me a compliment. At least with a straight face. Maybe I *could* get used to dating like a dumb blonde.

I briefly wondered why I hadn't chosen to become a bartender instead of a lawyer. Realizing that I was on a date with someone like Colin White—gorgeous, and apparently smart and successful—was almost enough to make me want to rethink my entire career plan. Was it too late to enroll in bartending school? Perhaps my life plan was fundamentally flawed. Hmm.

Colin held the door open for me and I walked inside the restaurant. As my eyes adjusted to the lowered light, Colin touched me lightly on the elbow and steered me toward the hostess stand in a way that I might have found offensive if he weren't so handsome. Amazing how his gorgeously sharp features made me want to forgive and overlook anything that I might ordinarily construe as negative.

He gave the hostess our name, and we were seated immediately, in part, I suspect, because the blushing woman appeared to be as taken in by Colin's warm smile and chiseled features as I was. I wanted very much to believe that his personality matched his good looks—that he was as sweet and wholesome as he was polished and perfect.

I knew I was deceiving myself. But tonight, it didn't matter. Did it?

"So, Harper," he began in a slow, confident, deep voice once we were seated. He looked across the candlelit table at me and smiled. "Your profile says you're a bartender?"

"Yes," I said demurely and then added a blonde-worthy giggle, because I feared my answer had sounded too staid and, heaven forbid, too intelligent. I flipped my hair over my shoulder for good measure and smiled as vacantly as I could at him. "I, like, love bartending," I chirped, trying to sound as excited about my job as possible. After all, I *was* kind of excited about it at the moment. It sure seemed to net me better men than my real job did. But I digress.

"Well, that sounds very exciting," he said in a voice that sounded almost patronizing. But perhaps I was reading into it. He smiled at me. "How long have you been doing that, Harper?"

"Oh, on and off for ten years," I bubbled. "I just love working behind the bar. It's such a thrill." I giggled for emphasis and he smiled more widely at me, apparently intrigued. I still couldn't understand what about empty-headedness seemed to appeal to guys, but hey, I wasn't going to knock it tonight. I could be as vacant as Colin wanted as long as it kept him gazing adoringly at me.

Hot guys never gazed adoringly at me. Ever. I hadn't realized how nice it felt. I wanted to bask in it for as long as possible, even if *technically* I didn't *quite* deserve the adoration, considering that I was being adored under false pretenses.

"I'll bet it is," he said warmly. He looked deeply into my eyes, as if he were about to say something momentous. "So what's it like, Harper? Being a bartender?"

"Oh," I said, then tittered for effect. "Um, it's, like, really awesome. I mean, I get to meet all kinds of, like, cool people. And I like making drinks." I batted my eyes in what I hoped was a convincing manner. Fortunately, he didn't appear fazed, so I assumed that my batting skills had improved.

"Really?" Colin asked, still appearing quite intrigued. I resisted the urge to squirm under his gaze. I wasn't used to being stared at this intently. It was a little unnerving, actually. "Tell me about it."

Okay, this was new. The guy actually wanted me to talk? That was great and very flattering. There was just one problem. I had never bartended, and I hadn't thought of planning this out ahead of time. I didn't know what to say.

"Um," I said, then hesitated. I glanced over to the restaurant's bar, where a blonde bartender—not a lot unlike me, I supposed—was shaking a martini. "I, uh, like shaking things," I said, then immediately cringed, because really, who would say a thing like that? But Colin merely smiled and nodded as if he understood.

"You must be good at it," he said, and I was about to smile back when I noticed that he actually wouldn't have noticed if I did, as he was currently staring at my breasts instead of my face. I cleared my throat, which got his attention. His eyes shifted upward with what appeared to be an abundance of reluctance, then he smiled slowly.

"Thanks," I said, narrowing my eyes at him. He smiled widely and went back to looking at my breasts.

After ordering drinks (A Limón and Sprite for me; a vodka gimlet for him. Aren't gimlets for sixty-five-year-old men?), we chatted comfortably, Colin asking interested questions ("So what brought you to Manhattan?"), me giving airheaded answers ("An airplane."), him asking me follow-up questions with an arched eyebrow ("No. I mean, why did you move here?"), me giving incomplete follow-up answers

("Oh. Because my friends had, like, moved here already."), and him staring at my breasts. All in all, it went well, I think.

We moved on to our main courses—a New York strip steak with a lime, onion, and garlic marinade for him and a big bowl of paella for me—and to another round of drinks (What was with the gimlets?). The more Bacardi that slipped down my throat, the more comfortable I felt talking to Colin as a dumb blonde. Interestingly, the act seemed to come more naturally when I was the slightest bit tipsy, much as I'd once discovered, on a trip to France, that I was a better French speaker when I was a few sheets to the wind. (Then again, does being able to enunciate *"Voulez-vous coucher avec moi, ce soir?"* before laughing hysterically at my own wit really count as fluency? Perhaps not.)

When we were finished with our meals, Colin suggested, with that arch of his eyebrow that seemed to get sexier with every Bacardi Limón and Sprite I downed, that we order two glasses of Martini & Rossi prosecco and split the restaurant's specialty flan for dessert. Never one to turn down sparkling wine—or dessert (Calories? What calories?)—I immediately agreed.

"I, like, love flan," I said, feeling a little drunk but still remembering to insert the word *like* everywhere. See? I was a natural. "I'm a flan fan."

"So, Harper," Colin began, apparently choosing to ignore my pun—a pun that was admittedly so bad that it probably didn't actually even qualify as a pun. "I have to ask you. What made you try out this dating site? You must meet guys all the time."

"Uh," I paused and cleared my throat to buy some time. Okay, so this was the problem with getting tipsy while acting. I was just a tad bit slower with my answers. "Uh, you first," I said finally. "You're really hot," I said (perhaps a little too bluntly). "I'm sure you meet women all the time."

"Okay," Colin said with a laugh. "Me first. Well, as you know, I'm a mortgage broker. Most of my colleagues are men. And the vast majority of the people I work with are couples, looking to buy their first apartment in the city. I can't exactly date those women, since they're coming in with their husbands."

"But there must be women looking to buy apartments, too," I said quickly, thinking of my own apartment. After all, I'd worked with a broker when I'd bought mine, although he had been about thirty years older than Colin and about two hundred pounds heavier. Just my luck. "You know, single women, I mean."

"Well, sure," Colin said after a moment of studying my breasts, which seemed to be the fallback position for his eyes any time he needed to think. He raised his eyes to look at me. Ah, so he *could* locate my face. Hurrah! "But those women don't need to go out with someone. They can take care of themselves."

I looked at him in confusion for a moment. I wasn't sure whether his words truly didn't make any sense—or whether I was simply having trouble understanding them thanks to the Bacardi-and champagne-induced fog I was currently in. I decided, however, that the fog wasn't that thick. No, he really wasn't making sense.

"What do you mean?" I asked after a moment, being careful to tilt my head to the side, speak in a high-pitched voice, and accentuate my question with a giggle and a vacant smile. "What does it matter that they can, like, take care of themselves?" I took a breath and added as blankly as possible, "I don't get it." Really. I didn't get it.

"Oh, baby, what am I going to do with you?" Colin asked with a laugh, shaking his head like he would at a child who had just said something adorably amusing. He glanced at my breasts again—perhaps to verify that I was indeed not a child but instead a grown woman—then raised his eyes back to mine and smiled at me, apparently satisfied with his substantiation of my womanhood. "You should know this," he said, his voice playfully chiding. "Men like to take care of women. I can't ask someone out who has enough money to buy her own apartment. That would just be embarrassing."

My throat constricted as I had a sudden flashback to Peter leaving me, telling me that men didn't want a woman who was successful. With some difficulty, I gulped, trying to get rid of the lump in my throat. I blinked a few times, then tried to smile.

"Like, I totally see your point," I forced out. I wasn't going to get up on my pedestal like I had with Scott the other night. I was going to ride this one out. "That would be, like, intimidating." I was going to say *emasculating* but figured that your typical dumb blonde wouldn't know that word.

Colin's face darkened a bit. "I didn't say I was intimidated," he said a bit defensively, but not unkindly. "Just that it wouldn't make any sense to ask one of those women out. You know what I mean. Obviously."

"Like, of course," I said, nodding enthusiastically. "Being a bartender and all. I *need* a guy."

"Right," Colin said warmly, leaning forward, placing his left hand on mine, and looking into my eyes. "I like to feel needed. Guys like that."

"I know," I said softly. Apparently mistaking my sudden quiet for flirtatiousness, Colin licked his lips, took another sip of his prosecco, draining the glass, and smiled at me. "Are you ready to get out of here, baby?"

"Yes," I said, daintily dabbing at my own lips with my napkin, which I placed on the table. I took a deep breath and looked Colin up and down—dark hair; perfect, chiseled features; a straight smile that wasn't unkind. He was handsome, no doubt about it. But he wasn't for me.

Too bad. Seriously, too bad. He had seemed so promising.

I sighed to myself and got up from the table. Colin, playing the role of perfect gentleman to perfection, quickly scrambled to my side of the table, where he pulled my chair out for me and pushed it back in when he was done. Then he smiled at me and placed a strong hand on the small of my back, sending a little shiver up my spine. But whether it was a shiver of desire—because he was so cute—or of apprehension—because he'd really thrown me with his words about successful women—I couldn't tell. I shook my head and told myself to stop worrying. I knew I would never see him again. As pleasant as he had initially seemed, I knew this wasn't the kind of guy who could or would ever appreciate me for who and what I really was.

For a moment, as we walked through the restaurant in silence with his hand still lightly on my back, I wondered what was wrong with me. I think some part of me had believed that I could win over a man like Colin with my charm and then reveal to him that I actually had more brains than he had initially believed. But that was crazy, wasn't it? Because the guys who were attracted to dumb blondes—like cute, funny, successful Colin—would never be attracted to a woman like the real me.

I knew I shouldn't have been depressed. After all, he had shown himself to be shallow. He had even spent a large portion of the meal staring at my breasts. He wasn't exactly a golden catch. But still... there was a part of me that wasn't quite getting all the reasons he was undesirable.

I shouldn't have felt sad and rejected. But I did.

Outside the restaurant, Colin surprised me by stepping in front of me, leaning down, and kissing me tenderly on the lips before I even saw him coming. It felt right, even while it felt foreign. I hadn't kissed anyone in longer than I cared to admit. And Colin wasn't Peter. That's all that mattered in that moment. So I kissed back and let myself get lost in him for a moment as he looped an arm around me and pulled me closer, while his other hand lightly cradled the back of my head.

When we finally broke apart, I felt a bit dizzy. I blinked a few times to get my balance and regain my shaken composure. Colin smiled at me slowly.

"Do you want to come back to my place?" he asked softly, reaching out again to tenderly thread his fingers through my hair. "I live close by."

I took a deep breath and closed my eyes, running through all the reasons why I shouldn't.

"Yes," I said softly, my lips still tingling. Colin grinned and looked down at my breasts again, and I suddenly realized that I couldn't. I absolutely, definitively shouldn't and wouldn't. I shook my head, took a step backward, and then said, "No. I mean, I'm sorry, but I can't."

Colin's face fell.

"What?" he said, shifting his gaze up to my face again. "Why not? You just said you could."

"I . . ." I paused, ready to feed him an excuse about having to bartend later that evening or something. But I stopped myself. "I just can't. I'm sorry."

And I truly was. I was sorry that I couldn't forget who I really was. I was sorry that I couldn't overlook all the reasons that I shouldn't go home with Colin. I was sorry that I would never be the right woman for someone like him. And I was sorry that he would never be the right man for someone like me. I was sorry because I had no idea where I fit. I wondered if I actually fit anywhere. Maybe I didn't.

"Thanks for a lovely evening, Colin," I said, as he stared at me slack-jawed, apparently unaccustomed to being turned down. "I had a really nice time."

"But . . . ," he began, glancing frantically from my face to my breasts, as if he didn't exactly know where to address his protests.

"Good-bye," I said softly, then turned to walk away up Third. I could feel his eyes on my back. But for once, *I* was the one who didn't turn around.

There was something about that that felt really good.

* * *

In the next two nights, I went out with Marco, the Prada buyer, and Douglas, the airline pilot.

Marco seemed interesting at the outset. He was broad-shouldered and slender around the waist, with curly blond hair, deep brown eyes, and tanned skin. Clad exclusively in Prada, of course, he looked every bit the classic style icon when I met him at Ruby Foo's for sushi and cocktails. He kissed me on both cheeks, European-style, and spoke with a thick Italian accent, although his English was nearly perfect. He had been living in New York for seven years and loved it, he said. His eyes sparkled with warmth when he talked about his job, which consisted mainly of supplying New York stores with the latest in Prada apparel.

If he hadn't stepped outside five times during dinner for a smoke and continually called me "dahling" in a way that sounded like old cheesy Hollywood, he would have seemed a lot more attractive. But even that, I could get past. After all, I smoked when I sulked, so it didn't bother me that much in general (even though Marco smoked like a chimney that never went out). As for the repeated *dahling*s, I could write them off as misguided European slickness.

But it was his intense fascination with models that got under my skin. I'm sure that it was immediately obvious that I—five foot six, thirty-five years old, and certainly not model-lithe—was not indeed one of the women who walked the catwalk for a living, yet Marco spent much of the meal telling me stories of his escapades with models in Italy and all of the many reasons why models were the best women to date.

"In New York, though, I've had to expand my dating selections a bit and date nonmodels, too," he said, as he paused between bites of his bacon-wrapped date perched on an endive leaf. "Thus, the women like you. Not models, exactly. But still good looking."

"I'm… glad?" I finally responded, not sure quite what to say. I looked at him quizzically.

"You should be flattered, *bella*," he said, leaning across the table seductively and staring into my eyes. I blinked and looked away. "My standards are very high."

"Lucky me," I said drily.

The next night, there was Douglas, the airline pilot. Like Marco and Colin, he was cute and successful. And the date started off well enough. But somewhere around the time I launched into the full-fledged bimbo act ("So how does a plane actually fly?" I asked, wide-eyed. "It seems too heavy."), Douglas launched into a strange soliloquy of his own.

"I used to fly in the navy," he said cheerfully, once he'd downed his first amaretto sour. (I was trying to refrain from thinking that it seemed like a girlie drink—but then he asked for extra cherries and a cocktail umbrella.) "And man, every time I landed my helo, I was Tom Cruise, baby."

"Helo?" I asked.

"Oh, that's navy talk for helicopter," he said, puffing his chest out proudly. "Toughest birds to fly, baby. Just like *Top Gun*."

I paused for a moment.

"But doesn't Tom Cruise fly a fighter jet in *Top Gun*?" I asked, keeping my eyes wide and vacant and tossing my blonde hair for effect. Douglas paused and stared at me, his chest deflating a little bit.

"Well sure," he said, then shrugged. "But he should have flown a helo. All the best guys do that." Then he paused and continued, apparently undeterred. "Anyhow," he said excitedly, "every time I landed my helo on the deck of my frigate—that's a ship—I always sang the *Top Gun* theme song out loud."

"But shouldn't you have been concentrating on your landing?" I asked blankly.

He just stared at me. "Well, it's not like I can land without music," he said, looking at me like I had suddenly sprouted a third eye or something. "Obviously."

"Obviously," I repeated. He stared at me for another moment and then burst into song.

"Highway to . . . the danger zone!" he shouted. All around the restaurant, heads swiveled to stare at him. "I'll take you right into . . . the danger zone!" he continued singing, belting out Kenny Loggins at me. Then he stopped and grinned. "Want me to take you into the danger zone, baby?" he asked, apparently trying to be seductive. It didn't exactly work.

"Um, no thanks," I said blankly. I had no idea what he was talking about, but I figured it couldn't be good. Especially if it involved more singing. Thanks to Douglas's solo, my ears were already feeling like they were in the danger zone, thank you very much.

"Now I fly for Blue Horizon Air," he said, grinning at me. "Small private company. Private charter jets. And I still sing every time I land my aircraft. I think of myself as an older, suaver version of Tom Cruise now."

"Oh . . . do you?" I asked finally, not sure what else to say. After all, I supposed he resembled Tom Cruise a little bit—dark hair, dark eyes, a wide smile, nice features. But he was starting to sound like a lunatic. Then again, it was debatable whether the original Tom was playing with a full deck. So maybe there were more similarities than I had initially thought.

"Yes," he confirmed with a nod. "And it totally works. I've only crashed twice." He held up two fingers and grinned.

My eyes widened.

"You've . . . you've crashed twice?" I asked.

He nodded cheerfully. "Yes," he confirmed as if it were the most normal thing in the world. "No fatalities, though. It's not like Tom Cruise can say the same. I mean, he's got Goose on his conscience."

"Huh?" I asked.

Douglas rolled his eyes at me. "Goose!" he repeated. "You know. Anthony Edwards? His buddy? You know, in *Top Gun*? Tom ejected? Goose didn't? Goose died?"

"Oh," I said, staring at him, thinking that surely this was some kind of a joke. "Of course."

"Harper," Doug said with a sigh, tilting his head and looking into my eyes. "You're such a good listener."

Needless to say, after the dates with Colin, Marco, and Douglas, I was left feeling pretty demoralized. They hadn't been horrible, exactly. But I had had to suppress everything that made me who I was—my intelligence, my job, my background, even my personality—to sit there and listen to their weird takes on the world.

The thing is, none of the guys had lied in their profiles. They were exactly what they said they were. But I had looked at them on paper—a successful mortgage broker, a successful Prada buyer, and a successful airline pilot, all of them very good looking—and assumed that they would be normal, maybe even somewhat desirable, although the fact that they had deliberately chosen the dumb-blonde version of me didn't bode well, I supposed. I had assumed that these were the kinds of men I was missing out on by walking around with a formidable brain in my blonde head.

But if I was missing out on men like these, was that really such a problem?

Then again, maybe the abysmal failure of all three dates was just a fluke.

Chapter Ten

The day after my date with Douglas, I met Jill and her husband, Alec, for lunch, the *Top Gun* theme unfortunately still lodged in my head, where it was playing on an endless loop. I was in a cheerful mood by the time I arrived at Jill's apartment, despite the fact that Alec would be there, too. I didn't exactly dislike Alec, but there was something about his uptight and often condescending nature that made me ill at ease in his presence. But, I reminded myself, Jill was happy with him. She had chosen to marry him. I had to check my judgment at the door. It wasn't my business.

"Harper, come in!" Jill was all Park Avenue princess in her pink short-sleeved sweater, black A-line skirt, string of white pearls, and perfectly highlighted blonde hair slicked back in a black headband. I stepped across her threshold, and she hugged me. "Alec and I can't wait to hear about your dates!"

I'd been so busy going on these dates that I hadn't had time to fill the girls in on the details—except through occasional short missives sent via e-mail while I waited on clients to arrive.

"We're going to talk about this in front of Alec?" I asked in surprise, hugging her back.

"I've told him all about The Blonde Theory," Jill said with a smile as she pulled away from me and shut the door behind us. "He thinks it's funny. In fact, I think he has some advice for you. I thought it would be fun to get a guy's perspective." Her eyes twinkled mischievously.

"Oh," I said, a bit bewildered. I hadn't exactly figured Alec for the advice type. But perhaps I had misjudged him. However, I had the vaguely uncomfortable feeling that Alec's advice wouldn't necessarily be something I wanted to hear.

Jill led me into the dining room of her enormous apartment. She had already set the rectangular glass table, and she gestured for me to take a seat.

"I have a tray of sandwiches in the other room," she said cheerfully. "I'll just call Alec and we can start."

Alec rounded the corner a moment later, and I stood to greet him. He looked even shorter than usual today, which, I supposed, was due to the fact that I was still in my heels, while he was in socks. I deliberately slouched as I got up to exchange chaste kisses on the cheek with him, European-style. He was short with brown, thinning hair, a narrow face, and a broad nose. He wore thin-rimmed glasses and, as always, was in a shirt and tie, even though he wasn't working.

"Harper, you're looking nice today," he said politely after we had greeted each other. "It's good to see you."

"You, too, Alec," I said as we sat down.

"And how's the practice going? Any interesting cases lately?"

I smiled. Alec did know how to make polite small talk well; I had to give him that.

"Just the usual, mostly," I said. "But I've been working hard. How about you? How are things at the hospital?"

Alec told me a bit about his new partner in the practice as well as some hospital politics that were affecting turnover among young doctors. We both looked at Jill with relief when she appeared in the doorway of the dining room with a tray of sandwiches. I suspected Alec didn't care about the ins and outs of my office any more than I cared about his. At least he didn't treat me like a leper because I was a lawyer, though. He had always treated Jill's friends with respect. I had to say that for him.

"So Jill has told me about the whole dating experiment, Harper," Alec began once we were all munching on Jill's perfectly prepared finger sandwiches, complete with crusts cut off. "What is it you're calling it? The Blonde Theory?"

"Yes, that's the name," I replied cautiously. I didn't know what he thought of the whole thing, and I wasn't entirely sure I wanted to find out.

"It sounds fascinating," he said, and I relaxed a little bit. "A great social experiment, indeed. Jill told me about your first date with that ophthalmologist. And you've been on a few more since then?"

"Yes," I confirmed. "Three of them."

I quickly filled them both in on the dates with Colin, Marco, and Douglas, ending with the whole *Top Gun* issue. They were both laughing hard by the time I concluded with my own off-key rendition of "Danger Zone."

"The problem is, these are guys who I thought would be my type, even though it's not like I had planned to actually continue dating any of them," I said with a sigh after I had sufficiently slaughtered the song. "But they're turning out to be more or less empty and shallow."

"What exactly *is* your type?" Alec asked. He leaned forward, looking truly curious. I thought about it for a moment, because I had never really put my type into words.

"Well, I suppose he'd have to be intelligent and somewhat successful," I began. "You know? Sort of like an intellectual equal?

I don't know that I could date someone who wasn't smart and didn't have a good job."

I don't know why, but I unintentionally thought of Sean, the cute handyman, the moment the words were out of my mouth. I hurriedly pushed the thought away. That was random.

"Fair enough." Alec nodded thoughtfully. "What else?"

I considered it for a moment. "And I usually like guys a little older, a little more mature, I guess," I said after a pause. I thought about it some more. "The guy would have to be a good conversationalist. I like bantering with a guy who has some wit and intelligence. So he has to be able to joke around with me in an intelligent way. He has to have a good job, too, not because I need him to be making money, but because I don't ever want to be in that weirdly unbalanced situation where I'm supporting the guy, you know?"

"Okay." Alec nodded.

"I'm not saying the guy has to make as much as me or more than me," I explained. "Just that I can't date someone who feels threatened by what I do."

"Okay." Alec nodded again. "So all these guys you've gone out with seemed to fit your requirements, no?"

"Yes," I agreed. "On paper, at least. But then they turned out to be…I don't know. Just not my type at all."

"Maybe you're wrong about what your type is," Alec smirked. Well, at least it looked like he was smirking. I wouldn't put it past him.

"I think I'm just meeting the wrong guys," I retorted quickly. Then I muttered, half under my breath, "Although it's certainly easier to meet them and keep them interested when I'm acting like a ditz."

"Alec has a theory about that!" Jill piped up excitedly, grinning at me and then nudging Alec. He took a thoughtful bite from his finger sandwich while I stared dubiously at him, waiting for whatever his great revelation would be.

"It's a theory some of my friends and I came up with a few years back," Alec began, then hastily added, "before I met Jill, of course." She smiled, batted her eyes at him and reached over to squeeze his hand. He smiled back at her before refocusing his gaze on me.

"Guys come up with dating theories, too?" I asked, momentarily trying to envision Alec trying to test something like The Blonde Theory. Hmm, I just couldn't see it.

"Well, not quite like you girls do," he said, rolling his eyes at me. "It was just that one night over drinks, I was talking to some of the other single doctors about something we had all noticed."

"And?" I prompted.

"And it doesn't have a fancy name like your theory," Alec said with another smirk. "But I guess you could call it the Star of the Relationship Theory, if you have to have a name for it."

"Star of the Relationship?" I repeated. Jill nodded enthusiastically. I guessed she had heard the theory before. I squinted at him and tried to prepare myself to take in whatever it was he had to say.

"Yes," Alec confirmed. "It's the theory that every relationship has to have one 'star,' so to speak, and one person who's willing to step aside and let the other one have the limelight the majority of the time. And most men like to be the one in the limelight."

I looked back and forth between Alec and Jill.

"And in your relationship?" I asked slowly.

"I'm the star, of course," Alec answered instantly. Jill hesitated for a split second, then nodded and smiled broadly at me.

"Meaning...what?" I asked slowly, feeling vaguely offended on Jill's behalf, even though I wasn't quite sure what he was saying yet.

"Meaning that I'm the one who earns the money, makes the big decisions, calls the shots, has the important job," Alec said smugly. I looked quickly to Jill, expecting her to look angry and offended. After all, wasn't Alec putting her down a little bit? Dismissing what she brought to the relationship? But she was just smiling tightly at him. I wondered if she was purposely avoiding my gaze.

"How does this apply to me?" I asked finally, staring down the gloating Alec, who looked very proud of himself.

"It sums up your problem in a nutshell," he announced proudly. "See, you have a good job, you make a lot of money, you're not afraid to make decisions, you can take care of yourself."

I paused.

"So?" I asked after a moment. I was beginning to understand where he was going with this, and I had a tight feeling in my chest as he continued.

"So," he continued dramatically. "No one wants to be with you because you're always going to be the star."

"Alec!" Jill chided quickly, shooting me a nervous look. "Harper, he didn't mean that *no one* wants to be with you. Right, honey?"

"No, of course not," Alec said a little too quickly. I narrowed my eyes at him. "I just mean that it's harder for you because men know right away that you're going to be the one wearing the pants in the relationship."

I shook my head. "I'm not like that," I said in frustration. "I don't boss guys around. I don't take control in the relationship."

"It doesn't matter." Alec shrugged. "As long as you appear to have it all—great career, good head on your shoulders, lots of money, and so on—you're going to have problems because guys are going to see you a certain way. It's as simple as that."

"Which is why The Blonde Theory is working!" Jill concluded dramatically. She grinned at me. "Doesn't it all make sense?"

I stared at her for a moment, then shifted my gaze back to Alec.

"So what are you saying?" I asked, trying to ignore the panicky feeling rising in my chest. After all, it wasn't as if this was news to me. Alec was just putting into words my entire dating experience, basically. But there was just something about hearing someone say it—especially a man—that made me feel a bit ill. "Are you saying that I'll never find anyone by being myself?"

"No," Alec said with a dismissive shrug. "I'm just saying that it will be hard for you. Really hard. Which is why acting like a ditz is such a good idea. You don't threaten guys right off the bat."

"That's not exactly the way I plan to meet the right guys for the rest of my life," I muttered.

"So why are you doing this, then?" Alec asked.

I looked at him for a moment, suddenly unsure of what to say. Why *was* I doing this? Was I really learning anything new? After all, I had always known instinctively that it would be easier to date as a ditz, so it wasn't like I was paving new ground.

"Just to see," I said softly.

"See what?" Alec pressed.

"I don't know," I mumbled. "To see how things change. To see what it feels like when guys aren't intimidated by me."

"They're not *intimidated*," Alec said, sounding almost defensive. I wondered for a moment why he seemed to be taking this so personally. Was *Alec* intimidated by me? Was this his way of putting me in my place, so to speak? "They just don't necessarily like a woman who has it together as much as you do. They know you'll never need them or respect them the way they want."

I glanced at Jill, who was nodding in agreement.

"See, Harper, I told you it would help to get Alec's perspective," she said cheerfully after a moment of silence, apparently choosing to gloss over the tension in the room.

"Er...yeah," I said tightly.

Alec looked at Jill and then back at me, a serious expression on his face. "If you want my advice, Harper, it would be to learn something from this Blonde Theory and act more approachable in the future," he said almost condescendingly.

"You're suggesting I just spend the rest of my life acting like a ditz?" I asked flatly, staring at him.

"Not the rest of your life." He shrugged. "But until you find a man." He chuckled a bit. "No offense, but it's not like you're getting any younger." Just when steam was about to start shooting out of my ears, his pager went off. Saved by the bell! He took it off his belt, where it was clipped, and glanced at it.

"Work call," he said tightly. He glanced at Jill. "Sorry, honey. I have to call the hospital. I'll be back in a second."

He stood and strode quickly out of the room. I heard his footsteps disappear down the hall, where he closed to the door to the bedroom. I looked after him for a moment, then shifted my gaze to Jill, who was looking slightly embarrassed.

"Sorry, Harper," she said, not quite meeting my gaze. "Sometimes he says exactly what's on his mind, and it doesn't exactly come out right."

"No, I think it came out just the way he intended," I said drily. I had to admit, he was probably right about a lot of what he'd said. I just didn't particularly like it. Nor did I like the smarmy, condescending way that the message had been delivered. I didn't much like the way he'd talked to Jill, either, come to think of it.

We heard the bedroom door reopen, and in a moment Alec came striding back into the dining room.

"Sorry, ladies," he said, leaning down to kiss Jill on the cheek. "That was the hospital. I have to get going. There's an emergency rhinoplasty I need to do right away."

"But you're off today," Jill said, looking up at him with a wounded expression on her face. "We were going to meet my aunt and uncle for dinner."

"I'm sorry, honey," he said with a helpless shrug. He reached down to ruffle her hair. She looked moderately appeased, but still troubled. "Duty calls. We'll have to reschedule."

"Okay," Jill sighed obediently.

"Nice to see you again, Harper," Alec said, turning to me. He reached out a hand and I shook it, thinking how odd it was that he insisted upon this formality with me, like we were two guys in a Wall Street boardroom. "Good luck with your Blonde Theory."

"Thanks," I said drily.

He grabbed his coat off the hook in the front hallway and disappeared out the front door.

"He's always doing that," Jill exclaimed in frustration the moment the door had closed behind him. She exhaled loudly and shook her head.

"Doing what?" I asked.

She waved angrily at the door. "Just disappearing like that," she said, looking upset. "The days he's supposedly off, he's always getting called in. It drives me crazy."

"Have you said something to him about it?" I asked.

She shook her head. "It's his job. What can he do? It's no use me getting upset about it."

"But you *are* upset," I pointed out.

"No reason to burden him with that," she said with a shrug, visibly pulling herself together and slipping back into perfect-wife mode. "Besides, he's off saving people's lives. Who am I to complain?"

I paused for a second.

"Jill, he's a cosmetic surgeon," I pointed out. "He's not really saving people's lives."

She looked at me sharply for a moment: then her face softened. She sighed.

"I know," she said. "But he's doing important work. Making people's lives better and all that. I understand why he has to go. Anyhow," she said, visibly switching tracks. She blinked a few times and smiled at me. "I'm glad we have some time alone."

"Why?" I asked, concerned. I put down the sandwich I was eating and looked at her closely. Was she going to confess some problem in her marriage that she had thus far been unable to talk about? Personally, I think I would have reached the limit of my patience within the first twenty-four hours of being married to

Alec. Maybe she was finally admitting that his constant condescension drove her crazy.

"Because it will give me the chance to go over The Rules with you," she said cheerfully. My heart sank. I was hoping that we could finally talk about Alec's shortcomings. But apparently that was a conversation for another day. Or, knowing Jill, we'd *never* have the conversation, because she'd be too busy pretending to herself that everything was perfect.

"What rules?" I asked.

She looked at me, astonished. "*The* Rules," she said. Images of the old-fashioned dating advice book flashed through my head for one horrifying moment until Jill clarified. "My mother's cardinal rules for dating. They worked for me. I know they'll help you with The Blonde Theory, too."

Oh great. Marianne Peters's dating rules straight out of the nineteenth century were almost worse than the outdated book. I'd grown up hearing about them and vaguely remembered them from the days when Jill used to babble about them ceaselessly, but I had never paid much attention. I'd always thought they were silly and antiquated. Then again, come to think of it, Jill was the one who had gotten married to the kind of guy she'd always dreamed of while I was stuck acting like a dumb blonde because I'd apparently been unable to date like a normal human being. So maybe there was some merit to the rules after all.

"Okay," Jill began dramatically while I reached for another sandwich quarter and looked at her apprehensively. "I know I've told you these rules before, but it's been ages."

"At least ten years," I agreed. I refrained from adding how silly I'd always thought the rules were and tried to keep an open mind. After all, it wasn't like Jill was trying to get the *real* me to follow them. I tried to remember that.

"Right," she said. "But it seems like you could use a refresher now. For use on all these dates you're going out on."

Jill apparently still believed wholeheartedly in her mother's rules, which were designed to result in a happily-ever-after marriage to a doctor, lawyer, engineer, or other high-powered, successful businessman. As an only child, Jill had been the sole focus of her mother's indoctrination efforts, and thus grew up believing in the rules the way other people believed in their religions. In fact, I suspected that Mrs. Peters's rules were very much like a religion to Jill, and her marriage to a well-established doctor like Alec only solidified their efficacy in her head.

I, on the other hand, had never believed in "rules" for dating, relating, or anything else. I believed in learning from experience, trusting your gut, and trying to play it smart. I didn't think there was a one-size-fits-all set of instructions that would land me my Mr. Perfect.

Then again, Jill *had* landed the man of *her* dreams (even if *I* wouldn't exactly consider Alec a dreamboat). And I was still conspicuously single. Perhaps I needed to reconsider my aversion. With that in mind, I listened with as much optimism as I could muster, although that was easier said than done.

"Okay," she said dramatically, while I concentrated on an egg salad sandwich quarter. She seemed thrilled to have an audience for once. "Let's start with the most obvious ones. Always let men open doors for you. Never second-guess a man. And of course, don't sleep with a man or even ask him up to your apartment on your first, second, or third date."

"Why not?" I whined, only half kidding. I smiled slyly at her, knowing my words would bug her.

She rolled her eyes at me.

"Never babble, and make the man work to find out more about you," she continued as if I hadn't spoken. "Never be an open book; always remain a mystery."

"That shouldn't be too hard since my new personality is a mystery to me, too," I said with a smile.

Jill rolled her eyes at me again. "Always listen attentively," she continued. "Always stand up straight. Don't touch him too much, because you appear needy. Always act just a little aloof, so that he feels he has to work to earn your admiration. Never act like you know more than him, though. That can be emasculating."

"Yeah, no kidding," I muttered. After all, wasn't my whole dating history a testament to that? Hmm, maybe I *would* have benefited from spending more time in the Peters household, listening to Mrs. Peters's rules. "It's not like I'll be acting like I know anything as a dumb blonde anyhow," I added.

"Good point," Jill said thoughtfully. "Maybe that's one of the reasons this Blonde Theory has been so successful so far. Because it's based on one of my mother's cardinal rules."

I snorted, then quickly apologized.

"Maybe you're right," I admitted reluctantly, hoping that Jill's mom, whom I'd always dismissed as somewhat shallow and materialistic, hadn't been right all along. That would be the ultimate slap in the face—to realize that I'd had all the correct dating advice in front of me at age twelve, and had chosen to ignore it. Oops.

"Just a few more rules for now," Jill said. "Make sure to let him know you need him. Not that you need a boyfriend, but that you need *him* specifically, because his wisdom is so indispensable to your life and you can't figure things out on your own."

I had to laugh at that one. "Is that really how you acted around Alec?"

Jill shrugged. "Let's just say he still thinks I don't know how to change a lightbulb or drive a car with a manual transmission," she said with a wink.

"You're kidding me," I said. "Six months into your marriage, he still thinks you need him to do things like that for you?"

She shrugged again. "It makes him feel important," she said. "Which, by the way, is another one of my mother's rules. Always let a guy know that you think he's very, very important."

"So basically just stroke his ego," I said drily. It seemed that most of the guys I'd been out with—even pre–Blonde Theory—had egos that were large enough already. I almost felt like I'd be doing the world a disservice by stroking them further.

"Oh yes, and always wear enough makeup," Jill added.

I raised an eyebrow. "That's one of the rules?" I asked dubiously.

She nodded. "My mom added that one when I was seventeen," she explained. "She told me then, 'Guys don't want to know that you have wrinkles, blemishes, or imperfections of any kind.' I think she's right."

"So basically, according to your mother's rules, women should strive to be perfect in every way except that they need men to help them do even simple things," I recapped.

She shrugged innocently. "Pretty much."

"Sounds like you've been trying out The Blonde Theory for the last twenty years," I said.

Jill just looked at me. She didn't have an answer for that.

Chapter Eleven

On my cab ride back to the office that afternoon, with Jill's Rules swirling through my head, I had a new thought about The Blonde Theory. What if it wasn't really about *me* anyhow? What if it wasn't that *I* actually intimidated guys? What if it was that they were so insecure to begin with, they were scared to date women who were smart enough to potentially see beneath their thin layers of power and prestige?

I thought about it all the way back to my office and was still deep in thought as I glided past my secretary, Molly, and sat down at my desk. Maybe these men *knew* deep down that they were complete duds and relied on the stupidest women they could find to build up their egos anyhow. In any case, these realizations weren't exactly helping me. I was no closer to discovering the secrets of successful dating than I had been a week ago. If anything, I was feeling more discouraged, especially after my little talk with Alec.

I was just mulling over that thought when Molly burst into my office, looking nervous, her eyes wide behind her thick glasses.

"Um, Ms. Roberts?" she asked, pushing her short brown hair distractedly behind her ears.

I cocked an eyebrow at her and tried to relax her with a smile. "Molly," I said, "I've told you a hundred times to call me Harper, not Ms. Roberts."

She was a fantastic secretary; don't get me wrong. There was just something about the doe-eyed twenty-five-year-old who filed my papers and booked my appointments calling me "Ms. Roberts" that made me feel about twenty years older than I was. After all, she wasn't *that* much younger than me. And after a year and a half as my secretary—and more than a hundred corrections from me each time she said "Ms. Roberts"—it seemed high time that she started addressing me by my first name.

"I'm sorry, Ms... Harper," she stammered.

"Don't worry, Molly," I said soothingly. "Everything okay?"

"Um, yes," she said. "But you have someone waiting downstairs in the lobby to see you. He's not in your appointment book, though, so I didn't know whether you wanted me to have reception send him up or not."

I checked my watch and frowned. I didn't have an appointment until four o'clock, and it was only two. This wasn't exactly a business where people did drop-bys, either. I was on the thirty-fourth floor of a Wall Street office building; it wasn't like my office was just a Midtown storefront where people with random ideas they wanted patents for could stream in and out.

"Molly, I don't think we had anything scheduled until later in the afternoon," I said finally. "Right?" I certainly hoped not; I had a ton of paperwork to do for a few clients whom I'd met with last week.

"No," she said hesitantly. "But the man downstairs insists you should be expecting him. I told him that he wasn't on your schedule, but he asked me to come in and check with you."

"Well, who is it?" I asked, starting to feel annoyed. Not at Molly, but at the stranger outside who felt he was due a meeting with me.

"He says his name is Matt James," Molly said.

"Matt James?" I repeated, dumbfounded. What could *he* be doing here? I flashed briefly back to our "date" at my firm dinner and blanched when I realized that any of my co-workers could see him in the hallway. Great, now they'd all think he really *was* my boyfriend, and I was being über-unprofessional by letting him come visit me in the office. What could he possibly want anyhow?

"Um, Harper?" Molly asked hesitantly, and I snapped my focus back to her.

"I'm sorry," I said, shaking my head. I was painfully aware of the fact that I was blushing. "Er, okay, send him up."

Molly nodded, looking a bit confused, and walked back out to the waiting area outside my office door. I hurriedly shuffled through the admittedly messy stack of papers on my desk and shoved them into one of the big drawers to the left of me. Then I quickly reached into my desk drawer, where I always kept my little container of Tarte blotting papers and mattifying powder, and quickly blotted as much nervous moisture as I could from my forehead, dusting powder onto my pink cheeks to conceal my blushing. I hadn't had a chance to screw my face up too badly since coming back from Jill's, so the rest of me looked relatively decent. I quickly shoved the little purple compact back into my desk and tried to look busy.

Not that I cared what Matt James thought of my appearance. I mean, why would I? It's not like I *liked* him.

"Hey, Harper," Matt's deep voice rang out a moment later as Molly pushed the door open. She shrugged at me as he entered. I looked up, still pretending that I was working on something very important, because after all, I didn't want him thinking that I just sat here and goofed off. I didn't. I had a job. A serious job. So there.

"Hello, Matt," I said, trying to sound as formal as possible. "Please. Have a seat. What brings you here today?"

He grinned at me as he crossed the room and sat down. Despite my best intentions, I couldn't help noticing how cute he looked. His thick, nearly black hair was unkempt and floppy, but in that intentional way common among the MTV crowd. It should have looked ridiculous on a man who was in his late thirties, but somehow it didn't. His green eyes looked particularly bright this morning, and his tan deeper than it had last time I'd seen him, leading me to wonder if he spent weekends in the islands—or twenty minutes a day in a tanning bed. Hmph. Flake.

He was dressed in dark-washed Diesel jeans, a black blazer, and a gray ribbed T-shirt that wasn't too tight but still showed me the contours of his well-developed chest.

I shook my head, trying to rid myself of the inexplicable pull I was feeling toward this guy whom I'd never date in a million years. After all, he was just a flaky actor. And he had seen me at my most embarrassing. Not good.

"You're looking lovely this afternoon, Harper," Matt said as he settled into one of the overstuffed leather chairs that faced my desk. He appeared to be smirking, or at least smiling with a slightly smarmy edge, so I wasn't sure whether he was actually complimenting me or disguising a little dig.

"Thank you," I said stiffly, all of a sudden aware of how uptight I must look in my blue starched blouse and my fitted black Ralph Lauren skirt suit. I cleared my throat. "Is there something I can help you with, Matt?"

"I see," he said, flashing me his wide, white-toothed signature grin. "No time to beat around the bush, right? You're all business." His expression was amused, which made me quietly simmer. What did he think this was, some kind of game?

"Well, this *is* my business, Matt," I said slowly, not caring that I sounded patronizing. "And *you're* the one who came to see *me*. So is there something I can do for you?"

He just smiled infuriatingly at me and craned his neck to look around my office, slowly taking it all in as I waited, tapping my fingers impatiently on my oak desk, trying to ignore the uninvited attraction I was feeling for him.

"Nice office you have here," he said finally, looking back at me and nodding his approval.

"Glad you think so," I said drily. My patience was wearing thin. The longer he sat here, the more I noticed the strong curve of his jaw, the adorably curly ends of his thick shock of hair, even the thickness of his dark eyelashes. Not only did I not have the professional time to waste on Matt James today, but I didn't want to keep noticing all his numerous attractive features. I was sure he went for twenty-one-year-old blonde starlets or something—not over-the-hill, destined-to-be-single-forever attorneys. So why waste my time noticing his perfect cheekbones, his well-defined triceps, or his perfectly straight teeth?

Besides, I knew I was still blushing. I *hated* that he made me blush.

"I hope you don't mind me just dropping by this way, Harper," Matt said, finally refocusing his attention on me. Man, he flashed that smile of his around a lot. I tried to resist its sparkle. I cleared my throat again.

"It's fine, Matt," I said brusquely. "But I do have quite a lot to do today. So if you'll just tell me why you're here..." I let my voice trail off and raised an eyebrow at him. He finally seemed to get it.

"Right," he said with a nod. "Sorry. I was just in the neighbor-hood and thought I'd drop by to talk."

"Matt," I said slowly, as if talking to a child. "You're in the neighborhood every day. Your studio is right down the street. And it's not like we're friends. Why would you stop by for a chat?"

"Not exactly a chat," he said, looking momentarily wounded and then quickly flashing me another of his incredible smiles. I had to admit, they were starting to melt my tough veneer. But I couldn't let him see that.

"What do you mean?" I asked, trying to keep my tone even.

Matt shrugged, stretching out his long legs and leaning back. "Fine, fine, I'll cut to the chase, if you want," he said, looking resigned. "I was actually hoping you'd be willing to talk to me about your job."

"About my job?" I repeated dubiously. I didn't have the faintest idea what he was talking about.

"Right," he said, nodding eagerly. "See, I just got a raise at work. They're going to be increasing the number of scenes I'm in this season."

"Congratulations," I said, still completely confused about what this had to do with me.

"Thanks. Anyhow, I was hoping you could... help me. I mean, I think I do a decent job of portraying a lawyer now. But most of my scenes are out of the courtroom. This next season, the writers want to give me more courtroom scenes. I just want to make sure I nail them. I need someone to help me make my scenes authentic." He paused and looked at me imploringly. "I need *you*."

I coughed and tried to ignore his last words, because of course what he *meant* was he needed me to help him with his scenes. Still, it was hard not to feel at least a little bit of something when a drop-dead gorgeous man sitting mere feet away told me he needed me. Especially a drop-dead gorgeous man who was not under the mistaken impression that I was a dumb blonde. Which, of course, made the possibility that he was actually flirting with me astronomically slimmer.

"Matt," I began. I paused and continued, trying to keep my voice flat. "Flattered as I am by your interest, I'm a patent lawyer. Not a criminal attorney like your character. I'm rarely even in the courtroom."

Matt nodded. "I know," he said urgently. "But you went to law school. I know you know how to practice criminal law. In fact, I know you were a criminal lawyer for your first year out of school while you studied for the patent bar."

I looked at him, startled. "How did you know that?"

"Emmie told me."

"You asked her about me?" I demanded, well aware that my cheeks were growing even hotter. I just hoped that this wasn't as obvious to Matt as it was to me.

He nodded and shrugged. "I was curious," he said casually. "Anyhow, will you help me?"

I studied him for a moment.

"I don't even understand what kind of help you're asking for," I said finally. The truth was, I didn't know how I was going to say no to him. I suspected that few people were able to; he could probably charm his way into just about anything.

"Nothing big," he said with a shrug. "I just want to come in sometime this week and talk to you. Pick your brain, so to speak. About legal terminology, closing arguments, courtroom behavior, that sort of thing."

I looked at him dubiously. He must have mistaken my hesitance.

"I'll pay you your hourly rate, if that's what you're worried about," he added.

"No, no, don't be silly," I said with a wave of my hand. I looked at him for a moment, then nodded. "Look, I don't know how I'm going to be able to help you. But you could come one day this week during my lunch break and I can answer whatever questions you have. Okay?"

He nodded enthusiastically. "I really appreciate it, Harper. I really, really do. You have no idea how much this will help."

I relaxed a bit and smiled back.

"Don't thank me until after we talk," I said, picking up a pen that lay on my desk and twirling it distractedly through my fingers. "I'm still a bit doubtful that there's anything I can really do to help."

"No, no, I know it will help," Matt said, shaking his head. "Okay?"

I paused for a moment, then nodded and buzzed Molly to ask which day I was free for lunch. She consulted my schedule and called back to tell me that I had an opening on Thursday at noon. I asked Matt, and he happily agreed to be back at my office the day after tomorrow for our lunch meeting.

"Great, great!" he enthused. He stood up and reached across my desk to shake my hand, which seemed oddly formal. Still, I grasped his hand firmly and shook back, as I always did with clients. He looked me in the eye and smiled broadly. I tried to ignore the beat that my heart skipped as he did so. "I'll see you Thursday at noon, then!"

"See you Thursday," I murmured as he hastily made his way to my door. I tried not to notice how incredibly cute he looked from behind as he left. Because that was really irrelevant. Wasn't it?

BY THE END of the workday, I had finished the patent paperwork I needed to do and met with a regular client of mine, Larry Bond, the director of development for Fisher Pharmaceuticals, a small drug manufacturer that brought me a lot of my business thanks to its productive research department. This year already, I had secured patents for the firm on two new eczema skin creams and a birth control patch with a low dose of progesterone. Today's meeting had been about a new pain relief medication that was in the final stages of development. Larry had wanted to get the patent ball rolling early, so we had pored over paperwork and documents most of the afternoon. I couldn't help but think, as we batted around statistics and figures, how completely unglamorous my job was. Boy, was Matt James in for a shock if he thought he could pick my brain about ways to spice up his portrayal of defense attorney Patrick Carr, lawyer extraordinaire. I was probably the most boring lawyer in Manhattan. Even though I loved it, patent law wasn't exactly full of made-for-TV excitement.

Between my busy day at work and unwelcome thoughts of Matt and his infuriatingly adorable smile, I had almost forgotten about the fact that I was more than halfway through The Blonde Theory. I didn't feel like I had learned much except the inevitable truth that I already suspected: Most men liked dumb blondes a whole lot better than they liked me.

THAT EVENING, FREE from The Blonde Theory for one night, at least, I had just changed into sweats and settled back onto the couch with a lap full of paperwork from the office when there was a knock at the door. I looked at the clock on the wall and frowned. Nine forty-five. What, was today National Drop In Unannounced On Harper Roberts Day or something? First Matt James and now a random evening visitor at my apartment?

I sighed and shifted my paperwork to the couch. Then I padded to the door, opened it, and blinked into the hallway. It took me a moment to recognize the man standing there. He was dressed in dark jeans and a button-down collared shirt, and his sandy hair was combed back.

"What are you doing here?" I blurted out, sounding much ruder than I'd intended to. I immediately flushed.

"Now what kind of a greetin' is that for the man who came to your rescue with a load of towels the other day?" asked Sean O'Sullivan, the handyman who had responded to my overflowing toilet crisis call on Saturday.

"Oh no," I groaned, slapping myself on the forehead. "I'm such an idiot! Your towels! I told you I'd be here Sunday for you to pick them up, didn't I? I am so sorry."

" 'Tis no big deal," he said, grinning at me. "You shoulda heard me inventin' stories for the benefit of my flatmate, though, about where the towels had gone to."

"I'm so sorry," I repeated again, feeling horrified with my own rudeness. I had, in fact, washed the towels. But then I had vanished to go on my series of blonde dates, with no thought to the generous handyman at all. "You should have called. I would have brought them over."

"Didn't have your number," he said with a shrug. "Just your address. Besides, I was on my way home from having drinks with a friend anyhow. You were right on my way."

"A date?" I asked before I could stop myself. Embarrassed, I clapped my hand over my mouth. Why did I keep blurting out the rudest questions around this poor guy? My foot seemed permanently poised to be inserted into my mouth in his presence. There was just something about his cleaned-up appearance and the faint whiff of cologne I could smell in the air that had made me assume he had been meeting a girl. But it was none of my business.

Instead of looking insulted, though, Sean just laughed. "As a matter of fact, yes." He leaned forward conspiratorially. "Turns out it didn't go very well."

"No?" I asked, despite myself.

"No," Sean echoed. "A bit of a daft bird, she was."

"Daft bird?" I asked with a small smile, halfway between confused and amused at his choice of words.

Sean nodded solemnly. "She wasn't that bright, if you get what I mean," he said. He leaned against the door frame and crossed his arms.

"I thought guys liked girls like that," I grumbled darkly, the sting from the first four Blonde Theory dates still fresh in my mind.

"No," he said, knitting his brow. He looked concerned. "What, is that what some bloke told you?"

I shook my head and sighed. "Just what I've learned over eleven years of dating in this city."

"Maybe you're dating the wrong guys, then," Sean said with his easy smile, his blue eyes twinkling at me.

I frowned and thought about it for a second. "What's that supposed to mean?" I asked finally, not sure if I should take offense or not.

"Oh, I didn't mean that as an insult, ma'am," he said, leaning away from the door frame, taking a step back, and looking a bit abashed. "I just meant, well, a nice woman like you should be able to meet a nice guy who appreciates you, is all."

"Yeah, one would think," I grumbled. I felt inexplicably annoyed at him, although there was really no reason to be. I looked at him for a moment, then shook my head. "Listen, I'll get those towels. I really am sorry. Is there anything I can do to make it up to you?"

"You could invite me in for a second so we're not conversin' here at your doorstep," Sean said with a smile.

I hesitated, then smiled back. "Yes, yes, of course, come in while I go get the towels." Sean nodded and followed me inside, where he waited in my front entryway while I went back to my bedroom to get the stack of towels I had folded after taking them out of the wash. My mind was on his comment about me dating the wrong guys, so much so that I felt almost lost in a fog of thought as I walked back to the entryway with the perilously high stack of towels. I placed them on the counter in the front hall. "Here they are, good as new," I said. "Thanks again, so much, for letting me borrow them."

"Of course," Sean said, winking at me. "It's not as if I was goin' to let ye live in a swamp, now."

I laughed.

"You definitely saved me," I agreed. Sean smiled then reached over to the counter to pick up the stack of towels.

"Do you need some help?" I asked, feeling guilty. "I can help you home with those if you want. It's the least I can do."

"No, no, that's not necessary." Sean laughed. He picked up the stack of towels, which didn't look nearly as large and teetering in his arms as it had in mine. "I think I can take it from here. But thanks for washin' and dryin' them."

"No problem," I said. "I'm just sorry you had to stop by to get them."

"My pleasure." He walked to the door and waited while I opened it for him. "Just remember what I said," he said as he stepped out into the hallway.

I stood in the door frame and cocked my head to the side. "What?" I asked.

"About guys," he said. "If they're not appreciatin' your intelligence, they're clearly not the right guys."

"Thanks," I murmured. Sean tipped his chin at me and said good night, then turned to walk away. I watched him go, feeling a bit insulted that he had felt it necessary to comment on my taste in men.

But for the rest of the evening, I couldn't shake his words from my head.

Chapter Twelve

The next night, at eight, I was waiting in the entryway to Ralph's, a fancy Upper East Side bistro with a trendy bar that attracted a lot of movers and shakers from the neighborhood. This time, I was scheduled to meet George Edwards, an electrical engineer who had responded to my dumb-blonde NYSoulmate.com profile. And despite myself, I was a little excited; he had a background in engineering, like me. We'd have a lot in common. Too bad I'd have to hide it to correspond with my profile. Thanks to my talk with Alec, and to my discomfort over Matt's random drop-in, I was filled with a renewed sense of resolve about acting like a ditz. Maybe Alec was right, although I hated to admit it.

Thanks to Emmie's indispensable assistance, I was decked out once again as a dumb blonde—this time in a strange, off-the-shoulder lime-green wrap shirt and a white denim miniskirt, paired with staggeringly high white heels, all from the wardrobe closet of Emmie's show. Once again, I had protested, saying that I felt naked and exposed in the outfit; once again, Emmie had oohed and ahhed in sympathy while teasing my hair and heaping too much lipstick onto my mouth and too much blush onto my cheeks. Once again, I felt like a bit of a clown as I waited alone at Ralph's for my Internet date.

At five minutes past eight, a man I recognized immediately from his NYSoulmate.com profile photo came hurrying through the door. My first thought was that he definitely wasn't the six foot one he had claimed on his profile; he'd be lucky to measure up to five foot ten. But I didn't care about height; it was just the odd realization that he'd fibbed about something so basic. Beyond that, though, he looked nice: dark-haired, square-jawed, clean-shaven, and dressed in navy pants with a pale blue oxford and a yellow tie. I vowed not to hold the height thing against him and to consider him with an open mind.

"Harper?" he said, approaching me with a smile.

I nodded and giggled, turning on the dumb-blonde charm. "Yeah," I bubbled. "And you, like, must be George?"

"That's me," he said with an easy smile that immediately relaxed me a bit. "Sorry I'm a few minutes late. Want to get a table?"

Ten minutes later, we were seated and talking easily. I was finding it easier and easier to act vacant and ditzy. The more dumb-blonde dates I went on, the easier the act seemed to become.

Better yet, George didn't seem half bad. Unlike the first four guys, who were pretty self-absorbed, George actually seemed to be relatively modest and, despite my feigned stupidity, wasn't treating me as if I were a second-class citizen. In fact, twenty minutes into the date, I was wondering why I couldn't have met him when I was actually acting like my real self; he really did seem to be just my type.

Then again, I had to consider the fact that he had responded to BlondeBartenderHotti's ad and not UptownAttorneyGirl's. And he seemed to genuinely *like* the dumb-blonde version of me, which didn't speak too highly of his judgment in women, I supposed.

He told me about his upbringing in Montana and his decision to move to New York after he had graduated from college. He told me about getting his first job in the city and how much time and effort it had taken to rise to his current position, as one of the top engineers at Con Ed. And he listened with rapt interest as I invented a fictitious background as a waitress in Ohio who had always wanted to move to the big city.

"And now I'm living the dream," I sighed, forcing a far-off, dreamy expression. I tossed my hair and batted my eyelashes for good measure. "I'm a bartender at one of the hottest bars in town."

"So, Harper," George began.

I enthusiastically bobbed my head, then tilted it to the side, widening my eyes. "Yes?" I chirped.

"I have to ask," he said. "Why would a beautiful, talented girl like you need to meet guys online? It seems like you could have your pick of guys at your bar any night of the week."

"Oh, George." I sighed dramatically. "It's, like, so hard to meet guys? At the bar? Because they don't want to get to know the real me?"

"And you're looking for more," he said, lowering his voice and leaning forward as if he expected this to be our great romantic moment.

I nodded enthusiastically. "Yes," I exclaimed, still bobbing my head, keeping my eyes wide. "I mean, there's more to me than just bartending, you know?"

He nodded thoughtfully, as if my words were completely normal.

"Of course, I can see that," he said solemnly. "And a pretty lady like you certainly deserves a guy who sees you as more than a bartender."

"Like, yeah," I agreed.

We continued to chat for another thirty minutes, through a second round of drinks, with George complimenting me frequently and asking thoughtful questions about my job and my life and giving me genuine responses to the few questions I asked about him while I intermittently took out my compact and studied myself vacantly in its mirror. When I had finished my second martini, I excused myself to go to the bathroom.

"I have to go freshen up," I bubbled. "In the little girls' room."

George nodded and stood up politely as I got up to leave the table. I turned around halfway to the bathroom to see if he was watching me, and indeed he was, with an appreciative expression on his face. I gave him a little pageant wave and wink before continuing on my way, my entire focus on not tripping in the perilously high heels strapped onto my feet.

In the bathroom, I stared at myself in the mirror for a long moment, confused and trying to collect my thoughts. George actually seemed decent. He seemed to be genuinely interested in me, and he didn't have the massive ego or self-absorption that my previous dates had. But I simply couldn't figure out why an intelligent man who seemed reasonably kind would be so interested in someone who clearly didn't have an ounce of intelligence to her name. It didn't seem fair. If the smart guys were going for the dumb girls and the *dumb* guys were going for the dumb girls, who did that leave for people like me?

Exactly. Nobody.

I used the bathroom, then stood in front of the mirror again, digging in my purse to find the horrid tube of lipstick Emmie had sent along with me. I had just retrieved it from the bottom of my bag when two women, one bleached blonde and the other an artificial redhead, both with melon-size artificial breasts stuffed into low-cut shirts, came tripping drunkenly into the bathroom, giggling at some private joke. They went into adjoining stalls, and I tried to ignore them while I applied my lipstick and fished around in my bag for my compact. The women were speaking so loudly, though, that they were impossible to miss.

"Your date is such a high roller," bubbled the girl behind door number one, the blonde, to her friend on the other side of the stall wall. "He's throwing cash around like it grows on trees."

"I've only been fucking him for two weeks," the redhead slurred back from her stall. "And I've already gotten a diamond tennis bracelet and a mink. How fucking fabulous is that?"

"His wife must be an idiot not to know what's going on," said the first girl with a haughty sniff. "You've been with him nearly every night. Where the hell does she think he is?"

The redhead laughed cruelly.

"He tells her he's stuck at the office," she slurred. "Married guys are the shit, man. You get the sex and the presents without the obligation. It's perfect. I feel like a princess."

I rolled my eyes at myself in the mirror. If there's one thing the woman in the stall *wasn't*, it was royalty of any kind. Hearing her talk so cavalierly about having an affair with a married man made me want to smash her over the head with something the moment she emerged from the stall. Of course that would be inappropriate, though.

I tried to focus on applying a fresh coat of mascara and brushing my hair. I had just turned to leave, trying my hardest to forget about the trampy women, when I heard the redhead say something else to her friend.

"I'm going to take my panties off," she said drunkenly. "And when we go back to the table, I'm going to whisper in his ear that he can fuck me right there if he wants to."

"Tiffany," the blonde said with a giggle. "We're in a *bar*. He can't fuck you here."

"He can do anything," the redhead slurred. "He bought me a mink. He can do anything he wants."

Sickened, I quickly hurried out of the bathroom and back to my table. But now I was curious, despite myself, to see what poor sucker Tiffany and her friend were with. After all, maybe this

warranted a paragraph in the Blonde Theory article I was writing
for Meg. I was just faking vacant stupidity. These girls were the real
thing, and they were pulling it off spectacularly. It sounded like
the redheaded Tiffany had some jerk eating right out of her hand,
buying her thousands of dollars' worth of gifts after just two weeks
together. I pitied the man's poor wife (she was probably home with
the kids) and hated him immediately, even though I hadn't even
laid eyes on him, for cheating on her—especially with some dumb
tramp who was clearly just using him. My blood quietly boiled.
What was wrong with men?

I turned my attention back to George, who actually seemed to
be turning out all right. I was dying to tell someone about the conversation I'd overheard in the bathroom, but I realized I couldn't
share it; it wouldn't exactly jibe with the image I was trying to
portray. I settled on babbling about my "career."

"So, George," I began, "have you ever been out with a bartender before? Because it's a very tough profession, and there's lots
to say about it."

Twenty minutes later, I had told George all about how to mix
a rum and Coke ("one shot of rum, and, like, some Coke"), a gin
and tonic ("one shot of gin and, like, some tonic water"), and a
white Russian ("I forget, but it's like, Kahlúa and milk or something. The recipe is taped to the bar."), and he had told me more
about his engineering job. But the whole time, I couldn't shake
the voyeuristic desire to figure out who the horrid redhead from
the bathroom was with. So after George had finished telling me
about how he had graduated sixth in his class from MIT ("Sixth is
still top ten," he had announced somewhat defensively), I excused
myself to the bathroom again, claiming that I needed to freshen
up my lipstick. George looked a bit confused but nodded, and
I smiled and got up from the table.

After I'd touched up my hot pink lips in the bathroom once
again, I walked back into the main room of the bar. It would be

another moment until George started wondering where I'd gone to. And my curiosity about the slutty redhead's date was still killing me.

I scanned the main room and didn't see the woman's flashy red hair, so I ducked into the smaller lounge, an offshoot of the main bar, which had a more intimate feel—and a bottle-service-only policy: Every table had to order at least one bottle of liquor. It was the restaurant's way of creating a VIP feel. I should have suspected that the two double-D twins would be in here. I saw Tiffany's head full of bright red hair immediately. I took a few steps closer to where she was sitting, giggling about something and hanging on her man. I tried to get a good look at her icky, cheating date, who had his back to me. From behind, he looked rather short and nondescript, with close-cropped dark hair and an expensive-looking charcoal suit. I took another step closer and was just about to try out another position when he turned his head to the right to summon the waitress.

I gasped involuntarily. I recognized him immediately and took a horrified step back. I blinked once and looked again, sure that I had seen him wrong. His head was still turned in my direction, though, as he beckoned the waitress impatiently. I stared, unable to look away. I had no doubt.

It was Alec. Jill's Alec.

For a moment, I stood frozen in place, a thousand thoughts racing through my mind. Surely there was some mistake, I finally decided. Perhaps the slutty panty-removing redhead wasn't with him after all. Maybe she was with the other guy at the table and Alec was just there...for a work-related reason or something. I knew I was grasping at straws.

But Tiffany the redhead quickly dispelled that thought by leaning over to whisper something in Alec's ear. He smiled and said something back, and I looked on in horror as she slid her hand under the table and into his lap. He shifted a bit, giving me a sickeningly clear view of what she was doing. And he was enjoying every second of it, a wolfish grin on his face.

I couldn't watch any longer. It was too horrible. My heart breaking for Jill, I backed quickly away and retreated again to the bathroom, where I stood, fighting the rising nausea inside me as I stared at the mirror, my eyes wide with shock.

I had to tell Meg and Emmie. They'd know what to do. But it wasn't the kind of conversation I could have on my cell phone from a restaurant bathroom. Much as I was enjoying being a dumb blonde with a guy who wasn't *entirely* self-absorbed for once (and who didn't sing '80s movie songs at the table), I knew I had to cut the date short in order to get home and call the girls. This was an emergency.

Breathless and trying not to cry, I returned to the restaurant's main dining room. I sat back down at our table and looked at George.

"I'm really sorry, but I have to go," I said quickly.

George looked crestfallen. "Oh no," he said, his brow creased with concern. "Did I do something wrong?"

"No, no, it's not that," I said quickly. "It's . . ." I searched my mind for an explanation, but my brain was already on overload, processing the horrific scene I had just witnessed. "It's just that . . . I remembered, I have to, uh, deep-condition my hair tonight." I blurted out the first thing that came to my mind. "I have an appointment at the salon tomorrow for a dye job, and they ask me to deep-condition the night before."

"Oh." George twisted his napkin in his lap. "Um, of course. I'm just disappointed. I was having a good time with you."

"You were?" I asked without thinking. I found the thought inconceivable, as our entire conversation had been devoid of any substance whatsoever. "I mean, um, of course you were," I bubbled. "I'm sorry I have to go. But thank you so much for the drinks."

"Harper, this may be forward of me, but can I take you out again?" George asked. "Since our date was cut short and all? I was really enjoying your company."

I stopped and stared at him for a moment. He wanted *another* date with me? Even though we seemingly had nothing in common? Even though he appeared to be a reasonably intelligent man who had no place dating an empty-headed bimbo?

"George, I..." My voice trailed off as I looked at him. He seemed cute and nice. It was just that he was deriving a bit too much enjoyment from being with the empty-headed version of me. "I can't," I concluded. "I'm sorry. I'm very busy. I can't."

I felt a swell of pride when I said the words. I had power in this situation, too, even if it didn't stem from anything intelligent.

"I have to go," I said. "But thanks again for a lovely evening."

And as I had on my last blonde date, I walked away without looking back.

Chapter Thirteen

Slow down, Harper." Meg's voice was groggy through the phone, but I didn't have time to wait while she slowly came to. "What's wrong?"

I had called her the moment I walked through my door, disregarding the fact that she and Paul were usually in bed early on weeknights. This was an emergency.

"I saw Alec," I repeated, unable to keep the urgency and rising panic out of my voice. "Jill's Alec. At dinner with another woman."

"Are you sure?" Meg asked, and I could tell that she had woken up instantly. "No, there must be an explanation."

"No!" I insisted excitedly. "There's not! I heard this woman in the bathroom talking about how she'd been sleeping with him for two weeks. And then I saw her, you know, *touching* him under the table!"

"Maybe you saw wrong," Meg said calmly. I paused and pulled the receiver away from my face for a moment, looking at it warily as if it might be able to tell me where Meg's common sense had disappeared to. Realizing that the phone wasn't about to impart any such information, I held it back up to my ear.

"No, I didn't," I said into the mouthpiece, as firmly as I could with a voice that wouldn't stop shaking. "I didn't see wrong. I know what I saw and I know what I heard. Meg, Alec is cheating on Jill!"

"You'd had how many martinis?" Meg asked, apparently still stubbornly skeptical. "And I've been to Ralph's. It's dark in there. Maybe it was someone who *looked* like Alec."

"No!" I exclaimed again, growing increasingly frustrated. "Meg, it *was* Alec! I am one hundred percent sure." I quickly recounted everything I'd seen and heard at Ralph's, then breathlessly waited for Meg's agreement.

She was silent for a moment.

"That doesn't make any sense," she said finally, her voice flat. "They've only been married for six months. How could he be cheating on her?"

"I don't know," I said miserably. "But he is. I'm sure of it. What do we do?"

She sighed and was silent for another moment. I held my breath.

"Don't say anything to her until we're sure," she said finally. I couldn't believe that she still wasn't convinced, but Meg always had been more optimistic than she should have been when it came to love. Perhaps that's what happened when you married your high school sweetheart and lived happily ever after, I thought glumly. I tried, as always, not to resent her a tiny bit.

"But—" I started to protest.

Meg cut me off. "Look, Harper," she said firmly. "I know it looks bad, especially if the girl was saying that stuff in the bathroom. But isn't it possible that she was lying to her friend? And that you were mistaken about what you saw at the table? Maybe it's not as bad as it looks. Maybe it wasn't even Alec."

Okay, this was downright delusional on Meg's part. Clearly I had gone to the wrong friend about this. I needed to call Emmie instead.

"Maybe you're right," I mumbled, not really meaning it. I had no idea what else to say, and my frustration level was rising along with my anger at Alec. Obviously I needed proof. If I couldn't convince Meg, how was I going to even broach the subject with Jill? I felt heartsick thinking of the conversation I'd have to have with my newlywed friend, who was so fixated on the image of perfection she thought she had created for herself.

I hung up with Meg and immediately called Emmie. I quickly recounted everything I'd seen at Ralph's.

"I was right," Emmie breathed softly when I had finished.

My breath caught in my throat. "What?"

"I thought I saw him," she said slowly. "About a month before the wedding. With another woman. I wasn't sure, so I never said anything to Jill or you guys. And I think I kind of talked myself into thinking I'd been mistaken. Who would cheat on his fiancée just a month before the wedding? But it must have really been him."

"Oh my God," I murmured, feeling sick to my stomach. "He's been cheating on her all along?"

"That little bastard," Emmie said, her voice soft and deadly. "I'll kill him."

From her tone of voice, I believed she might do it.

"What are we going to do?" I asked, since killing him was not actually an option, although it was certainly tempting. "Jill will never believe us if we just tell her. She wants to believe everything is perfect."

Emmie was silent for a moment.

"Let's follow him," she finally suggested.

"Follow him?" I repeated dubiously.

"Yes," Emmie said, sounding more sure of herself now. "The next time he tells Jill he's going to a business meeting or has been called into the hospital. Let's follow him with a camera. We'll take pictures. Then she'll will have to believe us. We'll have proof."

My stomach swam uncomfortably at the thought. "We're not detectives, Em."

"We can be if the situation calls for it," she replied, sounding a bit insulted.

"But, Em, he'll see us," I insisted, feeling discouraged.

"Not if we use the wardrobe closet to disguise ourselves," she said mysteriously. I felt a little glimmer of hope, even though my recent experience with the wardrobe closet had been less than ideal.

"You think?" I asked after a moment. Far-fetched as it sounded, it just might work.

"Definitely," Emmie said firmly.

We agreed that Emmie would sit in the coffee shop across the street from Jill's apartment the next evening and wait to see if Alec came out. I told her I would join her there after work; then I remembered I'd already made a commitment.

"Oh geez, I have a date," I exclaimed. I was supposed to have dinner with yet another NYSoulmate.com match, a political consultant named Jack. "I'll just call him and cancel."

"No," Emmie said. "We don't even know that Alec will go out tomorrow night. And you have less than a week left on The Blonde Theory. Just keep your cell on. If I see him leave, I'll call you and have you meet me wherever he winds up."

I DIDN'T SLEEP much that night. Whether Meg believed me or not, I knew what I'd seen. Poor Jill.

She had been so sure that she had finally stumbled upon perfection when she found Alec. And she had it all planned out in her head. She was living her dream—perfect, wealthy husband; perfect, expensive home; perfect, upper-class life. But it was all a sham. And she didn't know it yet.

It seemed her mother's constant nuggets of wisdom about dating had backfired. Sure, Jill had gotten everything she'd always thought she wanted, everything her mother had ever told her she needed. But she had forgotten to look for one basic ingredient in her perfect man: decency. I'd always had the feeling that she looked down her nose, just a little bit, at Meg, who would probably never make more than eighty thousand dollars a year (not bad anywhere else in the country, but pocket change in Manhattan) and who was married to an electrician probably making about half that. They lived in Brooklyn; they clipped coupons; they wore clothes they'd had for years instead of buying new wardrobes every season as Jill did.

But they were *happy*. Really, truly, genuinely, lasts-forever happy. And that was one thing Jill had forgotten about in her rush to drag Alec down the aisle so that she could live out the dream her mother had always insisted upon.

I SPENT THE morning yawning thanks to my nearly sleepless night. Molly brought me four cups of coffee (which forced me to make six trips to the bathroom; yes, I have the world's smallest bladder), but I still didn't feel awake at noon, when Matt James arrived for our appointment.

The sight of him was enough to stir me into at least a semblance of alertness, though. As Molly let him into my office, I couldn't help but notice how good he looked in a pale blue shirt, charcoal slacks, and a charcoal silk tie. He was downright gorgeous. Damn it.

"Wow, fancy," I said, teasing him slightly.

He shrugged and grinned at me as Molly shut the door behind him. "Well, I had a big meeting with some big-shot lawyer today."

"Anyone I know?" I asked with a smile.

"Nah, just a really gorgeous woman who was nice enough to give me a few minutes to ask her some stupid questions."

I involuntarily flushed in response. I certainly hadn't expected that. Then again, maybe he was sucking up because he was afraid I'd charge him for my time today.

"No need for compliments," I said brusquely, trying to ignore the heat I felt creeping into my cheeks and the rapid acceleration of my heartbeat. "This hour is on the house."

He raised an eyebrow. "Well thanks," he said softly. "But I still mean what I said."

His green eyes held mine for a moment longer than was necessary. Finally, I broke the stare and dropped my eyes to the legal pads on my desk, feeling nervous as I fumbled around for a pen.

"Uh, what I can do for you today?" I asked. I looked up at him again and noticed that he was still standing. So was I, for that matter. "Oh, I'm sorry," I said, shaking my head at my rudeness. "Have a seat."

Matt sat down in one of the leather chairs facing my desk and leaned back, stretching his long legs out in front of him as he watched me for a moment. The attention was making me increasingly uncomfortable, so I sat down beside my desk and hurried to start the meeting.

"So what can I help you with, Matt?" I asked brusquely, trying to sound as professional and detached as possible. No point in letting him know that I wanted to leap into his lap and make out with him. That wasn't very lawyerly. "I don't know that I'll be able to give you what you need since I don't practice criminal law anymore," I added tightly.

Matt grinned lazily at me. "Oh, I suspect you'll be able to give me what I need," he said with a wink. I struggled to ignore the potential double meaning. Clearly my mind was just in the gutter because he was so distractingly hot. And I, of course, was in the longest slump of my life. "Why don't you start by telling me a little but about what you *do* do then," he continued. "I mean, if you don't mind."

"No, that's fine," I said, relieved to be moving on to a topic I at least knew something about. It was better than sitting there wondering what kinds of girls Matt James liked to date, which was the thought currently tugging at the corners of my mind.

Admittedly, this was a complete waste of time. I knew he was just flirting. It was probably how he talked to every member of the female gender.

"Patent law is a very specialized area of practice," I began, trying to sound as formal and professorish as possible. I tried to recall the introduction to my first day of patent law class, but that had been an eternity ago. So I winged it. "Basically, it's my job to protect the inventions of my clients in a legally binding manner," I said stiffly. "I have a background in chemical engineering, so most of my clients have some sort of chemical aspect to their work, and I have to deal on a routine basis with people high up in management, marketing, and technical development in companies that my firm does business with. Booth, Fitzpatrick and McMahon is contracted to represent their legal interests in and out of the courtroom. I deal specifically with obtaining and protecting patents for new products they develop."

I paused for a breath, and Matt nodded appreciatively at me.

"Wow," he said. He gave a little laugh. "It sounds complicated."

I shrugged, feeling a bit embarrassed.

"It is sometimes," I admitted. "I have to do a lot of reading and keep up with everything from the newest developments in the industry to the emerging science behind biopharmaceuticals to the ins and outs of polymer chemistry. It's really challenging. But that's part of what I love about it."

I paused again and thought about it. It had been years since anyone had asked me about what I did on a day-to-day basis. My friends had a basic grasp, and they didn't need a reminder of my daily routine. Besides, I knew my job sounded very boring to almost everyone but other lawyers.

But hearing myself explain exactly what I did, to an incredibly handsome actor, of all people, sent an unfamiliar swell of pride shooting through me. I didn't appreciate enough how much I loved my job, or how lucky I was to be doing it. I had been spending so much time lately focusing on the fact that the men in my life were scared of my profession that I had almost started to resent the very thing I loved so much.

I went on to explain to Matt about our in-house technical library and online search facilities, which allowed me to research the background, precedents, and other patent applications that related to the patents my clients were seeking. I told him about how I had to go to several technological and scientific conferences each quarter, just to keep up to date with progress in various fields, and how I had to spend a sizable chunk of my time outside the office skimming research journals. I told him about my occasional trips to Washington, DC, to search through the hard copies of patents at the US Patent and Trademark Office. And I told him about what I considered the most frustrating aspect of my job—the fact that I couldn't discuss the specifics of my work with anyone, not even my partners in the firm.

Being a patent lawyer was a very isolated life, I explained, feeling a tinge of sadness. It was an area of law that called for the absolute utmost secrecy and discretion, which meant that I couldn't talk about patent applications with anyone, not even Molly.

"Wow," he said, shaking his head appreciatively. "Harper, I had no idea. I'm really impressed."

"You are?" I asked dubiously.

"I came here prepared to ask you all sorts of questions," he said, after a pause, still looking at me with an intensity that made me feel like squirming under his gaze. "But you've explained everything so well. Now I just have one thing I want to know."

"Yes?" I asked warmly, relishing, for the first time, the opportunity to actually give some advice to someone who didn't hate me or judge me because I happened to have done well in school or gotten a job I was good at.

"Why...," he began softly, then paused, shifting his weight in the chair and looking me right in the eye. "Why are you pretending to be a ditzy bartender to get dates on NYSoulmate?"

My mouth went dry, and I could almost feel my heartbeat grind to a stop in my chest. I sucked in a breath and stared at Matt, who was looking at me with what appeared to be genuine concern. "Wh...what?" I finally choked out.

"Why are you pretending to be a ditzy bartender to get dates on NYSoulmate?" Matt repeated in the same even tone of voice, still looking at me carefully but not, I noticed, in an unfriendly way.

"Um, what do you mean?" I asked, stalling for time by playing dumb. Which, might I add, I had been getting awfully good at lately.

"You're BlondeBartenderHotti," he said calmly. "I saw your picture." His tone was matter-of-fact, not mean.

But I felt attacked. "What were you doing on a dating Web site anyhow?" I blurted out instead of answering him. "What, a guy like you can't get dates without going online?"

Matt looked a bit wounded but shook his head. "It's hard to get people to see me for who I am instead of as an actor on a soap opera, you know," he said. He shrugged and held his hands out helplessly. "Like, for instance, I went to a good school, too. Yale, actually. I did pretty well. I'm pretty smart. I'm not just another dude who stands in front of the camera and recites his lines like a trained monkey. But most girls like you wouldn't even consider going out with a guy like me."

I was momentarily stunned. Matt James had gone to Yale? And, more unbelievably, he needed help getting dates?

"What do you mean, girls like me?" I asked softly, after a moment of silence between us.

"Smart girls," he said, looking a bit pained. "Accomplished girls. Girls who aren't just looking for a guy to wear on their arm. Or to bankroll their lifestyle. Or to brag about to their friends. Girls who have some substance and take pride in taking care of themselves."

I gulped and stared at him. I couldn't believe what I was hearing; I had always envisioned Matt James dating stick-thin model types (or at least artificial, sexed-up morons like Alec's redhead). Isn't that what actors did? Even C-list soap-opera actors? Why would Matt James be any different? He could have any woman he wanted. I cleared my throat.

"Are you being serious?" I asked, my voice sounding smaller and more timid than I'd intended it to.

Matt nodded slowly, staring intently at me. "You still haven't answered my question," he said. When I just looked at him, he added, "About the dating site. Why are you pretending to be a dumb blonde?"

My mind spun through the possibilities of what I would tell him. Maybe I could say that it was research for a patent application of some sort. Or that it was all just a joke. Or that it wasn't me at all—it was another woman on the site who looked like me.

In the end, I decided to tell the truth. I blinked quickly, suddenly fiercely embarrassed.

"Nobody wants to date me," I mumbled, feeling pathetic. I hated the loss of power that came with admitting what a loser I was in the dating world. I hated that Matt James, someone I barely knew—and beyond that, someone I was attracted to, despite myself—was seeing me with all my layers stripped away. I hated that in order to admit the reasons behind The Blonde Theory to Matt, I had to admit them fully to myself.

"What do you mean?" Matt asked, looking startled.

"Nobody wants to date me," I repeated, feeling more miserable and embarrassed with each word that crossed my lips. "Sure, I get dates here and there. But Matt, no one wants to keep dating me once they find out I'm smart. Or that I'm a lawyer. It's like I have a disease or something. Even with the guys who've stuck around for a few months—the few serious relationships I've had—it's always been an issue. I just thought... I just thought that maybe it might be worth trying to see what it's like to date without scaring people, you know?"

Somehow, the floodgates had opened, and I couldn't stop. I told him about The Blonde Theory: Meg's idea, the girls' enthusiasm, and the elaborate lengths to which we'd gone to pull it off. I told him about the dates I'd had so far and about my sinking feeling that I'd found my answer: that guys would only ever be into me when I acted like a dumb blonde. While I spoke, Matt watched me closely, not saying a word, simply nodding here and there when I finished sentences. I knew he was judging me—and his verdict wasn't going to be good.

Finally I finished and sat with a dry mouth, awaiting Matt's reaction. As the seconds ticked by, I began to deeply regret opening up to him. I regretted making the appointment with him, regretted feeling attracted to him, regretted telling him the truth. It had all been a big mistake. A big *stupid* mistake.

Then he spoke. "This Blonde Theory, as you call it...," he said slowly, pausing as if choosing his next words very carefully. "It doesn't...it doesn't make a lot of sense, Harper."

"Yes it does," I snapped back immediately, surprising myself with the vehemence of my own defensiveness.

"Harper," Matt said slowly. He looked down at his lap then back at me with an intensity that set my heart pounding. "Don't you realize that if you just act like yourself, the right guy will come along?"

I rolled my eyes, not even bothering to be polite.

"While I appreciate the insight, Matt," I said, my voice thick with sarcasm, which, of course, I was using to mask the intense discomfort I was currently feeling, "I've been trying that for the last twenty years or so. And it's not working yet."

"Your mind is just closed, then," he said simply.

I stared, incredulous. Who did he think he was, Dr. Phil coming to save me from myself? What did he know about being me?

What did he know about constantly being rejected simply for being yourself? What did he know about having someone you love simply walk out on you because you've done a good job at work?

"You don't know anything about me," I said coldly, aware in some remote way that the anger that was rising inside me was a bit misdirected.

"I think I do," Matt replied softly, without missing a beat, which just infuriated me all the more. I took a deep breath and tried to calm down. "So you're just looking for someone who will appreciate you for who you are?" he asked.

"Yes," I said sullenly.

"And you feel like you're going to accomplish that by pretending to be someone else?" he asked dubiously, cocking his head to the side.

Okay, when he put it that way, it *did* sound illogical. But how could I explain it to him? The Blonde Theory was just because I had to know: Was it my job that was scaring guys, or my personality? How could I explain that without sounding even worse?

The easy answer was that I couldn't.

"Yes," I said defensively. "So?"

"Fine, then I have just one more question for you," Matt said.

I didn't respond; I just sat there looking at him, hoping that he would know enough to get up and walk away, shutting the door behind him, so I could curl up and die of embarrassment in his absence.

But he didn't. He just gazed back at me, waiting.

"Fine," I said, finally coming to the realization that acknowledging him would, at least, speed his exit. "What else could you possibly want to know?"

Perhaps he wanted to ask about the time I'd wet my bed when I was four and sleeping over at my cousin's house. Or about the time in seventh grade when I'd started my period and didn't know it until the guy I liked mentioned the spot seeping through my gym shorts. Or the time in my sophomore year of college that I was arrested for underage drinking at a fraternity party. Because it couldn't get much worse than this.

"My question is..." He hesitated and looked me right in the eye. I squirmed. "Would you go out with me?"

"Huh?" I asked. This was definitely not the humiliating question I had expected.

It was worse.

"Would you go out with me?" Matt repeated.

"Like on a date?" I was quite sure he'd gone insane.

"Like on a date," Matt confirmed in a thoroughly normal and casual tone.

I thought about it for a moment, but of course I already knew the answer. The only thing worse than a guy knowing that I was intelligent and successful was a guy knowing that I was pathetic and sad and needy. Matt already knew too much. And now he was asking me on a pity date. Again! Why had I spilled my guts to him?

"No," I said finally, not even caring that I sounded rude.

"But why?" Matt asked, a bit taken aback.

"Because, Matt," I said wearily. I paused, and in my head, I was saying, *Because I hate that I let you see inside me. Because I know I'm not pretty enough for you. Because you're just asking me out because you feel sorry for me.* But aloud, I said, "Because I just don't think it's a good idea."

"Why not?" he asked, again looking shocked. Yeah, I'll bet he was shocked. Undesirable lawyers didn't usually turn down dashing actors, I imagined.

"It's just not, Matt," I said with as much finality as I could muster.

"How about tonight?" he asked cheerfully, as if I hadn't just rejected him quite plainly.

"I already have a date tonight," I said quickly and then realized, to my surprise, that I actually wasn't lying. I *did* have a date. With Jack Majors, the political analyst.

"Really?" Matt asked suspiciously, arching an eyebrow as if he didn't quite believe me. "Where?"

"At Bistro Forty-nine," I said haughtily, glad to have an actual answer to his question. "With a very nice, good-looking political analyst. So there," I added petulantly.

"How interesting," Matt said with a smile. "Well then, if you have a political analyst, what do you need some actor for?"

"Exactly," I said firmly, a bit disappointed, despite myself, that he was backing down so easily. I mean, no, I didn't actually *want* to go out with him. But I was worth fighting for at least a little bit. Wasn't I? Evidently not. I don't know why this seemed to come as a surprise to me.

"Well then," Matt said, rising to his feet. "I guess you know what you're doing after all. I'm glad we had this little talk."

He was?

"Me, too," I lied, standing up, too, and extending my hand across my desk in as business-like a manner as humanly possible. After all, if I ended this encounter the way I'd end a business meeting, maybe I could forget it ever happened. *Right.*

"Good luck with it," Matt said cheerfully. "The Blonde Theory, I mean."

"I appreciate that, Matt," I said formally. "And good luck to you, too. With your role on the show."

Okay, that sounded stupid. But Matt was smiling at me.

"I'll see you around, Harper."

And with that, he was gone, striding toward my office door and then disappearing out into the hall, closing the door behind him without looking back.

I sat down at my desk wearily after he left, burying my head in my hands and cursing myself and my endless stupidity.

Chapter Fourteen

That night, I met Jack Majors for an early dinner at Bistro 49, thoroughly distracted both by thoughts of Jill's husband, Alec, and by embarrassment over my encounter with Matt that day. Emmie was, as promised, hunkered over a double latte at the twenty-four-hour coffee shop across from Jill's apartment, and she had promised to text me if and when she saw Alec leave. Until then, I was to go ahead with my date. I tried unsuccessfully to push Matt's infuriating words from my mind.

Jack arrived just minutes after me, and I was pleasantly surprised by what I saw. As I had bragged, somewhat prematurely, to Matt James, Jack was in fact pretty attractive. He was tall and broad-shouldered with light brown hair, straight white teeth, and wide-spaced eyes that were big and pale green. His nose had an ever-so-slight Owen-Wilson-ish tilt to it, making me think he had broken it at least once. He had a mustache and goatee, and although I normally didn't like facial hair on men very much, it looked relatively decent on him.

"Shall we get a table?" he asked politely after greeting me with a sweet peck on the cheek and placing his hand on the small of my back to lead me inside. Tonight, I was wearing a neon pink dress that clung to my water-bra-enhanced curves and billowed out just below the hips into a flowy, asymmetrical hem that ended just above the knee. Again, it was something I wouldn't have been caught dead in as Harper the Attorney-at-Law. But as Harper the Dumb Blonde, it suited me just fine.

Not surprisingly, though, my enthusiasm for The Blonde Theory was waning. There was only so much that my ego could take, and the afternoon's embarrassing chiding from Matt James wasn't helping me much. It had taken all the energy I could muster to convince myself that this date with Jack Majors was worth going on.

But now that I was here, giggling through my annoyance at the day's events, I was rather glad I had come. Jack seemed nice, attentive, interesting. Unlike some of my previous dates, he was doing a good job with the normal give-and-take of conversation. Once again, I was faring much better as Harper the Harebrained than I ever had as Harper the Highly Educated. This thought frightened me more than a little bit.

"So Harper, tell me about yourself," Jack said kindly after we had ordered drinks. I kept the story condensed, as Emmie would have recommended, and just gave him the same short story I had given the others. I had been raised in Ohio, had come to the city dreaming of bigger things, and was now living the dream as a bartender.

"Fascinating," Jack said, and he really seemed to mean it.

Over drinks, he told me the story of how he became a political consultant. He had always been interested in politics and economics, and a college internship on Capitol Hill had led to several interesting opportunities. He had returned to Washington after he graduated from college, had worked on several campaigns, and had eventually partnered with a buddy to open a consulting firm.

"So I keep an apartment here and another one in DC," he concluded. "I'm traveling so much, I don't get to spend any real time in either city. But it's nice to have a home in both places. It means that the familiar is never too far away."

It did sound nice, and I told him so, with the requisite blonde giggles and hair flipping, of course.

"So, Harper," he asked me as our salads arrived. I tucked daintily into mine, trying to ignore my growling stomach and eat with the delicacy expected of a dumb blonde. "What made you put your profile up on NYSoulmate? I mean, my motivation was that it's hard to meet single women in my line of work, especially with all the traveling I do. But it seems like you must meet lots of guys all the time."

"Oh, Jack," I said in my high-pitched voice, following the words with a dramatic sigh. "You have no idea. I mean, I, like, totally like guys who are, like, successful? Like you? And at my bar? A lot of the guys who hit on me? They're just, like, kind of losers. So I said to myself, *Self. How can you meet really, like, cool, successful men?* And so I thought, *Okay, I'll try this dating site.* My friend Meg had to help me, though. I'm not so good with computers. And I'm, like, totally terrible at spelling."

"Your profile was nice," Jack said, winking at me.

"Oh, Jack," I sighed. "That's, like, so totally sweet." I paused and smiled innocently at him. "So I have to, like, ask. Other than my killer hair, what made you, like, pick me out of all the girls?"

Jack laughed. "Yes, your hair was—and is—great," he said. I touched a hand to my Aqua-Netted big bangs and smiled as if it was the most normal, attractive hairstyle in the world. And maybe it had been. In 1985. "But I think what really attracted me was that your profile made me think you'd be a really interesting girl to talk to."

Hmm. That was hard to believe. After all, everything about BlondeBartenderHotti's profile screamed empty-headedness. Was this akin to the *I-just-read-it-for-the-articles* explanation guys gave when their girlfriends asked why they still had subscriptions to

Playboy? I suspected so. I wanted to say that. But I settled for a squealed, "Really? That's, like, so sweet!"

Jack shrugged modestly. "Well, it's true, Harper," he said with a simpering smile. "And so far, so good, right? I'm loving our conversation."

"Oh Jack," I said. "Like, me too. Totally."

I had to know something, though. My afternoon encounter with Matt James had gotten under my skin just a little too much. And I felt the clock ticking on The Blonde Theory. I had less than a week to go, and I hadn't really learned anything tangible yet.

"Jack, I have, like, a question," I said after the waiter whisked our salad plates away. He smiled encouragingly, and I continued. "How come you wouldn't want to go out with someone, like, as educated as you? I mean, I totally know that I'm like, really smart. Don't get me wrong. But you went to college, and, like, you've seen the world and stuff. How come you didn't look for, like, a smart girl?"

"You're smart, Harper," Jack said patronizingly, as if I might just believe him if he used a sweet-enough tone.

"Duh, I know, silly," I giggled. "But what I mean is, like, why wouldn't you search the profiles for like a business lady? Or, like, a lady who's a doctor? Or a lawyer?"

Jack shook his head. "I like a woman who can listen to me," he said softly. "Women like that just want to talk about themselves."

"You don't like women to talk about themselves?" I asked, batting my eyes.

"No, no, I didn't mean that," he said quickly. "I'd love it if you want to talk about yourself, Harper. It's just that women who are really successful . . . well, all they want to talk about is their jobs, how important they are, how much money they make, you know? Like they're trying to prove something. I barely get a word in edgewise."

I felt suddenly sad. I forced a vacant smile and tried to think of something amusingly stupid to say.

"Well, I hope I don't, like, make you feel like that," I said finally. "I mean, I got, like, the bartender-of-the-month award last month at my job. It came with a free month of tanning at Sunny Ones. I hope you're okay with that."

Jack laughed. "I think I can manage," he said.

"Oh good," I sighed in relief. "I mean, it's like totally a good thing I'm not a lawyer or something."

Jack laughed hard at my little joke. "Yeah, right," he said between chortles. "You. A lawyer. Ha!"

I laughed along with him, but for utterly different reasons.

MIDWAY THROUGH OUR entrées, with Jack telling me about the latest political campaign he'd worked on and how he'd had to save a senator from accusations of alcoholism that were, in fact, completely correct, I heard someone calling my name.

I recognized the voice immediately, and my heart leapt into my throat. I froze and thought that maybe if I just stayed stock-still, he wouldn't be able to see me.

No dice.

"Harper. Well, what a coincidence!" Matt James said, sauntering up to our table with a smirk on his face and a slender brunette in a short black dress on his arm. "I had absolutely *no* idea that you'd be here tonight. What are the odds?"

I glared at him. How could I have been so stupid as to tell him where I was going for dinner? Why? Because in a million years, I would never have expected him to turn up here. With a date on his arm. Hours after he had asked *me* out. A sensation of what felt an awful lot like jealousy crept through me as I stole another look at his date, who was infuriatingly pretty.

"Hi, Matt," I said through gritted teeth. Had it not been enough that I had bared my soul to this man today? Now I also had to act like a ridiculous dumb blonde in front of him, too?

He was looking as gorgeous as ever, I noticed reluctantly. His hair was tamer than it had been this afternoon, but it was still spiked in dark, perfect, sexy peaks. His olive-colored button-up shirt offset his green eyes perfectly, and his teeth gleamed extra-white against a tan that looked suspiciously deeper than it had this afternoon. His broad shoulders were all too evident beneath his designer shirt.

Matt and his date stood there uncomfortably for a moment while I mentally gnashed my teeth, wondering why I couldn't have had the good fortune to be born a witch so that I could twitch my nose and turn him into a frog or something.

"Aren't you going to introduce me to your date, Harper?" Matt asked finally, his eyes sparkling with amusement. I plastered a smile on my face.

"Oh, like, of course," I chirped like the dumb blonde I was. "Jack Majors? This is Matt James. And his date, um . . .'"

"Lisa," she supplied helpfully, linking her arm through Matt's and smiling at Jack and me.

"Well, Matt, it was great to see you," I said, keeping my voice syrupy sweet. Why had he brought a date? And why did I *care* that he had brought a date? The realization that it was bothering me so much made me very, very uncomfortable. And mad.

"Harper," said Jack brightly, and I could almost see the lightbulb going on in his head. My heart sank because I knew exactly what he was going to say before he said it. "Why don't we ask your friends here to join us?"

"We'd love to!" Matt enthused, cutting me off before I had a chance to respond. Before I knew it, Matt has asked the maître d' to push up another rectangular table for two, to turn my private meal with Jack into a cozy foursome. I only hoped that Matt would sit close enough to me so that I could violently kick him in retribution under the table.

"What is wrong with you?" I hissed at him under my breath once he and Lisa had settled in.

"Whatever do you mean?" he whispered back, grinning, while Lisa and Jack exchanged pleasantries. "It's such a pleasure to *coincidentally* run into you, Harper."

"You are *such* a jerk," I hissed, giving him a good, and well-deserved, kick in the shin for emphasis. He winced but continued to grin at me. I wanted to kill him.

"I can't *imagine* what you mean," Matt continued in a whisper.

"And you just *had* to bring a date?" I immediately regretted having said this. But it was too late.

"Why, *Harper*, do I sense a little jealousy?" Matt whispered, his voice dripping with sarcasm. I contemplated stabbing him under the table with my dinner fork.

"No," I said so loudly that both Lisa and Jack looked up from their conversation in surprise, no doubt wondering what on earth I could be yelling at Matt about.

"Don't mind her," Matt said dismissively, that infuriating grin still plastered across his perfectly chiseled features. "We were just having a little disagreement about the ingredients needed to make a Sex on the Beach."

Jack arched an eyebrow at me.

"The cocktail," I hurried to clarify before anyone at the table got any ideas.

"Oh, I'd take Harper's word for it," Jack announced to Matt, nodding at me proudly. "She just told me she won the bartender-of-the-month award last month. Sounds like she knows what she's doing."

"Well, Harper, I can't believe you didn't tell me that," Matt said, widening his eyes in mock amazement. "What an honor. Please, let me buy you and your friend here a round of drinks to celebrate."

Matt ordered us a round of cocktails while I quietly simmered, glaring alternately at him and Lisa. She didn't seem to notice, and Matt simply ignored me.

Soon, I had learned that Lisa was a stockbroker, and Matt and Jack had briefly discussed their careers. Matt explained to the others that he and I had met when he and a friend used to frequent the bar where I worked.

Just when I was wondering whether it might be possible to obtain some arsenic from the kitchen to put in Matt's gin and tonic, my cell phone vibrated, alerting me that a text message had just arrived.

"Excuse me," I said in my high-pitched voice, flipping open the phone. Until that moment, I had nearly forgotten that I was expecting to hear about Alec tonight. I could feel the blood drain from my face as I read the message from Emmie.

ALEC JUST LFT APT. I'M FOLLOWING IN TAXI. CALL ME AS SOON AS U GET THIS. I'LL TELL U WHERE TO MEET ME.

"Um, excuse me," I said hastily, already pushing my chair back from the table and fumbling to remove my napkin from my lap. "I have to make a call."

Jack looked a bit wounded and Matt seemed to be paying a bit too much attention to the curves that my dress revealed as I stood up, but I didn't have time to worry about either of them at the moment.

My heart thudding, I hurried toward the back of the restaurant, went down the flight of stairs leading to the restrooms, and called Emmie as soon as I had pushed through the door to the ladies' room.

"I'm heading downtown in a taxi now," she said urgently as soon as she picked up. "I saw him leave, so I called Jill and pretended to be making small talk. He told her he was going to the hospital. But Harper, he passed the hospital five minutes ago. He must be going to see that girl. I think we've got him."

"I'll leave now," I said instantly. "I'll start heading downtown. Just call me as soon as you stop somewhere, and I'll have my cab take me there."

She agreed and we both hung up. I turned to push back through the ladies' room door, and to my surprise, I found Matt James leaning lazily against the public phone that hung on the wall outside the bathrooms.

"Going somewhere, Harper?" he drawled casually, grinning at me.

"Oh, cut the crap, Matt," I snapped. "I don't have time for this." I really didn't. I needed to get out of there immediately. Jill had to be my first priority now.

"I don't have time for this either, Harper," Matt said, his voice suddenly husky. He took a step closer.

Then, before I knew it, he was kissing me, pressing his gorgeous, surprisingly soft lips to mine. Time seemed to stop for a second. He had caught me so off-guard. I hadn't expected this. And it felt so . . . good.

Damn it.

As he pressed into me, parting my lips gently with his tongue. I didn't have time to think about how much I hated him, time to think about how much he had embarrassed me, or time to think about how inappropriate this was since we were both here with other dates. That's because time ceased to exist for the eternity that our lips were pressed together.

And despite myself, I kissed back.

Finally he pulled away, looking tenderly into my eyes, his long-lashed lids lowered seductively, his right thumb stroking my jaw ever so gently. I felt dazed, so much so that I couldn't think of a single sarcastic thing to say. That was a first. I opened my mouth but no words came out.

"That was nice," he said softly, still stroking my face and gazing into my eyes.

"Yeah," I agreed weakly. Then logic and awareness kicked in. I cleared my throat and hurriedly straightened up, backing away from him. "I mean, no it wasn't!" I exclaimed, indignation rising within me. "What the hell do you think you're doing?"

"Kissing you," Matt said, as if it were the most obvious thing in the world. Okay, well, I supposed it was.

"Why?" I demanded angrily. I wasn't really angry that he had kissed me, but I wished I was. That would make it easier to gloss over how nice it had felt. Why did he have to be such a good kisser? Damn it, damn it, damn it.

Matt looked taken aback. "Because . . . because I wanted to," he said finally.

"Oh yeah?" I challenged him. "What about your little girl-friend upstairs?"

"Lisa?" Matt asked, looking surprised. He paused, then laughed. "She's just a friend, Harper."

I hated the sense of relief that washed over me when he said the words.

"Yeah, well, it doesn't matter," I snapped. "Because I have to go. So enjoy the rest of your night with Lisa, okay?"

Matt looked bewildered and bemused at the same time. With one last desperate look at him, I dashed up the stairs, quickly made my apologies and excuses to a surprised Jack and Lisa, mumbling something about an emergency at the bar where I worked, then hailed a cab on the street.

It wasn't until I was leaning against the sticky leather of the taxi's backseat, trying to slow my pounding heart, that I realized my lips were still tingling. And that the only thought crowding my mind was how nice it would be to kiss Matt James again.

Damn it.

Chapter Fifteen

Emmie called me about five minutes after I'd settled into a cab to tell me to meet her at the corner of Second Avenue and 4th Street, in the East Village. Alec had gone into an apartment building on the southwest corner a few minutes earlier, and Emmie had staked out a spot across the street, in a window booth at a diner called Over the Moon on the southeast corner of the same block.

"Thank God you're here," she said, her face a mask of concern as I bustled through the door to Over the Moon ten minutes later, after begging the driver to get me there as quickly as he could. Emmie stood up quickly to hug me, and we both slid into the booth she'd been sitting in. "Here, put this on."

She quickly handed me an enormous khaki-colored hat that looked suspiciously like one that a beekeeper would wear—if the beekeeper in question had absolutely no taste whatsoever.

"Emmie, what *is* this?" I asked, regarding the hat suspiciously.

She shrugged apologetically. "It's all I could find on such short notice in the wardrobe closet. We need something that'll cover your face so Alec won't spot you."

I looked suspiciously at her. She didn't appear to be in possession of a second beekeeper's hat for herself.

"And what will *you* be wearing?" I asked in a tone as even as I could manage. Emmie sheepishly held up a wig of thick, dark, long hair.

"It's from a scene where my character dreams she's Cher," she said, looking a little embarrassed. I rolled my eyes. Okay, so she'd dressed me as a frumpy beekeeper and herself as a glamorous singer. This wasn't the time to address it.

Emmie quickly filled me in on her evening. She had sat for hours in the coffee shop across the street from Jill and Alec's apartment, watching. When she saw Alec leave, she had hailed a cab to follow him. Then she'd called Jill from her cell phone and, feigning pleasant conversation, asked casually if Alec was around. No, Jill had said. He had just been called into work for an emergency operation. That was right about the time Emmie and her cabdriver had sped right past the entrance to Alec's hospital while hot on his tail.

I felt instantly guilty that I had left Emmie to stalk Alec all alone while I was off on a date. I told her so. She waved me off. "Actually, except for the fact that I am dying inside for Jill, this stakeout has been kinda fun," she admitted. "Who knows, maybe I'll have to play a detective one day. My agent says they're going to be casting soon for a role in a new Brad Pitt–Cole Brannon film noir detective movie. Maybe I can audition."

A middle-aged waitress named Marge brought us coffee and seemed content to let us sit, unbothered, peering distractedly out the window. We must have looked like a pair of crazy people.

I was trying desperately not to think about Matt James and the way he'd kissed me in the basement of Bistro 49 less than an hour earlier, but the longer Emmie and I sat there, the more it was weighing on my mind. Finally, I nervously broached the subject with her while we both peered out the window.

"Matt James came to see me today," I said.

Emmie nodded. "Yeah, he told me he was going to come talk to you about your job."

"Right," I said slowly. "But he also told me he knew about The Blonde Theory. He saw my profile on NYSoulmate."

Emmie turned her head sharply and stared at me, a stricken expression on her face.

"Oh, Harp, I swear I didn't say anything to him," she said, looking concerned. "I would never do that. I can't believe he knew."

"I know you didn't say anything," I said soothingly. "He apparently figured it out on his own. But the thing is...he asked me out."

Her jaw dropped. "He what?"

I quickly recounted the whole conversation, then told her about his infuriating appearance at Bistro 49. Emmie stared at me wide-eyed while we took turns glancing out the window to keep an eye on the situation.

"And then, right after I got off the phone with you and was about to go back upstairs to tell my date I needed to leave," I concluded slowly, "he kissed me. In the hallway. Outside the bathrooms."

"Oh my God," Emmie breathed, her full attention turning to me. "Oh my God," she repeated.

"I know," I said miserably. I glanced out the window again to make sure that Alec hadn't reappeared. "And the thing was, the kiss was *great*. But what am I going to do? I mean, it's not like I like him. And he's *your* co-worker, for goodness' sake."

"Don't worry about me," she said dismissively. "I don't like him or anything. And I guess he's more your type. But I have to warn you, I hear that he's a bit of a player."

"Oh," I said, not entirely sure why my heart had just sunk. Of *course* he was a player. Why else would he ask me out then turn up with another woman on his arm? I was such an idiot.

"But you can't believe everything you hear," Emmie added after a moment, turning back to the window. "I mean, *I've* never

seen him do anything creepy to a woman. I don't even know anyone he's dated. He doesn't date the actresses at work like the other
guys on the show do."

Hmm, this was food for thought. I was about to say something
else, to protest to Emmie that I didn't really like him that much
anyhow so this was all a moot point, when there was a movement
in the doorway of the building across the street. Emmie and I both
gasped at the same time.

"It's Alec!" she exclaimed softly.

"And that's the girl I saw him with last night," I said grimly as
he emerged with his arm draped around the shoulders of a scantily
clad, familiar-looking redhead.

Emmie and I each threw down a five-dollar bill to pay for our
coffee and a nice tip for the waitress, and then we threw on our
"disguises": the ridiculous beekeeper hat for me and the glamorous
Cher wig for Emmie. Our waitress stared after us, a bewildered
expression on her face, as we rushed out.

We stayed half a block behind them and across the street as they
walked south on Second, his arm still draped around her. I couldn't
help but think he looked a little ridiculous (this coming from a
woman in a beekeeper's hat, of course). In her four-inch stilettos,
the redhead dwarfed Alec by almost half a foot. She was wearing a
very short black skirt, which left little to the imagination, and her
long, deeply tanned legs ended in expensive silver Choos. I was just
the teensiest bit jealous of her footwear. Was that wrong?

They turned right onto 3rd Street while we followed, still
hanging back half a block. They didn't appear to notice that they
were being tailed. Finally, they entered a small Italian restaurant
called Bella Toscana, tucked between a bookstore and a vintage-
clothing shop. Emmie and I let them go inside, then stood just to
the left of the window and conferenced about what to do next.

"We can't go in," I said, feeling I was stating the obvious.
"They'll see us, for sure."

"But we can't get a photo of them from out here," Emmie said urgently. "The windows are too dark. And we definitely need some kind of proof to convince Jill. Obviously, Alec will deny it."

Indeed, it was nearly impossible to see through the darkened windowpanes into the dimly lit restaurant. More than that, Alec and the redhead had been seated somewhere near the back, entirely beyond our view. Finally, after much debate, we agreed that Emmie would take her digital camera inside, act as if she were trying to find the restaurant's bathroom, and snap several quick zoomed-in photos from as close as she could get to their table. She would keep the camera in her handbag, with just the lens peeking out, so no one would notice what she was doing.

"Why do I have to do this instead of you?" she whined before going inside.

I smiled. "Because, Cher, you've dressed me in a beekeeper's hat and this Day-Glo pink dress," I said. "And it will be a lot more obvious than your jeans, T-shirt, and black hair. Plus, this whole crazy 'detective' plan was your idea." Emmie sighed and nodded. I wished her luck and crossed my fingers nervously as she slipped through the doorway of Bella Toscana, her ridiculous Cher hair billowing behind her.

The seconds seemed to be taking an eternity to tick by as I stood outside the restaurant, fingers still crossed, heart in my throat, alternately tapping my right foot impatiently and glancing in to see if I could spot her. Finally, I saw a flash of light inside and heard a male voice yelling. In a second, Emmie burst out of the doorway, wig askew, her face twisted with concern.

"Let's go," she snapped, grabbing my arm and dragging me with her as she turned left out of the restaurant, heading back toward Second Avenue.

"What is it? What's wrong?" I asked as I raced after her, marveling a bit, despite myself, at my speed in stilettos.

"He saw me," she said grimly over her shoulder. "Alec saw me."

Finally, two blocks later, when it became clear that no one was following us, we slowed and turned down 5th Street to lean against the side of a building and catch our breath.

"He saw you?" I repeated, panting.

Emmie nodded. "I guess I'm not much of a detective," she said glumly. "I took about four pictures. Then when I tried to zoom in a bit more to take a fifth, I must have accidentally reset the automatic flash on my camera. It went off as soon as I snapped the photo. He turned and looked right at me, and I know he recognized me."

"Oh no," I said, feeling a bit sick. Alec was a smart guy; he was probably already inventing excuses that he could tell Jill before we had a chance to get to her. That meant that we had to get to her *soon*. Like now. "Were the pictures okay at least?" I asked, hoping against hope that they were.

"Let's see," Emmie said nervously. She turned her camera back on as I crossed my fingers again. Without clear photos, it would be our word against Alec's.

"Bingo," Emmie breathed softly after a moment, sounding triumphant and sad at the same time. I looked over her shoulder at the photos and knew immediately why. All five of them were clearly of Alec and the redhead. It was obvious they were on a date; they were holding hands in one photo, she was touching his cheek in another, and in the fifth picture, the one where the flashbulb had gone off and illuminated the room, it was painfully obvious that they were locked in a passionate kiss across the table. We'd caught him red-handed with the redhead.

But it was hard to feel victorious knowing that the photos stored in Emmie's camera would be the death knell to Jill's marriage.

EMMIE AND I shared a cab uptown and called Meg—who was at the office closing a feature that had come in late—during the ride.

We quickly filled her in, and, sounding very sad, she agreed to meet us at the coffee shop across from Jill's apartment right away. Then we called Jill.

"Oh hi, Harper!" she said cheerfully when she picked up. "How did your date go tonight?"

"Fine," I answered hesitantly. "Listen, I have a problem I need to talk about with you. Can you meet me at the coffee shop across the street from your apartment in about twenty minutes?" Emmie, Meg, and I had decided not to say anything to Jill over the phone about the reason for our call. It would give her too much time to invent excuses in her head. We needed to present her with the hard evidence—the photos—from the outset.

"Harper, are you okay?" Jill asked with concern. "Should I call Meg and Emmie?"

"Um, no," I said. "I'm fine. I just need you to meet me right away, okay?"

"If you need me to, I will," she said slowly. "But Alec just called and is on his way home. He said he had something important to discuss with me. I think it's probably about the trip I had asked him to take with me." Her voice took on a gleeful edge. "I've been dying to go to France, and he keeps telling me that he's busy. But I have the feeling he's going to surprise me with tickets tonight, or something."

I teared up just listening to her. I was hating Alec more with every passing moment.

"Look, it won't take that long," I said. "Please. In fact, why don't you leave your apartment now? I'm on my way there. If Alec gets home before you leave, you'll just get caught up in a long conversation with him."

In reality, I was more worried that Alec would preclude our revelation by explaining it away before we had a chance to. But what could he say? That in the photo he was actually performing CPR on the redhead? That his medical emergency had actually been in a dimly lit Italian restaurant instead of at the hospital? There was truly no way out for him. But I feared that Jill, desperate to keep her life looking perfect from both the inside and the out, would somehow convince herself that his words must be true. Clearly, he had been deceiving her for months—in fact, for months even *before* their wedding if Emmie had been right about what she'd seen. The thought that he'd been cheating on my friend practically since day one made me feel physically sick.

"Okay, Harper," Jill agreed. "Are you sure you're okay?" Her voice was heavy with concern for *me,* which broke my heart.

"I'm okay, Jill," I said, my voice breaking a bit. "I just need you to meet me, okay?"

"I'll be there, sweetie," she said softly. "Whatever it is, don't worry. It can't be that bad."

Emmie rubbed my arm comfortingly as I hung up with Jill.

"It's going to be okay," she soothed. "She's going to be okay."

I nodded, but I didn't know if I believed it. Jill's whole life had been built on constructing her version of the perfect existence. And she believed so strongly that she had it. She thought she had done everything right, had fit everything into the preconceived ideals she'd started the game with.

It was about to come crumbling down all around her. I wished I could stop the fall. But no one could.

Emmie and I arrived at the coffee shop fifteen minutes later and found Jill sitting there with a cup of coffee in front of her and a look of concern on her face. When we both walked through the door, she looked a bit confused.

"I thought you were coming alone, Harper," she said, standing up to give us both hugs. I knew the somber expressions on both of our faces were making her nervous, because she started chattering. "But I'm so glad to see you both. Are you okay? I was so concerned when you called, Harper. I thought maybe something bad had happened on your date. Wait, why aren't you on your date?"

"I, um, got sidetracked," I said, exchanging glances with Emmie. Jill caught us looking at each other and became more concerned.

"Is everything okay?" she asked, her voice rising an octave. "You're scaring me. Is something wrong with Meg? Where's Meg?"

Just then, as if on cue, a fresh-from-the-office Meg bustled through the door of the coffee shop, dressed in a rumpled beige corduroy skirt and a navy blouse.

"Sorry I'm late," she mumbled, giving Jill a peck on the cheek and sliding into the chair beside her.

"We just got here," I said softly. Jill's eyes darted nervously among the three of us.

"What is it?" she asked. "What's going on? Are you all okay?"

Emmie, Meg, and I exchanged looks. Emmie nodded at me to go ahead. I wasn't sure why this was my job, but someone had to do it.

"We're all fine, Jill," I began. She looked relieved and nodded. I hesitated for a moment, then drew a deep breath. "Actually, this is about you."

"Me?" She looked shocked.

"And Alec," I added, watching her expression carefully. For a moment, her face fell, then she smiled brightly. I knew her well enough to know that the smile was forced.

"What do you mean?" she asked with levity that I knew wasn't real. "Alec and I are fine. Things are good. Like I said, I think he's taking me on vacation soon."

Emmie and Meg looked at me helplessly. I forged ahead.

"He's cheating on you, Jill," I said gently. I reached across the table and took her hands as her mouth fell open. "It's going to be fine. We're all here for you." I squeezed her hands tightly and nodded as encouragingly as I could.

Jill stared at me for a moment, then yanked her hands away. She stared first at me, then at Emmie, then at Meg, then back at me again.

"What are you talking about?" she finally demanded. "Alec isn't cheating on me. We just got married. Things are fine."

"Harper and I caught him in the act," Emmie explained softly.

Jill's eyes flashed and her nostrils flared. "Oh, so now you're spying on him? What, you two have nothing better to do than to follow him around?"

Emmie and I exchanged glances. We had been braced for sadness, outrage, and anger at Alec. But we hadn't expected Jill's fury to be fully directed at us.

"Don't be angry at them, Jill," Meg said in that soothing voice of hers. "They knew he was cheating on you, and they wanted to be sure before they said something. To be honest, I didn't believe them when they told me at first, either."

"He's *not* cheating on me," Jill said through gritted teeth, glaring at the three of us. "Look, I know you guys aren't *trying* to hurt me. But what is this all about? Why are you doing this? Are you mad that I'm married and you're not?"

She looked sharply at Emmie and me, and I felt like she'd punched me in the gut.

I finally said softly, "No. Of course not, Jill. We've never been jealous of you. Not about that."

"Oh c'mon," she scoffed. I couldn't believe she was being so mean. "No offense, but I know you two want to get married," she continued. "It's okay if you're upset that I got married first. But following my husband around is no way to behave."

"Jill, there are pictures," Emmie said flatly. I knew she was struggling to contain her instinct to snap back. Like me, she was offended by Jill's accusations, but she knew what was at stake here.

"What?" Jill asked softly, tears creeping into her narrowed eyes. "What pictures?"

"We took them less than an hour ago," Emmie said slowly. She reached into her handbag, turned her camera on, pulled up the first image, and handed it to Jill. "They're from a little Italian restaurant in the East Village."

"Alec doesn't go to the East Village," Jill protested, but her voice was weaker this time, less convinced. "He hates anything below Union Square." She looked at the camera, but she didn't take it, didn't look at the screen.

"It was definitely Alec," I said, as gently as I could while keeping my voice firm. "He was in the East Village because that's where the girl he's seeing lives."

Jill's eyes welled up with tears and she looked helplessly among the three of us.

"I can't believe you're doing this to me," she whispered. "He's not cheating on me. You *know* he's not cheating on me."

"Look at the pictures, Jill," Emmie said firmly, thrusting the camera at her again. Jill didn't take it but she did look down at the screen. I watched as her eyes widened and then narrowed again.

"It's not him," she said simply, looking away. "You're wrong. It's not him."

"There are more," Emmie said, pushing the button on her camera to go to the next shot. "There are five. Look at them, Jill. They're definitely him."

Jill hesitantly took the camera from her and stared long and hard at the second picture that, like the rest, had a time and date stamp indicating it had just been taken tonight. She was silent as she skipped to the third and then the fourth. When she landed on the fifth, the flashbulb shot of Alec kissing his redhead, she gasped aloud and lifted the camera up to look closer.

"No," she said finally, but I knew she was no longer protesting against us. The pictures didn't lie, and not even Jill could explain away their significance. She started to cry.

We sat there in silence for a full five minutes, a statue of inter-twined arms, comforting a friend we loved dearly. Emmie, Meg, and I looked at one another with concern as we rubbed her back, rubbed her arms, held her hands, while she looked down at her lap and cried silent tears. None of us knew what to do. There was nothing *to* do.

"I appreciate your concern," Jill finally said stiffly, pulling away from us and sniffing back tears. "But I'm sure there's an explanation for this. I know he wouldn't cheat on me."

I gaped at her. She was still in denial, even after seeing the photos. "Jill, I—"

"I'm going home now," she said, standing up without looking at any of us. She sniffed again. "I'm going to talk to Alec. I'm sure there's a logical explanation."

"Jill, you can't—" Emmie began.

"Stop," Jill cut in coldly. "Just stop. I think you've done enough for one night."

Gathering her purse up, she sniffed again and strode purposefully toward the door. She was gone before any of us could react.

"What just happened?" Emmie asked, looking helplessly between me and Meg.

Meg shook her head. "I was afraid she'd react like this," she said softly. "She's going to have to deal with this in her own time, in her own way. We just have to try to be there for her as best we can."

We all stared after her until long after she'd disappeared back into the perfect doorman entrance to her perfect apartment building, where she had been living her perfect life with her perfect husband.

Chapter Sixteen

I walked home that night, after Emmie and Meg and I had parted ways. We all felt sad and helpless and unsure what to do about Jill—even Meg, who always had an answer for everything. None of us was angry at her for blaming us. That was just Jill. The four of us were like sisters, and we had been through enough ups and downs together to forgive one another when the going got rough.

We talked for a little while about sticking around to see if Jill needed us, perhaps trying to get past her doorman to join her in her apartment so that we could support her when Alec got home. In the end, we realized it was a battle she needed to fight alone. She knew we would be there the moment she called if she needed us.

In the blocks from Jill's apartment to mine, I thought a lot about love, loss, and that which makes a relationship real. I'd spent so much time faking love and happiness in the past two weeks that I'd barely noticed my friend, who had been faking her own love and happiness, even to herself, for months. Perhaps she'd been faking that same visage of perfection for as long as we'd known her. Jill had never had a hair out of place, had never looked, seemed, acted anything less than perfect. I guess I'd always figured that, for the most part, she and her life *were* perfect. But maybe they never had been at all.

It made me think about this stupid Blonde Theory and the quest for perfection in my own life. Maybe I just wasn't meant to have it all. Maybe I'd gotten smarts and the perfect job, and that's all I would ever get. Maybe that would have to be enough, would have to be okay, would have to be something I conceded to in order to be happy for the rest of my life. After all, I was thirty-five. I'd never been in a relationship where the guy hadn't eventually walked away from me. Since Peter, in fact, I hadn't been in a relationship at all. Discovering these past two weeks that stupidity made me attractive in a way that kindness, intelligence, humility, and charm never had was sort of the final blow. Instead of making me feel better or somehow illuminating where I had gone wrong, The Blonde Theory had just left me feeling more alone than ever.

Maybe I needed to start being happy with what I had rather than wanting more than I was owed.

I was so lost in thought that I didn't notice the tall figure in the shadows of my fifth-floor hallway until I was jiggling my keys absently in the lock on my door. I didn't notice him until his hand was on my shoulder. I whirled around and started to scream, but he clapped a hand over my mouth.

"Harper, it's just me," he said, emerging from the shadows. I stared into his face for a moment, until he dropped his hand from my mouth.

"Matt?" I asked, my heart thudding, although I wasn't sure if it was from the scare or from the fact that Matt James was standing in the hallway outside my apartment, holding a bottle of wine, looking deliciously sexy as usual in a pair of faded jeans and a black ribbed shirt. "What on earth are you doing here?"

"I just wanted to see you," he said with a helpless shrug.

"At"—I checked my watch—"midnight?"

He shrugged again. "Well, you ran out of the restaurant after I kissed you, and I didn't know what to think," he explained sheepishly. "I've actually been waiting here for a couple of hours. I was starting to wonder if you weren't coming home." I didn't know what to say to him, so I just stood there for a moment, until he asked if he could come inside.

"Uh, yeah, I guess," I agreed, still a bit bewildered.

"Thanks," he said, his voice husky.

"Come in," I said softly. I was exhausted, both physically and emotionally. My feelings had been stripped raw by the events of the evening. Jill was still weighing heavily on my mind. And now here was this man in my hallway—the man Emmie had, just hours before, described as a "player"—and I was too tired to pretend to myself that I wasn't attracted to him. I just couldn't figure out why the feeling appeared to be mutual. The fact of the matter was, hot, sexy, successful, gorgeous (did I mention sexy?) men weren't attracted to me. Ever.

Once we had stepped into the front hallway and I had closed the door behind us, Matt held up the bottle of wine tentatively.

"I realize it's kind of lame," he said, smiling at me helplessly. "But I was hoping you might join me in a bottle of merlot."

I looked from Matt to the bottle then back at him again. I don't know whether it was the long day I'd had, my heartache over Jill, my frustration with dating in general, or the simple realization that things were never as good as they appeared and I therefore needed to stop counting on them, but I started feeling very cranky.

"Exactly what are you trying to pull here?" I asked wearily. I knew my wariness was entirely appropriate, no matter how innocently he was staring at me with those wide green eyes.

"What do you mean?" Matt asked, looking bewildered. "I'm not trying to pull anything. I'm just trying to say that I like you, Harper. I like you a lot."

"Oh, give me a break," I said, hating the way that my heart had jumped into my throat when he said that. After all, I knew he didn't mean it. I wasn't one of his soap-opera fans who believed the fictitious lines his character delivered to swooning leading ladies. "Seriously, what is this? Some kind of little joke? Ha ha, you've hit on the uptight lawyer lady, now you can get back to your real life and all your little model girlfriends?"

Matt looked at me blankly.

"This isn't a joke," he said. Was it my imagination, or did he look genuinely wounded? "Harper, I don't date models. I don't like models. Stupidity doesn't turn me on. Intelligence does."

"Oh yeah, brains are a *real* turn-on," I scoffed, rolling my eyes at him. "*All* the guys just *love* the smart girls. C'mon. Give me a break, Matt."

I sauntered into my living room, my back to Matt, doing my best to pretend I didn't care that he was here. What was he *doing* here? There had to be some sort of ulterior motive. But I was at a loss when it came to figuring out exactly what it was. And I *hated* being at a loss.

"Do you have a corkscrew, Harper?" Matt asked, ignoring my sarcasm as he followed me into the living room. "And maybe two wineglasses?"

My back still to him, I walked into the kitchen, removed a corkscrew from the drawer, and took two wineglasses from my glass-front cabinet. I walked back into the living room where Matt stood, holding the wine bottle and looking at me quizzically.

"Here," I said, thrusting the corkscrew and glasses at him. "Have a seat," I mumbled as an afterthought. "I need to use the bathroom."

When I returned a few minutes later, after trying to get ahold of myself while staring at my dark circles and growing crow's-feet in the bathroom mirror and marveling at the new pimple that had materialized on my forehead at some point during the day, Matt was holding two wineglasses filled with merlot.

As I approached the sofa, he stood and held out one of the glasses in my direction. "At least have a drink with me and hear me out."

Something in me snapped just then.

"Honestly, what the hell are you doing here, Matt?" I demanded, waving away his offer of wine. He slowly set the glasses slowly down on my coffee table and stared at me. "I mean, I've had enough for one night, you know? I just had to tell one of my best friends that her husband has been cheating on her. And that's after you appeared at Bistro Forty-nine with the sole purpose, apparently, of ruining what could have been a good date. So whatever your reason for being here, let's just get it out in the open. Okay?"

Matt regarded me carefully and seemed to take a moment to collect his thoughts before speaking.

"I'm sorry to hear about your friend," he said slowly. "And I know you don't believe me, but I didn't show up at Bistro Forty-nine trying to ruin your date. I just wanted to see you."

"Whatever," I sniffed. "Seriously, Matt, don't patronize me. I'm not stupid."

"No, you're not," Matt agreed. "But you're also not acting very smart right now."

I bristled. "And what exactly is *that* supposed to mean?"

"It's supposed to mean that I'm telling you something that should be relatively easy to understand, and you won't be quiet long enough to listen to me," he said, his brow furrowing into waves of frustration in a way that, I had to admit, was somewhat endearing. At least I was starting to get under his skin, too.

"And what exactly is that?" I asked, trying to sound obstinate.

"Harper," Matt said, taking a few steps forward until we were face-to-face, our noses barely six inches apart. He looked so deeply into my eyes that I started to squirm, mostly out of a desire to restart my heart, which I swear had stopped for a moment. "I like you," he said softly. "I don't know how many ways you want me to say it. I like you. I like you a lot."

"No you don't," I said stubbornly, not sure why I was protesting so much. But this was impossible. Guys like him didn't go for girls like me. Not when they knew the *real* me. Which Matt did.

"Harper, listen to me," he said, cupping my chin in his hands. My instincts told me to pull away, but I didn't. Because despite myself, his warm, slightly callused hand felt good there. "Harper, I like you for who you are. You're an incredible, intelligent, attractive woman whom I respect and admire. I know you're used to guys being intimidated by your job or your success. But Harper, I want you to listen to me: I like you *because* of your intelligence and your intellect and everything you are. Not despite those things, Harper, *because* of them. Are you listening to me?"

I finally heard him. I mean, I really, really heard him. And in that instant, it was as if all my other senses had kicked in, too. I saw his green eyes as if for the first time, noticing the little silver flecks in them that seemed to make them sparkle. I noticed his musky, manly scent, a mix between cologne and something else that was nearly irresistible. I felt his presence, just inches away from me, in a way I never had before. I felt my entire body suddenly flood with unfamiliar warmth, and I knew I was blushing from head to toe.

"Oh," I said finally because there was nothing else sarcastic or angry or unkind left to say.

Then he kissed me, and it was even better than it had been in the restaurant. It was long and slow and deep and deliberate, and I was no longer trying to resist. Instead, I kissed back, letting his tongue search my mouth, tentatively probing his in return. I pressed myself into him with desperation and longing I hadn't let myself feel in three years, my heart filling with something unfamiliar as he pressed into me.

Then, before I could stop myself, I started to cry.

"What is it?" Matt asked, pulling back a bit but still holding on to me tenderly, which just made me cry harder. "Did I do something wrong? Are you okay?"

I shook my head, mortified, wishing that I could stop the tears, but they seemed to be gushing out with a life of their own as if from a broken faucet I couldn't turn off.

"No, you didn't do anything wrong," I said between sobs. Could I possibly embarrass myself more in front of this guy? "It's just that...It's just that..." I paused and struggled for the next words, because they were hard for me to say. "It's just that that's the first time anyone has ever said anything like that to me."

Matt nodded, and I knew he understood. He pulled me close and held me as the tears poured out of their own accord. And slowly, as I sobbed into his shoulder, my feelings of inadequacy started to fade, leaving me only with an entirely alien feeling of belonging.

"Stupid Blonde Theory," I mumbled as my tears finally dried. Matt smiled and leaned down to kiss me again.

That night, Matt stayed over, and we had absolutely perfect sex. Three times. Slow, passionate, gentle, perfect sex with Matt gazing into my eyes, sometimes holding my hand, sometimes stroking my face, sometimes running his big hands tenderly through my hair or over the curves of my body. I had never known that sex could feel that way. I was in such a daze by the time we finally stopped that I completely forgot to set my alarm clock. And you know what? For the first time in my life, it didn't even matter that I was being irresponsible. I didn't even care.

Maybe there *was* such a thing as perfection.

WHEN I WOKE up in the morning, an hour later than I should have but after only a few hours of sleep thanks to our lovemaking marathon the night before, I felt strangely calm and at peace. I looked to my left and felt a sense of comfort at seeing Matt there, sleeping peacefully, his back to me, his rib cage rising and falling with the deep breaths of slumber. He was still there. He hadn't been a dream. The previous night hadn't been a dream. We had fallen asleep with him spooning me, and I'd never felt so safe in all my life. Not even with Peter.

Wanting to be close to him, I rolled to my left and wrapped my body around Matt's contours. He stirred, sighed, and settled into the curve of my body. I pressed into him, loving the feel of him against me, loving the scent of him, loving the fact that we had stripped down all the reasons why we shouldn't be together, leaving only us, the real me and the real him. And it was all going to be fine.

Oddly, I wasn't even worrying about the fact that I was tremendously late to work. I didn't have any meetings until the early afternoon, and I doubted the other partners would even notice my absence. I supposed I should call Molly, who was probably worrying about me, but I didn't want to move, didn't want to break the spell of perfection that had settled over my bed. If I could have, I would have stayed there forever.

It was another half an hour before Matt woke up. He came to slowly, stirring a bit first, then rolling over to face me.

"Well hello, you," he said with a lazy smile, blinking into the sunshine that had started to pour through the bedroom drapes.

"Hello," I said, smiling back shyly.

"Did you sleep well?" he asked. I nodded, and he smiled. He reached for me, wrapping his arms around me and pulling me into his chest. I snuggled against him, loving the feeling of being held so tightly by someone who really, truly knew me.

"That was some night," he said into my hair, as he rubbed my back. I breathed in the scent of his muscular chest.

"Yeah," I said dreamily, because what else could I say? It had been spectacular. It had been the kind of fireworks sex I'd seen in movies but didn't know really existed.

Perfection, I thought again. This was perfection. I hadn't known, until last night, that anything could really feel this way.

Matt started kissing me on the top of my head until I looked up at him. Then he started in on my forehead, then down my nose, across both cheeks, and finally down to my lips until we were kissing with the same passion we had last night. Again, his hands started roaming tenderly over my body, appreciating curves that I hadn't yet learned to appreciate myself.

We made love again, faster this time, with more of an edge of need and less tenderness than we had the night before, but it was still wonderful. It was wonderful to feel wanted and needed for all the right reasons. It felt wonderful to be filled by someone who wanted me for *me.*

"I'm going to jump in the shower," Matt said into my hair as I lay, breathing hard into his hard, sweaty chest after we'd finished. He gave me a quick peck on the top of the head and rolled over. "Do you have a towel I can borrow?" he asked over his shoulder, walking toward my bathroom as I admired the perfect, chiseled contours of his naked body from behind. *Perfect, perfect, perfect,* said the voice in my head.

"Sure, I'll get you one," I said, hopping up from bed and quickly sliding into one of the oversize T-shirts I usually slept in. I wasn't quite as comfortable with my naked body as Matt seemed to be with his. Maybe in time I would learn to be, though. Matt lingering on my curves didn't hurt my confidence any, that's for sure. He had spent almost half an hour last night touching and kissing the admittedly small breasts most men skipped right over. I'd always figured that men didn't like them much because they were so small. But Matt kept whispering how beautiful I was. I flushed at the memory.

I took out a towel from the linen closet, and looked at it for a moment in confusion before realizing why it looked unfamiliar. It wasn't mine. I looked at the stack of towels and groaned. *None* of them was mine. With the exception of my own towel, which I'd been using for a few days and hung in my bathroom, I had apparently given the Irish handyman the wrong stack when he'd showed up the other day. My linen closet was filled with the towels that apparently belonged to the buddy whose couch Sean was crashing on. I felt terrible; the poor guy had been so kind to help me, and I'd done nothing but screw him up, making him come over twice to pick up towels because I forgot all about him, then giving him the wrong pile to top it all off. I wondered if he had noticed yet.

I resolved to borrow one of the towels for Matt, because what else was I going to do, ask him to air-dry? Hmm, not that that would be such a terrible idea. I thought about it for a moment. Yes, more naked Matt, I could definitely handle that. I giggled and chided myself for being ridiculous.

The towels had made me think of the handyman, which made me think of his prophetic words. As I carried one of his towels in to Matt, I thought about what he had said in that endearing Irish brogue of his.

If they're not appreciatin' your intelligence, they're clearly not the right guys, his deep voice echoed in my head. I smiled. He was right. All the ridiculous men of The Blonde Theory had preferred me stupid. But Matt had appreciated my intelligence in ways no one ever had before. He had told me he liked me *because* of my intelligence and success, not *despite* them. And he *was* the right guy. I knew it. I said a silent *thank you* to the sweet Irish handyman for inadvertently steering me in the right direction.

Matt left after he had showered and slipped back into his clothes. His good-bye kiss was short and sweet, a tender peck on the lips as he ran his hands through my hair and told me again how much he'd enjoyed the night before.

"You're amazing, Harper," he had whispered, his breath brushing past my ear as I unlocked my front door for him. "I'll call you."

"You're amazing, too," I whispered back. He smiled. I watched him until he had disappeared down the stairs leading to the ground floor.

Perfection, the voice in my head said one more time.

AFTER MATT LEFT, I took a quick shower, snapped out of my daze, and checked the voice mails on my cell phone. Three concerned messages from Molly, wondering where I was, which made me feel instantly horrible. One call from Meg, wanting to talk about Jill. And one from Jill asking me to call her.

I called Jill back first, my heart in my throat, feeling horrible that I hadn't been available for one of my best friends in the middle of what was probably the worst crisis of her life so far. Some friend I was—curled up with a hot guy in my bed rather than tending to my friend's needs. I felt like a real jerk. This wasn't like me. Then again, it wasn't like me to have a hot guy in my bed, either. Ever.

Jill picked up on the first ring.

"Are you okay?" I asked right away. "I'm so sorry I didn't answer when you called," I added guiltily.

"Oh, I'm fine," she said, her voice sounding surprisingly chipper for someone who had discovered just last night that her husband was cheating on her.

"You...you are?" I asked, thoroughly confused. Last night was seeming more and more like an episode of *The Twilight Zone.* Maybe I'd imagined it all. Maybe Alec hadn't really cheated on Jill and Matt really hadn't showed up at my door. Maybe I was going insane. That would be a logical explanation for all of this, I supposed.

"Oh yes," she said brightly. "I just called to tell you not to worry about me. Alec and I talked everything through. Everything's fine. I also wanted to apologize for snapping at you last night. I know you were just trying to help."

I paused, not quite sure how to respond. Okay, so last night hadn't been *The Twilight Zone.* This morning evidently was. Of course I accepted her apology; I had never expected one because I knew exactly where she was coming from.

"Alec and you talked it through?" I finally asked, keeping my tone even.

"Oh yes," she said, laughing tightly. "It was just a misunderstanding."

I paused and chose my words carefully.

"A misunderstanding?" I asked finally, speaking slowly. "Jill, what do you mean? We caught him kissing another woman, whom he has been seeing for at least a few weeks. You saw the pictures. What, exactly, is the misunderstanding?"

"Oh, it's not what you thought," she said, keeping her voice light and cheerful in a way I knew was artificial. I just wasn't sure if *she* knew her lightness wasn't real, or if she had managed to brainwash herself into believing that everything was okay. "The woman was just a friend of his," she explained brightly. "A colleague at work. Another doctor. The kiss that you photographed, it was just a friendly peck. The woman is from France. That's how they greet each other over there, you know."

"Jill," I said slowly. "You can't really believe that."

"What do you mean?" she chirped back instantly. "Of course I believe it. Alec wouldn't cheat on me. Alec loves me. He explained everything."

My heart ached for her. I knew she wanted to believe that everything was perfect. But how could she possibly believe that Alec was innocent? *Did* she really believe it? Or did she just want *us* to believe it so that we wouldn't see that she was imperfect?

"Jill, I'm not saying he doesn't love you," I said finally. "But he *was* cheating on you."

"Harper, that's just a mean thing to say," she said stiffly, sounding wounded. "We're trying to work things out. I would appreciate your support."

I didn't know what to say.

"Look," I said finally, feeling helpless. "You *always* have my support, Jill. You know that. I love you. But I can't pretend that what happened last night didn't happen."

"Meg and Emmie said the same thing," Jill said, her voice heavy and tense. I could hear her take a deep breath. "Look, I know you're trying to help, so I'm trying not to be mad," she said. "But this is something Alec and I have to work on. And if we're going to fix this marriage, I am going to have to take him at his word. If he says he wasn't cheating on me, then he wasn't cheating on me."

I was silent. I didn't know what to say in the face of such blatant denial. I only knew that I had to stand by her as best I could. But that didn't include lying to make her feel better or accepting her lies as truth.

"Okay," I said finally. "Look, Jill, please just know that I'm here for you. All three of us are here for you. Whatever you need, we're here. Okay?"

"I appreciate that," she said, sounding relieved, her voice artificially bright and cheerful again. "I'm lucky to have such good friends."

If only she could admit to herself how much she needs us, I thought. Instead, I told her to hang in there and to call if she needed anything. We said our good-byes and I hung up feeling even more discouraged and worried about her situation than I had the night before.

Chapter Seventeen

I canceled the date I was supposed to have that night with another NYSoulmate.com match, because I obviously couldn't even consider going out with someone else while Matt was still so fresh in my mind. The scent of his cologne lingered in my apartment—and on my pillow, which, I admit, I had buried my face in appreciatively more than once since he'd gone. After thinking about it for an hour or so, I also called and canceled with Kevin Corcoran, the restaurant owner whom I was supposed to go out with the next night.

I was done with The Blonde Theory.

Sure, I probably had more dates to go on to complete my official obligation to Meg. But the fact was, I had my answer. Sure, it was easier to date as a dumb blonde. That was a depressing truth I'd have to learn to live with. But Matt James had taught me last night that it was possible to find a guy to appreciate me just by being *me*, too. I could include that realization in the article I wrote for Meg, so I felt sure I wasn't letting her down. Besides, I couldn't see how anyone could expect me to go on any more blind dates after the amazing night I'd had with Matt. I couldn't imagine spending another waking second with anyone else.

After apologizing again to Molly for my tardiness and after taking my 1 PM meeting with the head of development for Cambridge Pharmaceuticals, I called Meg to see if she was busy and then decided to head uptown to surprise her in her office.

After signing in at the visitor's desk and having my name cleared by the receptionist at *Mod,* who knew me from the numerous times I'd come in to see my friend, I was whisked up forty-six floors by one of the express elevators on the left side of the hallway. I stepped out into a hallway painted bright red and lined with blown-up covers of all the *Mod* issues produced in the last two years.

"Hi, Gina," I said to the receptionist, a beautiful girl with thick, dark hair, enormous green eyes, and porcelain Italian skin.

She smiled widely at me. "Nice to see you, Harper," she said. "I'll let Meg know you're here."

I flipped through an issue of *Mod* while I waited. The cover promised to help me to FIND A MAN TODAY!, to KEEP YOUR SKIN LOOKING 21 FOREVER!, and to PLEASE HIM IN BED TONIGHT! Well, all those things sounded good, but I doubted I'd absorb enough to make my reading worthwhile in the few minutes before Meg arrived.

Five minutes later, she came through the door to reception, dressed in a simple brown dress with three strands of wooden beads.

"Well, this is a surprise," she said, smiling at me as I put the magazine back on the table, stood up, and gave her a hug. "Everything okay?"

"Yep," I said. "I just wanted to talk to you about The Blonde Theory. Do you have a minute?"

In Meg's office, I took a deep breath and poured out the story of what had happened last night with Matt James.

"So I think I'm done with The Blonde Theory," I concluded. "I mean, I found out what I need to know. And then I found Matt."

Meg was silent for a moment, and I started to feel just the slightest bit uneasy as she regarded me thoughtfully.

"It almost sounds too good to be true," she finally said in an even tone. I nodded enthusiastically.

"Yes, yes it does," I agreed eagerly. "But Meg, it was amazing. I can't believe I've known this guy for a couple of years, and I didn't take the time to realize he could be the guy for me. I just assumed that an actor like him would never go for a lawyer like me."

"Hmm" was Meg's only response. I started to feel uncomfortable again.

"What?" I finally asked.

"It's just that…" Her voice trailed off and she seemed to choose her next words carefully. "It's just that I'm afraid you're jumping the gun."

"By finishing The Blonde Theory early?" I asked. "If you want me to go on a couple more dates to finish it out, I will. I don't want to let you down. And I'm sure Matt would understand. He's a great guy. But wasn't the point to test out whether dating as a dumb blonde would make my life easier? I *did* test it. And I feel like I have my answer."

"I wasn't talking about The Blonde Theory," Meg said after a moment, her eyes looking troubled. She sighed. "If you feel like you've learned what you needed to learn and it's enough for a fifteen-hundred-word article, that's fine with me. I'm concerned that you're jumping the gun with Matt."

"What are you talking about?" I asked, surprised. I thought Meg would be as happy for me as I was.

"It's just that it happened awfully quickly," she said slowly. "And you haven't even had a first date with the guy yet. I don't want to see you count on anything too soon."

What, now Meg was a skeptic? Romantic Meg, who had wanted to believe that Alec was being faithful to Jill, even when Emmie and I tried to tell her otherwise? Who was she to naysay my newfound happiness?

"Meg, it was perfect," I protested finally. "I really don't see any reason to worry. Like I said, I've finally found someone who says he likes me *because* I'm smart."

"I know," Meg said after a moment's pause. "I just hope you're being careful."

Although she agreed to let me end the Blonde Theory experiment early, I couldn't help but feel uncomfortable without her complete endorsement. And for whatever reason, she wasn't giving it to me at the moment.

Oh well. What did she know? She hadn't been there to see me and Matt together. She hadn't seen the incredible fireworks between us, the way he had touched me so tenderly, the way he had looked at me so lovingly. She didn't know a thing about the situation, and I wasn't going to let her pessimism get to me. Sometimes I felt like she was at least a little bit out of the loop after a decade off the dating market. She had been with Paul, her husband, since we had been teenagers. Maybe she didn't even remember what the first sparks of love were really like. But I did: I had experienced them in blinding brilliance last night.

We talked for a few more minutes about Jill and how sad we felt. Meg repeated that she thought we needed to give Jill her space for a bit and let her come to her own realizations in her own time. Then I told Meg I needed to get back to work.

"Listen," she said before I left. "I have another article on file that I can fill the August 'Dating Files' slot with. Why don't you take another month with the Blonde Theory article instead of trying to turn it around for me next week?"

I looked at her blankly.

"Why?" I asked. "I'm done with the experiment. I can have the article written for you by the end of next week."

Meg shrugged. "I'd prefer you take some time to think about things before you start writing," she said simply. "At least do that for me. Okay?"

I paused and nodded, not understanding at all where she was coming from but realizing that I owed her at least that if I was going to bail early on The Blonde Theory. We both stood up and she walked me back to the lobby, where we hugged good-bye.

"Give me a call if you want to talk," she said as I turned to leave. I looked at her in confusion. What would I want to talk about? Jill was having marital problems; Emmie was worried about an upcoming audition. For once, I was the happiest and sanest in our group. I shrugged and nodded.

"Thanks," I said simply, surprised at how short I sounded. Then, waving good-bye to Gina the receptionist, I took the elevator down to street level, grabbed a cup of coffee in the lobby, and took the R train from 49th Street back to my office downtown.

IT WAS EIGHT o'clock before I had finished my paperwork at the office. Like an insecure teenager, I had called home four times that evening to check my answering machine. I was growing increasingly insecure by my fifth call home.

No calls.

No messages.

No Matt.

That was okay, I reminded myself. After all, it wasn't like he had said he'd call me at a certain time. Or even that night, for that matter. It was just that I had assumed he would. I had been hoping that after I finished my long day of work, I could unwind with Matt somewhere, maybe a romantic little bistro where we could talk about our days as we sipped French Bordeaux or something. Meg was right; we hadn't even technically had a first date yet. It clearly didn't count that he had crashed my date with someone else. I supposed I wanted to have one with him. But that was stupid. Obviously he had things to do. I couldn't very well expect him to just drop everything for me, now, could I?

I called Jill to check on her before I left the office, and she thanked me stiffly for my concern but reiterated that I didn't need to worry. I sighed, made small talk for a few minutes, and then we said our good-byes. Then I called Emmie to talk for a bit, but she was on the way out for a date with a guy she'd met at the grocery store. I smiled and shook my head; she could always be counted on to bring home a new man from a random location.

Finally, I wound up home alone with a stack of paperwork I'd been putting off these last two weeks. As I yawned and dived into patent applications for a new chlorine substitute, a new pain reliever in powder form, and a new artificial sweetener, I felt suspiciously like I had two weeks ago, before The Blonde Theory had started. But that was ridiculous; two weeks ago, I'd had no luck with dating and no prospects in sight. Now I had Matt.

Even if he didn't *technically* appear to be calling me at the moment.

Chapter Eighteen

There was no call from Matt that night. There was no call from Matt the next night, which I also spent home alone. And there was no call from Matt on Sunday, which threw me into a full-scale panic. Nearly *three days* had passed, three days since we had slept together, three days since I had become convinced that he was the answer to my prayers (or at least The Blonde Theory), three days since he had said, "I'll call you." And I even knew for a fact that his absence wasn't because of something logical like, for example, he'd been hit by a train on his way to work and had amnesia. No, Emmie had seen him at work every day. And he hadn't said a word about me to her. Furthermore, she said he didn't appear to have been hit by a train or otherwise mangled or maimed.

It also occurred to me around Saturday afternoon that he had my number and my address...but I didn't have his. I hated the lack of control that gave me. And I was starting to hate him for not calling. Okay, that was a lie. I don't think it would have been possible to hate him. I just felt like I was going quietly insane while I wondered where he was.

Emmie had offered to say something to him, to ask him why he hadn't called. I thought about it for a moment, but then asked her not to. All I needed was for Matt James to feel like I was chasing him.

On Sunday afternoon, after two long nights, two packs of Marlboro Lights, a bottle of Bacardi Limón, two bags of frozen Reese's Peanut Butter Cups, and approximately four additional pounds on my waistline, I finally decided to leave my apartment—and thus the Matt-hopeful security of waiting by my phone "just in case"—to go for a jog in Central Park, where I sweated in the early-June heat and felt downright disgusting. Flavored rum, Reese's, and little else weren't exactly the perfect pre-workout meal. But I needed to clear my mind.

An hour and a half later, my mind wasn't any clearer, but my stomach sure hurt a lot more. I huffed and puffed my way back to my apartment, trying to keep my mind off the Reese's and liquor sloshing around inside. *Note to self:* No more candy-alcohol-cigarette binges followed by jogs in the park. Bad idea. Very bad idea.

At least I could now take a long hot shower, wash away the day's aggravations, and settle into a long evening of legal work, just like usual, while I waited for Matt to call. I knew he would call. He *had* to call. And I knew there was a logical explanation for why he hadn't already. In the meantime, I would distract myself by finding comfort in routine. I had never looked forward more to my stack of legal briefs and manila folders full of patent application paperwork.

As I rounded the corner to my apartment after emerging from the elevator (what, was I supposed to walk up several flights of stairs after an hour-long jog on an upset stomach?), my heart skipped a beat for a split second as I saw a man standing on my doorstep. For an instant, I knew that it was Matt, finally Matt. Then he turned and grinned at me and I resisted the urge to groan.

"Hiya," said Sean the handyman, who was most decidedly *not* Matt James. He straightened up. "I thought you'd never get home, then, and I'd be stuck on your doorstep all evenin' while you were out on a hot date."

"No chance of that," I muttered, warily regarding the stack of towels that sat next to him on the ground, which were clearly the reason for his visit. He saw me looking at them and gestured their way.

"Seems you gave me the wrong towels," he said sheepishly. "I'm beginnin' to think you're just tryin' to lure me back here, Miss Harper Roberts."

I laughed, despite myself, as I squeezed past him to unlock my door.

"I'd be a lot slicker than that if that's what I was trying to do," I said, gesturing for him to come into my apartment. He bent to pick up the stack of towels, his sandy hair flipping into his face as he did so, then straightened up. "Come in," I said.

"Sure thing." Sean followed me into the apartment, and turned to close the door behind him. In the living room, he set the towels down on the large glass coffee table filled, unfortunately, not with magazines but with stacks upon stacks of legal briefs. "I see you had a really wild and crazy weekend," Sean said, his eyes twinkling as he gestured to my mounds of manila folders and legal pads.

"At least I'm getting back into a routine," I said defensively, immediately aware that Sean would have absolutely no idea what I was talking about. After all, he didn't know that for two weeks, I had been masquerading around the city as a dumb blonde with no taste in men. He didn't know that I had such an immense stack of work because I'd been procrastinating for the last two weeks in favor of ditzy dating.

I looked at the stack, feeling discouraged. What a waste of time it had been, the whole stupid Blonde Theory. I had gotten so behind at work, and what had I gained? The knowledge that 95 percent of the men in bars and on dating sites would prefer a ditz to a smart girl? I has already known that; the experiment had just driven the hurtful, unhelpful point home. What I had acquired, I supposed, was simply a cementing of the knowledge that I'd gleaned when Peter left three years ago—the fact that making partner in my firm had effectively killed my chances of having an actual relationship with anyone. Well, anyone but Matt, who obviously valued me for who I really was. Now I was almost worse off than when I'd started this whole stupid experiment. I was way behind in my work. And I couldn't keep my mind on anything anyhow, because I was worrying desperately about the fact that there had *still* been no word from Matt.

I glanced over at the answering machine on my desk as an afterthought and almost fell over when I saw it blinking. I practically knocked Sean over as I dashed across the room to push PLAY.

"Harper? Hi, it's Matt," said the familiar deep baritone from the tinny tape of my answering machine. I grinned from ear to ear and only managed to restrain myself from doing a happy dance because there was a virtual stranger in my living room watching me. "I'm sorry I missed you. I was just calling to say hello and to apologize for not being in touch. Things have just been crazy at work, and I've had a lot going on that I had to deal with outside of work. I'll try you again later, but I just wanted to tell you what a great time I had with you the other night. I've been thinking a lot about you, Harper. Talk to you soon."

The machine clicked off and I just stood there, smiling at it. I wanted to play the tape again (and again and again) but refrained, because I knew that would appear a bit obsessive to Sean.

"Is that your boyfriend, then?" Sean asked after a moment, curious, no doubt, about why a seemingly intelligent woman was standing stock-still in her living room, grinning like a fool.

"Oh no," I said immediately. Then I reconsidered, tilting my head to the side and trying on the sound of it for size. *My boyfriend. My boyfriend, Matt.* I liked it. "I mean, not exactly," I clarified. "He's a guy I'm sort of seeing."

"Lucky bloke," Sean said. I whirled around to look at him, but he was just grinning devilishly, which I knew meant that he was teasing me. What, he didn't think I could land a boyfriend?

"Look, he's a really nice guy," I said defensively. "We have a great time together. He actually likes me for who I am, you know."

"Well, I'm glad to hear that," Sean said, still looking amused. "I didn't mean any offense. I really meant it. He's a lucky bloke. You seem like a very nice girl."

"Oh," I said. I paused, still not sure if he was serious. But I gave him the benefit of the doubt. "Thanks."

I went into the bathroom to get the towels and returned to find that Sean had made himself at home, settling into one of my plush couches like he owned the place. I resisted the urge to get annoyed at him; after all, I had sort of created this awkward situation by mixing up the towels in the first place, and he had been nice enough to trek over here, yet again, to sort things out. But I didn't feel like socializing with the handyman at the moment. I wanted to shower, dry off with my *own* towels, change, and pretend to myself that I was attacking my legal briefs with enthusiasm while really I'd just be biding time while I waited for Matt to call back. I wondered briefly why he hadn't left his number on my machine but dismissed it as an oversight. He would call back, of course. He'd said he would.

Still, I felt bad that Sean had gone to all this effort. I needed to make some kind of polite gesture, just to let him know I appreciated it.

"Do you, uh, want a drink or something?" I asked as I plunked down his roommate's towels on the coffee table, on top of my legal briefs.

"I don't suppose you have Murphy's on tap in your kitchen there," he said, nodding toward my open kitchen, which I was actually very proud of due to the large kitchen island I'd had installed and the top-of-the-line smooth-top stove I'd bought last year.

I laughed and shook my head.

"Just some bottles of Newcastle," I said, knowing that he would say no. After all, he'd described my favorite beer as *shite* just a week ago.

"That'll have to do, then, won't it?" I just stared at him. He was saying yes? He settled comfortably back into my sofa as if he intended to stay for quite a while.

"You mean you want a Newcastle?" I asked. "Even though you hate it?"

"Well, *hate* is an awfully harsh word," Sean clarified. "I could never *hate* a beer. Well, maybe some of your cheaper American beers. But one Newcastle won't kill me."

"Oh," I said, dejected. It looked like Sean would be staying, at least long enough to down one of my apparently distasteful beers. "Okay then. I'll get you one."

I returned a moment later with two freshly opened Newcastles, one for him and one for me. Then, on second thought, I went back into the kitchen and got myself a bottle of water instead. There were only so many things my stomach could take today.

"No offense," I began, as brusquely as possible as I came back into the room, "but I don't have much time to chat. I have to get cleaned up and get to work on all these briefs." I gestured to the impressive display of work in front of us, thankful that it was giving me the excuse that I was looking for to hurry Sean through his Newcastle. Why did he want to stay and talk with me anyhow? He was nice and all, but he was just the handyman who had helped me with my toilet problem and had been nice enough to stay and lend me some towels.

"Point taken," Sean said with a smile. "I'll finish my beer and be on my way."

I felt instantly bad. I hadn't meant to be so rude.

"I'm sorry," I said. "I didn't mean it to sound that way. It's just that, well, I do have a lot of work to do."

"And you'll be waitin' around for your boyfriend to call back, I suspect," he added.

"Well...yes," I conceded, blushing and not even bothering to correct Sean by telling him again that Matt wasn't my boyfriend—at least not yet.

"Ah, dating," Sean said, shaking his head in a way that made him look wise beyond his years—and as if the weight of the world were currently on his shoulders. "It's a roller-coaster ride, that's for sure."

"Yeah," I agreed, nodding and sinking into the love seat that faced the couch Sean was sitting on.

He took a long sip of his beer and held up the bottle for me to see. "I'm goin' as fast as I can," he said with a wink.

I shook my head. "No, I'm sorry, I shouldn't have been so rude," I said. "Take your time. Honestly."

An uncomfortable silence descended over us for a moment as Sean sipped his Newcastle and I sipped my water, feeling suddenly self-conscious about the way I looked, which was sweat-drenched, makeup-free, and probably completely haggard.

"So, uh, do you have a girlfriend back home in Ireland?" I asked, finally breaking the silence with the only question I could think of to make conversation.

"No," Sean said, shaking his head. His seemingly ever-present smile slipped a bit. "I did. I was dating the same girl for a long time. We broke up about a year ago. There hasn't been anyone serious since."

"Oh," I said, not sure how to respond. "I'm sorry," I added finally.

Sean shrugged. "Nah, it was for the best," he said. "Kara was a nice girl, really. But we just grew apart over time. We still talk on occasion. She's doing really well, now, and I'm happy for her."

"Oh," I said, trying to conceive of a situation in which I'd be happy to hear that Peter was doing well. I came up empty. Most of my fantasies about Peter ended with severe bodily harm. I admired Sean for having the ability to split up amicably.

"What does this Kara do?" I asked finally, just to make conversation.

"She's a doctor," he said dismissively. "A pediatric oncologist."

I almost choked on my water.

"You were dating a doctor?" I sputtered, immediately regretting that once again, I'd managed to sound both rude and classist.

Sean looked a little offended.

"Well...yeah," he said finally, setting down his beer on the coffee table and looking at me closely. "It really didn't matter what she did for a living, although I admired her dedication to the kids. Relationships aren't about what two people do for a living. Relationships are about how two people connect with each other."

I involuntarily snorted.

"Yeah, right," I muttered. Sean was staring at me, which made me start to squirm uncomfortably. I felt compelled to explain. "Look, you don't understand. Guys are scared to death of me because I'm a lawyer. I mean, not this guy Matt who I'm seeing now. He likes that I'm smart. But pretty much every other guy I've been on a date with gets really freaked out that I'm an attorney. How can you say that people's jobs don't matter?"

"Because they don't," Sean said slowly, looking at me doubtfully. "I would have dated Kara whether she was a chambermaid or the prime minister of Ireland. Who cares, as long as two people are compatible?"

"But how can two people be compatible when one has a better job than the other?" I asked in desperation. I knew I sounded rude, but I didn't care. What he was saying was ludicrous. "Or when one of them makes more money than the other? Inevitably, one of them is going to feel overshadowed."

"Why?" Sean asked. "Why would anyone feel that way if they were satisfied with their own life?"

I looked at him in exasperation. Why didn't he understand? Why couldn't he see how hard it was to be me?

"You don't understand," I finally muttered.

He gazed at me long and hard for a moment. "No, I guess I don't," he said finally, shaking his head. He wasn't smiling anymore. "Look, I know I have no place saying this. I know I'm just the guy who's come to fix your toilet and who you can't seem to get rid of. But I'm going to go ahead and say it anyway: Maybe you're part of the problem, too."

"What?" I asked, startled and offended. How dare he? What was he even talking about? He didn't know me. He didn't know my life. And now he was telling me that *I* was the problem?

"Let me ask you something," he continued, clearly choosing to ignore the fact that my entire body had gone rigid with anger. "When's the last time you went on a date with someone who wasn't a lawyer? Or a doctor? Or another job that people consider important or successful?"

I opened and closed my mouth then opened it again and just gaped at him. Who did he think he was? I didn't have to listen to this.

"What's your point?" I asked coldly.

"You haven't, have you?" he asked. My silence was all the answer he needed. "You only date guys you perceive as being just as successful as you are."

"That's not true," I protested, realizing as I said it that perhaps there *was* just the tiniest bit of truth to his words. "Besides, even if I *did* do that, it's not like I'm being elitist or something. It's because I *have* to. I can't date someone who doesn't have a good job. He'll only wind up hating me for being successful, just like my ex-boyfriend did."

"Ah," Sean said, nodding wisely, which just infuriated me more. "So that's what this is all about."

I stiffened. I felt like I was being psychoanalyzed, and I didn't like it one bit. "Don't act like you know me," I snapped.

"I *don't* know you," Sean said. "But I do know one thing. You're assuming that every guy is going to be like this ex-boyfriend of yours."

"They all are," I said sourly. "I think three years of testing out that theory has been enough to prove that to me, at least. Every guy I go out with eventually leaves because he feels threatened."

"Did you ever consider," Sean asked slowly, "that some guys out there might not *care* how much money you make? Or how successful you are? That maybe they value other things? That maybe all men aren't so intent on climbing some kind of corporate ladder? That maybe they haven't all lost sight of what's really important?"

"Yeah, right," I scoffed. "And where are these guys hiding? I sure haven't met any of them."

"Maybe you're not looking in the right places," Sean said slowly. He reached for his Newcastle and took another long sip, draining the bottle. Then he stood up and waggled the empty bottle in my general direction. "I'm pretty sure I've overstayed my welcome," he said a bit sheepishly. "If you can just tell me where to throw this out, I'll be on my way."

I silently stood up, yanked the bottle away from him, and walked into the kitchen, where I tossed it into the recycling bin under the sink. Then I returned to the living room and glowered at him.

"I'm sorry you had to come all the way back here for the towels," I said stiffly. I paused, and although it pained me to do so after he'd been so rude, I added, "And I'm sorry if I offended you by reacting with surprise when you said you had dated a doctor. That was very impolite of me."

Sean shrugged, then bent to pick up the towels that he'd come for.

"'Tis all right," he said. "I'm sorry, too. I shouldn't have said so much to you. You're right. I don't know you."

"No, you don't," I said as we walked toward the door. "It's not as simple as you're making it out to be."

"But it is," Sean said after a pause, turning to face me as I opened the door for him. "It *is* that simple. You're not dating the right guys."

"Yeah, well, you're wrong," I snapped. "You don't know me. And you don't know what it's like to be a lawyer and try to date."

"Okay then," Sean said with finality, clearly choosing to ignore my last comment. He forced a smile and nodded at me. "Anyhow, thanks for the towels. And for the beer. I'll be seeing you around, I guess."

"Yeah," I muttered. "See you around."

Then, without any additional commentary or pretense of politeness, I slammed the door behind him.

How dare he? My blood was boiling as I stalked back to the living room and threw myself down on the couch, glaring at the mound of towels that Sean had left behind. Even though they were mine, I had the illogical desire to open my window and toss them all out, just to rid myself of all things related to the irritating, know-it-all handyman. Who did he think he was? Sure, in an ideal world, his words made sense. But this was no ideal world. This was reality. And in my reality, guys were universally intimidated by me. What, I should be trying to date handymen or something because there might be one diamond in the rough who wasn't intimidated that my salary was ten times what he brought home every year? Yeah, *that* was really likely. *Gee, great thinking, Sean. Clearly, that's the answer to my prayers.*

Besides, he was just supposed to come fix my toilet. Not offer unsought commentary on my life and my dating situation. That was the last time *I'd* call a handyman service.

Anyhow, it was all moot. I had Matt now. What did it matter how intimidating I had been to men in the past? I had finally found one who respected and liked the fact that I was an attorney. For once, my success was a turn-*on,* not a turnoff. And I wasn't going to let the words of a rude handyman—or anything else—get in the way of my newfound happiness.

I took a shower and settled into the tedious process of drafting two new patent applications, knowing that Matt would call at any moment and make me feel better about everything.

Chapter Nineteen

*B*y Tuesday morning, I was fuming. *Fuming*. Matt hadn't called again. And all that had shown up on my caller ID from his Sunday-night call was UNAVAILABLE. I didn't know his number. I didn't know where he lived. I was reduced to a pathetic girl waiting by the phone all weekend, waiting for some guy to call. I had *never* been that girl, and yet there I was, biting my nails, eating ice cream, and feeling my eyes glaze over as I went through enough legal paperwork to make my head explode, all in an effort to distract myself from what I was really doing, which was waiting by the phone for a call from a guy who apparently hadn't thought twice about me.

What bothered me most was that it made *no sense*. He had really liked me. I *knew* he did. He was the first person who had seen me for *me* and hadn't run screaming in the other direction. How could I have lost him already? Through no fault of my own?

"How sad," Emmie said drily when I called her cell phone on Tuesday morning to complain. "He must have died over the weekend."

I couldn't help but laugh. That had been Emmie's answer every time a guy had dropped off the face of the earth following a date with one of us (although it seemed to happen to me a lot more than it did to her). "How sad. He must have died," she would always say, entirely straight-faced. "He was so young to go. Too bad."

But today, even though her words made me laugh, they didn't lighten the mood as they usually did. I felt terrible; I couldn't shake the feeling that perhaps I had done something to offend him on his way out the door, although I couldn't imagine what.

"Honestly, Harper, he's probably just busy," Emmie said after realizing that even her proclamations of certain death weren't helping me this morning. "Guys don't think about things the same way we do. You know that. It probably hasn't even occurred to him that he owes you a call."

"I don't want him to feel like he *owes* me," I mumbled. "I thought he would *want* to call me."

Emmie offered again to say something to Matt at work that day, but again, I turned her down. This wasn't junior high, where she could hand him a note that asked him to "check *yes*" if he liked me. Although I had to admit, I was behaving suspiciously like an insecure preteen. Maybe I would *have* to resort to a note, folded into those fancy triangles I remembered from my own middle-school days.

At nine thirty, an hour and a half before my first appointment of the day, Molly buzzed me to say that I had a visitor. I sighed. Somehow in the last week, everyone in my life had apparently unanimously decided to veto the calling-ahead rule in favor of the random drop-in. What, like I didn't have an important schedule at work?

My first thought, though, was that it might be Matt. Annoyed as I was at him for basically ignoring me for the last five days, I figured that a random drop-in would make it up to me, at least a little bit. I mean, in the time we had been together, Peter had never cared enough to go out of his way to drop in on me at all, even though his firm was a mere three blocks away. I'd always resented that he couldn't make a romantic gesture that minuscule. If Matt was able to swing by within a week of getting together with me, it would go a long way toward absolving him of his conspicuous absence over the last five days.

"Who is it?" I finally asked Molly after debating the possibilities in my mind.

"It's your friend Jill," she whispered into the phone. "And she looks upset."

"Oh my God," I said, my heart catching in my throat. "Thanks, Molly. Please show her in right away."

I was already crossing my office when the door opened seconds later to reveal a worried Molly, her eyes wide behind her thick glasses, and a red-eyed Jill, whose clothing and hair were disheveled like I'd never seen before.

"Thanks, Molly," I murmured, shooting her an appreciative glance as I wrapped Jill in a tight hug. Molly nodded, mouthed *Good luck,* and backed out, shutting the door behind her.

"Are you okay?" I asked, rubbing Jill's back as I continued to embrace her. I could feel her shoulders shake as she started to sob into my shoulder. "Did Alec do something else to you? Jill, I swear, I'll kill him."

In that moment, I think I really meant it. I was sick of men hurting me and the people I loved. I might as well take all my annoyance at the male gender out on Alec in particular. After all, he seemed to be the slimiest example of a man that I'd ever seen— worse, even, than Peter. At least Peter hadn't *married* me before revealing himself as a weak, sniveling jerk.

"No," Jill said, finally pulling away and looking at me with eyes so bloodshot I knew immediately she'd been sleeping little and crying a lot for the past few days. "He didn't do anything else. I've just been doing a lot of thinking. Can we sit down?"

I nodded quickly and led Jill over to one of the leather chairs facing my desk. She sank into it slowly, and gratefully took the tissue I handed her from the box on my desk. I sat down in the chair beside her and stroked her arm. She was silent for a moment as she wiped away her tears and then softly blew her nose in a far more feminine manner than I could have managed. I always sounded like a foghorn. It figured that even her nose blowing would be dainty.

Finally, between sniffles, she mumbled something unintelligible, her voice muffled by the tissue she was holding up to her face.

"What?" I asked gently.

"I have to leave him," she repeated. She sniffed and blinked a few times. "Don't I?" She spoke the last two words with finality, more a statement of resignation than a question. I didn't know what to say. She looked up at me, her face a storm of emotions, as if she were struggling to understand something. "Don't I?" she repeated, her voice a bit stronger this time.

I hesitated, then nodded. "Yes," I said simply. "You do."

I didn't know what else to say. I don't think that Jill *wanted* me to say anything else. She just nodded in acceptance and dabbed at her eyes with a tissue again. Her tears had slowed now, and she was looking down at her lap intently. It seemed to be difficult for her to look at me. I continued rubbing her arm comfortingly, waiting for her to say more.

"I need your help," she said finally, still not meeting my gaze. "I know you're not a divorce attorney. But you can still help me file papers, right?"

"Yes, of course, of course," I said quickly. "I'll do anything I can to help. One of my friends from law school, David Ahern, is one of the best divorce lawyers in the city. I'll get him involved, too. Okay?"

"Okay," Jill agreed softly with a tiny nod.

"You're doing the right thing," I said after a long silence. Jill, still looking at her lap and not at me, nodded.

"I know," she whispered. "It's just so hard."

Her tears began again, and I scooted my chair closer to hers so that I could wrap my arms around her and hold her while she cried. Her sobs racked her body in a way that shook me to the core.

"You were right, you know," Jill said, finally pulling back from me after several minutes of sobbing. She sat back in her chair and looked me in the eye, almost reluctantly.

"About Alec?" I asked.

Jill hesitated. "No," she said softly. "About me. About how I can't make something perfect just because I want it to be."

I stared at her. I couldn't remember ever having said that to her, although I'd thought it a thousand times, especially when she was about to marry Alec.

"But I didn't—" I started to protest.

Jill cut me off with a small, tear-stained smile. "I know," she said. "You didn't have to. I knew what you were thinking."

"Oh," I said, feeling tremendously guilty that my friend had felt so judged by me. I hadn't meant to make her feel that way. "I'm sorry," I said.

"Don't be," she said with a soft smile. "You were right."

I nodded slowly, and we sat there for several moments in silence.

"What made you change your mind?" I asked finally. After all, just days earlier, Jill had been insisting that things were okay, that Alec hadn't really cheated on her, that they were working on their marriage and that things would be perfect again.

She gave me a crooked half smile. "You did."

"Me?" I couldn't imagine what she meant. I'd been no different to her last week than Meg and Emmie had been. In fact, if anything, I'd been worse, by turning off my ringer while I went to bed with Matt and missing her call. *Matt.* My heart temporarily ached at the thought of him. *Where is he?* But that didn't matter now. What mattered was Jill coming to the realization that she needed to leave the man she had once thought was the embodiment of her dream of perfection.

"You and that dumb Blonde Theory," she said with another sad-looking half smile.

"I don't understand," I said.

"You had the courage to try it out, even though it went against everything you believed," she said. "And you learned that at the end of the day, even if things seem easier if you're pretending, you can't make things perfect by being anyone other than you."

"I did?" I asked without even thinking about it. I hadn't exactly put into words *what* I'd learned yet, but Jill's vocalization was surprisingly on target.

"Didn't you?" she asked.

"I guess I *did*," I said thoughtfully. I thought about Matt. I *had* been myself with him. And things still didn't seem to be perfect, although they had been five days ago when he'd shown up at my door and convinced me that he liked me for who I was. But if that was true, where was he now?

Jill's tears began falling again, and I reached out to give her a hug.

"I'm so sorry, Jill," I said, really meaning it. Even though she had grated on me over the years by acting like she was superior because she knew how to "land a man," as she put it, I never wanted her to hurt. I never wanted this for her. She was my friend. I wished she could have had that happily-ever-after she'd wanted so desperately.

"I'll be fine," she said, forcing a smile and drying her tear-stained cheeks with a fresh tissue. Her eyes filled again. "I'll just need your help. And Meg's. And Emmie's."

"Of course, of course," I said instantly. "We're all here for you."

She smiled again, a real smile this time.

"I know," she said softly, reaching out to squeeze my hand.

JILL STAYED FOR another hour, and my mind was still on her when my eleven o'clock appointment arrived. After I had talked to the head of research and development for BakersGrain, a new cereal manufacturer, about a potential patent for a cereal he had overseen the development of, I shut the door to my office, ordered Chinese delivery, and asked Molly to hold my calls. I just needed to catch my breath and get ahold of my thoughts.

But five minutes later, just as I was closing my eyes and leaning back in my chair, Molly buzzed me. I looked at my intercom in confusion; it was too soon for the Chinese food.

"What is it, Molly?" I asked, trying not to sound annoyed. Usually, she was great at leaving me undisturbed if I asked her for a few minutes of peace and quiet.

"Um, I'm sorry to bother you," she said guiltily. "It's just that there's someone here to see you." She lowered her voice, then whispered, "Matt James."

My heart skipped a beat and I sat straight up in my chair.

"Give me a second, then send him in," I said. "Thanks," I added as an afterthought.

My heart thudding in anticipation, I dug through my purse until I found some concealer, my Tarte blotting papers, some lipstick, and my powder compact. I quickly made repairs to my face as well as I could, ran a brush through my hair, then sat back in my chair, trying to look as calm, cool, and casual as possible. After all, I didn't want Matt to know that I'd been waiting by the phone for his call. How pathetic was that? I was *far* too busy to worry about him. Or at least that's what I wanted him to believe.

"Hey, Harper," Matt said a moment later as he entered my office. My breath caught in my throat. He looked as gorgeous as ever. He had had a haircut in the five days since I had last seen him, so his thick, dark shock of hair was noticeably shorter. His tanned, chiseled face was clean-shaven, and his green eyes looked gloriously bright against his olive-green T-shirt. His distressed jeans hugged him in all the right places, I noticed with near-physical pain as he turned to shut my door behind him.

"Hi, Matt," I said stiffly. I rose from my chair but didn't come out from around my desk. I looked at him warily, my heart pounding as I flashed back to the night we'd spent making love for hours, just days ago. I cleared my throat and was glad that my desk was a buffer between us. I was torn between wanting to jump him and rip his clothes off…and wanting to strangle him for waiting until Sunday to call and then not leaving me his number.

"Sorry that I was out of touch for several days, Harper," he said, as if reading my mind. He looked somewhat ashamed, and I instantly softened, then reminded myself not to get too comfortable, not to let him get away with it. After all, I'd *slept* with this guy. He owed me more than an appearance in my office five days late. So I simply grunted in response.

"I figured you were a bit mad," he continued with a guilty shrug. "Your friend Emmie was muttering something about dying and funerals or something this morning," he added, looking momentarily confused. "I still don't know what she was talking about, but it seemed to have something to do with you and me."

"I really don't know," I said stiffly, trying not to giggle. I made a mental note to strangle her—in the nicest of ways, of course—later.

"I just got really busy with some things around my apartment this weekend," he explained sheepishly. "I should have called you again. Really, that was terrible of me. I had such an amazing time with you last week. That's why I came over here today. I couldn't wait to see you again."

"Hmph," I grunted again, trying to project coldness in his general direction rather than the *I love you, I love you! Take me now!* vibes that I was fairly sure I was sending out instead.

Just then, my office phone rang. I stood there awkwardly for a moment, not sure what to do. Should I answer it? Or pretend that I didn't hear it or didn't care? Finally, realizing it might be Jill, I reached for the receiver.

"Harper?" It was Meg, her voice sounding urgent. "I'm sorry to bother you. I know you're in a meeting, but I asked Molly to put me through. You talked to Jill this morning?" Her voice was urgent, but I wanted to tell her that I'd talk to her later, that I was busy now. Matt had apparently appeared in my office to beg my forgiveness. (And perhaps, if I was lucky, also to fling my papers from my desk, throw me onto it, and make passionate love to me on the spot. Okay, maybe not. Maybe I needed to cut back on the number of times I watched *The Rich and the Damned*.)

"Yes," I said carefully, glancing at Matt. I suddenly had an idea. Immature as it was, it would be nice to make Matt feel at least a little bit of the insecurity I'd been feeling in his absence for the last five days. Fight fire with fire, so to speak. So, realizing that of course I would confuse Meg terribly, I said into the receiver, "Dinner tonight? Yes, I'd love to. I'll call you back in a little while." I hung up, ignoring Meg's surprised protests.

"Who was that?" Matt asked. I knew it wasn't my imagination that he looked a little jealous.

"My ex-boyfriend Peter," I lied with a cavalier shrug that belied the way my heart was thudding inside my chest. "I'm having dinner with him tonight," I added, as casually as I could. "He's interested in getting back together."

"Oh," Matt said, seemingly at a temporary loss for words. He drew a deep breath. "Okay then. I was actually coming over to see if you'd have dinner with *me* tonight. But I guess you've made other plans."

I suddenly wanted to leap over my desk, throw myself at him, and beg his forgiveness. I wanted to tell him that Peter didn't mean anything to me, that it hadn't been him on the phone after all, that I'd only been trying to make him jealous, as immature as that was. But I couldn't. Not after Matt had let five days go by without talking to me. Not after I had spent the last five days pining away for him.

"Yes, I have other plans," I said instead, my voice stiff. "Maybe some other time."

"Yeah," Matt said sadly, backing toward the door. "Maybe another time."

I watched him back away, wondering if this was it. Maybe I had been stupid to think that he actually liked me. Maybe he was about to back right out of my life. But I didn't want to let him go that easily.

"Why didn't you call me, Matt?" I blurted out suddenly, surprising myself with my frankness.

He looked surprised, too. "I did call," he said. "On Sunday."

"But you didn't call for three days. And then when you did, you didn't leave a number." The words were tumbling out of my mouth of their own accord. But the hurt that I'd been trying to ignore was suddenly bubbling to the surface. "It's like you didn't want to talk to me."

"Oh, Harper, that's not true at all," Matt said, looking ashamed. I felt a bit sorry for him, despite myself. "I'm so sorry. The other night meant a lot to me. I didn't mean to make you feel that way. Sometimes I just get so caught up in my own life that whole days pass by without me noticing. But I should never have done that to you. I shouldn't have made you feel that way."

"Oh," I said, not sure what to say. His apology seemed genuine, his eyes looked concerned, and his shoulders were slumped in what appeared to be defeat. He took another step closer to my office door and looked up to meet my eye again.

"I *am* really sorry, Harper," Matt said, his hand on the knob. "Honestly. I should have called. I really like you. I hope you know that. I hope that your, um, dinner goes well tonight."

Then he was gone, leaving me staring after him helplessly, not quite sure what I'd just done.

Chapter Twenty

I spent the rest of the day wishing that I hadn't spontaneously lied to Matt about my fictional date with Peter, who, of course, hadn't actually bothered to call me in the past three years. I wondered for a moment why, of all the names that could have come to mind, his was the one I chose to wound Matt with. It seemed sort of pathetic. Why was I still holding on to Peter, three years after he had summarily dumped me? It wasn't that I had any desire to get back together with him. It was just that I hadn't had any closure with him. It had been smooth sailing one day, and the next, the entire boat on which our relationship happily coasted had capsized.

For three years, I had let thoughts of him rule my mind. I had let the insecurities that he had planted when he left fester. I had let his weaknesses and fears rule and ruin my dating life. I was so terrified that every man would turn out to be as threatened by me as Peter was that I pushed away any chance of happiness. Matt had come to me today with an apology and a dinner invitation, and I had thrown it back in his face, like an immature child, simply because his behavior had left me terrified that he, too, would turn out like Peter. It was as if I was waiting for every man on the planet to flee in terror once he got to know the real me.

But this time, I had actively driven Matt away. He hadn't been about to bolt. But I had self-defensively lied, and in doing so, I had pushed away the only man who had been willing and ready to see and love me for who I really was.

As I sat home alone that night, staring blankly and miserably at the wall, I knew suddenly what I had to do.

I had to get to Matt. I was thoroughly confused, my insides a storm of conflicting feelings. But one thing was clear: I had to get to Matt and apologize before I permanently screwed up the one good thing that had come out of this whole Blonde Theory.

I called Emmie, who answered after the first ring.

"What's wrong, are you okay?" she asked immediately, her word tumbling out quickly on top of each other. "Meg said you were really weird on the phone today."

"No," I said, laughing, despite myself, at her blind concern. "It's fine. I promise, I'll tell you all about it later. But right now, I really need you to help me find Matt's number."

"Matt James?" she asked incredulously.

"I promise I'll explain later, Emmie," I said urgently. "This is just something I need to do now. Please?"

Emmie agreed and asked me to hold while she rifled through her address book, her Palm Pilot, and her file of paperwork from the show. A few minutes later, she was back on the phone.

"I can't find his number," she said. "But I have his address. Will that work?"

"Yes," I said urgently. "Can you give it to me now?"

"Just be careful," Emmie said with concern.

"Don't worry," I reassured her. "I'm finally doing the right thing. I know it."

I quickly hailed a cab outside and gave the driver Matt's address, which I had hastily scribbled on a Post-it note. While the cab sped downtown, darting in and out of traffic on Fifth, my heart thudded in my chest and I tried to think of what I would say.

I knew I needed to apologize. I'd acted immaturely, and I had risked blowing a really good thing. Yes, he had left me hanging for several days, but he had come to my office today with an honest apology. And instead of accepting it, I had lied and blown him off, just to make him jealous. I was ashamed of my behavior.

Twenty long minutes later, we pulled up across the street from Matt's building, a canopied doorman building on the west side of Park Avenue between 20th and 21st. I was just about to give the driver a ten and hurry out of the cab to make amends when a familiar figure inside the building's lobby across the street caught my eye. I froze and peered inside the glass entryway to Matt's building, my insides suddenly cold and twisted, my mouth dry. I recognized him immediately. It was Matt, with his dark hair spiked in that sexy skater way, a button-up shirt untucked over distressed, faded jeans... and his arms around a woman who looked familiar, too.

I stared. It was Lisa, the woman who had been with Matt when he showed up to crash my date with Jack, the political analyst. The woman he had dismissed as "just a friend," making me feel ridiculous for being jealous.

Through the glass, Matt was saying something to Lisa, bending close to whisper in her ear. She was giggling. I couldn't help but notice, with a rising feeling of nausea, that he still had both arms around her, wrapping her in a loose hug that looked almost romantic.

I shook my head at myself and blinked. I was being stupid. There was nothing going on. She was just a friend, as he had told me the other day. They had probably just grabbed a cup of coffee or a quick, friendly dinner together and were saying good-bye. Maybe he had even asked her advice about me. I was just on edge. Thoughts of Peter, his lasting legacy apparently, had soured me to such an extent that I was suspicious of everyone, even the people who I should be trusting most.

"Are you staying or going?" the cabbie barked, staring at me in the rearview mirror and snapping me back to the present. I met his eye in the mirror and smiled ruefully.

"Yeah, sorry," I said. "I'm going."

I started to reach over the seat with the ten-dollar bill clenched in my fist, and as I did so, I glanced back at Matt's building, just to make sure he and Lisa were still in the lobby. It would be easier if I didn't have to ask the doorman to call up to his apartment and announce an unexpected guest.

But as I glanced back into the glass-encased lobby, I froze, clenching the ten-dollar bill so tightly that the cabdriver had to practically rip it from my hand.

"Lady, I don't got all day here," he growled as he stuffed the ten into his pocket ungratefully. "This ain't a sightseeing bus."

But I couldn't move. I could only stare, glued to my seat, eyes wide, face pressed up against the cab window, as I watched Matt kissing Lisa. It wasn't the kind of kiss anyone would give to "just a friend." This was the kind of kiss Matt had given me just the other day.

The world seemed frozen as I watched, horrified, the man who had only hours earlier proclaimed his feelings for me passionately making out with another woman—a beautiful, glamorous, stick-thin woman.

"Go," I finally choked out to the driver, unable to tear my eyes away from the sight. "Go, go!" I barked, suddenly terrified that Matt would look out and see me. I'd look like I was skulking in the shadows, spying on him.

"Are you crazy, lady?" the cabbie asked, staring at me angrily in the rearview. "Now you *don't* want to get out? Make up your mind!"

"Just take me home!" I said, quickly telling him the address. "I'll tip you extra. Please, just go."

He rolled his eyes pointedly at me one last time in the rearview then inched back into the northbound traffic, muttering to himself.

As we pulled out of sight of Matt's lobby, I leaned back in the seat and closed my eyes, breathing hard. I didn't know what to think.

I knew one thing, though. This was my fault. I was sure of it. If I hadn't pretended to be going out with Peter just to hurt Matt, this never would have happened. Sure, there was no excuse for him kissing Lisa, and to be honest I couldn't understand it. But I knew it had to have something to do with the awful way I had treated him. Clearly, this was some kind of rebound coping mechanism on his part. After all, what had happened between us last week hadn't been a figment of my imagination. He liked me. I knew he really liked me—for who I was. And I had gone and screwed it all up. I had hurt him, and this was how he had reacted.

I opened my eyes and gazed out at the city inching by outside the cab windows. We were just east of the big, touristy area of Times Square now, and all around us couples seemed to be walking hand in hand. Sure, there were people by themselves, too, but in my current state I seemed only to notice the happy pairs—old, young, and everywhere in between—hand in hand, arm in arm, and side by side. Why couldn't I have that, too? Why wasn't I half of one of those happy couples, strolling through the streets of New York without a care in the world, knowing I had found the person I loved? How did I manage to screw it up, every single time? I pounded a fist into the beaten leather of the cab's backseat in frustration and ignored the driver's sharp glance in the rearview mirror.

If I had just followed my heart and forgiven Matt this afternoon, rather than trying to make some stupid point, this wouldn't be happening right now. For that matter, if I had just allowed my stupid career to take a backseat to my social life—even occasionally—I wouldn't be in this position in the first place. What was wrong with me that I felt like I needed to be the best patent lawyer in the city? Maybe Peter had been right all along, and I *had* treated him badly, *had* put my stupid, meaningless professional needs ahead of him. Granted, he had behaved abominably, but maybe I was to blame, too. The blame was certainly on my shoulders in this situation with Matt.

Why couldn't I get it right?

Maybe my lack of success in dating had nothing to do with my job. Maybe it had to do with *me*. Maybe I was too demanding. Maybe I expected too much of people. Maybe I was too disappointed in them when they did things that I perceived as wrong. Maybe I held people—including myself—to standards that were too high. After all, I had done that with Jill, hadn't I? I'd been so judgmental about her situation. Maybe I did that with guys, too. Maybe I didn't even give them the chance to love me. Maybe it was *me* who pushed them away, not my job and my success.

Regardless, I had somehow managed to screw up the only chance I'd had in three years to be with a guy who actually liked me for me.

As the cabbie pulled up in front of my building, I heard him audibly mumbling something about how he always wound up with "the crazies." Maybe he was right. I dragged myself out of the cab, sniffing back my tears as I shut the door behind me. Maybe I really was crazy. That would explain a lot.

An hour later, I had changed into an old pair of jeans and a T-shirt, but I hadn't bothered to clean up my tear-stained face. Why should I? I was destined to be alone forever, apparently. So who cared how I looked?

I settled back into my plush leather sofa, hating it for the first time, because it was the fruit of me working too hard. I frowned at my wide-screen TV as I snapped it on with the remote control, because it, too, was one of the perks that came from making a mid-six-figure income instead of actually being able to date like a normal human being. I sighed and glanced at the omnipresent mound of manila folders on the coffee table in front of me. Then, as an afterthought, I kicked them off the table with one swift shot of my right foot, sending them flying all over the room. In that moment, I hated them, hated this apartment, hated everything I had built for myself, because it meant I had neglected one whole area of my life—love—as if it meant nothing. And now it was too late to make things right.

I bit my nails as I flipped through the channels, a nervous, self-destructive habit that I often took to when things in my life seemed to be going south. Finally, I settled on a *Seinfeld* rerun and settled back to watch George and Jerry discuss whether the Yankees should be wearing cotton or polyester uniforms. I intently nibbled on the nail on my index finger, trying to forget that today had even happened. I longed to go back to two weeks ago, before I had started The Blonde Theory, before Matt had told me he was attracted to me, before Peter had "reappeared" in my life, and before the annoying Irish handyman had called me out and tried to force me to admit that *I* was the problem.

Fine, I admitted it. I *was* the problem. I had completely screwed everything up. And I apparently continued to do so.

I had just settled into a second episode of *Seinfeld,* the one where Elaine dates the close-talker, when there was a knock on the door.

"If that's that damned handyman again," I muttered as I heaved myself off my couch, glancing around for stray towels I might have somehow missed, "I'm going to kill him."

I opened the door, harshly, fully prepared to snap at whoever was on my doorstep, interrupting my sulking. But my eyes widened as I realized that it was Matt James standing there, a puppy-dog expression on his face, looking sad. His shoulders were slumped, and he was wearing the same untucked shirt and distressed Diesel jeans that I'd seen through the windows of the cab just an hour before.

"Matt," I breathed, a whole tidal wave of emotions flooding through me. I felt angry and hurt after seeing him with Lisa.

But more than that, I felt sad, hopeless, and very, very guilty. I had put this whole chain of events into motion. This was my fault.

"Hey, Harper," he said softly, hanging his head. "Can I come in?"

"Of course," I breathed, stepping aside so that he could cross the threshold. He looked glum, and I longed to reach over and pull him into a hug, but I was on edge after seeing him with Lisa and didn't know quite how to address it. Plus, I didn't understand what he was doing here.

"How was your date?" he asked softly after I had shut the door behind him. My eyes welled up, and I quickly blinked back the tears.

"Matt, I'm so sorry," I said, the words spilling out on top of each other. He turned to face me, and I looked him right in the eye even though I wanted to look away in shame. "I should never have said that to you. Peter never called. I don't know what I was doing. I don't know why I said that."

He just stood there for a moment, staring at me, before he reached out and wrapped me tightly in his strong arms, pulling me close. My body felt weak as he pressed me into his muscular chest. I breathed in the intoxicating scent of his cologne, loving the protective feel of being nestled against him.

"It's okay," Matt said finally, his words slow and soothing. "I forgive you. I understand. I really like you, and I don't want this to get in our way."

"I really like you, too," I said softly.

I looked up at him gratefully, waiting for him to continue. I was thankful we were clearing the air. I waited for him to tell me about Lisa and apologize for that, too, so that we could start over again.

But instead, he just continued to rub my back comfortingly and run his fingers through my hair tenderly.

"Let's promise that nothing like this will happen again," he murmured. "That we'll always be honest with each other."

"Okay," I agreed eagerly, wondering if he was about to admit his misstep with Lisa and explain what he was thinking. Still, no admission seemed to be forthcoming. Sighing, I took the lead. "What did you do tonight?" I asked innocently.

Matt released me and took a step back. He smiled down at me.

"I just stayed in by myself," he said, shrugging as if helpless to control his own actions and decision. "I couldn't stop thinking of you."

I looked at him for a moment, frozen in place. He looked back at me, his face innocent as a newborn baby's. Slowly, a thought began to creep into my mind. *He's an actor,* said a little warning voice in my head. I tried to ignore it. Surely he hadn't been acting with me.

"Matt," I said finally, choosing my words carefully and trying not to sound accusatory. I knew there was a logical explanation. "I went by your apartment tonight, to apologize. I wanted to tell you how sorry I was and how I didn't feel anything for Peter anymore. But..." I paused because the words were hard for me to say. I drew a deep breath and continued. "But I saw you kissing the woman you were with at the restaurant last week. *Lisa.*"

I said her name as if it were a bad word. Matt visibly stiffened. Then he shrugged.

"Yeah, okay," he said finally. "What's the big deal?"

"The big deal?" I repeated incredulously. "You were kissing another woman! Aren't you going to apologize?"

"Why?" Matt asked defensively. He shrugged again. "She's just my stockbroker."

"Your stockbroker?" I repeated, failing to see how this was any kind of an explanation.

"Sure," Matt said. "She's one of the women I date."

"*One* of the women?" I repeated, taken aback. I felt suddenly short of breath.

"Yeah. Is something wrong with that? I always date several women at a time."

"You... you do?" I asked slowly. I flashed back to Emmie telling me that there were rumors that he was a player but that he'd never dated anyone on set as far as she knew. I had dismissed her words. Now it appeared that the joke was on me.

"Sure," Matt said, looking at me as if I were crazy. "Why not? I'm an actor. I'm a good-looking guy. I'm in my prime. And women like you go crazy for me."

"Women like me?" I repeated incredulously. I was suddenly feeling very weak.

"Powerful women," he said, gazing dreamily off into the space behind me. "Doctors. Directors. Investment bankers. Women with balls. Figuratively speaking, of course. God, what a turn-on." He turned his attention back to me and smiled gently. "But attorneys are my favorite, Harper. They always have been."

I gaped at him, trying hard to grasp what he was saying.

"You only wanted to date me because I'm a lawyer?" I finally asked, appalled, my voice cracking on the last word. I felt as if my stomach might overturn.

"Well, yeah," he said, looking surprised. "And you're adorable and very cool, of course. But yeah, the whole power thing is a real turn-on for me."

"Oh my God," I murmured, horror flooding through me.

"What's the problem?" Matt asked, looking truly mystified. "I thought that's what you wanted. Didn't you want someone who wanted to be with you because you're smart and because you have a good job?"

I just stared at him, processing his words slowly. I'd been so flattered when he'd said he didn't like me despite my job but because of it. But I hadn't taken his words literally. I had assumed that he'd meant that my job was just *one* of the facets about me that he found attractive—not the primary one.

I felt sick. He had clearly slept with the majority of Manhattan's female upper echelon. I was apparently just another powerful notch on his belt.

"Please leave," I whispered finally, the sight of him in my entryway with wide, innocent eyes nauseating me. "Please just go now."

Matt looked at me blankly. "You want me to leave?"

I gaped at him. What, did he think his words would win me over and I'd want him to stay? That I was masochistically looking for someone to appreciate me only for my job and then dash out of my apartment to go sleep with the next single girl on the block with a six-figure income?

"Right now," I said firmly. My eyes were welling with tears, and I didn't want to give Matt the satisfaction of seeing me cry. Matt started to protest, but I cut him off with a deadly stare. "Now," I said coldly. "I'm not going to ask you again."

He stared hard at me, then finally shrugged, as if in defeat, and took the few steps toward my front door.

"Call me when you change your mind," he said with a small smile. Clearly, he wasn't accustomed to being rejected and didn't, in fact, recognize it when it was happening. "I won't hold this against you."

I didn't say anything. Trembling with anger now, I reached behind him, opened my door, and gestured sharply with a flick of my wrist that he should get out. Shrugging once more, he backed into the hallway and opened his mouth to say something else. But I didn't care what else he had to say. I slammed the door right in his face with a finality I hoped sent him the message that I intended, which was to stay away. Forever. I never wanted to see him again.

I stood there in my front entryway, trying to get the tremors racking my body under control. I didn't think I'd ever felt this angry—or this stupid. I couldn't believe I had believed him. A large part of my anger was currently directed at myself for being so desperate to find someone that I never paused to consider that Matt might not be all he was cracked up to be.

I closed my eyes and leaned against the door, breathing hard. There was only one thought in my mind at that moment, although I was trying as hard as I could to push it away, to deny that it was true. But it was no use.

Peter was right, the voice in my head repeated over and over. *You're never going to find someone who likes you for who you are.*

AFTER AN HOUR or so of feeling sorry for myself, I had a sudden, illogical, but nonetheless powerful desire to go home to Ohio. I wanted nothing more than to crawl into my childhood bed in the house I'd grown up in and have my mother tuck me in tightly and tell me to sleep well, everything would be better in the morning. But that was impossible. It was nearly 11 PM, and there was no way I could catch a flight to Columbus this late. Besides, even if I could, I had to be at work in the morning; I had an early deposition that I couldn't miss.

I knew I could go to Meg's or Emmie's or even Jill's, but I didn't want to talk to them. Not tonight. I just wanted to feel like I was home somewhere, somewhere no one would bother me or moralize to me about my situation or analyze my various shortcomings. I looked around me at my uncomfortably stark apartment, which I'd put little effort into making warm since Peter had left. In this moment, it didn't feel like the home I needed.

Finally, I gathered my manila folders, a change of clothes, and my makeup bag and headed out the door to the closest thing to home I'd known in the last eleven years: my office.

I doubted I'd be sleeping much tonight anyhow. At least I could dedicate my sleepless hours to the one thing in my life that hadn't rejected me: my job.

Chapter Twenty-one

"Harper?" A concerned voice was calling my name from what seemed like far away. "Harper?" The voice sounded clearer now, closer as I finally came to, emerging from a dream that quickly slipped back into the fogs of sleep.

I sat up and blinked, startled momentarily because I couldn't understand where I was. My back and shoulders ached, my eyes felt dry, and inexplicably, my left cheek was killing me. I reached up to touch it and felt, to my horror, a weird series of cubic imprints pressed into my skin.

"Harper?" the voice came again. I blinked a few times and focused, then jumped as I made eye contact with Molly, whose nose was just inches from mine. "Harper?" she asked again in that same concerned tone. "Thank goodness you're awake. Are you all right?"

I blinked and slowly looked around, my eyes adjusting to the harsh fluorescent light. I looked down and slowly realized that my cheek felt so strange because I had fallen asleep slumped over my computer keyboard. The J, K, and L keys had droplets of drool on them to prove it. My back and shoulders hurt because I had been slumped uncomfortably forward in my chair since sometime in the middle of the night. And my eyes were burning because I had been reading legal briefs and precedents online until I couldn't see straight anymore. Oh yes, and I'd spent much of the night crying.

"What time is it?" I asked Molly, my voice cracking, my lips sticky because my mouth was so dry. Out of nowhere, she produced a bottle of water, which she handed to me. "Thank you," I mumbled.

"It's only seven thirty," she said soothingly. "I'm the first one in. Don't worry. You have time to freshen up."

"Oh," I responded, suddenly acutely embarrassed and aware of how this must look. Who knew what was going through wide-eyed Molly's mind as she found her unconscious boss slumped over her desk? I probably looked like I'd gone on some drinking binge and then wound up here. In truth, I hadn't had a drop of alcohol; I had overdosed on pain and humiliation instead. "I wasn't drinking or anything," I mumbled defensively.

Molly nodded gravely, her eyes still wide. "I know," she said without missing a beat. "But what happened? Are you okay?"

"I'm fine," I said. "Just fine. Don't worry."

Still horribly humiliated, I stood up quickly and, ignoring Molly's attempts to help steady me on my feet, mumbled something about how I needed to go to the bathroom, then grabbed my makeup and clothing bags so that I could make myself at least halfway presentable.

When I returned fifteen minutes later, after washing my face, changing into the gray suit I'd brought with me, and applying enough makeup to conceal most of the ravages the previous evening had left on my face, Molly was nervously neatening stacks of papers and folders on my desk.

"Thanks for waking me," I said, eyes downcast, as I crossed my office and slid into my desk chair, pushing my overnight bag underneath my desk to get it out of the way. "I don't know what came over me."

"No problem," Molly said softly, looking at the desk and not at me as she continued to straighten meticulously. "Sometimes I like to get in a little early and get a jump-start on the day," she mumbled.

"I'm glad you were here," I admitted gratefully. I thought with dread of what would have happened if one of the partners had discovered me, drooling on my keyboard as if sleeping off a hangover.

"Is there anything…" Molly paused, her eyes darting around the room, then she started again. "Is there anything you want to talk about? I mean, is everything okay?"

I nodded.

"Thanks, Molly," I said, trying to sound as together as possible, although I think she and I both knew it was a charade. "Just a long night. That's all."

Molly looked up at me nervously.

"Did it, um, have anything to do with that guy? Matt James?" she asked. I looked up at her sharply. She blushed immediately and shook her head. "I'm sorry, I shouldn't have asked that. It's none of my business."

I sighed, then cleared my throat.

"No, no, don't apologize," I soothed, feeling bad that she was so nervous around me. Was I really that mean as a boss? I paused, then nodded. "As a matter of fact, yes, it did have to do with Matt. And about a million other things."

"I knew it," Molly said quietly, balling her right hand into a fist and slicing the air. "I knew it," she repeated. I looked at her, puzzled, and she looked back at me a bit sheepishly.

"Knew what?" I asked.

"There was just something about him that didn't seem right," she admitted. "I had the feeling he was up to no good."

"You did?" I asked, mystified. "Why didn't you say something, then?"

Molly blushed furiously and shook her head.

"That's not my place, Harper," she said. "I'm just your secretary. You've never talked to me about anything personal. I figured it wasn't my place to say anything."

I felt terrible. For a moment, I didn't know what to say.

"I'm sorry, Molly," I said finally. "I never meant to make you feel like that." Great, now I was alienating my sweet secretary, too. Clearly I couldn't even get things right with her. I was a complete failure at everything.

"It's not you," Molly said quickly. "You're a great boss. It just seems like something's been bothering you for a long time, and you never talk about it. And you've been acting so strange these past few weeks. I just figured it was something you had to deal with on your own. I didn't want to be rude."

I sighed. "Molly, I don't think you could be rude if you tried."

"Well," she said, pausing uncomfortably. She stopped neatening stacks of paper and straightened to look at me. "Is there anything you want to talk about? Only if you want to, I mean."

I studied her for a moment, her earnest face, her wide, honest eyes, and I felt a sudden, overwhelming urge to confide in her, no matter how awkward it was professionally.

"My best friends had this idea for something they called The Blonde Theory," I began, and before I knew it, I was wearily pouring out all the details of the past few weeks, starting with meeting Scott Jacoby, which felt like an eternity ago, and ending with the sordid details of last night's abysmal failure.

When I finished, out of breath and emotionally drained, Molly just stood there, looking at me. After a moment, I started to feel very uncomfortable. Maybe she hadn't been the right person to confide in after all.

"Um, Molly?" I asked finally. "Is everything okay?"

She nodded slowly, then cocked her head to the side.

"I don't understand," she said.

"What don't you understand?" I asked, confused. I thought my explanation of the whole misguided experiment and my immense failure had been pretty clear.

"I don't understand why you'd feel like you needed to do something like that," she said, looking perplexed. "I mean, you have everything. You're smart. You're pretty. You have great friends. You have a great job." She paused and looked me right in the eye. "Why would you want to pretend to be someone else?"

I sighed, frustrated. I hadn't considered the fact that Molly might not see how difficult it was to be me. She seemed so intuitive, I supposed I'd figured she would understand immediately.

"Molly, it's really hard for me to feel like I always intimidate guys and scare them away," I tried to explain. But she still looked perplexed. I pressed on, trying to get the point of my patheticness across as clearly as possible. "Don't you understand? No one wants to date me, because I'm a lawyer. It terrifies most guys. It's not like I need a boyfriend. But I'm starting to feel like I'm going to grow old alone."

"You just haven't found the right guy yet," she said.

I rolled my eyes. How many people were going to tell me that this week?

"You don't understand," I said, frustrated.

"No," Molly said, more forcefully than I'd ever heard her speak before. "*You* don't understand. I would give anything to be as smart and successful as you. You're, like, my idol."

Molly's words struck me speechless. I had never thought myself capable of being an idol to anyone—certainly not to my secretary, who wasn't all that much younger than me. Certainly I wasn't old enough to be anyone's idol... was I? I was flattered beyond words all the same.

"*I'm* your idol?" I finally asked incredulously.

Molly nodded. "I want to be a lawyer," she said. "More than anything in the world. It's just taken me a little longer to figure out what I love to do. And it's not like I have all sorts of scholarship offers or anything. So I'm putting myself through law school."

"You...you are?" I asked, thoroughly confused. I hadn't had any idea. How had I not known that my secretary was going to law school?

"Yes," she said, blushing. "Just one or two classes a semester. It's all I can afford. So it's slow going. But, Harper, I want to be just like you. I don't know how you don't see that. You're amazing. You have it so together."

I started to open my mouth to protest, but then I noticed how earnestly Molly's eyes were shining as she looked at me. I thought back to the conversations she and I had had the past year and a half, the way she had asked me small questions about cases I was working on, the way she had treated me with so much deference that it made me almost uncomfortable. And for the first time, I saw myself through Molly's eyes instead of through the eyes of the scores of men who kept rejecting me. It wasn't much, because it didn't erase the pain of my long string of romantic rejections, but it was something. I was so used to judging myself based on what Peter and every guy after him thought of me that I had forgotten to judge myself based on my own standards. There had been a day when I'd been as proud of myself as Molly was.

"Thank you," I said finally. I was dumbstruck by how clear everything suddenly seemed.

Molly smiled shyly. "You're welcome," she mumbled. "I'd better get to work now."

I watched her leave my office, my jaw hanging open. It wasn't until she had shut the door behind her that I snapped out of my reverie.

"I'm her idol," I said to myself, shaking my head in wonder. I smiled—a real smile this time—for the first time in twenty-four hours. "How about that?"

* * *

I WAS JUST packing up my things at six forty-five to go home when Molly came into my office, her eyes downcast and a slip of paper in her hand.

"You're still here?" I asked in surprise. Molly was required to work only nine to five, and most days she left around five forty-five or six—probably to head over to her night-school law classes. A new wave of guilt washed over me as I thought about the fact that I'd been too self-absorbed to have even known she was going to law school. What kind of person had I become?

"Yes," Molly mumbled. "I wanted to make sure you were okay."

Her concern almost brought tears to my eyes. I blinked quickly and smiled at her.

"Listen, thanks," I said earnestly. "But I'll be fine. Really. I don't want you to waste your time worrying about me." I felt badly for burdening her with my insignificant, self-absorbed problems while she had real issues to deal with.

Molly shook her head.

"It's not a waste of time," she said. She looked up at me nervously. "Actually, I've spent the whole day thinking about it. And I want you to do me a favor."

I hesitated for a moment, studying her wide, blushing face. She had never asked me for anything in the year and a half that she had worked here. Besides, she had more or less saved my job—or at the very least, my reputation—this morning when she had awoken me from my drooling-on-the-keyboard slumber. I owed her one. Actually, I probably owed her about a hundred. I wasn't exactly in the habit of agreeing to favors sight unseen, but I couldn't say no to Molly.

"Okay," I said with a nod. "Of course."

"You have to promise," Molly insisted. I studied her for a moment. What was it that she needed? At worst, it was probably some help with some briefs she had to write for one of her law school classes or something.

I hesitated, then nodded again. "I promise. What can I do for you? Do you need some help with some coursework or something?"

Molly shook her head, then glanced down at the piece of paper she was clenching in her hand. She looked up at me again nervously.

"I want you to go on a blind date," she said firmly.

"What?" I croaked, my heart sinking. I'd been on enough dates in the last two weeks to last me a lifetime or two. There was no way I was going to go down that road again. Besides, blind dates *never* worked when I was actually acting like myself. "No, I can't," I said, shaking my head.

Molly looked wounded. "But you promised," she said, her eyes wide and hurt.

I looked at her for a moment and sighed. "I know I did," I said. "But I didn't know that's what you were going to ask me."

"I know someone who would be perfect for you," she said slowly. "And whether it works out or not, at least I know he won't be scared of you because of your job."

"How do you know that?" I demanded, a little curious, despite myself, about the mystery guy. But not curious enough to commit emotional suicide by agreeing to a blind date.

"I just know," she said firmly. "He's the nicest, most decent guy I think I've ever met."

"Then why aren't *you* dating him?" I asked accusatorily. I resisted the urge to roll my eyes. If I had a nickel for every time one of my friends recommended a guy whom *she* wouldn't actually date but who was "just perfect" for me...

"Because I'm gay," Molly said, looking surprised. My jaw dropped. "You didn't know that?" she asked incredulously.

"Um, no," I said, feeling once again like a huge fool. I had seen this woman nearly every weekday for a year and a half, and I hadn't known that she was going to law school *or* that she was a lesbian? Wow, I really was a terrible person.

"Oh," Molly said, blushing again. "I hope that's not a problem. I just ... I just figured you knew."

"No, no, of course that's not a problem," I said quickly. "I just feel terrible that I didn't know. I never realized how little I knew about you."

Molly shrugged. "I kind of keep to myself," she said. "Besides, I figured some of the senior partners here wouldn't exactly approve. I guess I don't really make a big show of it or anything."

"Oh," I murmured, still feeling terrible. I hesitated, feeling like I had to ask her a question or express interest in her declaration in some way. "Um, do you have a girlfriend?" I asked.

"Yes," Molly nodded, peering at me peculiarly. "You've met her a bunch. Francesca. You know? The girl who goes to lunch with me a couple of times a week? The one who works at *The New Yorker*?"

"That's your girlfriend?" I asked incredulously. I *had* met Francesca, a tiny, dark-haired pixie of a girl with a cute, upturned nose and a spattering of freckles. And come to think of it, I had seen Francesca and Molly acting rather affectionately, hugging each other whenever they saw each other, giggling together at private jokes, touching each other's arms with an implied intimacy. I can't believe I had never connected the dots. "Of course that's your girlfriend," I added softly.

Molly smiled at me. "She's great," she said. "I'd love for you to get to know her better. If you want to, I mean."

"Of course," I said, again struck with a giant pang of guilt. "How long have you been with her?"

"Two years," Molly said. "She's perfect."

"Lucky you," I said softly. The more I thought about it, the more I realized that they *were* a perfect match. Huh. Maybe *men* were the problem. Why couldn't I have been born a lesbian?

Then there would have been no preconceived gender stereotypes, no expectation that I would have to be subservient while my partner brought home the bacon and wore the pants in the relationship, so to speak.

"Yes, I'm lucky to have found her," Molly agreed. "But it's hard, too, you know? I know I want to spend my life with her, but we can't get married in New York. And my parents basically disowned me after I came out to them. So it's not all good, you know?"

"I'm so sorry," I murmured.

I thought about it for a moment. I had been so absorbed in my own problems and my own dating difficulties these last few weeks—these last three years, in fact—that I had barely considered that other people had problems running much deeper than mine. I instantly felt even worse than I had before for harping on my own problems, and especially for whining to Molly about them.

"I'm so sorry," I murmured again.

"You apologize too much," Molly said gently. "You have nothing to be sorry for. But please, consider going out with this guy, okay? I'm telling you, he's perfect for you. At the very least, you need to go out with a guy who isn't scared to see the real you."

I sighed and studied Molly's face. Behind her thick glasses, her eyes were wide and pleading.

"Exactly how do you know this guy?" I asked suspiciously.

"He's in my study group for both of the classes I'm taking this semester," she said. "He's really smart."

"You want me to go out with some twenty-two-year-old law student?" I asked, surprised.

Molly laughed. "No," she said. "He's thirty-three. He already worked as an accountant for several years, and he just started law school this semester. He just moved to New York. He's sort of changing paths in life and wanted to give this a try. He's not that much younger than you, Harper. C'mon, give him a chance. Please?"

"But he's a student," I said. "Why in a million years would he want to go out with a woman who has already been working as an attorney for a decade?"

"I don't think that kind of thing matters to him, Harper," Molly said. "It shouldn't matter to you, either."

I was about to protest again, to tell Molly that there was no way it would ever work out between me and some law student who probably didn't have two dimes to rub together and was doing the same course work I'd done twelve years ago. Then I remembered the bizarrely prophetic—albeit insulting—words of Sean, the Irish handyman. *Maybe you're not looking in the right places,* he had said. Much as I hated to admit it because he'd been so rude to me, maybe he was right. I had only dated guys who made as much—or nearly as much—money as I did because I was so afraid of the men feeling inferior. But maybe this had all morphed into a problem of my own making. Maybe I *did* need to try going out with someone a little different.

"Fine," I finally agreed reluctantly. I really had no desire to go on yet one more horrible date. But Molly looked like she was on the verge of getting down on her knees to beg me. I'd been so obtuse about two things that were so obviously important to her—her school and her sexuality. If agreeing to this favor would begin to make it up to her, then I really didn't have any choice.

"Wait," I said after thinking about it for a minute. "I don't have to act like a dumb blonde or anything, do I? Because I'm done with that."

"No, you don't have to act like a dumb blonde," Molly said with a smile. "Just be yourself."

I nodded reluctantly, and Molly flounced out of the room to call the mystery man. Three minutes later, she was back, grinning from ear to ear. She told me I was to meet him tomorrow night at the The Long Hop, a British pub in my neighborhood. She scribbled down the name and address of the pub and the time

I was supposed to meet him on a notepad, ripped off the sheet, and handed it to me.

"Don't be late!" she said cheerfully.

I looked at the paper then back at Molly. I forced a smile and tried to feel better about the whole situation. Really, how bad could it be?

I had the sinking feeling those were famous last words.

Chapter Twenty-two

The next night at seven twenty, after a long day of work and an even longer day of explaining what had happened with Matt to a disappointed Meg, Emmie, and Jill over lunch, I sat at the corner of the bar at The Long Hop, drumming my fingers nervously. The place was emptier than I'd expected it to be; apparently this was the lull between the bar's buzzing happy hour and its post-10-PM hip nightlife, complete with DJ and dance floor. But at seven twenty, it was just me, a handful of other people who looked about my age drinking at the bar, a pair of guys playing darts in the corner, and a lone bartender who was languidly drying martini glasses while whistling to himself.

I was casually hip in my favorite pair of slim-cut Robin's Jeans, a black Amy Tangerine tee with the Chinese symbol for happiness stitched across the front in pink, big silver hoop earrings, and a pair of silver stilettos. I had washed and dried my hair and reapplied my makeup after work, and I was feeling more confident than usual as I waited for my mystery date.

Despite my begging, Molly had offered few details about him except to say that he had blondish brown hair, was on the tall side, and had a smile that would turn her on if she weren't a lesbian. I wasn't exactly sure how I was supposed to take that. She refused to even tell me his name; she had simply said that he would find me.

I felt inexplicably nervous and unsettled as I waited, the moments ticking by slowly. The mystery guy was supposed to meet me at seven thirty, and as I checked my watch and saw that it was seven thirty-one, I started to get a bit annoyed, which I knew was insane, because obviously I was supposed to give someone a window of more than one minute before getting peeved. I supposed it was because I was on edge anyhow. I didn't really want to be here. The last thing in the world I wanted to be doing was going on another date. I wanted to be at home pouting instead. I still felt wounded and humiliated after the incident with Matt. I figured that I certainly didn't need yet one more thing to bring me down another notch—particularly not yet another bad blind date.

"Harper?" A deep male voice cut into my thoughts, and I turned, expecting to see my mystery man. Instead, my jaw fell open.

"You've got to be kidding me," I muttered, shaking my head as I tried to get ahold of myself. It was Sean. The smug handyman Sean. "What on earth are you doing here?"

Great. Just what I needed. The preachy handyman, sticking his nose where it didn't belong yet again, ruining my date by psychoanalyzing me or something.

"I might ask you the same thing," he said with a grin, apparently oblivious to the fact that I was shooting little daggers at him with my eyes. "This is my bar, you know."

"What, like you own it?" I asked flatly.

He laughed, low and deep. "No, of course not," he said in that thick brogue of his that I found attractive, despite my annoyance at him. "I mean, it's the pub I come to all the time. The one that has Murphy's on tap. Remember?"

"Yeah, your precious Murphy's," I muttered. I was starting to suspect that another Murphy's was at work here: Murphy's Law.

How else could you explain why the irritatingly chipper handyman seemed to materialize every time I was on the verge of romantic disaster? It had at least been somewhat understandable when he showed up at my apartment a few times during the series of towel mix-ups. But this was ridiculous. Apparently the universe thought it would be supremely funny to plunk him randomly onto the bar stool next to mine as I waited for a date I was dreading. Suffice it to say, I wasn't amused.

"Still a bit mad about the other day, are ya?" he asked with a lilting grin.

"It's just that my personal life is really none of your business," I said stiffly.

"Ay, that's for sure, then," he said. "So what are ya doing here all by yerself tonight?"

I rolled my eyes at him. Hadn't we just discussed the invasion of my personal life?

"Havin' a night out at the pub alone, are ya?" he persisted.

"No," I snapped. "For your information, I'm waiting for a date."

"Oh, are ya now?" he crowed. "So who's the lucky lad?"

"For your information," I said as haughtily as possible, "it's a very friendly—and very cute—law student who's about my age. Okay? He'll be here any minute. You'll see."

However, with the minutes ticking by, I was growing increasingly sure that Molly's perfect guy wasn't going to show. It was almost seven forty-five. If he didn't arrive, it would be a new low in humiliation, as Sean the handyman would have a front-row seat to my downfall.

"He sounds like a nice guy," he said with a wink.

"I'm sure he is," I said. "Not that I need your approval."

"Of course not," Sean demurred. "But I *am* glad to see that you're datin' outside your comfort zone."

"What?" I asked crossly.

"Agreeing to a date with a lowly law student, I mean," he said, nodding approvingly. "I do believe you're making a change for the better, Miss Harper Roberts. I think you're opening your mind. Good for you."

"Thanks," I said drily, wishing to end the conversation and feeling awkward, because of course Sean was right. As usual. How was it that he seemed to know more about me than I was capable of figuring out on my own? It was really annoying. I craned my neck, hoping I might catch sight of a cute, sandy-haired law-student-y guy approaching me with a charming grin on his face. No such luck. I slumped my shoulders and turned back to Sean with a sigh. "Is there something else you need?"

I hated sounding so mean. But I really didn't need him standing around judging me. Especially as it was growing increasingly obvious that this fantastic date of mine was going to be a no-show. I was just about ready to throw in the towel on dating altogether. Clearly, I was disastrous at it.

"Well, aren't ya gonna ask me what *I'm* doing here tonight, all by myself?" he asked, the dimples in his cheeks growing deeper as his grin grew wider.

"Sure," I conceded. Perhaps indulging him would make him leave more quickly. "What are you doing here tonight all by yourself?" I asked in a tone tinged with just the slightest bit of mockery.

"One of the girls from my study group set me up on a blind date with her boss," Sean said without missing a beat, his eyes twinkling. "Any idea where I might be able to find a single, thirty-five-year-old patent attorney around here?"

I gulped. My mouth was suddenly very dry, and I felt as if I might fall off my bar stool.

"What?" I croaked.

"My friend Molly," he said "She's in the two night classes I'm taking for law school this semester. We study together. And she told me somethin' about her really nice boss, who, for some strange reason, doesn't think that she's as appealing to men as she really is."

I stared.

"*You're* the guy Molly is trying to set me up with?" I asked, a little breathless. It slowly began to register. He *was* really friendly, even if his helpfulness was sometimes misdirected or unwanted. He *had* specifically said that a woman's career wouldn't matter to him. And he *did* have an adorable smile, I had to admit, although it was considerably less charming when he was wearing it while making me think about my problems. "But that's impossible," I protested. "She said she was setting me up with someone who used to be an accountant."

"Harper, you've got to learn to look beneath the surface, ya know," he said. "I've been taking law classes at NYU starting six weeks ago. It's what I came over to the States for. It's what I decided I wanted to do with my life. Tax law, actually, considering my background is in accounting. Did you know that? That I was an accountant in Ireland?"

"No," I said weakly.

"Ay, I musta forgotten to mention it. Anyhow, it was time for a change, time to get out of Cork, like I told ya. So here I am, attendin' NYU. It's no easy feat makin' the loan payments, which is why I'm crashin' on my friend's couch and workin' part-time to put myself through school. It'll be a long few years, but I'm hopin' I can save enough this summer to start going to school full-time this fall."

I stared at him for another moment, until a thought occurred to me.

"So this was all your idea, then, was it?" I demanded. "What, was this supposed to teach me some kind of lesson about life or something?" That figured. Although I'd been dreading it for the most part, there was a small part of me that had been looking forward to the date. Instead, it was Sean, and he had apparently taken me on as some sort of project. No thanks. I didn't need to be anyone's project.

Sean looked surprised, then he smiled again.

"No, actually," he said, "I had no idea Molly worked for you. I don't exactly go to study group talkin' about overflowing toilets and such, ya know. But I had given Molly some advice about a problem she was havin' with her girlfriend a few weeks ago, so we got into a conversation about datin' and such. I suppose that's why she felt comfortable asking me to go on a date with her boss."

"*She* asked *you*?" I said skeptically. "With no idea that we knew each other?"

"Absolutely." Sean nodded. "I swear it on the grave of me mother. She didn't tell me your name until after I'd agreed to the blind date."

"And when she said my name?" I asked carefully. "How did you react? You probably wanted to change your mind, right? But you're here out of some sort of obligation? Some sense that you need to teach me a lesson?"

"No," Sean said, looking surprised. "I'm here because I really want to be. I told Molly that I already knew you. And then I told her that I already liked you."

"You *what*?" I replied. "That's impossible. I've been nothing but rude to you."

"Ay, because I've been stickin' my nose where it doesn't belong, I suspect," Sean said. "I can't really blame you, now, can I?"

"I haven't exactly been overly friendly either," I muttered reluctantly. I studied him for a moment, not sure what to think. I hadn't even considered going out on a date with someone like Sean—not even that first morning when he showed up at my apartment and I noticed abstractly how cute he was. He was right: I hadn't bothered to look beneath the surface and see him as anything more than a handyman. It hadn't occurred to me that there was more to him than met the eye. I'd been so closed-minded that I'd only seen him as the guy who had the power to fix my toilets, not as someone who could be intelligent, kind, and, well, datable. I'd been so caught up in my own insecurities about how men felt about me and whether or not they felt threatened by my job that I had unconsciously dismissed anyone whom I assumed didn't fit. It wasn't that I thought I was too good for someone who had a lower-level job than me—far from it. I was deathly afraid of falling in love with someone and then seeing him walk away, like Peter had, as soon as the financial and status differences between our jobs became too much to bear.

I thought about Jill and the disaster she had stepped into by marrying someone who fit into her preconceived mold of the "perfect guy" without taking the time to really get to know him. I thought about Emmie, who was the same age as I was but didn't seem all that worried about her romantic future, although I always seemed to be fretting about winding up old and alone. I thought about Meg, who loved her job but loved her husband—a jovial, down-to-earth electrician—more. And I thought about Molly and the many challenges she faced.

I knew then, with a sudden clarity I'd been lacking, that I had to change my perspective. I'd been thinking of things all wrong, basing every dating decision on my experience with Peter, assuming that every man who came after him would think just like he had. And by selecting guys who were, for all intents and purposes, a lot like Peter, I had spent the last three years morosely confirming my own theory and slipping deeper and deeper into self-doubt. But maybe Sean had been right when he had suggested, last week, that at least part of the problem was within me. Troubling as that was to consider, maybe this whole dating conundrum that I'd been experiencing the last three years was, at its root, of my own making.

Finally, I focused on Sean, who was smiling as he waited for me to speak again. His eyes were big and blue; his sandy hair was tousled, and he had a small cluster of freckles across the bridge of his nose that I'd never noticed before. He had deep dimples, broad shoulders, and, as Molly had pointed out, one hell of a gorgeous smile. I flushed a little as I noticed how attractive he really was for the first time. It would take awhile to adjust the way I'd been thinking for the past three years, and indeed to really, truly learn to open up again without throwing up my defenses. But as far as I was concerned, there was no better place to start.

"So are you going to just sit there?" I finally asked Sean, smiling at him. "Or are you going to take me out on a date?"

Sean's grin grew wider and his blue eyes twinkled enticingly at me.

"Well, Miss Harper Roberts," he said, nudging me playfully. "I thought you'd never ask."

> *It's nice to be included in people's fantasies,*
> *but you also like to be accepted for your own sake.*
>
> —Marilyn Monroe, world's most famous blonde, in 1955

EPILOGUE
Two and a half months later...

S ometimes in life, everything seems to fall into place all at once. The clouds clear, the heavens shine down on you, and everything is perfect. The things you didn't understand before are suddenly in focus; all the little problems you were facing are gone, and you know that there are only good times ahead.

Unfortunately, that wasn't the case with me. Never had been. But at least I had two new pairs of amazing shoes that I could wear while skipping from catastrophe to calamity, purchased with my fee for writing the article about The Blonde Theory for Meg. I was wearing one of the pairs tonight: gorgeous zebra-striped Manolo sling backs with a two-and-three-quarter-inch heel and a little black bow tied neatly over the tiny keyhole opening on the top of my foot. They had set me back $565 but were well worth it. My other pair of new Manolos—black crepe mules with a crystal ring at the top of each shoe and a two-inch heel—had set me back $656, leaving me roughly $200 to treat the girls to a meal, which is exactly what I was doing tonight.

It was a night to celebrate, for sure. Meg had gotten a small raise at work a week earlier, a gigantic triumph, as her company was notoriously cheap. Emmie had finally, at long last, scored a role in a real movie. She had only two lines, and it would take her only two days to actually shoot the scene, but she was playing actor Cole Brannon's ex-girlfriend in a movie that co-starred George Clooney and Matthew McConaughey and was already being talked about as the breakout hit of the following summer. She hadn't stopped talking about it since she'd gotten the call from her agent. Molly, whom I had invited along to celebrate with us, had just finished her law school semester with A's in both her classes and had decided, at my urging, to enroll in three classes next semester instead of two. I had promised her that she could lighten her workload with me if she needed to.

But the real reason to celebrate tonight was that Jill's divorce from Alec had become final that day. I had sat by her side in a room full of lawyers as she signed the divorce papers once and for all. I hadn't known what to expect from her. Tears, perhaps? Regret? Sadness? Fear at being alone again? But instead, she had turned to me and smiled once everyone else had left the room.

"I guess it's time to throw my mother's rules out the window and get back out there to start dating again," she had said ruefully.

"Do you miss him?" I asked softly. I knew she was doing the right thing but couldn't for the life of me imagine what she must be feeling.

Jill tilted her head to the side, as if considering the question. Then she smiled. "No," she said finally. "I don't miss him. I miss what I *thought* he was. But that was never the real Alec anyhow, was it?"

As I watched my three best friends and my secretary—who had begun to turn into a good friend—smiling and laughing over enormous pitchers of sangria and an almost shamefully large spread of appetizers around a table at Pipa, a tapas restaurant just north of Union Square, I leaned back and smiled. This was what life was about. My friends were like family to me, and it warmed my heart to see them all doing so well. Never before had we all been so happy at the same time, I thought. One of us was always facing some kind of crisis or disaster. But for this frozen moment in time, we were all content, and our lives were all moving in the right direction. Everything just felt right, and that felt good.

As for me, I wasn't dating Sean anymore. I had, for about six weeks, and it had been great. Molly had been right: My career hadn't intimidated him in the slightest, and he'd been wonderfully supportive of everything I wanted to do. We had a lot of the same interests, and both of us understood the other's busy schedule, so there was none of that resentment that had crept into my relationship with Peter when I had to work long hours.

But the chemistry just wasn't there. We were great as friends, but there were none of those sparks that I knew came along with great love. When we finally slept together, after four weeks because it felt like it was about time, the sex was, at best, lukewarm. I was always happy to see him, but my heart never leapt and danced inside me like I knew it was supposed to with someone whose love would rock the foundations of my world. After six weeks, we'd talked about it, and I discovered that he was feeling the same way. We split amicably and had been close friends ever since. In fact, he'd even gotten me hooked on his precious Murphy's beer, and at least one night a week, I met him at The Long Hop to play darts and "grab a pint," as he said.

I suppose I felt a bit of regret that it hadn't worked out with Sean. He was one of the nicest guys I'd ever met, and in a lot of ways we fit perfectly together. But if there's one thing he had taught me, it was that I should never have to settle. And I would have been settling if I had decided to be content with someone I knew in my heart wasn't the love of my life. It would have been the perfect ending to the whole Blonde Theory mess, though, if my Mr. Right had been there all along, wouldn't it?

But there was really no need for a perfect ending. I knew that now. Sure, I was thirty-five, and the older I got, the harder dating got because my standards grew higher while the number of decent, available men grew constantly lower. And it was even harder for me, because I knew that a lot of guys *did* feel threatened by my job or by my intelligence, which further shrank my dating pool. But even though Sean hadn't turned out to be the guy for me, he had taught me a very valuable lesson: There were still guys out there who could accept me for me, without being scared of my job or my income or my intellect. If I could learn to open my mind to them and take a chance, and if I could withstand the inevitable bad dates and rejections that would come my way, I'd eventually find someone who loved me for who I was without wanting me to change or quit my job or become a housewife. Not that there would be anything wrong with those decisions, but they wouldn't be *me*. That's just not what I wanted for my own life. And I shouldn't have to lower my standards just to make someone else happy. I knew that now.

I would never be an empty, vacuous shell of a person or a giggling, uncomprehending ditz who was ready to fall into bed with the first guy who walked in front of her crosshairs. I knew that's the kind of girl a lot of guys wanted. And sure, my life might have been easier if that's who I was. But I wasn't. I was me. And for the first time in three years, I was really, truly proud of that. For the first time in three years, I was learning how to see myself through my own eyes—not through the eyes of my ex-boyfriend or the men who rejected me without getting to know me.

"I think it's time for a toast," Meg said, breaking into my thought process as she picked up the glass pitcher. "Who needs more sangria?"

After she had filled all of us up, she raised her glass. The rest of us followed suit.

"To friendship," she said. "We're lucky to have each other, girls." We all smiled, nodded, and clinked glasses.

"To Emmie's movie," Jill said with a grin, and we all clinked again.

"To Jill getting rid of that creepy husband of hers," Emmie said, shooting Jill a look. Jill smiled, and we all touched glasses again.

"To all of you," Molly said quietly. "I've never had a group of friends like you before. Thanks for inviting me along tonight." We clinked glasses again, then the girls went silent, all of them looking at me, waiting for my toast.

I hesitated, then shrugged. "Here's to The Blonde Theory," I said with a grin. "It was just about the stupidest thing I've ever done. But at least we learned something."

Laughing, the girls clinked glasses again then dug back into the appetizers, chattering happily. As I bit into a bacon-wrapped blue-cheese-and-walnut-stuffed date, perched delicately on an endive leaf, I looked around the table once more and realized something else. This was the life I had built for myself. I had a career I loved, a self-confidence that was in the process of returning, and a group of the best friends in the world. And man or no man, I knew I'd be happy. I was me. Despite my generous helping of faults and shortcomings, despite the many things I wanted to change about myself, despite the things I knew I needed to do to become a better person, I was glad about that.

At the end of the day, there was no one I'd rather be.

About the Author

I've always been a blonde. I come by it naturally. My mom's blond. My sister, Karen, is strawberry-blond. My brother, Dave, is dirty blond. It just runs in the family. And while I admit to occasional encounters with stereotypical dumb blondes out and about, the majority of the fair-haired folks I've met are pretty darned intelligent. My mom can debate politics better than almost anyone else on the planet. Karen's currently at an Ivy League university earning her second master's in public policy. Dave's brain has been a veritable atlas-slash-sports almanac since he was about two years old, and now he's majoring in economics at the same university Karen and I graduated from. And lo and behold, somehow I squeaked by as the valedictorian of my high school class (Go Northeast Vikings!) and graduated from the University of Florida *summa cum laude*, blond hair and all.

But like many blondes—and many non-blondes—I've sometimes wondered how much easier my life might be if I could simply giggle my way through my days, batting my eyelashes, flipping my hair, and checking my brain at the door. After all, sometimes it seems that's what guys are looking for, right? But, through a bit of trial and error, I've learned that most of the time, guts go a lot further than giggles, and brains count more than batted eyelashes—in dating and all other areas of life. I still battle with insecurities, but at the end of the day, I'm pretty sure I'm better off being me.

And who is "me"? Well, among other things, I'm the author of the novel *How to Sleep With a Movie Star*, which, incidentally, is a work of fiction and not a how-to book! I swear, I've never slept with a movie star! (But Matthew McConaughey, if you're reading this, um, feel free to give me a call.)

In addition to being an author, I'm a freelance magazine writer who has been published in *People, American Baby, Glamour, Health, YM,* and a variety of other magazines. I also appear regularly on *The Daily Buzz,* a syndicated TV morning show on in over a hundred cities around the country. I have a great group of friends and a wonderful family, and when I am not out spending too much money on clothes I don't need, I am probably either a) obsessing about when I can next visit Paris (my favorite city in the world), b) trying to plan a wine and cheese party that never quite comes together because of scheduling conflicts and my own inability to clean my house, c) watching *Sex and the City* reruns that I've already seen a hundred times, d) reading, or e) writing (okay that was an easy one).

I live in Orlando, and although I profess my undying love to Mickey Mouse annually through the purchase of a Disney World annual pass, there's also a lot more to do in this city than hitting the theme parks. I love eating out, picnicking by Lake Eola, going to the beach, going to wine bars, going out downtown with friends, listening to live music, and did I mention *shopping*? So check out my Web site, www.kristinharmel.com, and drop me a line to say hello. I'll probably be here, waiting by the phone for Matthew to call, resisting the urge to giggle, bat my eyes, and flip my blond hair.

Kristin

Words of Wisdom from Five Famous Blondes

1. *"Beauty, to me, is about being comfortable in your own skin. That, or a kick-ass red lipstick."*
   —Gwyneth Paltrow

2. *"It's never too late—never too late to start over, never too late to be happy."*
   —Jane Fonda

3. *"To be brave is to love someone unconditionally, without expecting anything in return. To just give. That takes courage."*
   —Madonna

4. *"There's something liberating about not pretending. Dare to embarrass yourself. Risk."*
   —Drew Barrymore

5. *"People think that at the end of the day a man is the only answer. Actually, a fulfilling job is better for me."*
   —Princess Diana (in a 1995 BBC interview)